Praise For Lexi Blake A~~~ ~~~~~s And Mercenaries...

"I can always trust Lexi Blake's Dominants to leave me breathless...and in love. If you want sensual, exciting BDSM wrapped in an awesome love story, then look for a Lexi Blake book."
~Cherise Sinclair USA Today Bestselling author

"Lexi Blake's MASTERS AND MERCENARIES series is beautifully written and deliciously hot. She's got a real way with both action and sex. I also love the way Blake writes her gorgeous Dom heroes--they make me want to do bad, bad things. Her heroines are intelligent and gutsy ladies whose taste for submission definitely does not make them dish rags. Can't wait for the next book!"
~Angela Knight, New York Times bestselling author

"A Dom is Forever is action packed, both in the bedroom and out. Expect agents, spies, guns, killing and lots of kink as Liam goes after the mysterious Mr. Black and finds his past and his future... The action and espionage keep this story moving along quickly while the sex and kink provides a totally different type of interest. Everything is very well balanced and flows together wonderfully."
~A Night Owl "Top Pick", Terri, Night Owl Erotica

"A Dom Is Forever is everything that is good in erotic romance. The story was fast-paced and suspenseful, the characters were flawed but made me root for them every step of the way, and the hotness factor was off the charts mostly due to a bad boy Dom with a penchant for dirty talk."
~Rho, The Romance Reviews

"A good read that kept me on my toes, guessing until the big reveal, and thinking survival skills should be a must for all men."
~Chris, Night Owl Reviews

For His Eyes Only

Other Books By Lexi Blake

EROTIC ROMANCE

Masters and Mercenaries
The Dom Who Loved Me
The Men With The Golden Cuffs
A Dom is Forever
On Her Master's Secret Service
Sanctum: A Masters and Mercenaries Novella
Love and Let Die
Unconditional: A Masters and Mercenaries Novella
Dungeon Royale
Dungeon Games: A Masters and Mercenaries Novella
A View to a Thrill
Cherished: A Masters and Mercenaries Novella
You Only Love Twice
Luscious: Masters and Mercenaries~Topped
Adored: A Masters and Mercenaries Novella
Master No
Just One Taste: Masters and Mercenaries~Topped 2
From Sanctum with Love
Devoted: A Masters and Mercenaries Novella
Dominance Never Dies
Dominance Never Dies
Submission is Not Enough
Perfectly Paired
For His Eyes Only
Arranged, Coming April 25, 2017
Love Another Day, Coming August 2017

Lawless
Ruthless
Satisfaction
Revenge, Coming June 20, 2017

For His Eyes Only

Masters and Mercenaries, Book 13

Lexi Blake

For His Eyes Only
Masters and Mercenaries, Book 13
Lexi Blake

Published by DLZ Entertainment LLC

Copyright 2017 DLZ Entertainment LLC
Edited by Chloe Vale
ISBN: 978-1-937608-60-6

McKay-Taggart logo design by Charity Hendry

This is a work of fiction. Names, places, characters and incidents are the product of the author's imagination and are fictitious. Any resemblance to actual persons, living or dead, events or establishments is solely coincidental.

Acknowledgments

Thanks to my whole team. Kim Guidroz, the best editor in the business. My lovely betas, Stormy, Riane, and Kori. All around cheerleader, Liz Berry. Proofreader extraordinaire, Fedora Chen. Social media queen, Jillian Stein. The best publicist a writer could have, Danielle Sanchez and the whole gang at Inkslinger. My husband and kids. In a world like publishing where the ground is constantly shifting, these people form the bedrock of my career and I love you all!

Sign up for Lexi Blake's newsletter
and be entered to win a $25 gift certificate
to the bookseller of your choice.

Join us for news, fun, and exclusive content
including free short stories.

There's a new contest every month!

Go to www.LexiBlake.net to subscribe.

Prologue

Martha's Vineyard, Massachusetts

Nikolai Markovic eased out of bed, desperate to not disturb the woman beside him. The floors creaked under his bare feet and he went still, his eyes going to her sleeping form.

God, but she was lovely. Dark hair spilled out over the pillow and he couldn't help but think about how she'd clung to him, how innocently she'd looked at him, her eyes widening with sweet shock as he managed to draw the first orgasm out of her.

I knew it would be good. I knew we would be good.

She'd whispered the words right before she'd fallen asleep, her body plastered against his.

She'd whispered something else, too. Something he couldn't forget.

I love you, Nick. I always have.

He should have gently explained all the reasons he wasn't good for her, should have been kind and put her into a cab and sent her back to the world she belonged in. Instead, he'd closed the door, locking the two of them in his shitty motel room. She deserved more than to have lost her virginity in a forty-dollar-a-night motel room. She should be back with her wealthy family, enjoying the ocean and eating a late supper. She should have saved herself for some well-raised intellectual who could have fit into her family and given her the life she needed, rather than selfishly taking what he wanted.

Was he actually thinking of doing this? Was he considering running away with Hayley Dalton, who was barely twenty years old and had stars in her eyes?

Did he think she could save him?

He had some money saved up. They could go to Seattle where she was in her last year of college. He could buy them a small house, get a job in security, and for once in his life settle down and breathe. He could get her pregnant and then there would be no looking back. He could have a family.

He shoved his legs into his jeans and tossed on a T-shirt. He needed to breathe right now and he couldn't do it with Hayley here. Not when all he wanted to do was get back into bed and roll on top of her. She would spread her legs and welcome him inside her body. Hayley loved him, and not with some small part of herself. When Hayley loved, it was with her whole heart. She was all in.

It felt good to be loved. It made him remember that once he'd had a home and a family, and life had been good. Life had been more than running from place to place. More than doing whatever dirty jobs he could find so he could keep running. So he didn't have to think about everything he'd lost.

He palmed the key and his wallet. There was a soda machine downstairs by the check-in desk. He would get a drink and sit for a moment.

He would think about it, think about putting her in his car in the morning and driving west and never looking back.

They could start all over. He could forget his past and build something for once.

Desiree kicking him out might be the best thing that ever happened to him. She'd ended their toxic relationship and he didn't have to feel guilt at moving on.

A light sense of joy bubbled up inside him. Hayley loved him.

Oh, she was a foolish girl to love him. She shouldn't, but she'd made the mistake and now he could take her and make her his.

He locked the door behind him. Was that the sun coming up over the horizon? How quickly the night had gone.

Hayley. He got a stupid grin thinking about her. He was too old for her. Not in years. In years he was only a few older, but he'd been aged by experience.

And she was reckless, as she proved by showing up at his motel the night before. Reckless and naïve and maybe she could use someone to watch after her, to protect her when she had those crazy ideas.

She was smart and kind and needed someone to ensure no one took advantage of her.

Unlike Des, who needed no one at all.

"My cousin? Really, Nicky? She's twelve."

He stopped and tried to shove down the white-hot anger that flared at the sound of her voice. How long had he followed her mindlessly? "She's twenty years old and I wasn't doing anything else for the evening."

She chuckled, the sound deep and sexy. He would give her that. Des radiated sex. "Sure. That's what sent you into the arms of my little cos. Boredom. Don't be ridiculous. I know you better than you know yourself. And I know Hayley's been mooning over you forever. Ever since we started dating."

He finally turned. She was leaning against the Benz she'd rented for the family gathering out at Martha's Vineyard. He wondered how many of her upper-crust family knew what Des did for a living. Certainly not Hayley, who seemed to be the odd poor kid in a family of wealth and privilege that spanned two countries. "Is that what you call it? Dating? I thought I did favors for you and you fucked me."

"Poor Nick. Where would you be if I hadn't found you? In some Gulag in Siberia, if you were allowed to live at all." She brushed her hair back. In the early morning light, he could see that her makeup was flawless. But then she was always perfectly done up.

15

Unlike Hayley. Hayley was always a little messy and she rarely paid attention to wearing the "right" clothes or perfect shoes. And still there was a fresh, sexy beauty to Hayley that called to Nick.

"I would be. Putin would have seen to it." He'd left the SVR the day he'd met Des. SVR was nothing more than a new version of the KGB. He'd joined to help his country and because he was addicted to the adrenaline of the job. He'd rapidly learned his boss was, as Americans would put it, an asshole. A money and power grubbing asshole who cared about nothing but keeping his lofty place in the world.

She straightened up and her perfect mouth turned down. "I don't blame you. She's a lovely girl. I like Hayley and I pushed you last night. I said some things I shouldn't have said. It wasn't well done of me, but then you know I like to play games."

"I think I'm tired of games, Des." It had been a crazy ride with this woman and he couldn't help but have feelings for her. Des had saved him. Des had gotten him out of Russia, and in return, he'd become one of the many people she relied on for information and backup. He'd been crazy about her in the beginning, but being one of many lovers was wearing on him.

Hayley offered something different. Maybe he was getting old because the thought of staying in one place, with one woman who cared about him, seemed like a good thing to do.

Des moved in, giving him a view of her perfect breasts. She gazed up at him, her lips pouting. "But you're so good at them, love. I'm sorry about what happened yesterday. I was overwrought. I have some business dealings that are going a bit awry and there are a lot of changes coming up, but I should have been kinder to you."

This was what Des did. She ripped his heart out and then came back with sweet words and even better sex.

Not this time. Not when he'd just had Hayley. Not when he'd made love for the first time in years instead of fucking. Hayley had let him touch her, let him spend hours kissing her and caressing and feeling like he was worth more than an orgasm. "I'm out, Des. I wish

16

you all the best. I'll always come if you need me, but I want to try with Hayley."

Her eyes closed briefly, and when they opened, there was a sheen of tears there. He'd never actually seen her cry. Not even when he'd had to dig a bullet out of her thigh.

"That hurt more than I could have imagined. I think I love you, Nick. As much as I can love any man. But I love her, too. She's my cousin. She's one of the best people I know, and given who her father is, that's saying something."

Hayley was smart and resourceful. She was kind. "I'll take care of her."

Des's jaw firmed. "Will you?" She stared at him for a moment and he had to wonder what she was planning. "You can't love her. You barely know her."

"I feel something for her I haven't before and I've known her for a few years now. When you bring me to these family outings, I spend most of my time with her. I've come to care very much for her." She brought him peace. When he was with Des, it was like his life was a roller coaster filled with thrills and moments when he simply held on for dear life. He'd been hooked on the adrenaline of the life they led, but he felt such peace with Hayley. Such beautiful peace.

"I get that, Nick. I really do. Like I said, I love her. I get that I hurt you. I don't mean to, but this is who I am. I'm never going to be faithful and I'm never going to want to settle down. But neither will you. Not for long. You're hurting because of what happened to Katja. You miss your sister and I was a terrible bitch to you earlier. I lost my temper. It's no surprise you're having a crisis."

"It's not a crisis. It's time to grow up." He wasn't sure she would ever understand him. "Breaking things off was the best gift you could have given me. What we have is toxic. I hope you can see that. It's not normal what we do to each other. There's passion and yes, there is some love, but, Des, there's no peace between us and there never will be."

"Because we're not normal," she said, her voice going low. He

17

could hear the impatience in her tone. "There's nothing ordinary about our lives and you won't last more than a few months in Hayley's world. I got some information last night. It's why I'm here. If you can walk away from this information, then I'll be the first one to cheer at your wedding. If you can't, then, by god, Nikolai, admit that you belong with me."

He wanted to walk away, to back up the last ten minutes of his life and be upstairs and safely in bed with Hayley. No temptations other than the soft heat of her body and the peace he felt when he connected with her.

But he could see in Desiree's eyes another temptation. It was one he'd never been able to resist.

Vengeance.

"You found the man who killed my sister?"

Des put a hand on his arm, invading his space as she had a thousand times before. "Yes, and this is going to get bloody. He's *Bratva*, my love. I have ties that go deep with that group, but helping you means moving to the private sector. I'm leaving MI6. We'll take out the Ivanov syndicate and then I thought we might spend some time making serious money and seeing how the other half lives. It would be nice to be out in the open about our work for once. Have you heard of a man named Damon Knight?"

She talked on but all he could see was months and months ahead. Months of blood and sacrifice and pain. That man had murdered his sister.

What would Katja want for him? Katja had been a fierce operative, one of the best, and yet somehow she'd managed to maintain her sunny, bright smile. Katja would have loved Hayley.

Katja had spent her final hours in agony, tortured by the *Bratva*, left behind by her own agency.

Even with Des's help, it could be a year or more before he finished the job. How much blood would be on his hands then? How many bodies would he have left behind? How many people would pray to see him dead?

He glanced back at the motel room where Hayley was sleeping.

Des had gone silent, but she wrapped her arms around him from behind. "I know, Nick. I know how much you want to stay, but we both know you won't. Please don't hurt her. She doesn't deserve it. Make the break clean so she can move on with her life."

His heart actually ached and yet he found some odd comfort from Des. Desiree had been the one constant in his life since that terrible day. His sister had died because she wouldn't give him up. Des had saved him, risked her own life to get him out of that hellhole he'd been left in.

What did he owe them? His sister and Des?

"You're being too kind," he said. "It makes me suspicious."

She sighed against him. "I'm getting something out of this, too. I get to keep you for a while longer. Like I said, I do love you. I know it's not enough right now, but someday you'll see that this is the right thing for the both of you. Hayley could get hurt, and neither one of us could stand it. Even after we've finished our work, there will always be someone after you."

Des was right. There would always be something. His world was blood and death, and Hayley was studying history. She was going to be some kind of teacher or professor. She wouldn't have any idea how to handle his world.

She would end up like his sister.

"I'll tell her I'm leaving." He broke away from Des.

"I'll start the car," she promised. "We have a plane to catch. We'll be in Moscow by this time tomorrow. I won't let you down. We'll do this together."

He walked back up to his room, his heart a heavy thing in his chest.

Chapter One

London, England
Five years later

Hayley stared up at the big building in front of her and wondered what the hell she was doing here. She should be anywhere but here. Anywhere on the planet.

Except home. Which had blown up.

It had been a ridiculously rough two days.

So this was The Garden. It didn't look like what she thought it would. Shouldn't it be way more gardeny? The stone structure looked pretty much like the rest of the buildings in London. Elegant, graceful, so very British.

A bit like Desiree.

Did he still mourn her?

Five years had passed and she was still a nervous idiot girl, with her heart thumping in her chest at the thought of seeing Nick Markovic.

She thought about the note in her pocket. It had come with the shipment of Desiree's things from her apartment in Tokyo. Not that Hayley had known Des had an apartment in Tokyo. It had taken over two years to go through all of her cousin's somewhat shady dealings and get through the odd requests of her last will and testament. It had all come down to the money going to Desiree's mother and father, the property to her sister, and the contents of her Tokyo apartment getting shipped to Seattle along with two letters. One made out to Hayley and one to Nick.

And then the world had blown up.

"Damn it, Des. What have you gotten me into now?" She muttered the words to herself because it wasn't like she had anyone to talk to. Five years had passed and she couldn't walk into Nick's office with a hottie on her arm because there were no hotties to be had. Five years and all she had to show for it romantically was a string of bad first dates and one boyfriend who slept with his undergrads.

Way to go, Hayley. Time to stop looking for dick. You've had the best dick you'll ever have. Start turning to women.

She scored super low on the Kinsey scale. The sweet sanity of lesbianism wasn't happening for her, but the sweet release of death would if she didn't get her butt off the street.

Someone had followed her. Someone had been waiting for her as she'd gotten off the plane at Heathrow. She'd barely given them the slip by slinking into the bathroom and stealing another woman's coat and scarf and blending in with the crowd. Had whoever was stalking her been smart enough to be a chick or a man more confident in his own masculinity, she would be a dead girl.

She glanced around, but the Chelsea street was quiet save for a few joggers and day-to-day folks milling about.

But that didn't mean no one was watching.

She settled her backpack on her shoulder. That damn backpack contained everything she owned in the world. Every single thing.

If she'd skipped her office hours, she wouldn't be here at all.

She walked up to the building and pressed on the doorbell.

"McKay-Taggart and Knight Security Services. Do you have an appointment?" A female voice came over the speaker.

Naturally she couldn't open a door and walk into the lobby. "Uhm, I don't, but I'm here to see Nikolai Markovic."

"I'm sorry. You look super interesting and all, but we only work by appointment," the sunny voice replied. And she sure didn't sound British. That accent was pure Cali girl. What was a California girl doing as a London receptionist?

"I'm not here to see him professionally." She was, but she certainly wasn't going to pay him. Nope. All her cash was gone, too. Not that the seven grand plus change that she'd saved up would have bought much of Mr. Super Security's time. Apparently when Nick and Des had gone private, they'd gone extremely posh, as her cousins would say.

"Oh." A long sigh came over the line. "Look, I'm so sorry. Nick's pretty good with the quick hookup, but he never goes back for seconds, if you know what I mean."

"Believe me, no one knows that better than I do." She had to get off the streets and fast. She was getting nervous. Who knew when Nick would get off work and if she could catch him as he went home? She had no idea where his home was and apparently he was completely unlisted. All she had to go on were Des's instructions. "But the matter is of some urgency."

Like I could be dead in the next couple of minutes if no one will let me in.

"Dude, are you pregnant?"

It took all she had not to roll her eyes, but she knew an opening when she saw one. She couldn't risk Nick sending her away without actually laying eyes on him. Maybe he wouldn't, but it was a chance she couldn't take. "I am. We're only a few months along, but I need his medical records. I need to talk to him."

"I was joking," the voice shot back. "Seriously, you're preggo? And it's Nick's. Shit. I'm not the normal receptionist but even I know we're not supposed to let people in without an appointment and vetting but god, this is awesome gossip. Like better than reality TV. It's a real dilemma. Follow protocol and don't get my ass handed to me or let the pregnant chick in and pop some corn. Are you an assassin?"

"No." What the hell kind of place did Nick work in? Were they all high? "But that's what I would say if I was an assassin."

"Yeah, you would," the voice replied.

"Okay, would an assassin know that he has a mole on his right butt cheek that looks a lot like a heart? I know because I saw it when we made our baby. It's a girl, by the way." Her father had taught her to use all her resources. Make the lie sound plausible.

Her father had been an excellent liar. And thief.

"Okay, I have to know, but seriously, I am a trained assassin so if you're coming here to mow down Nick with some sweet, sweet moves, I got some of my own." There was a buzzing sound and the door opened.

Hayley walked through despite the weirdness of that particular exchange. She would rather walk into a trap than get shot on the street.

She found herself in a lobby, but it certainly didn't look like the lobby of an office building. Maybe a plush doctor's office or like a place where wealthy women met for tea.

"Sorry, we're short-staffed right now." A second door opened and she was greeted by a young woman with shiny black hair and a ready smile. She was petite but there was something about her that gave Hayley pause. Her father had spent a good portion of her childhood training her to look for what he would call "easy marks." It was so nice to be raised by a con man. Still, the training sometimes surfaced and she knew in an instant that the woman in front of her wouldn't go into the easy mark column. "The boss and his wife are getting back in this evening and they're bringing most of the group back. Today you've got me, the lost boys, Teresa, and Nicky."

She wasn't going to ask why the cast of Peter Pan was apparently here, but the relevant fact had been stated. He was here. In this building. Nick. The man of her dreams. The focus of the most humiliating moment of her life.

"I only need to see Nick. If you could please tell me where his office is."

23

"You're not pregnant, are you?" The woman's face fell and suddenly there was a gun in her hand. A nice semiautomatic, from the looks of it. She didn't hoist it up, but it was there at her side. "I was hoping for a juicy scene. Things have been boring around here. Okay, I'm going to need you to leave now."

"Does she have to, Kayla?" A man with a heavy Scottish brogue stepped in the lobby. "She's quite pretty. Hello there, love. You don't want old Nicky. He's a bit dull. Well, he has been for the past few months. Don't remember a damn thing past then, but some women like that. I'm truly trainable."

The woman he'd called Kayla rolled her dark eyes. "You see what I have to deal with? There's so many of them. So pretty and such a big bag of cats when it comes to memory. And no, she can't stay. She no longer amuses me so she's gotta go."

Hayley stood her ground. "So you can tell by looking at me that I'm not pregnant."

"Your shoulders are up around your ears and your eyes slid off me when I walked in the room," Kayla explained. "You're uncomfortable, not victorious that you get to face down the dude who knocked you up. You don't want to see Nick, but for some reason you are happy to be inside this building."

So the chick was excellent at reading body language and Hayley had totally forgotten how to sell a con. It wasn't her fault. She'd spent the last few years studying world history, not working a long game.

"I still need to talk to Nick, and if you think for a second that gun in your hand is going to get me moving, you're wrong. Look at my body language right now and tell me if I'm lying." Hayley held her hands up, showing she wasn't hiding a weapon. "I'm not here to hurt him, but I'm not leaving without talking to him. Shoot me, but you're not getting me out of this building any way other than an ambulance. And I think you're bluffing because you don't even have the safety off that gun."

Kayla held her place, but there was something extremely dangerous about her stillness. Like a sleek panther waiting for the right time to pounce. "Why are you here?"

The hot Scottish guy held a hand out as though he knew exactly how dangerous the situation could get. "Why don't you let me talk to the girl, Kayla? There's no need to get nasty."

"I'm not letting her stay so you can flirt, Owen. I know it's been quiet around here, but you do know the rules." Kayla turned back toward her. "Talk. What do you need Nick for?"

Perhaps it was time for a bit of truth. "Because Des sent me. Desiree was my cousin and I inherited the contents of one of her many hidden safe houses. Part of those contents delivered to me included two letters written shortly before her death. One to me and one to Nick. The one to me advised that if I ever found myself in danger, I should get to Nick and give him his letter as quickly as I could. So here I am. Always the obedient cousin."

Kayla holstered the gun. "Damn. Now I can't let you go, but I can give Nick the option. Give me the letter. You can stay here in the lobby with Owen, and Nick will let me know if he wants to see you."

Not on her life, since that was what it might come down to. "If he wants the letter, he sees me."

Kayla frowned. "I know how the family felt about Nick. He's my friend and I'm not putting…" She stopped, staring for a moment. "You're Hayley. Oh, my. That's way better than some knocked-up chick showing up."

"Hayley? That's a pretty name for a pretty girl," Owen said with a smile. "Does that mean we get to keep her?"

"It means Nick's going to want to see her," Kayla shot back. "Desiree told me about her sweet cousin Hayley. Apparently Des had to save her from Nick's raging lust when she was an innocent twenty-year-old. Hayley, that is. Not Des. I don't think Des was ever innocent. Not even from birth."

Hayley felt her skin flush with embarrassment. Naturally Des had talked. Des always talked. She'd had a love-hate relationship with her cousin, but then most people did. Des had been larger than life and sometimes meaner than Satan. She could also be kind to people she cared about.

He wasn't for you. His life is too rough. Better to leave him with me. I know why you did it and I don't blame you, but I care too much about the both of you to allow it to happen. Ta-ta, love. If you ever need me, you know my number.

That was Des. She would pluck the love of Hayley's life right out of the bed they'd made love in, then promise to always be there.

"If you're done making fun of me, I'd like to see Nick."

Kayla sighed. "I'm not making fun of you. I just have the world's most boring sex life and I live for other people's drama because I can't seem to find any of my own. You know the sex you have while spying tends to be bad. Do you honestly think that pompous parliament guy I had to screw to prove he was defrauding the country and selling weapons to foreign dictators was good in bed? Because he wasn't. He was as selfish a lover as he was a political figure. Come on. I'll keep my mouth shut and this can all happen behind closed doors and I'll go back to playing Monopoly with the lost boys. Half the time they forget what they're playing at all and wander off. Like I said, my life is super sad."

Kayla turned and opened the door.

Owen stomped up to Hayley. "Now you've made the lass sad."

Kayla shook her head. "Don't mind Owen. I'm fine. Though my life kind of sucks right now. I got left behind on the whole wedding-in-paradise thing because I'm avoiding an ex-lover who I might or might not have spied on."

"You could give her something." Owen held the door open for Hayley.

Give the crazy chick something? Like what? She didn't owe the gorgeous, dangerous woman a damn thing. So why did she feel guilty that Kayla's shoulders were slumped? Fine. It wasn't like she didn't know all the stuff anyway. Des had obviously told Kayla that Hayley and Nick had a relationship. "Nick wasn't selfish. He was an incredibly giving lover right up to the point that he left me for my cousin. Still, he did pay for my cab. So there's that."

26

When Kayla turned, her smile lit up the room. "Seriously? That's awesome. And Des could be a total bitch. A likable bitch, but a bitch, and not in the super-cool, I-want-a-squad-with-her way. Nick always seemed like a guy who would want to settle down at some point, and that was so not Des's scene, if you know what I mean."

Such an odd woman. Hayley stopped because Kayla wasn't the only thing that was odd.

She was in a garden. A real live, ground-to-six-floor-roof garden.

It was the single most stunning room…building…she wasn't sure what to call it…that she'd ever seen. She looked up and down and all around and what she saw was green and calm. There was a skylight overhead, and she realized the whole building was centered around this atrium.

"It's prettier at night," Owen said, standing beside her. "At night the blooms open and the whole world feels fresh and young."

Kayla put a hand on his shoulder, a sheen of tears in her eyes. "It does, buddy. It's beautiful at night."

Something passed over Kayla's face, something Hayley didn't understand. Something about Owen.

It wasn't her problem. She had too many of her own to deal with. She was going to dump this problem in Nick's lap and find a way to move on with her life. She wasn't going to get drawn into these people's problems. They were Nick's people. Not hers.

She didn't have people anymore.

"The elevator's over here. Nick's office is on the third floor." Kayla pressed the button that called the elevator. "Owen can show you in. I have to stay down here and monitor security until they get back from lunch. Don't go too hard on Nick, okay? Sometimes he talks about you when he's drunk or half asleep. He only ever talks about you in Russian, but I know a few words.'"

You could be the one to lead me out of this hell. You could be my guide, Hayley. I don't know how to live in the real world anymore. I want this. I want you.

She shoved the words aside because they'd meant nothing. "I'm sure he was talking about Des. She was everything to him."

Kayla nodded. "They were an interesting pair, to say the least. She was quite a character. Des knew how to keep a person off balance. She kind of delighted in it. I think he's still hurting even years later. Like I said, go easy on him."

The elevator door opened and Owen stepped in. He was such a gorgeous man despite the fact that his clothes somewhat hung on him. He had that red hair one only found in Scotland and Ireland. He smiled readily, but he looked as though he'd been through an illness. There was a gaunt look to his face that told her he'd been through something and was only now seeing the other side.

"Come along then, darlin'. Let's get you up to see that big Russian bear and then perhaps you'll let me show you around a bit. I've been told I've lived here for a few years. Of course, after the doctor got hold of me and pumped me full of her drugs, I forgot all about that and now the noggin is mostly empty. Don't let that be fooling ya, though. I've quickly learned all I can about this place."

Doctor? Before she could ask the question, Owen was continuing on.

"Yeah, this place is fascinating. I think you'll love it here. Especially at night."

"When the flowers bloom," she said, thinking of what Owen had mentioned.

"And when the whole damn place turns into a sex club." The gorgeous Scot winked her way. "That's when the fun starts."

"Wait. What?" Hayley felt her jaw drop, but the elevator doors had opened and Owen walked through.

"He's this way. Yes, I think you'll like it here." Owen moved down the hall.

Hayley wondered exactly what she'd gotten herself into.

* * * *

Nick looked up as he heard the knock on his door. It was a bit of a lifeline, that distraction. It might keep him from giving in and pulling the vodka out of the bottom of his desk. He needed to keep that particular demon at bay until tonight when he could lock himself away and no one needed to know he couldn't get to sleep without it.

No one ever needed to know that even the vodka couldn't banish the ghosts that haunted him. The ghosts of both the dead and the living.

Five years had gone by and he still thought about that moment in the motel parking lot. That had been the moment that had decided his life. He'd chosen vengeance and death over peace and possibility. So often in his dreams he went back to that moment and chose again.

"Mr. Markovic?" Owen stood in the doorway and Nick felt the guilt that always rose in him the minute he saw his partner. Owen had been his closest friend and yet Nick hadn't seen that he was in trouble. Owen was a shadow of his former self. Owen had betrayed the team on their last major mission and he'd paid dearly for it. He'd sold out Theo Taggart to Hope McDonald, a doctor who liked experimenting on military men. Owen had done it to save his mother and sister, though McDonald had murdered both despite Owen's help. She'd then given Owen a dose of her experimental memory drug that had not only wiped Owen's mind clean, but made him sick for months.

Nick knew he should have seen what was happening under Owen's sunny exterior.

He'd lost a ton of weight, but sometimes when he smiled, Nick could see a hint of his old friend. "I'm sorry to bother you. I'm helping Teresa manage the front office."

He was nosing around Teresa was what he was doing. Despite the fact that the man had been wretchedly sick, he perked up around the sub.

He didn't remember that he'd already screwed the poor girl over and she'd likely never give him the time of day.

What would it be like to forget all his sins?

"It's all right. What do you need?" He wasn't getting anywhere with the files in front of him. Files on the six men who, like Owen,

29

had their lives decimated by Hope McDonald. The doctor was dead, but her legacy lived on in those men they'd taken to calling the lost boys. Men with families and lives somewhere out there. A puzzle Nick hadn't been able to solve yet.

"There's someone here to see you."

Nick straightened up. He didn't have any appointments today. There was nothing on his calendar at all because he was working the lost boys' cases. He didn't get clients walking in off the street. McKay-Taggart and Knight didn't advertise and The Garden wasn't a normal office building where one could wander in. No one knew where he worked. Unless it was someone Damon sent. He relaxed a bit. "Is Ezra back from wherever he's been?"

Ezra Fain was a CIA agent they'd been working with a bit as they tried to figure out who the lost boys were.

Owen shook his head. "No. It's a woman. Pretty thing, too. Says she knows you. Quite insistent."

"Yes, I am. Could you please move? I'm not leaving until I see him."

Nick froze at the sound of that husky American accent. It couldn't be. He hadn't seen her since the day of Desiree's funeral, and even then it had been from a distance because the family wouldn't let him in. He'd watched her, remembering the way she looked when she'd clung to him, wrapping her body around him while he drove into her.

And he'd remembered the way she looked when he'd told her he still wasn't leaving her cousin.

Hayley Dalton pushed past Owen, barging into his office. She looked every bit as delicious and curvy as she had that night they'd spent together five years before when she'd found him after a nasty fight with Des. She'd offered him comfort and he'd taken her up on it.

He'd spent one perfect night in her arms and in the morning he'd gone back to his own terrible reality.

She'd been the funny, sweet, smart girl he'd enjoyed talking to when he was forced to spend time with Des's horrible family. He'd liked her and he would never, ever tell her how close he came to walking away with her.

Especially not when she despised him. Not when she blamed him for her cousin's death.

"You owe me, Nick. You owe me and I've come to collect."

He was quiet for a moment. She was here. Right here in his office. She was standing there like a young Valkyrie demanding her due.

For the first time in years, Nick felt his heart rate tick up, his blood start to flow, like he'd been a clockwork man all this time and someone had wound him up slightly.

He stared at her for a moment, taking in the changes five years had brought. She was still breathtaking with dark hair and clear blue eyes, but she'd lost the charming awkwardness that had once marked the way she carried herself. She'd grown into her body, becoming both vibrant girl and devastating woman. She'd once shyly asked him to marry her, to run away with her and let her show him how well they could work.

The woman in front of him didn't ask. She demanded.

Damn but that did something for him.

"Would you like to come in and have a seat?" He was pleased with how even his tone was as he sat back, gesturing for her to sit in the chair in front of his desk. "Owen, thank you for showing my friend to my office. Perhaps later we can meet up for a drink."

Owen frowned. "Kayla wants me to listen in so I can give her all the gossip."

Kayla was a brat of the highest order. "Tell my dearest friend that she should be minding her own business."

"Apparently her business is boring right now," Owen said with a shake of his head as he closed the door.

And left Nick alone with one of two women who dominated his dreams for the last five years. "You're looking well, Hayley."

"You look tired, Nick."

He would give her that. "My job here is stressful at times."

"Your job at the sex club?"

He bit back a laugh. It was said with the intolerance of youth. "No. I don't actually get paid to go to The Garden at night. I was talking about my job here at McKay-Taggart and Knight. We work in the security field."

"So the sex club is just for fun?"

He wished she would stop sounding like a prude. "I'm sure my boss makes money off it, too, but I don't find that part of my life stressful."

She was still frowning, the expression causing the cutest line in the middle of her brow. "Nick, are you screwing with me? Like you used to? There's not a sex club, is there?"

Like he used to. He would tease her. Tell her all sorts of crazy stories about life in Russia and how he'd been forced to ride through the twenty-foot snowdrifts in order to get to his schoolroom. He would spend his time with Hayley at the family functions Des had taken him to. Hayley had been a changeling—a sweet soul left amongst the vipers. "There certainly is a club. These offices support McKay-Taggart and Knight. The club, bar, lounge, and locker rooms are all on the first floor and they support the dungeon."

Hayley was pacing, her petite form moving back and forth across his office. "Dungeon?"

How much would he have to explain? "Have you ever heard of BDSM?"

Her clear blue eyes rolled. "I'm not stupid, Nicky. I've heard of BDSM. I read books."

If she knew about BDSM, she read some dirty books. And the fact that she'd called him Nicky and not Mr. Markovic sent a thrill through him he hadn't been expecting. "Then you understand that it's more of a lifestyle club. Some sex might happen, but it's not like there's a nightly orgy."

She turned a lovely shade of red. "I should have known Des would end up in a damn brothel."

For the first time, anger flared through him. "It's not a brothel.

It's a place where people find themselves. If you're so sure of who you are, then you have no need of it. Good for you, Hayley. You've done something many can't. You're a whole twenty-five years old and need no more experience. I'm sure you have a husband by now who takes good care of you."

"You know damn well I'm not married."

"No, I don't. Believe it or not, since the moment Desiree was buried, I haven't kept in close touch with your family. Not that they would allow me to do so. I wasn't even allowed to attend the funeral. I only knew your father had died because his accident made the news." It was a huge open wound. He and Des had been…friends…lovers…something to each other for more than half a decade and he'd been barred from her final passage.

He'd been forced to stand back, a hundred yards away from where she'd been buried.

She hadn't wanted to be buried. She'd wanted to have her ashes scattered across the globe by him, but her family had gotten a lawyer and now she was confined to the family crypt.

Somehow the thought of Des being trapped hurt him. Despite all the turmoil they'd had in their life together, he'd still cared for her. He'd thought about marrying her. Even though he'd known not to ask because marriage would have been like the crypt to Desiree.

Hayley's arms went over her chest, a protective gesture. "I was against them barring you. Des wouldn't have wanted that. You have to understand. My aunt and uncle didn't know what Des did for a living. For years she told them she was working for the United Nations and that was why she traveled so often. They believed her. They thought you were trying to drag her down."

He knew the story. He didn't need it repeated to him. "It doesn't matter."

"It does." She took a step back and seemed to calm herself. Her hands came out in front of her, wringing slightly. "She would have wanted you there. She would have been angry about you being kept out. I should have said something."

He shook his head. "It wasn't your place. You need your family. I shouldn't come between you."

"I haven't seen my English relatives in years. Not since I started college. I don't go to many family functions anymore," she admitted. "It wasn't like they were lovely people or anything. I don't know exactly why my dad insisted on going to those reunions. We were always looked down on as the poor relations."

He'd wondered, too. Her father had seemed like a secretive fellow. Des would only tell him that Paul Dalton was a small-time con artist and part-time poker pro. Hayley's childhood had been a never ending up and down, with the ground always shifting under her. "Des loved you."

Hayley smiled, a wan lifting of her lips. "As much as Des could love anyone."

Yes, she would have said the same thing. Des's love always came with a warning. "Yes. So why are you here? How exactly do I owe you, *dushka*? I can think of many reasons you would come to me for retribution or compensation."

Her skin flushed and he wished he'd been a bit more temperate in his speech.

Her jaw firmed and she placed her hands on his desk, staring him down once more. "I don't think I need to remind you exactly why you owe me personally. I will remind you of what you told me that day. You said if I ever needed something, you would help me."

"Are you in some sort of trouble?"

Her eyes slid away and she started to pace. Not once had she stopped moving. "Yes. I need protection, but more than that, I need a safe place to stay and I need an investigator to figure out why someone would blow up my house."

Nick found himself on his feet in an instant. "What do you mean?"

Sometimes Americans spoke in hyperbole. He'd gotten used to it. Walt, a doctor on the team, talked about "blowing" stuff up all the time. What he really meant was changing things and rapidly. Surely that was what she meant.

"I mean my little two bedroom in the suburbs went *kaboom,* and not because of a gas leak like the cops are trying to tell me. Do you honestly think I could afford that place on my own? I bought it with the money my dad left me and I'll never be able to rebuild it for what the insurance will give me. If they give it to me after they figure out it wasn't an accident. Everything I owned was in that house. Every dish I've bought. Every stupid glitter turkey I picked up at an after-holiday sale because one damn day I was going to have enough friends to have a Thanksgiving party. Every book. Everything."

He didn't hold back. He knew he should, but he couldn't leave her standing there alone. He crossed the space between them and opened his arms, wrapping her up and holding her.

She was stiff in his arms for a moment, and then her body cuddled closer and she let him hold her. "I could have been in that house. I didn't have anything scheduled during office hours and I thought about going home early. It was only luck that I didn't."

She could have been lost forever and no one would have contacted him to let him know. He would have thought about her forever, never knowing she was gone. It struck him forcibly, the idea lodging in his gut like a stone weighing him down. He held her tighter.

"I'm so sorry to hear that, *dushka*. You can't imagine how… You're safe now." He let his hand find her hair, touching the silk of it while her body shook.

She held on to him and cried for a moment. Her arms suddenly clutched him as though she was afraid he would let go.

He could have told her he had no intention of letting her go. None. He held her close and let her cry.

"We'll get you new things. I promise. I won't allow you to be uncomfortable." Her childhood had been a vagabond existence. She'd talked that night about building a different life.

Imagine it, Nicky. We could have a house and friends who are always there. Friends we don't have to track down. We could have a comfy couch and we would sit on it every Sunday morning and read the paper while we drink our coffee out of dumb mugs we bought for each other. You know. The kind that says World's Greatest Lover *or some silly thing.*

She'd needed the shelter of a permanent home and she'd built it all by herself, and now it was gone.

And she'd come to him. When her world had gone dark, she'd run straight into his arms.

"I'll take care of you, *dushka*. I promise. I'll make sure you're all right and I'll deal with the authorities. You don't have to worry about a thing." His mind was whirling and he knew what a damn bastard he was. That hadn't changed, but other things had in the last five years.

What kind of man was he that he could hold her while she cried, and all along think about the fact that all those reasons he'd walked away from her five years ago were gone now.

There was no Russian mob vendetta on his head, no vengeance he needed to seek. His job was a bit dangerous, but stable for the most part. He was more likely to be involved in tracking down corporate spies than the more dangerous kind. He had money saved up and he'd been granted British citizenship. He was stable and secure.

She felt so right in his arms.

She gradually calmed, her sobbing relenting to low shudders of her body against his. When she looked up, her eyes were red and yet she was still so beautiful. He stared at her, trying to remember the last time he'd seen such honest emotion. Only in scenes, really. It was the only place he allowed women like Hayley close to him.

Hayley reminded him of the boss's wife. Penelope Knight was that open. Smart and funny and unafraid to allow her emotions to show.

Damon Knight was a happy man.

How long had it been since he'd been happy? Maybe not since that night he'd spent with her. Not truly happy. He'd had moments of passion, moments of fierce joy, but not a single time when he was content.

Not until this one. How shitty was it that he was happy her house had burned down because it had sent her to him? Okay, he wasn't happy that her house was gone, but he wasn't sad that she was here in his arms.

Did he deserve her here? It didn't matter because she'd made the choice. She had wealthy family to turn to, but she'd come to him. She'd made her decision.

She sniffled and started to pull away. He immediately let go because he intended to take things slowly this time. The first time she'd come to him, he'd allowed his passion to take the lead. This time he intended to let his head rule over his damn cock. She'd been through enough. She needed to feel safe, and groping her wasn't going to accomplish that.

"I don't think talking to the authorities is going to help." She wouldn't look him in the eyes. She stared at the floor as she started to pace again. "I mean, feel free to talk to them, but I would prefer they not know where I am."

"They have to know where you are. There are many forms for you to sign. You have insurance, right?"

"Of course, but it's bigger than insurance settlements."

He wished he was still holding her. "Any number of things could have happened. If the police believe it was a gas leak, why would you think differently? Who have you angered, *dushka*? Surely your students aren't going to plant explosives simply because you gave them a bad grade."

"It's not about me. At least I don't think so."

He couldn't imagine it, either. She was too kind and giving to call this kind of evil to her through her actions. "Have you had a boyfriend you turned away?"

That he could see. God knew he understood what it meant to be obsessed with a woman.

"There was one guy, but I seriously doubt Harrison would know how to build a bomb. No, he's the kind of guy who would come after me in print. He makes a hobby out of tearing apart my professional papers. I tried to tell him that it only made him look like an idiot and his arguments are specious at best, but he still comes at me from every angle. Well, every literary angle. He's an ass but not a killer."

As he suspected. "You're more than welcome to stay with me. I'll handle everything, but I think you have to consider that the police are right and this was a gas line explosion."

Her eyes came up, fire flashing there. "No. This is what you don't get to do. This is what you owe me, Nick. You will work this case and you won't charge me. You'll provide me with a place to stay that's safe and you will believe me when I tell you this wasn't an accident."

"You're not the type of woman people try to kill. Why would you think this wasn't an accident? It doesn't make it any less tragic and it won't make me want to help you less. You don't need an excuse, Hayley. I'm happy you're here. I want you here. Why don't we go to dinner and we can talk this out? You don't need some crazy story to make me interested in you. I've always been interested."

"You arrogant bastard. Do you honestly believe I traveled halfway across the planet with some crazy, made-up story so I could maybe spend another few hours in your bed? If you're bored and have nothing else to do, of course. We both know I'm not your type."

He'd said those words trying to make the break with her as quickly as possible, trying to spare her the pain of regret. If she hated him, she would move on. Now it seemed to him neither of them had moved on. He was drifting aimlessly and she'd apparently had one serious boyfriend in five years. "I didn't mean word I say that night. Please to come to dinner with me. I'll explain. I would love nothing more than chance to explain."

He was well aware his accent was thickening and he was dropping articles. It did when he got emotional and forgot to try to blend in.

She held a hand up as though she needed to keep some obstruction between them. "I didn't come back here to crawl into bed with you, Nikolai. I came back because you're the only person I know who I don't mind putting up against these bastards. Here's a news bulletin for you. I don't have gas in my home, nor is there a line anywhere near my house. They're lying and I don't know why."

"There could have been natural gas beneath the ground. The Pacific Northwest has many earthquakes."

"Fine. It was all in my head. It's all nothing more than science and the poor choice of living space. Fine. Explain away the cop who tried to shoot me."

"What?"

"I thought they were being so kind. A little chintzy with the cash, but kind. They put me in a crappy motel, but it wasn't until I went to get some ice that I realized I was the only one in the motel. It was deserted, at least the part they put me in. I was walking back to my room when I saw him."

"Who? Do you know this man's name?"

She shook her head. "Officer Harris. I recognized him from the police station. He'd been in uniform then. When he showed up to kill me, he'd changed. I watched as he kicked in my door. There was a gun in his hand. I didn't see anything after that. I ran. That was two days ago."

His chest felt tight. She was going to give him a damn heart attack. "Where have you been? How did you get to London? Bloody hell, woman, why did you not call me?"

She frowned his way. "First, stop yelling at me. Second, are you all right? Because you went pale and your eyebrow is twitching."

"Because heart is about to give out."

"Suck it up." There was no sympathy in her eyes. "You're of no use to me at all if you have a heart attack. So, to answer your questions. I hid in the woods until I managed to hitch a ride."

"You did what?"

"Well, I couldn't call a damn Uber. They require a credit card and I had to dump mine." She paled a bit. "I'd taken my backpack with me because I wasn't sure I could carry everything. Thank god I did or I wouldn't have had anything at all. Still, I knew better than to use the cards and I dumped my phone. I caught a ride to Portland with a dude driving electronics in from Canada. Or that's what he said. I was unaware there was a massive Canadian electronics manufacturer. I had some suspicions that he was hauling either stolen goods or bootleg meds. I've heard they do that now that the American healthcare system is in such disarray. And I don't blame them. Do you know what birth control costs if you don't have health insurance? Oh, I'm sure the docs will pass out the little blue pills like they're candy, but do they think about who bears that burden?"

"Hayley! Focus."

She'd always gone on and on when she was nervous. He used to find it charming. Now he simply wanted to get to the part of the story where she told him who he could kill.

Because vengeance, it turned out, was still on the menu.

Chapter Two

Why did he have to look like that? Couldn't five years of debauchery have given him wrinkles or something? He'd been working over a sex club. Shouldn't that show on his face? But no, not Nikolai Markovic. He was still every bit as stunning and masculine and sexy as he'd ever been. His shoulders were just as broad, his face as swoon-worthy. And that stern look he gave her kind of did something for her.

She'd never seen that look from him before. He'd always been so friendly and tolerant of her quirks. Now he was staring at her like he was ready to murder someone.

And yet, she'd totally known he was a killer. Not killer. It wasn't like he did it indiscriminately. He did it when he had to make sure the country was safe. Whatever country he was protecting at the time. Now that seemed to be England.

And she was supposed to be focusing. And not on his chest. Not on his big, broad, muscular chest. "So, like I was saying, I hitched a ride and managed to not get serially murdered. Which, considering that I was in Washington state, is something of a miracle. So I get to Portland and ditch the trucker, who was super creepy, at a gas station and make my way to the suburbs. I remembered that was where Dodi

Basra ended up. She was my father's friend and one of the greatest identity forgers on the planet. She gave me a passport, and I need you to send her three grand because she's the only reason I'm alive and here in England. She got me a passport and booked my extremely low-end flight here, which consisted of three layovers, including a lovely nine hours in Cleveland. So I'm tired as hell and I need you to start investigating. After you hand over the keys to your place because I need a nap."

He frowned her way, the expression doing absolutely nothing to take away from how hot he was. God, she hoped he had a guest room because the couch would suck and she would need a couple of walls between them to keep her sanity.

Nothing had ever felt as good as having those big arms around her. So safe. So fucking right. She'd been able to cry. She'd held it all in for days, but once she'd felt Nick's arms winding around her, she'd been able to cry and it felt so good. Like a crazy heavy weight had been lifted.

"Why would someone come after you in such a fashion?" Nick asked, his voice dark and deep.

Yeah, he'd never used that voice on her before either. It was like dark chocolate. A little addictive. She had to shake her head to force herself back to reality. "I don't think they're coming after me. I think they're coming after Des."

His whole body shut down in an instant, his shoulders lowering, his head dropping. "Des is dead. There's no reason to hurt her now. She can't be hurt."

She could hear his damn subtext. Des was never able to be hurt. Not really.

No. He'd made his choice. She wasn't going to empathize with him now.

She wasn't here to fix what had gone wrong with Nick. She wasn't here to rekindle some stupid flame. She was here to take him up on his offer and to make sure she survived the next few days. That was all.

She damn sure wasn't here to cry on his chest and lift her head, hoping he would kiss her.

She was so tired. That was why she'd cried in his arms. That was why it felt so good. It wasn't Nick. He was simply big and strong and might possibly help her out. She slumped down into the chair in front of his desk and immediately regretted it. Nick loomed above her, his icy eyes staring down. It was a reminder of how big he was, how strong. How serious he got when he pressed her down into the mattress, right before he leaned down and kissed her senseless.

"You were going to tell me why you think this is about Des."

The sound of Des's name coming from his mouth was enough to make her sit up straighter. She wasn't the same idiot girl she'd been five years before. "I don't know how much you know about Des's will."

"I told your family I wanted nothing from her. I have everything I need to remember her."

"Well, she left me the contents of her apartment in Tokyo."

His lips curled up. "There wasn't all that much. It was a tiny place, but she did have some sentimental items there. And she kept some jewelry and cash in all her safe houses."

Her cousin, the spy. "Yes, it was quite a bit of cash and it was all kept in a book safe. I thought it was weird that Des would read Dickens. Then I figured out it was a safe. I got it open and found a few things."

He reached out, touching the red and gold Venetian glass heart she was wearing around her neck. It had been in the small safe along with the two letters, seven thousand in yen that was now ash, and two sets of passports and visas Des would have used if she needed to slip out of the country.

"I remember seeing her wear that. I thought it rather odd since Des never wore less than the best. If I was going to buy her jewelry, I knew it would be expensive."

Because everyone laid jewels at the feet of Queen Desiree. "I bought it for her when I was fifteen. My dad took me to the yearly

43

retreat at Martha's Vineyard and Des was always so nice to me."

"She liked you very much. She always said of all her family, if she could have chosen her sister, it would have been you."

Damn. She'd spent five years hating Des and yet she still teared up thinking about her. So many conflicting emotions had come out when she'd seen that dumb heart that had cost her fifty dollars. She'd saved up for months to get it. She'd watched as her larger than life cousin had opened her other presents. Hermès. Chanel. Van Cleef and Arpels. Hayley had cringed as Des had opened it, but she'd proclaimed it lovely and immediately traded her Cartier collar for the cheap glass.

Even as guilt had swept through Hayley, she'd felt the need to wear that heart. The necklace and letters were the only things that had survived.

"Yeah, well, I'm sure after what happened, she didn't think that way anymore." She'd gone after her cousin's lover. Oh, at the time, Des had told her that she and Nick had broken up and she wouldn't be seeing him ever again, but Hayley had broken the girl code.

Thou shalt not go after thy cousin's leavings…even if he's everything you've dreamed of in a man. Even if you're a stupid girl who thinks she's in love.

Nick chuckled, the sound deep and deliciously dark. "She said that a few months before she died. She got news that you were going for your doctorate. She always said you were a smart girl."

"How did she know that?" And why would Des care? Des had been so damn complex. Kind when she should be cruel. A true mean girl when she wanted to be.

Hayley had been so humiliated that night, but sometimes when she thought about it, she could still hear Des talking to her after Nick walked out.

He would hurt you, sweetie. He's not in a place where he can be what you need him to be, but who knows? The world has a way of changing on us. We have to be ready when it does. Go to school. Become the woman you were meant to be. You'll thank me one day.

One day, maybe you'll even forgive me.

She took a deep breath and tried to banish the thoughts. Guilt and anger and sorrow. It was a boiling cauldron of emotion she got when she thought of her cousin.

"I believe she was in touch with your father before she died." He sat back up, his features going grim once more. "I was sorry to hear of your father's passing."

She'd gotten the flowers he'd sent. Not that there had been much of a funeral. His ashes had been presented to her and she'd had them interred in the family crypt. The same one that held Des's ashes. It had been seven months before and she'd thought so much about looking Nick up and seeing how he was doing.

She'd ignored the impulse the same way she intended to ignore all her impulses when it came to Nick Markovic. "Dad never mentioned he'd talked to Des. I know sometimes he'd call her when he was playing in Europe, but I don't think they regularly kept in touch."

"They spoke more than you know." The words were said with the crisp bite of a man who didn't want to delve into the subject. Probably because talking about Desiree still hurt him even years after her death. "So you received the package from Tokyo and then your house exploded? There was no request for information? No contact at all with someone who was interested in what you inherited?"

She could barely keep her eyes open. Now that she was sitting and had a nice cry, she was so damn tired. The events of the last few days were hazy. "Not that I remember. I would certainly remember it if someone threatened to kill me."

He sighed. "You need sleep. Come, I'll take you to my room until I can have Teresa set up one for you."

She was curious to see where he lived. Had Des lived with him? Had they set up a nice flat here in this quiet part of London or had they gone swanky and upscale? "How far away is it?"

He held out a hand. "It's two floors up. Are you hungry? Teresa or one of the other subs won't mind preparing something for you."

Subs? Submissives. Like her romance novels. He lived in a sex club and had a bunch of submissives who wouldn't mind taking care of his ragged old one-night stand.

She stood up suddenly, avoiding his help. "I'm not staying here."

He frowned. "The Garden is the safest place I know. You can have your own room if you like, or if you feel safer, you can stay with me. I'll take the couch."

"I'm not staying here, Nick. I'm not going to bed down in some orgy club. You think that would make me feel safe?"

His eyes went cold. "You think someone will hurt you here? You think I would allow that?"

She would be incredibly hurt if she had to come out of her lonely room looking for a bottle of water and managed to run into Nick and his likely harem of women. He'd talked about the subs so casually. Were they his submissives? Des had laughed about it once. It had been a sex game to her. She'd always said Nicky took it too seriously. It was one of the things they'd fought over. Hayley knew they hadn't been monogamous. Why wouldn't he have a harem of subs to do his bidding now?

She hadn't thought this through. "I'll find a hotel."

He moved in front of her. "With what? How did you get from the airport to here? Do you have any cash at all?"

He had her there. She had about ten dollars left of the two hundred she'd borrowed and she didn't have a credit card. "I need to borrow some cash and I need to find someplace cheap. A youth hostel, maybe."

At twenty-five, she wasn't exactly the college student they typically took in, but she certainly looked ragged enough.

"Hayley, be sensible. No one is going to touch you. That's not how The Garden works. Unless you go down to the club, you won't even see anything."

Sure she wouldn't. She wouldn't see who he'd moved on with when she couldn't move on at all. Maybe it was the horror she'd been through. Maybe it was all the tension and strain and lack of sleep, but she simply couldn't be rational. She couldn't stay with him. It was too much. Seeing him, being close to him, brought back too much heartache.

If she didn't get out of here soon, she was going to cry again, and she couldn't be vulnerable around him.

"I'm finding a hotel whether you help me or not. I bet that Scottish guy will loan me a couple of pounds." She glanced toward the door. Surely someone would help her.

God, she had no one. She couldn't go home. Not until she figured out what was going on. Her father had died months before. Des before that. Her mother had passed while she was in college. She couldn't risk bringing any friends from home into this. Not that she had many. Academia turned out to be pretty cutthroat.

"Owen barely remembers his own name, much less has any cash on him. We don't let him out much because he ends up getting lost."

Then she was on her own. It struck her that she was acting like a damn crazy person, but she couldn't quite bring herself to stop. She'd come to ask for his help. He would figure out who was coming for her, but that didn't mean she had to see him.

Tomorrow she could go north and visit her aunt. Who hated her and thought Americans were all barbarians.

She strode out the door and almost immediately ran into a gorgeous blonde woman. She nearly knocked her over, and it was only the other woman's quick hands that saved the tray she was holding.

The blonde looked up at Nick. "I'm sorry, Sir. I thought you and your guest might like some tea."

"Thank you so much, Teresa. It was a kind gesture, but I'm having a bit of trouble with this particular guest." He stared her way. "Go back to my office, Hayley. There's no reason to cause a scene."

Teresa. The sub who wouldn't mind making her some lunch.

Naturally Nick had moved from Des to gorgeous Teresa.

What had she been thinking? Somewhere in the back of her stupid head she'd thought that she would walk in the room and what?

47

That time would dissolve and he would choose again? That he'd realized his mistake and would fall into her arms?

Such a stupid girl.

She hadn't given him the letter, either. She was an awful human being, but she wasn't going to do it today. After she'd had some sleep and some food she would be better. Then she would be capable of acting her age.

She held a hand up. "I'm sorry, but I can't stay here. I'm not the type of person who stays at a sex club. I'm respectable and I intend to stay that way."

"This is ridiculous."

Yes, of course he would see it that way. "Could I please borrow a few pounds? I'll figure out the rest later, but I have to find a hotel."

The smile on his face didn't come close to being amused. "A few pounds won't get you into a hotel in Chelsea. If you insist on playing the prude, I'll have to go along. Teresa, please let Kayla know I'll be back in the morning. I assume you won't eschew my investigative services because of the building I happen to live and work in. Or am I too dirty to even look into the situation for you?"

She felt tears pierce her eyes. Naturally he put the worst spin on things. The only real spin he could since she wasn't going to admit how sick the thought of watching him with other women made her. "I don't have anywhere else to go."

"So beggars can't be choosers," he said, bitterness evident. "Well, I assure you I won't expose you to my filthy lifestyle. I think that's how your aunt put it the last time I was in a room with her. Filthy foreigner. Disgusting lifestyle. I suppose you've gotten closer to that side of the family. Come along, then. I'll find you someplace respectable to stay."

He strode toward the elevator and she was left with the blonde staring at her like she was some kind of monster.

"He's a good man. He didn't deserve the hell your family put him through. My tea is excellent, and I won't even go into how amazing my biscuits are. You don't get my tea. My tea is only for filthy, disgusting people." Teresa turned on her heels and walked away, tea tray in hand.

The first food she'd been close to in hours and hours.

She blinked back tears and forced herself to hold her head high.

She joined Nick in the elevator. It was a quiet ride.

* * * *

Nick opened the door that led to the lobby with a sick feeling in the pit of his stomach.

He had no idea who the woman walking beside him was.

Hayley had been sweet, kind, nonjudgmental. She'd been the bright light. Even when he hated being paraded in front of Desiree's relatives like some shock-and-awe campaign against an enemy, he enjoyed the time he spent with Hayley. Seeing her became the only reason to go to any of Des's family functions at all.

Had five years really changed her? Or had he been duped into believing the sweet exterior?

Well, everyone knew he was stupid when it came to the women of Hayley's family.

Kayla popped her head out of the reception room. "Hey, is everyone okay? I got a call that you're going out. You know the big guy is coming back in a few hours. I don't think he's alone. He asked me to make sure you, Robert, and Ari are prepared to give a full briefing on the state of our team of lunatics."

"Ari asked you not to call them that." He wasn't in a mood to joke, and damn it, if Damon wasn't coming back alone that could only mean one thing. Freaking Ian Taggart. The only man in the world who could give him more hell than Damon.

"I should send back those T-shirts then, I guess." Kay simply shrugged off his dark tone. "All I'm saying is if you're about to go off on some sex binge, you better make it quick. Damon wants that meeting early tomorrow. I tried to tell him that he's going to have some righteous jet lag, but he just said some British things about carrying on and stiff upper lips and pip pip and all that. I shut up."

49

"Damn it." Now he had the added problem of needing to work tonight to get that damn briefing finished. "How many Taggarts do I have to deal with?"

They were their own small army when they got together. Each more sarcastic than the next. They were on their way back from Loa Mali, an island country off the coast of India where the youngest Taggart brother had gotten married to the mother of his child. The Taggart children were the only ones he could truly handle. They were all small and sweet and cute, and soon they would begin to talk and probably sound like their fathers…

"It's just Big Tag and Charlotte. They're worried about the nice group of men who happened to lose their memories and most of their manners to the crazy doctor lady. Also, I'm sure none of them was military or worked for various government and or criminal organizations. I'm sure they were regular Joes. Tucker was probably a barista or something."

Perhaps it was all Americans who spoke the language of sarcasm. "I'll be here in the morning. I need someone to watch after this one while I work. Do we have anyone who can do close cover right now?"

"She needs a bodyguard?" Kay suddenly looked more interested. "Brody's back. I could assign one of the boys to her. They're pretty good at following orders when they're not trying out foods to see what they're allergic to. That started as a fun game and ended in an EpiPen to Jax's leg."

"I'll stay inside," Hayley said quietly. "I should be fine. I traveled under a false passport."

Kay leaned against the registration desk. "Then why were you so freaked out about getting inside? You looked totally paranoid for a chick with nothing to worry about. Also, you wanna explain why Teresa was so sniffly on the com system?"

Nick put out a hand. He did not need Kay to get all high and mighty on her squad horse. Or whatever she would call it. "I'll handle this."

"I wasn't trying to make her feel bad. I simply don't want to stay here. I want to go to a hotel," Hayley said, her voice so small.

In the dim light of his office, he hadn't seen the shadows under her eyes. She looked pale and beyond tired. He sighed. His anger drained away. She was still so young despite all her accomplishments, and to the outside world his lifestyle could be controversial, to say the least. He did owe her and right now that meant putting aside his anger and getting her the rest she needed. He could deal with everything else later. She mattered now.

"I'm taking her to the hotel around the block. Could you have Brody meet me there in ten minutes?" He would rather have Brody than one of the lost boys.

"I'll let him know," Kay promised. "And Nick?"

"Yes?"

"I'm so expecting a debrief on this when you get back."

Because she loved gossip. And because Kayla Summers would never leave him alone in this. She would push and poke at him until he finally spit out what was bothering him. She would pry into his business until he growled and threw up his hands and gave her what she wanted. Kay was the little sister he'd...well, she wasn't blood, but she was here. "I promise I'll tell you everything I know and then we can talk about figuring out the problem."

"So you're not trying to fly solo on this one?" Kay asked, her brow arched over one eye.

He might have tried, might have played it close to the vest to protect her privacy, but he wouldn't be able to. It seemed too big, and the truth was Hayley might feel safer if she had another operative on the case. Someone like Kay. "No, I'll talk to Damon about it when he comes home. We'll treat it like any other case. I will pay."

"Nick," she began.

He put a hand up. He knew damn well how much a full-time bodyguard and investigative services would be, but he didn't have another option. She couldn't pay and he wasn't going to leave her out there to die. "I'll text you the room number when I get her settled in. She has nothing, Kay. She needs clothes and toiletries."

"I can get them. I need some cash though," Hayley began.

He shut her down with a stern glare. "You will stay in the room and with a guard until such time as I decide you're safe enough to be on your own. And don't spit bile my way. I owe you a debt. I acknowledge this, but that means I'll give you my best work. It doesn't mean that I will coddle you. You asked for my help. Part of that help will be to protect you from yourself."

She didn't look at him, merely stared at the floor. "All right. I'll stay where you put me."

If only he could believe that. He felt guilty but shoved it aside. He wasn't the one who had made a massive fuss over nothing. He wasn't the prude here. He was trying to help her.

She looked so defeated and that damn near killed him.

He opened the door and strode out into the late afternoon air.

It would be better when he turned over the physical portion of guarding her to someone else. Brody and Kay could take shifts.

Unless Damon came back and put them on other assignments.

Would he leave her care to the lost boys? They weren't bad men. He simply didn't know any of them well enough to trust them. Hell, they didn't know themselves. No one had figured out who they had been.

"Can you slow down?"

He stopped and turned. She was struggling to keep up with him. He glanced around. The neighborhood was quiet at this time of day, but it would soon pick up. The businesses around them were beginning to shut down and employees would be running for the Tube or coming up out of it to get to their flats. "I'm trying to get you inside before we get crowds. It's easier to watch for suspicious people when the streets are empty."

Not that they were ever truly empty. He glanced up and down the street. This wasn't a place he felt uncomfortable with. The security staff at The Garden would be watching. There were cameras everywhere, though they were fairly subtle. Once they left the block that housed the club and office, they would be on their own.

This was a bad idea. He could feel it in his gut, but he wasn't going to fight with her. Once he had her secured, he could put a guard on her, spend his days and nights figuring out which one of Desiree's never-ending schemes had gotten them into trouble now.

"I'm sorry about pissing off your girlfriend," she said as she shuffled beside him.

He led her to the corner and waited for the light. Traffic was picking up. "Teresa isn't my girlfriend."

She stood beside him, her hands on the straps of her backpack as she stared at the light. "Sorry. I suppose you call her your submissive or something."

Was she jealous? "Hayley, Teresa works for the club and does some secretarial and assistant work for the company. She isn't mine. I don't have a girlfriend and I don't have a sub. And for the record, if I did have a sub, she would be my girlfriend. I wouldn't separate the two. I don't have intimate relations with anyone I work with."

Her eyebrows rose slightly. "I think Des would disagree."

"Des is the reason I no longer do that." The light changed and he nodded her way, beginning to lead her across.

"I didn't think you did much besides work," she muttered.

"I spend time in the club. My life has become insular the last few years." There was a hotel up ahead. He wanted to keep her close enough that he could run if he needed to get to her. "I work. I sleep. I occasionally play at the club, but mostly I drink. If I'm lucky, I meet a woman and spend a few hours with her and I forget. Most nights, I'm not lucky."

"Nick, I'm sorry." She reached out for his arm, pulling on his sleeve.

He stopped, not moving under her touch. There was so much pain and anger between them. When he'd held her in his arms, he thought perhaps they'd put it behind them, but their sad history was still here. A wall between them that he wasn't likely to climb. "I'm sorry, too. I should have known the years wouldn't change your opinion of me."

She shook her head. "I'm tired. Can I get some sleep and try to figure out the completely fucked-up web of emotions I have surrounding you? I know you thought of me as some kind of naïve child, but I'm human. I screw up and I say things I don't truly mean. I need some time to think."

She needed some space as well. He could see that plainly. He needed it, too. "I'll settle you in and you can sleep and in the morning, we'll talk again. We'll be professional about this."

He wasn't so sure he could ever be purely professional about her, but he was going to try. She deserved that. She deserved to find her academic knight in shining armor. Some man who'd never slit a throat or fought for his life. A man who could love her with a whole heart.

She nodded but he could see the way she flushed. "Good. That sounds good. I'll be better tomorrow. I need a nice meal and a bed. Tomorrow I'll be myself again."

He doubted that. She'd lost a lot in the last few years. It couldn't help but affect her. She'd lost Des and then her father and now her home.

He started to walk toward the hotel. It was a small, family-run hotel, but he knew the man who served as their head of security. At one point he'd worked for MTK. He was a sure thing, and that was why Nick was willing to leave her there. It was a boutique hotel with fewer than eighty rooms.

"So you really live in that place?" Hayley asked as she walked beside him.

"Most of us do. It's easier this way. We spend most of our time working and often must be away. While I'm gone, someone will take care of my place and handle my mail. I don't have to worry." He liked living in The Garden. It wasn't the way the American division was situated, but it seemed to work for them.

"So everyone's single?"

"Most of us are. My boss, Damon Knight, has a wife and child. They live on the top floor. His son is very young. I'm sure at some point he'll have to make some decisions about whether The Garden is a good place to raise children." He'd overheard Penny Knight talking about finding another home for her growing family. Even with the whole top floor, they were feeling confined when they talked about another child. "So soon it will be more like a dormitory. It's good to walk downstairs for work and to have a dining room where meals are served. Many, many days, I never leave the building."

"That sounds horrible," she said as they reached the alley that was a shortcut to the back of the hotel. "So if you're not working, you rarely leave? You live in one of the most amazing cities on the planet and you don't leave your house?"

It wasn't a house. He had a room in a building that he rarely left. Why should he? What was out in the world for him? Still, seeing it through her eyes made him wonder how pathetic an existence it was. He worked. He drank. He sometimes found a woman to top. Sleep. Start over again in the morning.

"Yes, well, that's the glamorous life of a spy." Not that he did much actual spy work anymore. He sometimes helped out MI6 or the Agency when he was asked to.

She stopped in the middle of the alley. "Nick, I truly am sorry. I was mean to say those things."

Weariness stole over him. Had it really been years since he found any joy in life? Since he woke up excited about the prospects of the day? "It's all right. It's not the lifestyle for you."

He was beginning to wonder if it was for him anymore. Even that part of his life had become rote and predictable. Unchallenging.

"I wouldn't know. I've read about it, but that's all. It's unlike me to be so intolerant."

"I suppose it was a surprise. You always wanted to live a respectable life. This lifestyle, it's not seen as respectable in most circles."

"Is the lifestyle why Des told me you weren't right for me that night?"

He stopped. He hadn't been aware Des had actually spoken to Hayley that night. He'd packed up as quickly as he could and when he'd come out of the motel room, Des had been waiting in her Benz. "She said I wasn't right for you?"

She turned to him, the shadows of the buildings around them casting her in a pale light. "She said you weren't in a good place. Not the place I needed you to be in." She shook her head. "I'm sorry. I don't even know why I mentioned it. Are we close?"

Oh, but he so wanted to know what Des had said that night. He had a million questions.

It was the slightest sound that alerted him to the fact that they were no longer alone. Nick turned, expecting to see some hurrying businessman taking a shortcut to get to the Tube station or a lost tourist.

The man who entered the alley didn't appear lost at all. The gun in his hand rather told Nick he'd found exactly what he was looking for.

With a curse, he threw himself in front of Hayley as the bullets started to fly.

Chapter Three

Hayley slammed against the brick wall, her left side flaring with pain. She managed to not hit her head and was about to explain that situation to Nick, who seemed to have lost his damn mind.

That was when she heard it. A ping and then the sound of metal slamming into metal.

Someone was shooting at her. At them. It wasn't just her anymore. Now Nicky was here and whoever was shooting wouldn't care that he wasn't involved. They wouldn't stop everything and give him the option to leave.

"Stay still." Nick pressed her down as though he could shove her between the massive trash bin and the wall.

She felt something wet on her hand. Dark liquid had splashed across her hand and arm.

Blood.

"Oh, my god. I think I'm hit." She tried to figure out where the bullet had gone in. She'd heard sometimes gunshot victims could go numb and not feel the actual effects until they were out of the situation.

"You're not. I am. Don't you dare pass out on me." Nick cursed and looked around.

She wasn't going to pass out. She was made of sterner stuff than that. "Where are you hit? How many of them are out there?"

"It's nothing. It barely grazed me." Nick held a hand up. "Now, hush."

Footsteps echoed down the alley. Two, then three. Nick had gone perfectly still. He pressed against her, completely covering her with his body.

"Miss Dalton, it won't work. I've got you in a corner and there's only one way out," a deep voice said. He spoke with an upper-crust British accent. "So if you care at all about your male companion, you'll come out and get this over with. I would rather bring you in alive, but if you won't comply, your body will do."

Nick was bleeding. Nick had been shot. She'd brought this to his doorstep and she didn't even understand why. Adrenaline raced through her, waking her up and bringing things into focus.

She was tired and scared and tired of being scared and really, really pissed off.

"Who the hell are you and what did I do to get your damn panties in a wad? Did I give your essay on the War of 1812 a bad grade? Because guess what buddy, you probably deserved it," she shouted before looking at Nick. "How bad is it? Can you still shoot him?"

Nick grimaced, trying to contort his massive body behind the trash bin. "I would if I had a blasted gun. I don't run around London armed. As I pointed out to you earlier, I don't tend to run around London much at all."

Damn it. What the hell kind of spy didn't walk around armed to the teeth? She looked down and he had a board in his hand.

Gun versus board. She kind of thought she knew how that one would turn out.

"This is your last chance, dear. The people I'm working with want you back in the United States. Do you wonder how they found you so quickly? Your friend was more than willing to give you up. Well, she was once we took a couple of her fingers. I don't think she'll be helping out criminals anymore."

Dodi? They'd found Dodi and now they'd found her. Confusion was a festering pit in her gut. What had she done to deserve this? She knew one thing for sure—she wasn't getting anyone else killed. It would be better to know why her life seemed to be ending than to watch Nick die and then die herself.

"Let me out." She tried to stand up.

"Hush." He crowded her, hunched over but on his feet. "You run the minute I move. You run back to The Garden."

She couldn't leave him. No matter what had happened all those years before, she couldn't run when he was facing down a man with a gun. And if she wasn't leaving him, then she definitely wasn't going to curl into a ball of fear.

"You should do as she says. I don't know who you are, mate, but you've gotten yourself involved in something nasty. You need to walk away. This is far bigger than you can imagine." There was the sound of his shoes against the concrete. Two more steps. Three more.

How far away had he been? How much longer did they have before he was on top of them?

She watched as Nick's fist curled around the broken board. Any minute now he would attack the man and he was such a big target. He was already hit and he would only get one real shot with that board of his.

Her brain raced through all the possible scenarios and they led to one conclusion. The man coming after them had the advantage. They had no weapons. He had the high ground. Nick likely wasn't thinking about taking this man out. He was probably giving her a chance to run while this asshole killed him. That was the most likely scenario.

She couldn't allow that to happen. All the fear and horror of the last few days morphed into pure will. She eased out of her backpack, maneuvering her arms and catching the straps in one hand. "I'm coming out. Don't hurt him. I'll go with you if you won't hurt him."

"Let's see you with your hands up. Come out easy and if I see a hint of metal, you should know I'm going to shoot," he explained.

But this time she heard the slight tremor in his voice. He wasn't unaffected. He might be a professional, but he apparently understood how dangerous all of this was.

"Don't you dare," Nick started.

She ignored him, concentrating on listening to her opponent. This man wasn't the police or he would have identified himself as such. Despite the fact that they were off the main street, they were still in public and he wouldn't want to involve civilians.

It was all about the bluff. Her father had made a living at the poker table. He'd taken her around the world when he had custody. He would teach her to listen to the other players.

Never play the cards in your hand, sweetheart. Play the men and women around the table. They will follow your lead.

She needed to lead him. He was in a heightened state of awareness, the same way she and Nick were. That was something she could use against him. He would be so focused on any movement coming from their direction that she might be able to distract him and give Nick a slim but fighting chance.

So still. She was still, every cell of her body focused on her moment. One chance. That would be all she had and if she missed it, Nick would be dead. She felt Nick begin to move and that was when she tossed her backpack across the alley with enough force that it hit the other side.

She heard the ping of the man's gun going off, but Nick was on his feet.

Hayley rushed to get up in time to see Nick bring the board down on their attacker. The other man managed to move so Nick missed his head but got his arm. The gun clattered to the ground.

Nick punched out, but the other man was smaller and obviously well trained. He kicked up, catching Nick in the gut. She could see the ragged place on his jacket where the bullet had ruined the material. There was blood clinging there, but he moved like he hadn't been hit at all.

Her heart was somewhere in the vicinity of her throat, but she had to stay calm, had to wait until she could help him again. This wasn't over. Two against one was pretty good odds, even if one of them was hurt and the other hadn't been to the gym in a while.

Nick groaned as the assailant managed to kick him again. He punched out with his good hand, this time connecting with the man's chin. There were only the sounds of grunts and groans, the majority of the fight taking place in utter silence, as though neither of the combatants wanted the attention.

She caught sight of the gun. It was across the alley, near her backpack. She had to get that damn gun. She wasn't sure Nick was going to win this particular fight. She couldn't take the chance.

Hayley ran for the other side, glancing over.

Her attacker pushed Nick away. Nick went down, his body slamming against the metal of the trash bin. The man in the suit started for her. He grabbed her arm, easily shoving her toward the brick wall. Pain slammed through her as she hit the wall and heard Nick's low growl behind her.

Hayley tried to kick back but couldn't connect. Stupid short legs. Where was Nick? The last time she'd seen him, his head was slamming into that bin. Was he still conscious? Panic started to rise inside her. She started to throw her head back only to have him push her again.

"Stay there, you slag. I swear the money better be worth it," he growled in her ear. "No one mentioned a man. It was supposed to be one lone and desperate girl. I'm getting double for you."

She went still. She couldn't hear Nick. "He's just some guy who was helping me find a hotel."

"I doubt that," the man said. He was shifting behind her, likely trying to figure out how to get that gun back in his hand without letting go of her. "He fought like a professional. I thought I was the only one who'd figured out you were in London. I guess I had some competition."

She heard the slight sound of shoes against the concrete and braced herself.

Nick attacked, throwing his big body into the man holding her.

Hayley dropped to her knees as Nick and the other man slammed against the wall.

The gun. It was still out there. She had to get the gun and then she could stop all of this.

She scrambled, her knees bruised and aching as she reached for the gun. Cool metal filled her hands and she managed to turn. Her hands shook as she held the gun up.

Nick sat with his back to the wall, his skin pale. "Don't bother with that. He's dead. Damn it. I hit him too hard."

He was dead? They were safe? Well, except for the police, who would come and then make a report and then everyone on the planet would know where she was.

Although apparently someone already did know.

"I'm glad he's dead." She knew she shouldn't be, but the man had tried his best to kill her. Her mother would be shocked at Hayley's first impulse, which was to kick the shit out of that body to make damn sure he was dead. Her sweet, granola, hippie momma who had died when she was seventeen. She was looking down from heaven with that stern frown she'd gotten whenever Hayley had come home from spending time with her dad and found a hidden stash of junk food in her backpack. Nope, she couldn't follow her momma's path now. Nonviolent protest would have gotten her killed. It might be time to saddle up and do things her father's way.

"Well, I'm not. Dead man can't explain why he was hunting you," Nick shot back. "Also, dead man can't be tortured, and I'm feeling like torturing someone, Hayley. None of this happens if you are not such a stubborn girl."

Well, that was putting it baldly. "I didn't ask to have my home explode. I didn't ask to apparently have international assassins put on my ass. That's so not fair."

"Now you sound like surly teen girl." He stopped and took a deep breath after muttering something in Russian. Nick pulled his phone out of his pocket, pressing a single button. It wasn't more than two seconds before he began to speak. When he opened his mouth this time, he barely had a hint of his accent. "It's Nick. I need a cleanup crew."

A cleanup crew? For the body? She glanced down at the man who had attacked them, trying to see anything at all familiar in his face. Her stomach turned. The man's dark eyes stared up at her, no animation behind them at all.

"I know. I know I've been gone for five minutes and now I have a dead body. Yes, I work fast. Damn it, Kayla. It was not sexual frust…she's alive. Yes. No. I don't know. Please get Owen and Brody and get them quickly or I'll have the police on my ass."

He got to his feet and brushed off his slacks as he hung up the phone. He reached down and pulled the man's body behind the bin where they'd hidden.

Nick turned to her, his eyes narrowing. "You will stay at the club."

She simply nodded because no amount of heartache was worth getting murdered. She'd been stupidly stubborn and she wouldn't make the same mistake again. "The club sounds great."

Nick frowned and guarded the body.

And Hayley finally took a deep breath. "Do you think we could…"

"Shhh," Nick shushed her. "I have to listen for people coming down the alley or we'll have the police called on us."

Her tummy grumbled. Damn. Not even a murder attempt and a dead body mattered to her empty gut. She was standing in an alley with a pissed-off Russian bear and a nasty old dead body, and suddenly she wished she hadn't insulted Teresa because apparently Teresa was like Gandalf standing in front of the kitchens telling Hayley that she shall not pass.

"Maybe you could talk to…"

Nick sent her a glare that shut her down.

Her stomach made an audible sound.

Nick sighed. "You are pain in my ass."

Like she'd never heard that before. What a freaking day.

Chapter Four

"Are you fucking kidding me? Is this like when a cat tosses a dead mouse at his master's feet? Nick, I told you. I don't need gifts, but this one is pretty cool. Look, baby, we just got back to the real world and we already have a dead body to deal with."

Nick stopped, his eyes closing, and he nearly did it. He nearly prayed. It was right there on the tip of his tongue to ask God that Ian Taggart not be standing in the middle of the conference room.

"I thought I would at least have time to unpack and perhaps take a shower before we had our debrief, Nikolai. Honestly, I thought it could wait until the morning since we recently got off a nine-hour flight. It looks like cleaning up and sleeping will have to wait." Damon Knight stood beside Taggart, the two men staring down at him.

And then he felt it. Hayley moved beside him, one hand on his back as though he would provide safety and security from the predators in the room. Smart girl since these two men were far more dangerous than the one they'd met in that alley. If these two lions had been the ones who wanted to take her apart, they would be picking their teeth with her bones by now.

"Well, paradise was fun but we were getting pretty bored there at the end. I'm afraid I can only stand about a week or so of peace and quiet." Charlotte Taggart joined her husband. She was a stunning woman with strawberry blonde hair and ties to the Russian mob. Luckily not the syndicate that had killed his sister. Her cousin ran the Denisovitch syndicate, one Nick had found fairly friendly, as murdering thieves went. Her eyes softened as she looked at him and began speaking in his native tongue. Though she sounded perfectly American when she spoke English, her Russian proved she'd spent much of her childhood in Moscow. *"Ty vyglyadish ustavshym, Nikolay. Yesli khochesh otdokhnut, ya pozabochus ob etikh dvukh. E skazhi dyevochke, chto boyatsya ne nuzhno."*

Sometimes he missed hearing his own language, but now was not the time to go soft. He replied to her, but stuck to English. "I don't know that she's afraid enough. Hayley, meet my bosses. The Englishman is Damon Knight. He runs the London office. The American is a man named Ian Taggart and this is his wife, Charlotte. They were supposed to get in late this evening."

"We left Loa Mali a bit early," Damon explained. "The wedding was wonderful. It was nice to get away, but it was time to come home. Now I see that I should have gotten us home a bit earlier. Would you like to explain why there's a dead body in the small conference room?"

He'd had Owen and the boys move it in there because the lighting was best for what he needed to do. "I have someone cleaning out the freezer as we speak, but I thought it would be easier to get the photographs we'll need if we properly laid him out."

Damon frowned fiercely. "Are you planning on having an autopsy? Because that might best be done, I don't know, perhaps at the bloody medical examiner's office. What were you thinking?"

"We can skip the autopsy," Taggart slid in. "I got this one. Dude got his head bashed in. I saw brains and everything. I don't get why we need to open him up and measure his organs and shit. Head met something harder. Something harder totally won."

This was the joy of dealing with Taggart. He needed to calm

down. His heart was still thudding in his chest half an hour after the attack. He needed a drink, but first he had to stay calm and handle Taggart. He focused on his English, on sounding as calm as he wanted to feel. "The man attacked me and my client as I was taking her to a secure hotel. I did not bring the London police or Scotland Yard in because of the sensitivity of her situation."

"Your client?" Knight asked. "I wasn't aware we were taking on clients while I was gone. Have you decided on new protocol in my absence? Clients will be vetted, their cases presented to a majority of the group, and the group will decide on whether or not we take a case. Madam, I don't know what my employee told you, but I haven't taken your case so until such time as we do reach a verdict on your status as a client, I have to ask you to leave the conference room. I need to speak to Nick alone."

Her hand slipped into his, her small palm practically pleading with him for safety.

Damn it. He could walk away from her when she was playing the brat, but he'd never once been able to toss aside a woman who needed him. It was like he had a damn switch and she'd flicked it on. He squeezed her hand and drew her up to his side. "She's Desiree's cousin. If you won't take her case, then I will put in for leave and take it on myself. If this isn't acceptable to you, then you'll have my resignation in the morning. I ask that she be allowed to stay here until I make arrangements for us."

Damon cursed under his breath and ran a hand over his head. "All right, then. I still want to talk to you privately. I'll expect a full briefing on her case first thing in the morning in whichever conference room doesn't contain a dead body. I suspect we're going to have to get rid of him."

"Acid," Taggart began.

"No acid," Charlotte said at exactly the same time as her husband, as though she'd known exactly what he was going to say.

"Baby, come on. I'm still on vacation. Why do you take this away from me?" Taggart was grinning at his wife like he was begging for the best Christmas present of all time.

She simply shook her head. "Absolutely not. I don't trust you with acid. You would go overboard and get it all over, and I like your skin the way it is. You're not careful enough when it comes to bodies. I blame it on your time in the Agency. You always had someone to back you up so you treated getting rid of bodies like playtime. That's not the way it is in the mob. We had to be super careful or we got shipped to Siberia. You know what they don't have in Siberia? Harrod's. Or anything nice and beautiful and glamorous. So I wasn't going. I learned. We've gotta burn the sucker. We go in undercover at a suburban funeral home and have our dear cousin John cremated. I can have the paperwork in a few hours. No funeral. He was pretty mean. Once we've spread his ashes all over the ocean there's no way the cops can pin it on Nick."

"God, I love your mind," Taggart said, his arm sliding around his wife's waist. "It's almost as sexy as your boobs."

"I promise I will dispose of the body once I have what I need for identification," Nick replied quickly because the Taggarts had been known to lose sight of the mission when they started in on the romantic stuff. And their version of romance could include some odd, rather violent things. "I'll have the situation as I know it ready for a meeting with the group in the morning. I'm going to settle Hayley into the empty room and then try to run the photographs through facial recognition."

"Send the pictures to the Dallas office," Taggart offered. "It's morning there and Adam's software is better than anything you have here. We're still negotiating terms of use since that bastard son of a bitch is leaving to start up another company, but he'll get the job done for now."

"Because he's a nice man and he's not trying to screw you." Charlotte's eyes rolled as though this was a conversation they'd had more than once.

He'd heard that two of the Dallas operatives were leaving the company. Adam Miles and Jacob Dean were starting their own firm, one that specialized in missing persons. It wouldn't exactly compete with McKay-Taggart, but rather complement the company. "I would be grateful for his help. I'm trying to keep her off the radar until I can figure out what's happening."

Knight nodded. "Get her settled in and then come to my office. I do want to talk to you privately. Now more than ever. I'm going up to make sure Penelope and Ollie don't need anything."

Charlotte sighed. "I suppose I'll go check on our kiddos, too. Kayla stole them the minute we walked in. I should have helped her but it's been a long time since we had an office full of dead bodies. The younger employees need to step up their game. I think I'll get a snack on the way up. Do we know if the kitchen is open?"

It wasn't a play night, but the kitchen would be open to anyone who wanted to cook. They tended to take turns, though they'd always given Owen an out since he could ruin toast. But supper wasn't for another hour and they'd been planning on ordering in.

Hayley stepped up, letting her hand drop from his. "I will kiss your feet if you show me how to get to the kitchen. I haven't had a thing but airplane food in days."

Charlotte gave her a ready smile. "Of course. We'll go see what we can find. Nick, you get the key to her room and I'll find something to feed her. You actually look a bit like Des. Right around the eyes."

Ian stepped up behind his wife. "I'll go take care of our demons. You help out the girl. I think we're going to hang out here for a few days. We owe Des a lot. Don't worry about this. We'll take care of you…do you have a name or are we calling you Des's cousin? Think about it. Names can be meaningful. If you've got one of those crazy names, you might go with Des's cousin. This is your shot."

He was about to tell Tag to leave her alone when Hayley gave him a brilliant smile.

"I'm Hayley, Mr. Taggart. It was my mother's maiden name. I quite like it so if you want to make fun of it, you'll have to wait until I've rested for us to fight. We're in England so we have to duel like proper gentlemen. I'll find a glove to smack you with in the morning.

I'm too tired to do away with you tonight."

Taggart laughed and put out his hand. "I will remember not to impugn your name. It's nice to meet you, Hayley. As my wife said, we owe a great debt to your cousin. I welcome you as a client, and know we'll do our best to protect you. And my Charlie here will feed you. She's good at that."

His Charlie would also gently interview Hayley to figure out exactly what was going on. Hayley could handle Charlotte. Oh, not in a fight or anything, but Charlotte meant what she'd said about Des. She would honor the fact that Hayley was family.

Would they take care of her if Damon Knight fired him in the next hour or so?

The thought of walking away…hours before there had been a bit of temptation to the idea. He'd thought about walking off and letting go and not caring about anything. Now that Hayley was here and he'd seen the danger she was in, he wasn't sure he could let go.

Hayley moved back to him, her head tilting up as she looked to him. "Is it all right? You did mention that you were in charge. After what happened in that alley, I'm totally okay with that, but I could use some food."

She was so tired and yet she was looking to him, asking for his permission because she was in danger. She couldn't fucking know how that affected him. He wouldn't want that in normal life. He would want a partner, but something about a woman looking to him for help when the chips were down did it for him.

He was sure Ariel, the group's resident profiler, would tell him that had to do with Des, too.

He shoved that idea to the side. He wasn't in a mood to fix himself and he wasn't sure he wanted to fix that particular part of himself. Perhaps it was time to let the other Doms in the room know where he stood on this. He reached down, smoothing her hair back. "Go and eat, *dushka*. I'll have your room ready in a few moments. Do you want a room to yourself or would you prefer to stay with me? I can sleep on the couch if it makes you feel more secure."

She sniffled a bit and seemed to think about it. "I would rather stay with you. I know I shouldn't, but the thought of closing a door and being alone right now…I wouldn't be able to sleep. And I'll take the couch. I'm sure it's far better than what I've been sleeping on."

She started to leave, following after Charlotte like a tired duckling. When she got to the door, she turned. "And Nick?"

He watched her, not quite ready to let her out of his sight yet. "Yes, *dushka*?"

"It's good to see you. And thank you." She turned and walked out into the corridor.

He was in so much fucking trouble.

* * * *

Hayley knew she was in trouble the minute she walked into the kitchen. She'd followed Charlotte Taggart through the building, trying not to stare at the winding vines and trees that made up the bottom floor. No. That's not what Nick would call it. He would call it the dungeon.

It didn't look like a place of pain and torture. It looked like a decadent dream.

Luckily the kitchen looked like a place where she could get some food. Unfortunately, they weren't alone.

A stunningly gorgeous woman with rich, dark skin and jet-black hair sat in the kitchen, a cup of tea in front of her and a book in her hand. She glanced up and a warm smile crossed her gorgeous face. She spoke with a pure, upper-crust British accent. "Charlotte, welcome back. I saw Penny earlier and she said you and Ian and the children were staying for a few days. I'm so happy to see you again. We didn't get to spend much time together at the wedding."

Charlotte leaned over to give the other woman a hug. "It was a crazy affair. Besides, it seemed to me Robert kept trying to get you to himself."

The other woman shook her head. "Well, you know I am his therapist."

Charlotte stood back up. "I thought he was trying to find a new one. Something about a conflict of interest."

The other woman waved it off. "Not on my part. You know I don't ever date people I work with."

"From what I can tell, you don't date at all." The redhead turned back to Hayley as she walked across the tiled floor to the refrigerator. "Ariel Adisa, this is our new client Hayley. She was Desiree's cousin and apparently she's smack dab in the middle of a shit storm. And she's hungry. Do you want a sandwich?" Charlotte opened the door to the industrial-sized fridge. "It looks like there's roast beef. Or I could make some eggs. Eggs and toast should be pretty easy on your stomach. It sounds like you've had a rough couple of days."

Before she could reply, the doors opened and Teresa entered. The Garden, it appeared, was a hopping place. The submissive/office assistant had big, lovely brown eyes that managed to spark flames when she caught sight of Hayley.

Teresa frowned Hayley's way. "Is there something I can help you with?"

Charlotte shut the door, a carton of eggs in her hand. "Oh, hey, T. How's it going? I was making a snack for me and the newbie before we hit the sack. Jet lag sucks. How many times zones you been through, Hayley?"

"A lot." She'd been so mean and she wasn't sure how to fix it. She could handle it if someone didn't like her, but this was different. She'd hurt Teresa's feelings and she couldn't abide that.

Teresa crossed over to the stove. "I can help you, love. It's nice to see you again. Would you like some tea with that? I've got some chamomile to help you sleep. Of course, I also know where the boss keeps the good brandy as well."

Ariel smiled at that. "You're going to get a spanking, dear."

Teresa perked up. "Well, isn't that horrible. I shall have to give Charlotte an extra shot to make it all worthwhile."

So many beautiful, self-possessed women. Hayley didn't fit in at all. She wanted to shrink away.

Charlotte set the eggs down. "You're a lifesaver. I think we could both use some booze. This one here is having a crap day."

Teresa sniffed and turned toward the cupboard. "If you say so."

Charlotte's eyes widened as she looked back to Hayley. "Did you manage to piss off the sweetest sub in the club?"

Tears welled. She'd pissed off everyone in the last couple of days. Some people she didn't even know. "I was surprised to find out Nick lived over a dungeon. I said some things I shouldn't."

"I believe she called The Garden a sex club," Teresa corrected primly as she pulled out a bottle of brandy. She whisked her hand over the stove where Charlotte was putting a frying pan. "Don't you dare. You're our guest. Sit down and relax. I'm quite good with eggs. Omelets? I've got some veg prepped for tomorrow's breakfast but plans always change, you know."

Charlotte sank into the chair across from Hayley. "A sex club? Well, I've had some pretty filthy sex here, but some take exception to calling it that. Better to call it a lifestyle club or go with the classic dungeon. It's coded language that kind of ends up meaning sex club."

Ariel sighed. "I'm not sure I like the sound of that."

Teresa set the drinks on the table. "It's about more than sex and you know it."

"I know that, too." Hayley saw a small opening and decided to try to wedge her way through. At least Teresa hadn't spat in her drink. "I took a class in the history of sex and gender politics. It covered some kink. And a psych course in sexuality."

"Yes, I'm sure we're all deviants," Teresa said under her breath.

"Oh, no, I went to college in Seattle. The emphasis was on BDSM as a model of consent."

Ariel arched a perfectly manicured brow her way. "Yes, I've heard Dr. Banning was pressing her research that direction. Some have said BDSM and its language are a good way to present the idea of sexual consent to adolescents and college-aged kids. I read her latest paper. I liked her ideas."

At least she found someone who didn't hate her. "The professor thinks most sexual partners would be happier if they talked about sex the way people in the lifestyle do. So I know I was being insulting when I said what I said."

Teresa opened the fridge and began her preparations. "And yet you managed to be insulting anyway."

Charlotte sat back in her chair, the brandy in her hand. "You said you were surprised that Nick was living here. Where did you think he lived?"

Hayley didn't want to talk, but this was her penance. It looked like she would be staying here and she didn't want her presence to hurt the other women. She knew far too well what it felt like to be an object of scorn. "I guess I pictured him still living wherever he and Des had lived. Some nice townhouse here. Maybe a swanky flat. I know they lived here in London most of the time, but they had places all over the world. I thought they would live somewhere where they could be alone. Maybe that's why he moved here. Maybe it was too hard to be in the home they shared."

Teresa turned, her face suddenly sympathetic. "How long has it been since you saw your cousin? I mean before she died. Were you two close?"

She was too tired to lie. "Three years before she died. Five all together. Not since the day I tried to convince Nick to marry me instead of Des. That's why I was pissy about finding out he was living over the club and was an active member. I'm so sorry I said the things I did. I was jealous. He told me you were a sub and I figured you and he…"

Teresa stepped toward her, reaching out for Hayley's hand. "Oh, sweetheart. No. Nikolai and I have never been together. We're better friends than play partners. I have played with a few of the boys, but the only one I ever slept with turned out to be a complete wanker. And now he's forgotten the entire incident and I can't hold it over his head. It's quite annoying. Honestly, I'm looking for someone I can get serious with, and every woman at The Garden knows it's not going to be Nick."

73

"Because he loved Des." She knew it. Nick and Des had a crazy, passionate, once-in-a-lifetime love. "He won't be able to love again."

Charlotte looked to Teresa. "Is that true? Because I thought they were a rather odd couple the few times I met them. I saw them as convenient lovers."

Hayley shook her head. "No. You don't understand how they were. I was a kid when I first met Nick. Des brought him with her to a family event. My father would make me go to at least three a year to keep up relations, as he would say. They were horrible because everyone there was awful with the exception of Des. She was always nice to me. And then she brought in Nick and I had the biggest crush on him. Maybe it was more about them. They were so passionate, so crazy about each other. And then they would fight and they were passionate about that, too. I think I wanted someone, anyone to be that passionate about me."

There was a heavy moment of silence where the three other women in the room looked to each other, seeming to have some kind of silent dialogue Hayley didn't understand at all. She felt small and insignificant among these women who seemed to know each other so well. Finally Ariel leaned forward.

"Before her death, Desiree and Nikolai lived here in The Garden. They started living here as soon as they hired on," the psychologist explained. "And they kept separate rooms. They did spend time together, but as a person who is an expert on relationships, I would say their sexuality wasn't very intimate."

Hayley shook her head. "No, they were in love. They were so in love."

"Obsession isn't love, and I think after a while they were more habit and affection than anything else," Ariel said. "I can understand how from the outside they would look passionate, but there's a certain psychology that happens when sexual chemistry butts heads with actual soul-deep connection. Call it obsession. Call it codependence. Call it what you like, but I think that's what happened with Nick and Des."

Teresa patted her hand and walked to the stove with purpose. "You're going to feel much better when you've had some decent food. Airline food barely counts as food at all. You sit back and let T take care of you, love."

Charlotte grinned. "See, that wasn't so hard."

Ariel was looking her way, her eyes curious. "How old were you when you met Nick? If you don't mind my asking."

There was something soothing about the woman's voice. And it wasn't like she hadn't spilled her guts out all over the table. "I was fifteen when Des first brought him to one of our family events."

"You're American," Charlotte pointed out. "Des's family was British and wealthy. So I assume the American relatives were wealthy as well."

The brandy was starting to warm her belly nicely. Teresa had been right. It was good stuff. "Not all of us. I mean I guess at some point we were. My mom and dad never married and she always told me she had no idea why my father associated with them. Apparently he found out he belonged to a branch of the family that had come to America and then kind of lost touch. We weren't entirely welcome, but Dad kept trying. I think Des enjoyed the idea of her posh family having a member who made his living playing poker."

Charlotte leaned in. "Your dad is a professional poker player?"

"Was. He died earlier this year. He was in Macau for a tournament and he ended up in the wrong cab apparently. He and the driver died in a crash. Not surprisingly my English relatives didn't show up for his funeral. But anyway, it was kind of how I bonded with Nick. At least three times a year we would end up at some reunion or family holiday, and they didn't like Nick any more than they liked me and Dad."

"Yes, I've known the type," Ariel said. "I'm surprised your father allowed you to be around that kind of disdain. It can be hard on a teen."

It hadn't always been so bad. "Des was nice. I know she could be hard to take sometimes, but she was always nice to me. I looked up to her."

"Desiree was a lovely woman," Charlotte agreed.

"Oh, she was a crazy bitch. Can we not sugarcoat it? I know the woman's dead and how she died made her a saint or something, but Des could cut you to the quick, and sometimes she'd do it for fun." Teresa had a spatula in her hand and the scent of something heavenly wafted from the stove. "And some of the things she would do to Nick were damn near unforgivable."

Ariel held up a hand as though this was something that had been discussed more than once and she wanted to stave off a real argument. "Des and Nick had a contract and Nick signed it."

Teresa shook her head. "I have no idea why."

"But you have to honor the contract," Charlotte replied. "Nick was a big boy and he knew what he was getting into. It wasn't like he didn't take advantage of their open relationship."

That woke her up even more than the thought of food. "Open relationship? I thought they got rid of that after…well, after what happened with me. When he left he told me that he and Des had worked everything out and that he was happy with where they were. Are you telling me I've felt guilty all these years when they never stopped sleeping with other people?"

"They never lived together. They would go off on assignments together and play husband and wife, but that was the only time they would ever cohabitate," Ariel stated plainly. "I can't go into the psychology behind it because that would push the boundaries of what I owe my coworkers, but I will say, he's certainly got his reasons that a relationship like that would feel more familiar than something different. Something softer and more peaceful."

"Yeah, let me say I've had both and there's zero question in my mind which I'll choose. I've had some serious crazy love-him, hate-him sex, and while it was wild and amazing, it had nothing on waking up in the morning with my husband after a long night with the baby and having him kiss me everywhere, having his hands on my body and him whispering how much he loves me." Charlotte raised her glass. "I will leave the angsty romance to the younger women."

"Well, of course it's better with your husband. You probably didn't really love the other man." Hayley's mind was going back to that night. Even as he'd taken her clothes off, she'd known it had been different for him. He'd been so gentle with her, kissing her for what felt like forever. She'd wondered afterward if that had been what made him sure of his decision to leave. She hadn't been passionate enough in bed with him.

Charlotte's lips curled up in a secret smile. "Oh, but you're wrong. The hate sex was with the same man. It was always Ian. Always. The funny thing is you can't keep that level of passion up naturally. Not if you want any peace at all in your life. The world catches up to you and life catches up and you either grow together or apart. You find yourself in this place where you know that your marriage is an act of love and one of pure willpower. You're not always happy, but you're content because you know that man isn't going to leave. You're in it for life because you need each other. So you make slight changes and bend in ways you didn't think you would and find out you're happier for doing it. You change in small ways for your children and suddenly you're making decisions based on what's best for your family and not yourself, and you realize he's doing the same for you. People looking out for each other, that's what makes a family."

"Desiree never let that man have a bit of peace in his life." Teresa placed a plate in front of Hayley. Eggs and toast with cheese. Some people would call it nursery food, but it was so what she needed. "She was addicted to drama and adrenaline and she made him a player in the soap opera of her life."

Hayley couldn't help but think of the way Des would make an entrance. She would storm in and out of everyone's lives. There was always something going on, some fight, some trial, someone who had done her wrong.

What kind of life had that been for Nick?

"And yet he continued to sign that contract," Ariel pointed out. "I

77

know you like him, but every story has three sides. His and hers and the truth."

"Spoken like a true shrink," Charlotte said with a grin.

"What do you mean about the contract? A contract for what?" Some of what Ariel was saying sunk in. Nick had stayed.

"Nick and Des took the lifestyle seriously. Well, Des took the parts she liked seriously," Teresa explained. "Once a year they signed a contract that covered all aspects of their relationship. Des ensured that she kept the relationship open. She wanted the right to have sex with anyone she liked."

"I think Des would say she was keeping her job options open," Ariel interjected. "Sometimes it's the easiest way to get information."

"Nick has certainly done the same," Charlotte pointed out. "Sometimes our business can get a little dirty."

She didn't like the thought of Nick fucking for information.

Ariel reached out, as though sensing what was going through her head. "You do understand that the work we do here can save lives."

"He worked to save my brother-in-law's life. Try not to judge him or Des too harshly. They did what they had to do to get the job done," Charlotte explained. "I know the tendency is to shame Des for having a healthy sexual appetite, but she didn't lie to him. She wasn't going behind his back. Desiree might have had some issues, but she didn't hide them. Nick and Des's relationship was what it was. No one should judge them for it. We weren't there."

But Hayley had been. At least she had been for one night.

"I know to someone who doesn't understand the lifestyle, a contract could seem cold, but it's actually an important tool." Ariel sat back, toying with her teacup as she spoke. "It's how we tell our partner what we need and expect. That was Des's way of explaining in plain language to Nick what she would and wouldn't give to him. A contract keeps things simple between two people."

"Or more." Charlotte winked up at Teresa as she placed a plate in front of her. "I have friends who share a wife. And I know some subs who serve the same Master. Anything goes in our world as long as you're honest and honor your partner."

A contract. She hadn't asked him for a contract that night. She'd simply offered herself up on a platter and only had thought to ask for what she wanted after she'd slept with Nick. Would it have turned out differently if she'd tried it his way?

She started to eat as Charlotte told her war stories from the dungeon. Contracts gone wrong, as she called them.

But Hayley was already thinking. She would be stuck with Nick for a while. As long as it took to figure out why someone was trying to kill her.

It might be time to work a few things out of her system. Perhaps his as well.

She just needed courage and maybe someone who knew a thing or two about the lifestyle.

Chapter Five

Nick walked in the door to Damon's office wondering if he wouldn't be the one out on the street in a few hours. His boss's office was elegant. Masculine and yet comfortable. It was the office of a man who had his foot in both worlds. The expensive furniture bespoke the successful business he ran while the pictures of a smiling wife holding a bundle of baby was testament to the fact that Damon Knight had figured out his life. He knew who he was. A husband and father first and then a man of business.

Nick had to wonder if he'd ever been anything but a killer.

"Why don't you have a seat, Nikolai?" Damon gestured to the seat in front of him, sliding off the reading glasses he'd taken to wearing in the last few months after Penny had nagged him into it.

What would it be like to have a woman who cared enough to nag? Who watched him so carefully she could figure out that his headaches came from the deep and vain need to pretend his eyes were still perfect? "Of course. Although if you're planning on firing me, you could simply say so and we could avoid a lengthy talk. I'm sure we're both tired."

Knight sat back, a frown creasing his face. Nick was certain that perfect face of Knight's had served him well when the man had been one of MI6's deadliest agents. "I'm intrigued. Why would I fire you?"

"Well, I thought the dead body in the conference room was a start." He had to play this cool if he was going to keep his job. And there was no doubt he wanted that outcome. Now more than ever. He could give Damon half a dozen reasons to fire him. He'd been Owen's partner and he hadn't seen the trouble his best friend had been in. He drank too much. Far too much. He wasn't half the operative Des had been and he'd failed to save her, too. He couldn't save anyone who counted.

He kept his mouth shut because he was a selfish prick.

"I have to say I wish I hadn't come home to a body in the conference room," Damon admitted. "Perhaps we should designate a space when bodies come up."

"I thought you would be more angry."

Damon waved him off. "I was a bit put out. I was planning on going right to bed, but Ollie slept on the plane. The whole plane ride. Now the little guy is awake along with all those Taggart children. Perhaps it makes me an utter coward, but I might have used the dead body excuse as a way to run. I left Big Tag up there with his two crying twins, his infant son who can't seem to go an hour without making poo, and my son, who's wailing for his supper. Now that I've had some time to reflect, that dead body actually saved me from a rather uncomfortable evening. Though I do wish Dante and Sasha would stop poking the poor bloke. I swear those boys are the worst. It's like they lost all maturity when they lost their memories. They've got the mentality and sex drive of bloody seventeen-year-olds."

He wouldn't argue with that. He was just happy one of the things Sasha remembered was how to speak English. That boy had a worse accent than Nick himself had when he'd first joined SVR. It was one of the things Nick had noted about Sasha in his report. The dark-haired man hadn't been a Russian operative. If Sasha had been in the program, that deep accent would have been trained out of him. Of course Sasha also hadn't been poor since his English was quite good.

It was one more mystery to be solved.

"They're curious," Nick said. "Sometimes I think they're reveling in having no responsibility. No past. And then I also worry that they feed each other and make what they're going through seem normal."

"Ariel thinks they need each other," Damon replied.

"I'm sure they do, but besides Robert, not a one of them seems interested in figuring out who they used to be, if anyone's even out there looking for them. It's like one of those American college clubs. You know, the ones with all the parties where someone ends up murdering a hooker."

"You watch far too much telly, I fear. Or too little. I believe you're talking about a fraternity and I think you're right about the lads pushing reality to the side a bit, but Ariel thinks they need it for now so we all must indulge it a bit longer." Damon stared at him for a moment as though assessing how to continue. "I don't want to talk about the lads. I need to talk about Des."

"Desiree's been dead for more than two years. I should think if there was something to say, you would have said it by now."

"I rather hoped I wouldn't have to." Damon's jaw went tight. "You know I worked with her for years before she came here."

"You two were in MI6 together. I knew that." Was he about to get some seedy backstory about how they'd been lovers? Des had claimed she'd never slept with their boss during their time together serving her majesty. She rarely lied to him. She didn't have to when the truth was a much more effective weapon.

"I had some reservations about hiring her on here."

"She never mentioned that. I suppose that was because of me. I know she made it a term of her employment that you would take me on, too."

Damon waved that idea off. "Not at all. I would have hired you in a heartbeat."

Somehow Nick found that hard to believe. "Then you didn't do as much research as I thought you would."

"Are you talking about what you did to the Ivanov syndicate?"

This was exactly what he wanted to avoid. Talking about all his sins. "I don't know what story you hear, but you should understand, it was bloody. I kill them with my own hands. I kill them all."

"No, you did not," Damon said quietly. "You killed ten of the top men and six others. The men who killed your sister. The men who had a hand in her death. You killed every single one of them and left the rest alive. You effectively killed the syndicate off, but there were a few men who you let go. Do you want to explain why?"

"There is nothing from that time I wish to talk about ever again."

"You let them go because you were merciful. Those few men had no part in Katja Markovic's death. They had been too young at the time or hadn't joined the group. One of them had joined because he had no other choice but death, and you let him go. You rained death down on that group and yet still found mercy on those who deserved it. And that was you, not Desiree. You. I know that because I've worked with her. How hard was it to hold her back? She loved the kill."

Nick felt shaken. He'd stopped thinking about it, hated thinking about those seven months of his life when everything had been blood and violence, or sex that felt a bit like violence. He had been forced to hold her back. She'd wanted to take them all down, but a few had no blood on their hands. No blood of his, and he would have been a horrible hypocrite to take them out because of their affiliations. "It was my mission. I was in charge. I made the decisions."

He wasn't going to give her up now. She'd been his partner. She'd been the one to bring him the intelligence when everyone else had disavowed him. No one would work with him. Only Des. He wouldn't tell Damon how he'd been forced to stop her from bombing a house with innocent family members where their prime target had been visiting. He'd wanted to kill the man but had not found it in his soul to take down others to quench his thirst.

Des had called him a coward. Told him he was too weak to get the job done.

"You don't have to tell me. I understand," Damon said. "Can I ask you a question?"

"As long as you understand I might not answer."

"What reason did she give you for her resignation from MI6?"

Here it was. One of those questions he didn't want to know the answer to. Des never lied about her sexual partners. Never cheated on him behind his back when she could do it to his front.

Stop. He couldn't do that. She'd never promised him anything more than she'd given. He wasn't going to make her into a villain. "She didn't give me a real reason. I think she probably left for me. She found out some vital information around the same time that she tendered her resignation and that led her to come back to Russia with me. When we were done with syndicate, you gave us both jobs, as she'd told me you would. Hiring on here was her plan, not mine. I wouldn't have come to you because I was a failed operative. You only hired the best."

"Failed operative? Because you didn't go through with the Crimean mission? Because you figured out that Putin was trying to foment a rebellion that didn't exist so he could waltz in and take over territory that held the key to providing natural gas to Europe?"

He'd figured it out quickly. He'd been sent to find those who were discriminating against natural Russians and found out it was mostly other operatives creating a situation for the media. He'd watched as fellow operatives hurt innocent people for the cameras, claiming to be the opposition.

"I tried to walk away." He'd been such a fool. He'd walked in and told his commanding officer why he was leaving. He hadn't thought about the consequences, hadn't thought that his actions could cost more than him.

It had cost Katja everything.

"You refused to participate in an operation you believed in your heart was wrong. You followed your conscience. Do you know how many agents at your level manage to maintain a conscience? Most of the high-level operatives I know shed their consciences long ago."

"My conscience cost my sister her life."

"I understand. Well, I've read the reports. I suppose I don't truly understand. She was leaving SVR as well?"

Nick nodded. "She believed the way I did. She saw the same things, but she went back in one last time. There was a man she cared about and she believed he was in danger. She asked him to come with us. That was when she found out her lover was a plant. He turned her over to the Ivanov syndicate. I was caught and turned over as well. The syndicate did the dirty work Putin does not want even his SVR agents to know."

"Yes, MI6 made that connection as well. Ivanov gave the government plausible deniability when it came to certain operations they didn't want to acknowledge. I'm sure they've found another syndicate to work with by now."

"I would have suffered the same fate as my sister had MI6 not been working in the region."

Damon nodded. "Yes, Desiree was active in that operation. She extracted you."

"She saved me."

"She had her reasons. Bringing you in gave us valuable information and likely saved her job."

"I don't understand." The conversation made him restless, but he had to admit he was intrigued.

"Des was in trouble with our boss," Damon explained. "She always had…projects on the side. Projects that weren't exactly company approved, if you know what I mean."

Ah, now he got it. "Yes, she figured she should make a bit of cash on the side when she could. I never agreed with that, but I couldn't convince her to give it up."

"She brokered information." Damon stated the truth plainly. "She made millions off it."

He was uncomfortable again. This was one aspect of Desiree's life he'd tried to have very little part in, but he had participated in those dark days after his sister had died. "I helped her from time to time."

"I know. You were her muscle for a few years. I also understand why you did it. You felt obligated to her. And you loved her."

She'd been everything to him for a while.

And then he'd met Hayley. Then he'd known what it meant to sacrifice again.

"I loved Des, but I also knew what she did. After we settled in here, I stayed out of most of her extra operations." Now that he knew Damon hadn't been fooled, he had some questions. Why on earth would McKay-Taggart and Knight hire Desiree and her "muscle"? The answer washed over him like a splash of cold water. "MI6 asked you to watch her."

Damon's eyes were grave in the low light of his office. "Like I said, I would have hired you in a second. I would not have hired Desiree without some intervention. It wasn't only MI6. The Agency was concerned about her as well. Ian and I decided to comply with their requests. A year into the investigation, she died. No one saw that coming. It's taken years to comb through her business dealings. She had connections everywhere and more aliases than I care to keep up with. We're still finding caches she kept in various places."

"Why didn't you come to me? I could have helped. I might not know everything, but I'm sure I could make the process go faster. I suppose this is why Hayley is only now receiving her portion of Des's estate."

Damon sat up. "Des sent her something?"

"Well, her lawyers did," Nick clarified.

"I would like to see what she received."

"Her house blew up shortly after the shipment."

Damon groaned and his head fell back. "Bloody hell."

"I don't have all the information yet. She's only been here for a few hours. I haven't questioned her beyond a cursory interview, and then she insisted on finding a hotel. That was when we were attacked. I sent the photographs to Adam Miles in the Dallas office. He thinks he should have something by morning."

"And now she's agreed to stay here?" Damon asked.

"Yes, I think almost being murdered in the alleyway tipped the scales in favor of safety versus her disdain for me." At least something good had come of it.

"Disdain?"

He shouldn't have mentioned that. "We have a history."

"Of course you do if she's Desiree's cousin," Damon replied, not unkindly.

Now that he was here, he couldn't lie to Damon. "We have a sexual history."

Damon's eyes widened. "I see. Well, perhaps we're going to need a bit of fortification. Scotch?"

He leaned over, opening the drawer to his desk and extracting a bottle of expensive Scotch and a couple of glasses. He poured out two fingers each and passed one over.

"I probably shouldn't but I'm going to." He could use it. He downed the Scotch quickly. "I thought this conversation was going to be about my recent failings, not the ones that felt like ancient history."

"History has a way of repeating itself," Damon said thoughtfully. "How long was this affair? I only ask because I need to know as much as I can if she's going to be a client. I need to know that you can be professional with this woman."

Honesty hurt sometimes. "I can't. Not in any way. I know I should recuse myself, Damon, but I cannot do this either."

"Damned if you do and damned if you don't. Yes, I know that feeling." Damon took a short sip and put the glass down. "I always meant to have this talk with you when we got back from Loa Mali. This talk wasn't meant to scare you straight or some shite. It was meant to drag you out of the place you've been in since Desiree died. It was meant to make you see that she's not worth giving up the rest of your life. I intended to explain the real truth behind what would have happened if she hadn't died when she did. We were roughly two weeks away from bringing her up on charges, Nick. The only thing that was holding me back was you."

The idea shook him to his core. "You didn't want to put me in jail?"

"I knew you weren't the problem. Des had started blackmailing some important people. Did you know anything about that?"

That pit was back in his stomach. "No. I didn't know. She and I had been fighting in the last few months of her life. She was more secretive. I thought she was up to something, but I didn't want to know. Now I have to wonder if it doesn't have something to do with why people are trying to kill Hayley."

"Yes, I think it's time we untangled Desiree's web. I know you loved her, but she wasn't good for you."

Somehow it was getting easier and easier to think about Des. In the beginning, the thought of her had been a deep hole in his soul, but now he was starting to be able to smile at some of her hijinks. And roll his eyes at the worst of it. He was balancing again, seeing her for who she was. The good and the bad. There was relief in that. "Sometimes she was very good for me, but yes, this I know. She was never going to marry me and I would always want to settle down in the end. Des was addicted to adrenaline. She wasn't going to give this up. Hell, this job wasn't enough for her. I don't think she did it entirely for the money. She did it for the thrill, for the power. I don't know what I would have done if you had arrested her."

A faint smile creased Damon's lips. "Of course you do."

He knew. He would have owed it to her. "I would have broken her out. I would have taken her away. She saved me, Damon."

"And you paid her back a thousand times. You have to let that go. You have to let so much of that go. I wasn't planning on firing you, but I was going to ask you to go on a sabbatical. I think you're going to turn down that request, aren't you? You know Big Tag and I can protect Hayley. You've been burning the candle at both ends since the day Des died and you've been mired in guilt over what happened to Owen. Don't you see you need a break?"

"I should have seen something was happening. Des was my lover and Owen was my partner. I don't think taking a break is going to make me a better operative."

"Do you think you're the only one who's ever felt the way you do? We all have, but somehow we move on. Des was brilliant at deflection and Owen didn't want you to know. He could have asked for help from any of us and he chose not to. I understand that his mother and sister were at stake, but you know as well as I do they would have stood a better chance if we'd been involved."

They even had protocols in place if an operative thought they were being watched. Why hadn't Owen used them? Why hadn't Nick seen that Owen was going through hell? "It doesn't matter now, and yes, I know you could protect Hayley, but I owe her. I'm not leaving."

"I could make this a requirement of your continued employment."

Nick stood. The meeting was obviously over. He wouldn't, couldn't let anyone else watch over her. "Then you'll have my resignation on your desk in an hour and I'll take her with me when I go. We'll disappear and no one will find us again."

He wouldn't go into the reasons why they were trying to kill her. Investigating would open a door and he would care about nothing but protecting Hayley. If he had a team around him, he could investigate, but if they were on their own, his only goal would be keeping her alive.

His mind went down a list. They would need new identities, several. They would need a place to live, off the grid if possible.

Damon stood up as well, shaking his head. "Or I could have some faith, as my wife would say. Perhaps this is what you need, a job you can actually care about. You'll have anything you require. You're in charge. Let me know how we can help. And I will expect more information in the morning. Conference room at ten a.m. And dear god, no more bodies."

He felt a piece of his soul settle. Damon wasn't kicking him out. He hadn't realized how much he'd come to depend on Damon and this team. They'd become his family, The Garden his home.

He didn't have to leave. He held out a hand and shook Damon's. "Sorry, boss. No promises. Besides, you know you were getting bored around here."

Damon smiled. "I will never admit that. See you in the morning. Take care of that girl. She's yours for now."

He turned to walk out, his boss's words sinking in. Hayley was his for the length of this op.

He prayed he could be good enough to keep her alive.

* * * *

Hayley stepped out of the kitchen after thanking Teresa for the food and saying goodnight to Charlotte, who was making a snack for her twins. Moments before, the big guy had stalked in carrying a tiny bundle and herding two toddlers who looked an awful lot like their mother. She'd stared for a moment, not quite putting together the dangerous man she'd met earlier with the harried father who begged his wife to find some grape jelly because their girls were rebelling.

"They're an interesting family," Ariel said as she walked beside Hayley. "I'm always fascinated by how tender the hardest of men can be when dealing with their children. I confess, I wasn't close to Ian or Damon before they married and had children, but from the stories I've heard they weren't the type of men a lot of people would think of as father material. Of course, that's because most would simply look at their jobs and not the underpinnings of why they choose to do their jobs. If they understood a man like Taggart or Knight, or even someone like Nikolai, they would see that fatherhood would come quite naturally to them."

They walked down the short hall that led back to the lush indoor garden. She knew she shouldn't ask, but couldn't quite stop the question from coming out of her mouth. "What do you mean about Nick? I don't think I've ever heard him talk about wanting a family. I thought he did when I was younger, but I think that was me turning him into my dream man. He seemed to prefer that it stay just him and Des."

"*Seemed* I think is the proper wording here. What do you know about Nick's background? Do you know anything about his family before he left Russia?"

"I know they're all gone now. He never talked about how he lost them, but he spoke of them often. He loved his family. One of the only times Nick was ever rough with me was because he found out I'd been asking Des how his sister died. He wasn't rough physically, but he got a little nasty. He told me to mind my own business and didn't talk to me the rest of the weekend." She hadn't seen him again for another five months and when she had, he'd acted like nothing had happened between them and she'd been happy enough to let it go.

"That's his story to tell, but he was close to them. He wasn't the typical operative with no ties to the world. He was recruited out of the Army. He went into SVR for the same reason he went into the Army. Not because he needed the money or for the sake of the adrenaline. He went in because he loved his country and wanted to protect it and those he cared about. The recruiters fed on that protective part of Nick. I've known some men who get into the business because they love the thrill of the chase and the kill. There's a predator inside those men that won't be held down, and this is the perfect business to let loose. You might look at a man like Taggart and think he's the predator, but when you scratch his surface, you find the protector. Like Nick. And I think Nick would be an excellent husband and father if he could find the right woman. Well, and forgive himself, but again, his story to tell."

She pressed through the double doors and Hayley found herself in the darkened garden. What had been lovely in the daylight transformed to something truly spectacular at night. The lights had been left low, the path illuminated by soft walkway lamps. Night-blooming jasmine accentuated the vines and trees.

"It's beautiful, isn't it?" Ariel ran her hand over a tree trunk. "I love it here at night. I love it even more when it's quiet and peaceful. Don't get me wrong. I enjoy the club, but there's something perfect about this place when the lights are low and the world seems peaceful. When I look up and see the moon through the rooftop, it seems like all things are possible."

"It is lovely," Hayley admitted. "But I worry I won't fit in here."

"Do you need to? One would hope you won't be here long. I suspect you'll want to return to your life in the States once the danger to you has passed. You have a job there, correct? A life?"

She'd begun to think it wasn't much of a life. "I have a job. I think. I might not anymore. I've missed several days' worth of classes and I don't have tenure yet. I teach history at a university in Seattle. No one cares about history anymore. I teach a bunch of freshmen world history and they mostly snore through my lectures. They're trying to get through the required basics so they can move on to their majors. I guess I don't have to fit in. It's not like I fit in a lot of places. I went to eight different schools growing up. My mom was a wonderful woman, but she would get into trouble and we would move. She was constantly trying to start a new life. I still don't know how Dad managed to find me sometimes. He would show up and he and Mom would fight and then I would spend a couple of months on the road with him before he got bored and dropped me back off at my mom's. I was always the new kid. I suppose I have a pathological need to fit in because I never felt comfortable anywhere."

"Not even in Seattle?"

She'd only ever felt that soul-deep recognition of peace once in her life. She'd felt it when his arms had been around her, when they'd been skin to skin, and she'd known she was where she was meant to be. "No. I keep thinking if I stay there, put in my time, one day I'll wake up and my house will feel like home and I'll belong there."

Ariel smiled, but it seemed a sad expression. "Oh, darling girl, what you have to figure out is that home isn't a place. It can feel like it should be, but that's nothing but a veneer, a story we tell ourselves so when the real foundation of our lives is gone, we can still feel connected. Home isn't a place. It's people. It's who we love and who loves us. You want to believe if you simply plant some roots, buy a home, stay in one place, the world is going to change, but it can't if you don't open yourself up. I suspect you're quite hard on yourself, and probably harder on others than you think you are."

She didn't like that description of herself at all. "Wow, you seem to know a lot about me in a whole twenty minutes."

If the good doc was bothered, she didn't show it. She merely leaned over, touching the flowers gently. The stark white of the jasmine made a gorgeous contrast to the deep, rich color of Ariel's skin. The moonlight flashed and brought out the glimmers of gold and brown and black that made up her skin. She was beautiful and Hayley felt so gauche compared to her.

Nick was surrounded by lovely, accomplished women.

"It's my job to assess people fairly quickly. You told me you moved around a lot and that you feel as if you never fit in. No one likes to hear this but most of our issues come back to us. If you don't fit in, it's usually because you're not looking for the right things. Perhaps when you were younger, you wanted to fit in with the popular crowd when you should have been seeking friends in other places. Did you want that? Did you want to be the popular girl?"

"I wanted to be liked, that's all." She'd tried in a million ways. She'd tried to be a cheerleader for a while. Tried to join in on a volleyball team. All that had gotten her was a broken arm and the realization that she wasn't an athlete. She'd liked the newspaper and the people there, but that had been one of her shorter school stays.

"But that's the funny thing about the world," Ariel continued. "There's something for everyone if we look in the right place. If we open ourselves to new experiences, we find out things about ourselves we didn't know. Do you blame your parents for how hard it was growing up?"

"Of course," she replied. "Children need stability and I never had that."

"Ah, so your mother was difficult."

Hayley shook her head. How did she make her understand? "Not at all. My mother was wonderful. She just moved around a lot. She would get into trouble with the rent or fight with a neighbor and we would move. When she would break up with a boyfriend, she would need a fresh start. Sometimes we drove until we found an apartment we could afford. Sometimes we'd live at friends' houses until Dad came through with some cash."

"I can see where that would be difficult. Never knowing where your next meal is coming from or if you'll have a place to live has to be terrifying for a child."

"I never missed a meal." Funny how years later, she could see through different eyes. "Not once. She would tell me we were going on an adventure and we would be off, but she always found somewhere for us to go to. She always made sure someone was around to pick me up from school. Sometimes they were kind of weird people, but they were always nice to me."

"Love is stability," Ariel said solemnly. "We don't get everything in life. Sometimes we have to look at what we have been given and be grateful for it. There are people who have money and every privilege the world can afford them, and without loving parents, they feel lost. I know you're going through something terrible, but you've been given an opportunity to change your life. If you don't like it, that is. Sometimes great things can come from pain and horror, if we let them."

"I hope so." Somehow she wasn't sure she saw that happening here. She went back to that moment when she'd been told her house exploded and realized what she'd really felt was numb. Shouldn't she have been hysterical? Shouldn't she have called a friend to hold her hand? She'd sat alone and calmly gone over everything with the police. She hadn't cried at all until she'd seen Nick. "I'm supposed to wait for Nick. Can I do that down here? I could use some peace and quiet."

"I'm not sure I should leave you alone." Ariel looked over to the front of the building. "Though we do have guards on the doors."

"Ariel?" A man stepped onto the stone path. He was tall and well built, wearing a T-shirt and sweatpants, sneakers on his feet, as though he'd walked straight out of a gym and into the forest. "I'm sorry to bother you, but you didn't answer your cell."

"I'm so sorry, Robert. I left it upstairs charging. What's wrong?"

Ariel moved toward the man as though drawn to him, stopping only once there was barely more than an arm's length between them.

"It's Dante. Something set him off," the man named Robert explained. "We've got him restrained, but I'm worried he's going to hurt someone."

Ariel looked back at Hayley. "Please excuse me. I have to deal with this. Robert, could you run up to my office and get my kit? I don't want to have to sedate him, but I might have to. Hayley, please don't leave The Garden. If you need to go anywhere…"

"I'll go back to the kitchen," Hayley promised. "I'm not planning on running. I swear. My infantile rebellion died the minute I almost got Nicky killed. I'm staying put until he comes to get me. Go. Do what you need to."

Ariel and Robert disappeared down the path.

And Hayley was left alone. Oh, she'd been alone for the last few days, but she hadn't been safe. This was the first time since the incident that she'd been alone and unafraid that someone was going to murder her. If Nick said this place was safe, then it was safe.

He'd only lied to her the once. When he'd told her how much he wanted her, how happy he'd been to hold her in his arms.

Hayley took a deep breath and tried to let go of it. Sometimes it felt like that night had haunted her forever. How long would she compare every single man to Nick Markovic and find them all wanting? How long would she be angry with him for choosing Des?

Her hand went up to the glass heart she'd given Des all those years before. Had she loved Nick or had she wanted to be Des?

She glanced around the quiet garden, taking it in in a way she hadn't appreciated anything in forever. Something had sparked inside when she'd talked about her mother…her bohemian, silly, somehow stalwart mother. She would stop when she saw a beautiful spot and force Hayley out of the car. Sometimes it was a historic site and she would read the words on the monument. All of them. Sometimes it was a mountain in the distance. Sometimes it was nothing more than a beautiful field of never-ending Midwest land.

Take it in, baby. You might not see it again. Remember it because it could all be gone tomorrow and only you'll be able to tell the tale of what it means to be standing right here. Right now.

How long had it been since she'd lived in the now? She'd rejected it because her parents never seemed to believe in a future or a past, so Hayley had put her roots firmly in both, always believing something better would happen and never enjoying the now.

When she'd had her first paper published, had she celebrated? Nope. She'd gotten a nervous pit in her stomach that it would be the only paper she ever published if she didn't immediately get to work on another one. Her days had become an endless round of what ifs and should bes.

She breathed, this time not to expel anxiety but to experience the moment. She closed her eyes and let the cool air creep along her skin, making the hair rise, but not in a bad way. It was like a tickle over her flesh that reminded her she could feel. The scent of jasmine played through the space along with the loamy smell of the earth and trees. Hayley opened her eyes and looked up. Sure enough, the moon was there, a full presence in the sky above. It filtered through the glass-top roof and lit up the garden like a spotlight.

This was where Nick lived. She'd made light of it before, but there was something magical about it. Did he stand here in the glow of the moon and think about Des? Did he ever think about that night they'd spent together?

Possibilities. Ariel had told her when it was quiet and the moon shone down, the world seemed ripe with possibilities.

What possibilities were out there for her? She'd lost everything she'd worked so hard for. Her house was gone. Her job would likely be gone, or at least the majority of her momentum would be derailed. She was the youngest of the junior professors there. Someone would quickly fill her place.

She would be one more missing girl who would have to put her life back together.

Hayley sat down on one of the stone benches that dotted the

space. She let the feel of cool concrete touch her hands as she listened to the quiet hum all around her. What would she be doing right now if tragedy hadn't happened? It was a Wednesday night. Afternoon back in the States. She would be closing up her last class of the day, cramming something in her face because she'd forgotten to pack her lunch. It would be some piece of junk she found in the vending machine. She wouldn't take the time to go to the cafeteria because she would have research to do. She would wave at some of the faculty but turn them down when they asked her to go out and have a drink.

Had she given up because she couldn't be the popular girl? Had she done exactly what Ariel had accused her of doing? Gone into her shell because things hadn't worked out the first few times? The first hundred times? She'd convinced herself she needed to be Des to be successful.

Maybe she hadn't looked closely enough.

"I thought you would be with Charlotte."

She closed her eyes and let that voice stroke over her. She'd never forgotten his voice. Deep and lush and tinged with exoticness. Nikolai. "I was but then the kitchen got crowded. I thought I would wait out here for you. Ariel was with me for a while, but she had some sort of emergency. Someone named Dante."

She didn't look at him, preferring to stare up at the sky. It was enough to simply be here.

"Ah, he has certain triggers. It's sad. He can't remember a damn thing about his life, but somewhere deep down, his consciousness remembers something terrible." She felt him move toward her, his big body making the stones vibrate slightly as he walked. "Sometimes he forgets where he is and tries to fight his way out. He never remembers the episodes. Or he never admits to it. I think it would be terrible to know something is out to get you, but not to remember why. But then you know a bit about this. Are you all right?"

"I'm better than I thought I would be." She was tired but now that she'd been fed and knew she was safe for the time being, it didn't seem an insurmountable thing. She turned her head, looking up at him and finally saying what she should have hours before. "Did I thank you for taking me in?"

She'd been so upset, so embarrassed at the thought of seeing him again that she hadn't let it sink in. He'd accepted her immediately. She hadn't been forced to fight to make him see he owed her. He'd simply opened his arms and let her in.

He'd taken off his coat and ditched the tie. He looked casual and a bit tired, and still so sexy it hurt to look at him as he stared down at her. "I wasn't looking for gratitude, *dushka*. I only want to see you safe."

"Because I'm Des's cousin?" She shouldn't ask, but after the day she'd had, she couldn't make herself stop. It would be good to know. So much of what Ariel had said weighed on her. Nick had chosen Des, but she would never have given him the stability he seemed to require. It was so much of a mystery, and maybe she would be happier if she simply solved it.

He sighed heavily and sat down beside her, his body brushing against hers. "No. Because you're Hayley."

"I missed you, Nick." It was better to say it because it was the truth. Better to say all of it. Her mother had been right. She had stood in a place and time and after it was all destroyed, she was the only one who could tell the truth about that moment. The whole truth. "I miss Des, too, but god I've missed you. I don't know how or why, but you always made me feel safe."

"I don't know why. I wasn't good enough to save Desiree."

She was quiet for a moment before finding the courage to ask her next question. "How did she die? No one will tell me anything except that she was in the Caribbean and she got shot. I went to the funeral with Dad, but no one would tell him much, either."

She hadn't seen her British relatives since the funeral, and then a year later her own father had died and none of them showed up to support her. She'd been cut off entirely.

"I'm sure they tell you a bit." His voice had gone low, accent thickening. "I'm sure they tell you I am the reason she is dead."

All their problems seemed to melt away and she was fifteen again looking at the most beautiful man she'd ever seen. Wanting so badly to make him smile. When she'd first met him, she'd had the worst crush on him and he'd treated her like a little sister. He'd been kind and paid attention to her when no one else would and she'd somehow seen past his smiling exterior to the pain he'd hidden. At the time she hadn't understood why he hurt, but she'd wanted so much to ease it. She let her hand slide over his. "I know it wasn't your fault."

He stared down at the place where their hands met and for a moment she worried he would pull away. Instead, he flipped his hand over, capturing hers. "Why do you think that?"

Warmth spread through her as he threaded their fingers together. "Because unlike the rest of the family, I believe Des was everything you said she was. A spy. They still believe her cover, but Des all but told me she worked for MI6 and that you had been in the KGB, though now there's a different set of letters. All you spy guys are big on letters."

"SVR. It means the same. I expected that she would tell her family after we left the government work and started here, but she liked the idea of keeping it from her mother and sister." His thumb made circles over her skin as he started to talk again. "We were on a mission in Grand Cayman, working with a former CIA operative. We were pinned down. She took a crazy chance and it didn't work out. I should have been closer to her."

She leaned against him. It was starting to make sense. "No one stopped Des when she wanted to make a point. Was she showing off?"

"Perhaps. She always got competitive when there were other female operatives. She wanted to be known as the best, to have every eye always on her. In this case, she was up against one of the truly finest women I've worked with. A woman named Erin Argent. Gifted agent. I've wondered if she wasn't trying to prove to the men that she was smarter and better than Erin. Still, I should have been closer."

Now she understood what Ariel had said about forgiving himself.

"Nick, you have to let that go. She made the choice. You would have saved her if you could."

"And my sister?" Now he did withdraw, his hand releasing hers as he moved away. He put a good foot and a half between them. "My sister died because I couldn't save her, because I made a choice that put her in harm's way."

They were in dangerous territory, but she wanted to keep him talking. "How old was she?"

He stood suddenly and put out a hand. "It matters not. I'm merely saying that perhaps you should not feel so safe with me. You should talk to my team tomorrow and make your decision then."

"I want you."

His jaw straightened, face tightening. "You should not."

"If you force me to take another bodyguard, I will, but I would prefer it if you stayed with me. I know I was a bitch earlier, but I didn't realize how much it would hurt to think about you with other women. I guess I'm not as over you as I thought I was."

"Another reason for you to stay away, *dushka*. I wasn't good for you then. I'm toxic now. What you need, I'm not the man who can give these things to you."

"I don't know what I need anymore. I got what I wanted, Nick. I got the cushy job and the house. I had a boyfriend for a while. He was super smart and popular amongst the faculty, and I was bored to death because all we talked about was work and publishing and getting ahead. We looked good on paper. My life looks good on paper, but I don't know that I've felt as much over the last five years as I did walking through your door today. I was knocked over by it. My house blew up and it didn't affect me the way seeing you again did."

He paced, his feet thudding along the stones. "Do you understand where you are? The man you knew back then had never been in one of these places. The man you knew then didn't understand what he needed from a woman. You see plants and romanticism but take a closer look. What's hidden amongst all this pretty greenery? Sometimes I think I prefer Taggart's club. It's all on display. There's no question about what it is and what people do there."

She looked around, but she'd already seen some of what he was talking about. "The X thingees on the back wall? And the bench with the restraints? I'm fairly certain what they're used for. I'm not a virgin. I mean, you know that. You were kind of there when I punched that card. But I've punched it a couple more times. Maybe not so many that I got a freebie, but there have been a few. I've had sex since the last time you saw me."

She was babbling. It was what she did when she got nervous. She said the stupidest things.

He arched a single brow arched over his eyes. "You've had sex that involved a St. Andrew's Cross?"

That's what it was called? She vaguely remembered the term. "No, but I let a doctoral candidate tie me up. He was a specialist in Victorian era England. He also showed me how doctors back then cured hysteria. There was a reason women complained so much. He was quite good at it."

She'd preferred his manual manipulation techniques to actual intercourse with him.

Nick stared down, his eyes fastened on hers. "When he tied you up, did he spread your legs out? Did he restrain all your limbs? Did he put a spreader bar between your ankles so your pussy was always on display for him? So he would have access and could fuck you with his fingers or his tongue or his cock? Did he turn you over and spank your pretty ass until it was red and you would feel him all the next day? Speaking of your pretty ass, did this man of yours play with it? Did he lube you up and force you to take a plug because one day he intended to shove his cock up your asshole, to take it and make it his because every single inch of you was intended to be owned by him?"

She could barely breathe. Every filthy word from his mouth had gone straight to all those parts he talked about owning. Her nipples had hardened. Her pussy had gone a little soft. Her anus had squeezed, but that might have been an act of self-defense. She wasn't sure about the back door action he talked about, but the rest of it…he'd asked a question. She should probably answer if she wanted to disguise the fact that all she could think about now was sex. "No. Uhm, I did get a lecture on Victorian erotica."

His hand came out, finding her hair and tangling in it, forcing her chin up so she could look in his eyes. "That's what I would do to you this time. I was a different man back then. I was capable of tenderness. I don't think I am today. I would be rough and I would take my pleasure from you."

"Without giving anything back?" Somehow she didn't think Nick could play that way.

"Oh, you would get something back. You would get pleasure. Orgasms. You would scream out my name and beg me for more. I would train you to come at my command and, *dushka*, I'm not talking about you walking to me. But that would be all you get."

He was forgetting something. "I would get protection, too. I would get safety from murderers and I would get orgasms. I'm sorry, Nicky. You're going to have to explain how that's a bad deal for me."

He stopped, letting her hair go and taking a big step back. "I didn't mean to do that, Hayley. You're tired and I'm tired. You've had a rough couple of days and I'm sure I look familiar to you."

She wasn't letting him off that easily. "Do you know what else I might get, Nick? I might get over you. I might figure out that what we had that one night five years ago wasn't anywhere close to as good as I remember. Don't you owe me that, too?"

He took another big old coward step back. "I'm not having this conversation with you tonight."

She stood, facing him. "I'm fine, Nick. Yes, I'm dead tired, but I can think and express myself. The brandy we found is helping with that."

Nick's eyes came up and he turned suddenly as the doors to the back rooms scraped against the floor. Charlotte was walking out, holding the baby bundle in her arms while her husband followed her, a girl clinging to either side of his muscled body.

"You fed her alcohol?" Nick asked. "Without consulting with

me?"

Ian Taggart stepped in front of his wife as though Nick was threatening her.

Charlotte waved her husband off. "Don't play the caveman. Nick's not coming after me. After all, they don't have a contract or anything. She's a client. I'm one of the owners of this business. I can help her out in any way I like."

There was something almost taunting about the way Charlotte spoke to Nick.

"Oh, this is a plot." Ian stepped back. "I don't get in the way of her plots."

Charlotte frowned, cuddling her baby. "It's not a plot. It was brandy and she'd had a shitty day. It's called being a good girlfriend." She turned back to Nick. "Apparently someone's feeling possessive, but according to Hayley he's got no reason to. They aren't exactly together."

"She's my client," Nick insisted.

"And again, I'm your employer and I'm hoping to be her friend. It doesn't sound like she has many of those. When you two have a contract between you, I'll honor it. Until then, there's no bond for me to honor. I'll treat her the way I would any unattached friend. I'll watch out for her," Charlotte explained.

"Stay out of it. You might be my boss, but you'll be gone long before I figure out her situation." Nick held out a hand. "She's my charge and I'll deal with her as I see fit. If you have a problem with that, take it up with Damon, but he knows what happens if he tries to take away my right to protect her."

To protect her. Not to love her. Not to pleasure her. Hayley looked at that hand waiting for hers.

It had to be enough for now.

She placed her hand in his. "I did hire him. I kind of didn't know I was getting a whole team." She didn't fight him at all as he dragged her close. It looked like Ian Taggart wasn't the only one who could play the caveman. "Also, you might rethink the taking-me-on-as-a-

103

client thing when you understand I have a fake passport and almost no cash. Oh, and an Oyster card, but it's almost empty. So I hope your offer of friendship also includes a discount."

Charlotte's lips curled up. "I think we can work something out. After all, you brought us a dead body. It's the gift that keeps giving."

"I'll handle it, Hayley," Nick said, beginning to walk toward the elevators. "You don't have to worry about money."

But all he had to offer her was orgasms. Maybe it was time to start watching him. She'd paid so much attention to the words coming out of his mouth that she hadn't watched what he was doing. She'd walked into his office and started creating drama like she was still twenty years old and wanting so much to be in their chaotic world.

She'd offered him peace that night and thought he'd rejected it. Now he said he was a changed man, a toxic man, but she looked up at him and all she could see was a man who still needed some peace.

Was she fooling herself? Or was he lying to himself?

She tripped on one of the rocks, a light shuffle of steps. She started to rebalance almost immediately, but before she could gain her footing again, she found herself up in the air. Nick swung one arm under her knees, the other around her back, and hauled her close to his chest.

"You're too tired to be up and this is what comes from you drinking too much." He turned, holding her tight, and faced the Taggarts. "You see, she could have killed herself."

Charlotte merely nodded, her eyes wide with what seemed to be mirth. "Yes, I can see that, Nick."

Ian's girls seemed to be trying to climb their father like he was a jungle gym. Every time she was sure one of them was going to tumble to the ground, he would catch them with the ease of a man who'd done this all before. "I'll make sure Charlie doesn't give her the heavy stuff anymore. No more…brandy. Yeah, and when is the wedding?"

Nick grunted and turned again, striding toward the elevators.

"Use protection," Taggart called out. "Unless you're ready for monsters of your own."

"I would flip him bird if I had extra hand," Nick muttered under his breath.

Ah, teamwork. She brought her right hand up and gave the man her middle finger, though she had the grace to wince. "Sorry. That was actually from him. I think you're both lovely. He's in a bad mood. He'll be better tomorrow."

A brilliant smile crossed over Ian Taggart's face, taking the man from grimly handsome to movie star hot in a second. "I like your girl, Nick."

Nick frowned as he moved into the open elevator. He turned. "She is client. Nothing more."

But he managed to press the button for his floor and then settled her close. He was silent as they rode up.

It was a start.

Chapter Six

Nick stared down at the report in front of him, but all he could think about was the night before.

What had he been thinking? He'd practically molested Hayley. Oh, he'd only used words, but if she could have seen what was going through his brain at the time, she would have run out into the street and begged for the assassins to come and get her.

Then he'd picked her up and she'd cuddled against him like a kitten who needed affection.

He'd put her to bed and closed two doors between them because one wouldn't have been enough. Instead of sleeping on his couch, he'd made a pallet on the floor of his office so he would be as far from her soft, sexy form as possible.

"Morning, Nick." Owen smiled as he strode into the conference room. "What do we have on the agenda this morning? Damon said I could sit in on the meeting and maybe try to help out with the lass a wee bit."

It was more likely Ariel's doing. She was convinced letting Owen try to find some normalcy would ease some of his issues. "Please pick up one of the reports the Dallas office sent us. It appears Mr. Miles has an identity for our would-be assassin."

Owen grabbed one of the reports and poured himself a cup of coffee before returning. "Where's your girl? Actually, where is everyone? I thought we were starting soon."

"They're on their way up. You didn't go to the breakfast? Apparently Teresa wanted to welcome back the boss with a buffet." He'd basically fled when he'd looked over and seen Hayley sitting down with the Taggarts. She'd looked up at him, all fresh faced and smiling, offering him a place beside her, and he'd run. He'd told her he had to prepare for the meeting and not to leave unless she had an escort. He'd done it all with a frown on his face because he'd wanted nothing more than to sit beside her and pretend for a moment that he was bringing a woman home to meet his family.

Thank god for dead bodies.

Owen sat back in his chair. "I don't seem to like breakfast."

He had to smile. "You rarely used to eat before noon. You would pound the coffee, but skip breakfast. Now if lunch came and went, you became very difficult to live with. Some days I would shove a sandwich in your face so you would stop whining."

Owen stared down at his coffee. "You know more about me than I do."

He shouldn't have mentioned it. "We were partners once. That's why I know. Ariel thinks you should figure these preferences out on your own. You never know. They might have changed."

"Were we friends?" Owen asked. "You said we were partners, but that doesn't mean you liked me. I get the feeling there are a couple of people around here who don't, though I'm unsure of why."

"Again, that's something Ariel feels is best left up to you. But I can tell you that you're not going to get anywhere with Teresa." He felt bad watching Owen chase after the sub.

Owen winced. "Ah, I thought I might have screwed that up in another life." He straightened up. "You know what? I'm still going to try. That woman has an arse to die for and I think there's a tender heart in there. I've been practicing me puppy eyes. She'll give in. Your girl's a pretty one."

Nick went back to staring at the report. "She's not mine. She was Desiree's cousin. Now she's my client."

Who had been tired the night before and that was why she'd said the things she'd said. This morning she'd seemed much more sensible. After she'd had some sleep and a shower and had straightened herself up, she'd been quiet and seemingly reflective. She was probably embarrassed by what had been said the night before.

I would get safety from murderers and I would get orgasms. I'm sorry, Nicky. You're going to have to explain how that's a bad deal for me.

He was going to make sure she understood that his protection wasn't based on whether or not she slept with him.

Because he wasn't sleeping with her. He couldn't hurt her that way again.

"So she was your old lover's cousin," Owen mused. "The lover you weren't exclusive with and who wouldn't marry you. The pretty girl who looks at you like you're the sun in the sky is her cousin."

"She looks at me like she would look at a man who can save her."

"I can save her." Owen's eyes lit up, his brows waggling. "Maybe she'll look at me like that."

Anger flared through his system. "Don't you dare. I told you I would take care of her."

Owen's arms crossed over his big chest and Nick knew he'd been had. "Well, that answers the question with more honesty. You can pretend, but you like the girl. And if you honestly don't then you need to know that the boys got a good look at her last night. If she's going to be hanging about, she should be ready for some serious male attention."

"What are you talking about?"

"The lads talked it over last night and decided there's no dibs on this one. They all saw her at pretty much the same time. They looked over that dead body and saw her walking out in the hall and that was when the fighting started. We all sat down and decided no dibs on her. She'll get to pick. You should know that Sasha and Jax have decided if she picks either of them, they're willing to share. I don't play that way. That's something I do know about meself. No need for you to be telling me that tale. If there's going to be some sharing in the bedroom, it's going to be the traditional kind between a man and a woman and her stacked best friend. That's what I say."

"You tell those boys to stay away from her or they will be dealing with me. They will not like to be dealing with me. I will put up with many things from them. They can poke all the corpses they like. They can punch each other. I do not care. They touch Hayley and I will be caring."

"Wow, now you do sound Russian. A scary Russian. Still, I think if you don't want the girl, shouldn't she be allowed to choose? Think about it. It could be fun."

"Are we talking about the lost boys and their battle for the new chick?" Kayla strode in, her hair in a high ponytail. It bounced as she walked, a testament to her seemingly ever-sunny personality. "I had babysitting duty last night and they kept talking about her even after lights out. Bad boys. I had a plan though. I think we make them compete in a beauty pageant. Hayley gets to judge."

"I'm judging a beauty pageant?" Hayley followed behind Kay, and both women were followed by Charlotte Taggart and Penelope Knight. It looked like the women on his team were rapidly accepting Hayley.

That was not necessarily a good thing. The women on his team could create chaos like no others.

"That sounds like fun," Charlotte said with a smile. "I think we should require Speedos for the bathing suit competition. No boring board shorts. If Hayley's picking a lover, she needs to see some booty."

Hayley stopped, her cheeks going the sweetest color of pink. "Wait. What?"

Penelope put a hand on her arm. "They're teasing you, dear.

Don't worry about it. The lads will be polite. Though you should expect some suitors while you're here. Especially if you come down to the dungeon."

Now Nick was the one flushing. "Excuse me?"

Hayley shook her head as she joined him at the table. "It's nothing. I was just talking to the girls. Did you get the report? Penny said the Dallas office had found something."

He was all too aware that they weren't alone. Damon and Ian walked in with Brody Carter and Walter Bennett. The four men settled into chairs as they joined the women. Nick held out a chair for Hayley. He would have to remember that he couldn't leave her alone for a minute or someone would be whispering in her ear, giving her ideas she shouldn't have.

Like visiting The Garden on a play night.

It wasn't happening.

"Good morning, everyone, and it's good to know the place didn't burn down while we were gone." Damon sat at the head of the table, Taggart to his right.

"Damon, you know they always do a wonderful job while we're gone," his wife admonished.

"Well, darling, I wasn't talking about Brody and Nick and Walt," Damon replied. "I was referring to our guests."

"Hey, I stayed behind, too," Kay protested. She winked Nick's way. "I held down the fort and watched the boys."

"You're practically their leader," Damon said with a shudder. "You're the one who let them watch *Dumb and Dumber* and introduced them to illegal fireworks. You're the Mother of Pranksters."

Kay grinned. "They're so much fun. Can we keep them forever?"

Ian gave her a thumbs-up. "As far as I'm concerned, they're yours."

Damon held up a hand. "That's a discussion for later. Let's focus on the present. Most of you have met our new client. Nick, can you tell us what you've learned about Hayley's situation? I assume you stayed up late to discover the details."

"I told him everything I knew," Hayley said quickly.

He didn't need her to defend him. He also didn't need to think about how nice it felt to have someone try to come to his rescue. "I did. If you look in the folder in front of you, you'll find the police report on what happened to her house. I've pulled the record on the two police officers who were in charge of her case. There're also copies of the media reports surrounding the explosion."

Taggart thumbed through the report. "The police offered to put her up for the night? Not her insurance company?"

He hated that she might feel embarrassed, but he couldn't lie about what everyone around that table would know. "They did. There's no record of them calling in a social worker or of her filing an insurance claim."

"I didn't have time to," she said. "Also, all my insurance records were kind of in the house. I was going to call the next day, but I was almost murdered...oh. The police don't offer that kind of service, do they? I should have been directed to a shelter if I didn't have anywhere to go. Not unless there was something wrong or criminal with what happened. They don't protect homeowners from random gas explosions. Wow. I wasn't thinking at all."

There it was, the dawning that she'd been played all along. He'd come to that same conclusion around three a.m. this morning. "No, they don't typically put citizens up at motels. There's no record of the department approving your motel for the night. The cop who put you up for the night paid cash. Do you recognize the police officers in the photographs?"

She stared down at the pictures he'd included in the briefing folder. "I remember them. I dealt more with the fire department, but these two were nice to me."

"Was either one of them the officer who showed up at your motel room?"

She shook her head. "No, he was a different officer. Officer Harris. Jeremy Harris. I told you that. He was the last officer I dealt with. I was actually really surprised because I thought I was going to have to find a hotel myself, and I was so stupidly numb at the time I wasn't sure I would be able to figure out where to go. The other officers I dealt with asked where I would go and I told them I would figure something out. When Officer Harris showed up, I figured they knew I didn't have anywhere to go."

"There's no Jeremy Harris at the precinct that responded to your call. I don't think he was a cop at all. I watched some of the news coverage and he was in some of the shots. I managed to pull an image before he turned away from the camera. Turn to page five."

She gasped as she found the picture he'd carefully pulled with Walter's help.

Walt leaned in. He was a physician by trade, but he was kind of their go-to for all things technical. He was an all-around genius. "It's grainy, but I was able to clean it up enough that Adam could use his facial recognition software."

Kayla held a hand up. "Wait, before we get to identities, I want to know why we think someone's after her. What would a college professor have that could be worth killing over? This seems an extreme way to protest a bad grade. I would have kept it to some light vandalism."

"I don't think this is about her work." He'd briefly considered it and discarded the idea. There was no such thing as coincidence. Not in his line of work. "She received a shipment from Desiree's estate roughly eighteen hours before her house was destroyed. It was a matter of public record so I can't pinpoint who might have known from there."

Penny sighed. "So you think this is actually about Desiree. If it is, why would they still be coming for Hayley?"

Damon was staring at Hayley as though he could figure her out strictly through study. "They think she knows something. Did you have an alarm on your home?"

Hayley shook her head. "No. It wasn't the kind of house people burglarized, and alarm systems don't come cheap. I put up a *beware of dog* sign. Apparently that only works if you have a real dog."

"So we can't tell if they went to her house first and couldn't find what they were looking for," Ian began.

"Or if they panicked and got rid of everything they could," Brody continued in his thick Aussie accent. It had taken Nick a while to get to the point he understood what the man said, but Nick could never question his devotion to the team. Brody Carter was a good man to have at his back.

"I think that might be the most likely scenario. From what I can tell, her neighborhood isn't exactly quiet," he explained. "I looked it up on a couple of sites and it's known for being a part of the college campus scene."

"If you're asking if it's a quiet place, then no," Hayley explained. "It's why I was so shocked they didn't kill someone. There's always something going on. A party or people out exercising or protesting something. I'm only a few blocks off campus so I'm surrounded by students."

"It was probably done by a professional," Ian said. "Did you ID the man who tried to kill her? Was he a pro?"

"He was a known associate of a criminal organization here in the UK. You've heard of the Clerkenwells. They're based in Islington and work primarily in drug trafficking, extortion, and prostitution." This was what concerned him. "Adam identified him for us. His name is Martin Donaldson. As far as our contacts at MI5 and Scotland Yard know, he's a mid-level drug dealer. He's not a known assassin."

"And the man in Seattle?" Damon asked.

"What we know about him is on page ten. He's connected to two murders. Both victims were involved in high-profile lawsuits. They would have been considered whistle-blowers. The FBI suspects he's killed at least three more, but they can't directly connect him."

"So we have Desiree sending her something and at least one known assassin and one mobster after her," Charlotte mused. "What was in the shipment? Has Hayley made a list?"

"It was the contents of her Tokyo apartment. It was a bunch of boxes." Hayley bit her bottom lip as she thought. "I only opened one of the smaller boxes. It had some stuff from her desk, I think. Some pens and a couple of cell phones. I looked through a few of the notebooks."

Damon sat up in his chair, leaning toward Hayley. "What was in those notebooks? Did she keep a log of the missions she worked?"

"Or was she writing a bloody memoir?" Penny sighed. "I'm sorry, but I wouldn't put it past her. She joked about it often enough."

"She wasn't joking, love," Brody interjected. "That was her version of a threat." He swung his gaze to Nick. "Sorry, mate. Only being honest."

He held up a hand. "No need. You couldn't shock me if you tried."

"Why would she threaten to write a memoir?" Hayley asked.

Hayley, on the other hand, could be shocked to her core. He didn't want to hurt her. She'd hero-worshipped Des through her younger years, but she needed to know what they were up against. "Des liked to make sure she had a way to keep everyone in their place. If she couldn't get some dirt on someone, she would use casual threats like joking about writing a tell-all about what we do here."

Hayley stared down at her clasped hands. "Well, there wasn't anything like that. Not that I understood. There were three notebooks. One was completely empty. One was written in Cyrillic, and the other was a bunch of numbers. The only other things in the box were pens and some CDs and a couple of pieces of jewelry. There was some cash stuffed in a travel pouch. It was in yen."

"Why did you only open one box?" Ian asked. "What happened to the ledger? I would like to see that."

"Was there a ledger of what the other boxes contained?" Damon spoke over his partner.

"And don't discount the empty notebook," Walt insisted. "There are plenty of ways to cover ink. I'd like to see it."

He hated those clipped tones, the quick questioning, as though if they could fire enough words her way, they could trip her up and force her to make mistakes. "She's not being interrogated here. She's not the enemy."

She held a hand up, her face strained. "It's all right. They're trying to help. I was busy at the time and honestly, I didn't want to deal with all the...emotional baggage that came with memories of Des. I put it off. The only reason I opened the small box was I looking for the letter from the lawyer. My intention was to donate everything to a local charity."

Damon turned a bit pale. "That could have been a disaster in the making."

"So you're saying that Des sent me something and that's the reason these assholes are after me? All that's left is the necklace I'm wearing, some of the cash and...a letter she sent me."

Something about the way she cut off her words made him wonder if she was lying, but he wasn't going to call her out here. "What did the letter say?"

"Can I see the necklace?" Kayla asked. She looked over at Walt. "We should take it to the lab and make sure there's nothing extra in it."

Walt nodded. "It would be like Des to hide information in something she could wear."

Hayley's hand went to the heart around her neck. "No. It was a sentimental thing, I think. I gave it to her on her birthday one year. She kept it because it came from me."

"Is that glass?" Walt asked.

Hayley nodded. "It's not expensive, but I thought it was pretty. She liked it. She kept it all these years so she must have liked it."

Damn Des. He knew her. She didn't do anything out of sentimentality. He looked down at the necklace. It was small, but he could see the chain was held by a hook that went down into the heart. It would be simple to take it apart. "I think you should let Walt and Kay look at it."

Her hands moved up and around her neck and she quickly undid the clasp of the necklace, handing it over. "I don't see what she could do with it. It's just a necklace."

Oh, but he knew. She would have found it funny to use the cheap piece of jewelry to hide some of her secrets. He didn't want Hayley to think about it. He passed the necklace to Walter, who started examining it as Nick tried to dodge that particular issue. "Can I read the letter?"

"There's nothing in the letter except some advice. I would like to keep it to myself." When she'd walked in the room there had been a happy vibrancy about her. Now she seemed to pull back into herself.

"Hayley, I don't want to invade your privacy, but this is a serious matter. Whoever is after you managed to follow you from Seattle all the way to London," Damon pointed out.

"From some of the things he said, I believe he had inside knowledge. It's in my report about the incident in the alley. He said he had a head start. I think that means more like him will be looking for her as time goes by. We need to put out some feelers to our contacts and find out if they've heard anything at all." It went without saying that they would have to be careful. He didn't want anyone at all to know Hayley was here. "We could file her as a missing person. Perhaps we could get a feel for what's happening in Seattle that way."

Ian pulled out his cell. "I can have someone there in a few hours. I'll send in Alex and Eve. Adam will provide documentation that Eve is a relative. We'll work the case from that side. I'll also put out some feelers to my Agency contacts."

"I'll do the same here," Damon agreed. "I've got some Interpol contacts as well. Nick, I hate to ask, but do you know of anything Des was involved in that might have this kind of a reaction? I know she was blackmailing certain powerful people, but that would have ended after her death. MI6 dealt with all her known extortion plots, but I don't think they checked on a place in Tokyo. It might have gotten lost in the shuffle. They insisted on handling it in house, and sometimes things get prioritized improperly."

"Blackmail?" Hayley shook her head. "I don't understand. My cousin was a spy. She wasn't a criminal."

Ah, but sometimes there was a fine line between the two. "Des had many dealings in the information world. Don't worry about it."

"You mean she bought and sold intelligence, don't you?" Hayley sniffled as though fortifying herself. "All right. The letter only said that if there was any trouble, I should go to Nick. She told me I shouldn't hesitate to call him if I needed something. You can read it. And there was one for Nick, too. I didn't say anything because…well, because I'm a selfish bitch. It seems to run in the family. They're both here." She reached into the bag she'd carried with her and drew out two letters, placing them on the conference table in front of Nick. "That's everything I know, everything I have."

"I'll read them privately." He leaned in so he could speak quietly to her. "No one else has to unless there's something important. And I had nothing to do with Desiree's business."

She wouldn't look at him. "I didn't think you did."

He slid a hand over her clasped ones. "Of course, you did. You probably still do and I don't blame you. Talk to Damon. I'll tell him to open my files for you. I don't want you to be afraid of me. I cared about your cousin, but I didn't agree with everything about her."

"You would let me read your file?" She looked up at him, her eyes big and wide and trusting.

Fuck, he didn't want to, but he couldn't say no to her. Not after what she'd been through. "Yes, but you should know I'm not always the hero."

She gave him the faintest smile and then turned to the front of the table. "I'll help in any way I can. If I remember anything else, I'll let you know. What more do you need from me?"

"I need you to stay inside the building," Damon replied. "The city is full of CCTV cameras. I don't want to risk your face showing up on one."

"Have we considered the probability that it already has?" Charlotte asked. "Unless she was extremely careful, she would have shown up on the security cameras at Heathrow and in the train station. Did you take the Express?"

117

"Yes, but I tried to keep my head down as much as possible," she replied. "One of the few things I bought was a cap. I put my hair up and wore sunglasses. I had a jacket that hid my body pretty much. I rode the Tube here, but again, I kept my eyes on the ground in front of me."

"You thought this through pretty well for a civilian," Brody pointed out.

"My dad was weird. He was paranoid, I guess. He played poker for a living so he was all about keeping as much information to himself as he could. Sometimes, though, I think he got in trouble with casinos and maybe even the mob because he definitely tried to keep a low profile," Hayley explained. "When I was with him, he wanted me to do the same. That's where I learned how to avoid security cameras. Still, I can't promise one didn't pick me up."

"I'll have some of the lads look through the feeds to see if they can find you," Penny offered. "I'll talk to Robert and put them on it. It's good for them to have something to do."

"And apparently they are very good at looking at my client." He needed to make something plain. "Damon, if they start bothering her, we're going to have a problem."

Owen spoke up for the first time since the meeting had begun. Nick hadn't realized it. It was a big change. Owen used to laugh and joke and generally annoy the hell out of Damon for the fun of it during meetings. Today, he'd been quiet and serious, taking notes as he read along in the reports. "They ain't bothering her. They're lonely and she's unattached. It would be good for the lads if we had some subs they could play with, and by play with I mean fuck until their eyeballs don't work anymore."

That sounded like the old Owen.

Except he'd turned a lovely shade of red and turned to Hayley. "Not you, of course. They'll be polite around you. Maybe you should come down and have dinner with us. Get to know us. You're going to be here for a while."

"Absolutely not. She's staying away from that group. She's off

118

limits."

"Off limits? What does that mean?" Hayley asked.

"It means you really need to use protection." Ian sat back, as though ready for a show. "There's something in the water, man. Unless Nick here got himself snipped."

"I am not snipped," he replied, aware that irritation was rising. It should be plain to everyone that he was in charge of Hayley and he would make the rules when it came to her safety. That certainly didn't include putting her in a roomful of horny, memory-wiped men.

"Then condoms are your friend, buddy," Ian continued.

He was going to have such a talk with Ian.

Damon held up a hand as if that alone could stave off the fight that might be coming. "Both of you stop. Nikolai has strong ideas about how to protect Hayley, but if she's staying here for a while, I don't see a reason why she should need to stay in your rooms twenty-four seven."

"I'm not staying in my room all the time. I'm not a prisoner. Mr. Knight, I promise not to leave the grounds, but I can't be stuck in a room and I don't need someone watching me constantly. I understand that I could be here for a while and because of that, I would like to be given something to do," she said. "I need a job."

"You don't need a job," Nick insisted. "You have a job back in Seattle. I told you I would handle the fees if I need to. You don't have to pay the firm back with manual labor."

"I don't think that's what this is about, Nick." Charlotte winked Hayley's way. "She's going to be bored and there are only so many super-hot romance novels I have with me to entertain her. She needs something to do so she doesn't go insane, and that includes at night. She can't hop out to the West End, so Penny and I decided that we want to sponsor her here at The Garden. It's only Thursday through Saturday, but it'll give her something to look forward to."

He felt his blood pressure tick up. He actually felt it. That was probably a bad thing.

Penelope took up Charlotte's line of thought. "And I can

certainly find you things to do around here. Teresa can take you under
her wing. We'll treat you like any other submissive in training.
Damon, she'll need a contract and we'll need to interview training
Doms for her."

"I think that sounds lovely. I woke up early this morning and read
a few of the books Nick had on the subject. I found them fascinating."
Hayley was smiling as though they were discussing an outing for tea
and not her joining a sex club. "And it might be fun to meet some new
people."

New men. She was talking about meeting Doms.

He took a deep breath and even as the words came out of his
mouth he knew he would regret them. He also knew he wouldn't take
them back.

"I forbid it."

* * * *

Five hours later, Hayley sat in the small window seat in Nick's
living room overlooking the street below. She'd been told the window
was tinted so no one could see inside and the panes themselves were
bulletproof. She stared down at the people walking and talking. A fine
rain had started, but it didn't seem to faze the Londoners. They went
about their business, holding umbrellas or newspapers over their
heads or simply letting the rain fall.

It fit her mood.

The door opened and the reason for her grim state stepped inside.
Nick shrugged out of his jacket and hung it on the coat rack next to
the hoodie she'd worn every day since fleeing Seattle.

She was safe. She was warm and fed and that had to be enough.
She managed a smile. "Hey."

He set two bags on the table. His apartment was rather sparse,
with few feminine touches. The dining room table was devoid of a
centerpiece or tablecloth. The living room consisted of a single couch,
a television that was absolutely the biggest thing in the room, a coffee
table, and a media center with what looked like every game system

known to man. She'd explored his apartment, trying to get some measure of who Nikolai Markovic was five years later, but all she could tell was that he liked vodka and video games and read mostly nonfiction.

"I bought everything on your list plus a change of clothes," he replied, his deep voice rumbling. "I thought you might want to do the rest on the Internet. I can have someone pick up the parcels for you. You can use my laptop and charge to my credit card."

She forced herself to move, swinging her legs around. It wasn't like being mad at him would solve anything. He didn't want her in that part of his life. He was either embarrassed by her or she'd read him wrong and he didn't want her in a romantic or even plain sexual fashion. She'd made her play and lost.

It was going to be a long couple of weeks, but she was grateful for the help he was willing to give her and she didn't intend to be a whiny houseguest.

In fact, she intended to be the thoughtful one who made life easier on him. While he'd been out, she'd been planning and plotting to take the tension away. He couldn't possibly want to sleep on the floor in his office for weeks, and he'd made it plain that he wasn't going to be sneaking into bed with her. That left a few options open.

She looked through the bags. He'd bought shampoo and conditioner and moisturizer. All the toiletries she would need including tampons, which she'd put on the list more out of spite since she was weeks away from needing them. He'd also bought jeans and two shirts, a six-pack of underwear, two bras, and a pair of pajamas. Staid, practical underwear and flannel PJs. She ran her hand over it.

It was not at all what he would have bought Des. She'd seen some of the gifts he'd bought her cousin. Des had shown her while Hayley sat in her bedroom. She'd shown her sexy lingerie and perfume. Des had wrinkled her nose at some of it, declaring it a bit gauche, but Hayley had thought the teddies and filmy nightgowns had been beautiful, the perfume exotic.

He'd bought her unscented deodorant.

He'd also completely forbidden her to walk into The Garden on play nights.

She needed to look to his actions to find the truth. It was right there in that plain white cotton bra.

She gave him what she hoped was a gracious smile as she placed the items back in the bags. "Thank you so much. I appreciate it and I promise I'll keep the receipts so I can pay you back. I'll look online tonight while you're out and pick some clothes. Nothing expensive, I promise."

She wouldn't need pretty dresses to sit around the apartment and not be murdered.

"You don't need to pay me back. It was nothing." He rolled up his shirt sleeves, exposing muscled arms.

Hayley chose not to argue. She would simply keep costs down and pay him back one day. "Well, thank you anyway."

"And I'm not going anywhere this evening." Nick turned and hung his keys on a hook by the door. "I'm going to work here. I have a meeting with Walter in an hour or so, but otherwise, I'll be in my office if you need anything."

"Oh. I thought you would go to the club."

"I will work on your case," he promised. "I'm not going to leave you alone while I go out and play, if that's what all that business this morning was about. You should have simply asked me before causing that scene. I told you I would protect you and I will."

She sighed. "I wasn't worried about being left alone, Nick. I thought it sounded like fun."

His gaze came up to meet hers. "I find that interesting because only yesterday it was a perverted way to live. Only yesterday you were so offended you wouldn't stay here."

Was that why he'd forbidden it? She knew it was utterly ridiculous for a man to tell her he forbade anything, and her first instinct had been to tell him to go to hell. Unfortunately, Charlotte Taggart had gotten there first. And then Kay had started in on him. Even sweet Penny Knight had called Nick a barbarian and harangued him about joining the modern world.

She'd shut them all down because no matter how poorly he was behaving, she owed him for saving her, and she wasn't going to let her boredom make him uncomfortable. Yes, she was curious, but mostly about him. He didn't want her there and that meant she would honor his wishes.

"I explained that, Nick. I'm sorry I mentioned it at all." She wasn't going to start an argument with him. Especially not when he seemed to want one so badly. He seemed anxious, his eyes tight, his shoulders taut. There was something in the grim set of his eyes that let her know he was still feeling the effects of the drama from earlier in the day. Had he caught hell from the others even though she'd tried to shut it all down? "I won't again. I'm not welcome there. Got it. But I do think we should talk about the living arrangements. Since I'm going to be here for a while, I don't want to cramp your style. You should go to the club if you want. I understand you go there every night The Garden's open. I think I should stay in one of the empty apartments."

"There are no open flats," he replied, his tone dark. "The Taggarts are in the guest suite and we have Robert's men to deal with. There are already six men sharing three rooms on that floor. Unless you would rather they crowded in further so you're comfortable."

"That's not what I'm saying." Why wasn't he listening to her?

"Excuse me, but it's exactly what you said. You don't like the accommodations I can provide you with so you seek to take someone else's," he shot back, that grim look turning dark. His hands found his hips and she had to wonder if this was what Nick looked like when he was interrogating a suspect. "I'm sorry, but this is all I have to offer you so you will have to make do."

"Please, Nick, decide if I'm too stupid to know what I want or if I'm the evil queen of the world who demands everyone bow down to her." She owed him but she wasn't taking this. She hadn't earned it. "I never said anything bad about your place. It's fine, but I seem to make you uneasy. I can stay with Kay until the Taggarts leave. She offered earlier today. She's got a pull-out bed. You can be comfortable and I can have a bed, too."

"No." He turned on her, walking back toward the bathroom.

She stopped, her whole body going rigid. *Breathe. It's all right. He's had a bad day and he's touchy.*

Wait. She'd given in on everything and he was still being a jerk. "What do you mean no?"

He stopped in the doorway but didn't turn. "I meant no. It's a word indicating the negative. You will not stay anywhere but here. You will not do anything without my permission. I'm your bodyguard."

Oh, that so wasn't how a bodyguard worked, and now she kind of knew how to talk to him. She'd woken early, jet lag doing its thing, and because she didn't want to wake up Nick, she'd skimmed through a few of his books, including *The Loving Dominant* and *Screw the Roses, Send Me the Thorns*. They'd been painfully clear on who was truly in charge of the relationship. It wasn't him.

Those books had spoken to her. Those words, the philosophy had meant something to her.

They'd made her question if she'd been going about her romantic life in the entirely wrong way. Now she was wondering if she was going about *everything* the wrong damn way.

They weren't in a relationship like that, but she could translate the meaning into the relationship they were in.

"I told you I won't put myself in danger. That's all you need to know. I'm taking my bags and staying with Kay. It will give us both the distance we need. You can be you and I can be me, and we don't have to step on each other's toes. I'll see you in the morning. You know where to find me." She wasn't taking orders from him that she didn't have to. She meant what she'd said. She wasn't stupid. Kay would be an easier roommate, and she didn't seem to mind the company. Nick obviously did.

He turned on her, moving far more quickly toward her than he had in retreat. "You will do as I say and that will be the end of it.

You're my responsibility."

"Don't you mean burden?" He was pushing her buttons, and her patience was starting to fray. "Would you treat me like this if I'd walked in as a paying customer? Do you routinely force your will on clients?"

"You are not merely a client and you know it. If you want a different guard, you should have gone someplace else," he replied. "You should have gone to one of your friends, perhaps. Oh, you don't have any who would save you. Maybe one of these lovers you speak of. They would not take you in?"

"Why are you being such an ass?"

He took a deep breath, as though attempting to bring himself under control. "I'm trying to be reasonable. I cannot have you running crazy through this place. You have no idea what can happen, who is waiting for you out there. I trust many of these men, but not the ones I do not know. Damn it. Not even the one I know best of all because he no longer knows himself. Do you understand what this lifestyle can do to you?"

Did he think she was some kind of moron? "Are we back to me going to the club? I understand that everyone here is freaking human and I need to be careful, but that doesn't mean I hide myself away like a shrinking violet virgin."

He stopped and turned, the dark look on his face nearly making her call back her words. "Oh, but you practically are a virgin, *dushka*. You have no idea what you would see down there. You certainly have no idea what would happen to you if you walked into that dungeon without a collar around your pretty neck. Is that what you want? Do you want men fighting over you? Do you think that will make you feel like a woman? Yes, perhaps it would. You could put on a corset that showed off your lovely breasts and a tiny thong that would neatly split the cheeks of your ass. You could walk around and know that every Dom in the room wants you. Know that every single one wants to be the man fucking you tonight. And you can turn them all down or worse. You could play with them. Would that make you feel better?

Would that give you more confidence? You could take Robert's boys and make them sweat, select one and let him think he's special. Let him think he's the only one you really want and then let him see you with the others. Put him in his place. Is that the kind of game you want to play? It won't go well for you."

Tears sparked in her eyes as she realized what she was listening to. She'd walked into Nick's office and had only thought about how it affected her. She hadn't thought about all the feelings it could bring up in him. She certainly hadn't thought that they wouldn't necessarily be about her. Desiree was still there. She was still firmly between them, but Hayley wondered now how friendly that ghost was. What the hell had been in that letter from Desiree to Nick? What had she said to put him in this mood? "Oh, Nicky, if she did that to you, she was so wrong. I wouldn't do anything like that. I only wanted to explore the place. I wanted to understand why it means so much to you. I'm not her."

He frowned, shaking his head as though she was speaking some kind of foreign language. "Not her. I wasn't... Don't read into things. Is this what they teach you in that ivory tower you live in? Don't psychoanalyze me, Hayley. You won't like what you find."

"I'm trying to be civil. I'm trying to be kind. You're making that difficult for me. That's why it's best that I leave. My being here upsets you."

He moved into her space, his massive body a reminder of how small the hallway was. "Everything about you upsets me. Do you think that will change if you're two doors away? Do you think that will magically disappear if I walk into my club and you're there sitting at another man's feet?"

Something was happening. She could feel the air crackling between them, but it wasn't like before. Before there had been sweetness and affection, and she couldn't feel anything like that now. No. This wasn't love and comfort. What rolled off Nick was pure lust.

She needed to walk away. Hell, she should run. He wasn't the lover she remembered, the one who'd carefully taken her virginity.

126

This was the Dom and he was hungry, and if she let him he would eat her alive.

"I told you why I wanted to go. I was curious and I wanted to learn something about you." She could barely breathe. He was so close she could feel the warmth of his body.

"Learn not to push me." He took a step back.

That deeply disappointed her. It wasn't sane, but it was true. "But it's okay for you to push me. It's okay for you to order me around like some submissive. All the orders and obedience. None of the pleasure. I think I'll pass. I'm going to speak with Mr. Taggart. He said he owed Des. I was stupid to come here. I'll go back to Dallas with them and then you don't have to worry about my upsetting you ever again. Consider the debt paid, Nicky. Until I can leave, I'll stay out of your way."

She turned to go. If he wanted to be a massive asshole, she could walk away.

Her hand was almost on the door when she was whirled around, the breath fleeing from her chest as she thudded against him.

He held her arms, the pressure almost to the point of pain. "I told you, you're not going anywhere, but it's clear to me you need more than words. You say you're doing this so we'll be comfortable?"

Her whole body warmed, nipples hardening. Her body didn't give a shit that he was oozing danger. All it could sense was the fact that he was also oozing sex. Her heart could read the signs. There was no way this turned out well, but her heart wasn't screaming as loud as her damn pussy. "I told you my reasons. You can't want to sleep on the floor. You won't sleep with me. You know there's enough room. Or I could be comfy on the couch."

"Too close. The couch is far too close for my comfort, but then I'm beginning to understand that there might not be a way out of this." His hand moved up, fisting in her hair as he tugged lightly.

"Please, Nick." She hated the whine in her voice, but there wasn't anything she could do about it. Now that she was here, she wanted him. She shouldn't. It was wrong and foolish and she simply didn't care. She put her hands on his waist, letting her body cradle to his. "I want to know. I want to know if it was all an illusion or if it was every bit as good as I remember. I think about it every night."

"You were always reckless. Always. Whatever happens now, it's not my fault. You forced us into this, *dushka*. You will have to pay the price."

His mouth came down on hers and she forgot about everything but the way he made her feel.

Chapter Seven

Nick knew it was a horrible mistake, but he couldn't stop himself. He was on the edge and her soft, breathy words had sent him right over it.

It had been a day to test his limits. No one seemed to understand that he was trying to keep her safe. Safe from the outside forces, but also safe from him. Safe from this.

God, he'd wanted to keep her safe from this.

His mouth found hers, drawn like a magnet to her pillowy lips. Like everything about Hayley, her lips were soft and sugar sweet. So fucking sweet. Years and experience couldn't change how it felt to drag her against his body and put his mouth on hers. Right. It felt right.

He let his hands sink into the silk of her hair and used it ruthlessly to control her. Yes, that was what he needed. Control. Even as his cock started to swell, his mind was still working to justify his actions. He was bad for her, but wasn't it worse to let her get into more trouble? That's what would come from allowing her to have her way. Lots of trouble.

It was better this way. Yes, this was how he would protect her. Control her with sex. Give her what she needed in bed in return for obedience.

Control. That was the key.

Control. Damn it. He needed some.

Her hands ran up his sides. "Please, Nick. I need you. This is what we should have done in the first place. I never stopped wanting you."

He'd never stopped thinking about her. Even as he'd slept with her cousin. It was so fucked up, and that was one more reason to step away from her, but her tongue came out, running over his bottom lip. Pure fire licked along his flesh and he knew he wasn't going to stop. He was going to have her no matter the cost.

He slammed his mouth over hers, demanding entrance. She clutched him, opening up for him. Heat pulsed through his system and he was done thinking. Done worrying. Done ignoring his instincts. She was right. They'd been foolish to think for a second that they could be on the same continent and not have it come to this.

He'd forgotten. After all these years, his brain had turned that night into something purely emotional. He'd forgotten how much he'd needed her, how deep the ache to have her went.

He'd never wanted anyone the way he did Hayley. Not anyone.

"I want to see you." He moved his hands down, skimming over her clothes to find the hem of her shirt. "I want you naked."

He stood back, though being apart from her made him ache. He tossed the shirt aside. He'd bought her clothes and some underwear, though he'd ignored his impulse to buy her frilly, silky lingerie. He'd stood in the middle of Harrod's and touched the La Perla lingerie and seen her in it. And he'd walked away because he'd had some sense back then.

He didn't have it now. Now lingerie seemed unnecessary. Naked was all he needed.

Her skin had flushed to a pretty pink, but she didn't hesitate. Her arms went behind her and she twisted until her bra came off. She tossed it aside and her breasts bounced free. Gorgeous, round breasts with pretty pink nipples. Not tiny nipples. Nice sized. The kind he

130

could play with and suck and bite. The kind that he could use to make her whimper and moan and beg him to stop and not stop. Beg him to continue to lave her with his tongue and teeth and then spread her legs and fuck her hard.

He reached out and placed a hand on her breast. Her head fell back.

"I can't be gentle this time." He thought he should warn her, though he wasn't sure what he would do if she protested. He wasn't sure at this point that he could let her go.

"I want you, Nicky. I want the real you."

He cupped both breasts, feeling how soft they were, the silky texture of her skin, before rolling her nipples between his thumbs and forefingers. "Do you want the real me, *dushka*? The real me is a Dom. The real me wants to push all your boundaries. The real me wants to peel back your layers until we find the real you."

He pinched her nipples and watched her whole body react. Her pupils dilated and the pink of her skin deepened. Her nipples tightened and she gasped.

"Please, Nick."

Oh, yes, everything about this pleased Nick, but he needed more. He needed to know just how much control he had. He'd felt out of control for the last decade of his life. Even the relationships he'd had, his control had been nominal. He wanted it with her, wanted to know she would do what it took to please him. "Unbutton my shirt."

She didn't hesitate. She moved right in, her hands pulling his dress shirt out of his slacks and reaching eagerly for the buttons. She worked hard and fast, not well. She had to go back twice when she skipped buttons, but he stood there, patiently allowing her to undress him. Not so patiently, but he was enjoying watching her and the way her breasts moved.

Why had he bought her a bra? He should have left off the underwear. She wouldn't need it now. She'd made her bed and he was going to lie in it with her and she would be naked in it. She would be naked as much as possible.

She finally managed to unbutton the last of his shirt and she stepped back, her eyes on his chest. This was what he needed. She looked at him like he was a fucking work of art.

Ten feet tall. That was how he felt. "Touch me."

She flattened her palms against his chest and sighed as she moved over him. "You're so beautiful, Nicky."

Only a few people ever called him that. He liked it coming from her mouth, but it made him soft. He couldn't be soft again. He'd used up all his softness and it wouldn't come back again. "Sir. Call me Sir when we're intimate."

It might give him the distance he needed.

Emotional distance. He didn't want any physical distance. Not a fucking centimeter.

She looked up at him, her hands moving over his skin like she couldn't stop touching him. "Like they would in the club?"

This was dangerous territory but suddenly it seemed like something they needed. He could put her under contract for the length of the case. It would outline their relationship properly, give him rights the others would have to respect. It also could scare the shit out of her, but he was willing to take that chance. If he was upfront and honest about what he could and couldn't give her, he wouldn't have to feel guilty. He could take what he wanted and send her on her way when things were done because he wouldn't have lied to her. "You said you were curious."

"I am. This is about control, isn't it? You need this."

He hated how vulnerable he felt when she looked at him like that. When she stopped and stared up at him with those clear-as-day eyes, he could feel her seeing right through all his walls. "I need it, *dushka*. I wish I didn't, but I do. Think about this. My needs could end up hurting you."

She let that sink in, her hands still soothing over him. "Physically or emotionally?"

That was an easy question. "Both. I'll want to play, Hayley. I'll want to discipline you and you might not like it."

132

"Is the intention to hurt me? Or does it turn you on that I might enjoy it?"

"Am I a sadist? I feel more masochistic now because I'm letting you touch me when you could walk away." She was driving him crazy. Her nails ran over his chest, lightly scoring his nipples, and he could feel his dick pulsing. "I need to know you trust me. I need to know you're mine for however long we choose. I want to use the play to push your boundaries sexually, to open you up to me. But the truth is you're in control. You can walk away or stop me at any time because it only works if it works for you. Consent is required every step of the way. You say no and I stop everything."

He would die if she said no. Or he would need to go and find someone to beat the shit out of. A couple of Robert's men never said no to a sparring session that often ended in one of them requiring Walt's skills as a physician.

"Okay. Does this mean I can't do anything to you unless you give me permission? I want to kiss your skin, Sir."

He didn't need that much damn control. "Unless I tell you, you touch me all you like when we're fucking." He should leave it at that, but he couldn't. He'd hurt her too badly before. "I need you to understand that this is fucking. This isn't making love. I…lied to you the first time. I can't do it again."

Except he was lying right now. He'd made love to her that first night, but admitting it would only hurt them both.

She leaned in, her lips finding the skin right under his neck, and it took everything he had not to shudder with pure pleasure. "All right. I've tried it the other way. This is fucking. This is for pleasure and comfort."

He wanted to argue with her, but she was right. This was for comfort. She agreed. He could do what he wanted. He'd been open and honest and now she was naked and licking a path right where he wanted her to go. "Unbuckle my belt."

"Yes, Sir." Her eyes had gone soft. "I already like it, Sir. Who am I? Do I have a nickname or do you call me sub?"

Never. He would never call her by a name he would use because he couldn't remember. He sank his hand into her hair and gave it a gentle twist. "You're Hayley."

"Or *dushka*," she replied with a smile. "I like it when you call me *dushka*."

"It means sweetheart. I don't throw it around. I don't use it on anyone anymore. Anyone but you."

"I don't call anyone else Sir." Her hands worked the buckle of his belt. "Are you going to let me get my mouth on you this time? If we're going to do this while I'm here, then I want everything I didn't get last time. I want all of it, Sir. I don't want to lie in bed years from now and wonder how it would have felt. I want to know."

Everything. She was offering him the fucking world and this time she wasn't some wide-eyed kid who didn't know what she was getting into. She'd agreed that this would last as long as she was here. Carte blanche. That was the right term. Sexual carte blanche. "You want it all, I'll give it to you. And you will definitely put that hot mouth on me. Do you know I've dreamed about your mouth, that sassy, sexy fucking mouth? I want you to kiss my cock. I want you to lick and suck it deep inside. Can you do that for me, *dushka*? Can you get on your knees and suck my cock?"

"Yes, Sir. I can do that. I want to do that." She eased the belt open and drew apart the fly of his slacks.

She dropped to her knees, looking every bit like a sweet, hungry sex goddess. Her hair spilled over her shoulders and almost to her nipples.

He shoved down his slacks and boxers, not bothering with his shoes. They didn't matter. He wasn't getting into bed with her. This would be quick and hard and satisfying and then he would go back to work and think, really think about the contract that would protect them both. He would have it all in place before he slept beside her.

But the last thing he was thinking about now was sleep. "Touch me. Take me in your hands and stroke me. Get me hard."

Her lips curled up and he could practically read her mind. He was insanely hard, but he wanted the words between them. He wanted to start her training. Her job when they were playing was to arouse him and obey him. His job was to pleasure and protect her.

She put her hands together, rubbing them. Warming them.

The innocence of the gesture did something to Nick. The thought fled quickly as she touched him, her fingers brushing over his cock, sending a shiver through him.

"I always wanted to take my time," she whispered before leaning over and licking the head of his cock.

He couldn't stop the groan that came from his throat.

He'd taken his time that first night. He'd kissed her and run his hands over her skin, trying to explore her. He'd held her down, his dominance coming through even as he'd tried to shove it back.

That was what he'd done. He'd tied up his lovers or held them down. He took their pleasure seriously, but held them all at arm's length.

He didn't want to do that with her. He didn't have to. They had an agreed upon end date and he'd promised her everything.

There was a whole club downstairs, a garden of decadent delights, and it would all seem vibrant and new with her at his side.

She held the hard stalk of his cock while she ran that butterfly tongue over and around him. Heat flashed up his spine, but he took a deep breath. He wanted this, wanted this moment when he stood over her and watched her give him pleasure for the simple fact that he'd asked her to.

She licked the flat of her tongue on the underside as she tightened her hold on his cock.

"Yes." He could hear his accent deepening, let go of trying to sound like he fit in. "Do not hold back on me. I want you dirty, Hayley. I want that part of you that can't hold back. That part of you that one day is going to beg for me to fill your throat with my come."

She didn't respond, merely hummed around his cock, the vibration sending waves of pleasure through him.

He let his hand drift down as he allowed the sensations to wash over him. He breathed in and out, taking in the scent of her shampoo and their arousal.

"Cup my balls. Touch them, too. I want to feel you on every inch of my cock." He'd missed this that first night. He didn't intend to miss it again. She was right. It was better to know than to have to dream about it. The real thing would be something he could recall and think about for the rest of his life. He would lie in bed and remember how good it felt to have her tongue on him, to be her Master.

Fuck, he knew it was a slippery slope, but he was falling right down it.

"More. Take more. I'm not going to stop. Take it all. Everything I have to give you." He took control, gently guiding her. "This is how it's going to be. You should think about this. I'm going to ask you to sign a contract with me, but think about how demanding I'm going to be. Think about how much I'm going to want from you. While you're here, you'll be at my beck and call. You'll live with me, sleep with me, obey me when it comes to your safety, and when I decide you need it, you'll be disciplined by me."

She hummed around him again as though trying to respond. Unfortunately for her, she had a big cock in her mouth. He looked down to where she was swallowing him whole. Her eyes were closed, but her hands drifted around to cup his ass as though she was trying to keep him close. He could have told her absolutely nothing would stop him now. He was far too close to the edge and he intended to go over it.

She worked his cock until every thrust was a complete acceptance. In and out, he fucked her mouth, glorying in the soft velvet heat of her. He felt the scrape of her teeth, but it was nothing but one more sensation to be had. He thrust in and felt the soft spot at the back of her throat and couldn't stop himself. His cock pulsed and then he felt the swell of white-hot release. It shivered down his spine and lit his whole body up in a way it hadn't in years. Because she was more than a fuck. In the chaos of the moment, the idea slipped inside his brain and he couldn't quite reject it.

He thrust in, letting the tension drain even as his hands softened on her hair.

Hayley didn't stop. She sucked and licked and swallowed down everything he gave her.

Because she wasn't some piece of porcelain. Because she wasn't some pretty perfect thing to put on a pedestal.

She was a woman and he had to start treating her like one.

She could be a hell of a woman if he would let her, a voice inside him said. She could be his woman if he worked hard enough.

She sat back on her heels and a wave of pure possessiveness went through him.

This was all a mistake.

Hayley smiled up at him. "I knew it would be like this."

She'd said it that night, too. She'd said the same thing as she'd reached for him, holding him close.

He was doing it again. The truth washed over him like ice water, waking him up to the fact that he was fooling himself. He'd promised he would get the contract between them before he moved on. It hadn't taken more than one push from her and he was ready to shove his cock deep and pretend she was his for the time being.

He glanced at the clock. He'd even forgotten about his meeting with Walter. A meeting intended to ensure Hayley's safety.

He'd learned nothing in five years.

"Nick?" Hayley was still sitting there, still gorgeous and naked and waiting for him.

He reached down and pulled up his boxers and slacks, his hands shaking. "I'm late for my meeting."

"What?" She sounded breathless and now she seemed to be figuring out that things weren't going the way they should.

He needed her dressed. He couldn't look at her breasts and not want to touch her. He was going to lose control again if she didn't cover up. He reached into the bag and pulled out the nightgown he'd bought her along with the plain flannel PJs that he'd thought might be some kind of armor against him. He tossed her the gown. "You should cover up."

She paled but stood quickly, as though she couldn't get the gown over her head fast enough.

He was a dick. He was a horrible prick of a man, but he couldn't do this again. He couldn't fall madly for a woman who wouldn't ever truly need him, who might fuck him when it was convenient, might enjoy him for brief periods of time, but he could never be essential to Hayley.

He had his hand on the door when he heard her sniffle.

And now he was the asshole who'd made her cry.

He let his head hit the door.

"Did I do it wrong?" Hayley asked quietly. "Because if I did, you could tell me. You don't have to make me feel like shit. You know, it's awful what you just did. Was that some kind of revenge? Was it something you've been waiting to do? Show the stupid girl how she can never get the guy?"

Let her. Let her see how pathetic you are, how utterly devoid you are. Let her see how empty you've been for fucking years and then she'll know the real measure of you.

It would be easier.

"I was wrong to do that. I'm sorry. I was wrong to offer you anything at all. You can stay with Kayla. I'm going to hurt you again and I didn't mean to do that."

"So the contract then? That was a lie?"

He should turn and face her and tell her everything that came out of his mouth was a damn lie. "I changed my mind."

"Coward."

Yes, he was definitely that. "I'm sorry, Hayley."

She suddenly wrapped her arms around him from behind. He hadn't heard her move, but now she was hugging him, resting her head against his back. "I'm not Des and you didn't change your mind. You felt something for me and that scared you. That's not wrong, Nicky. I feel something for you, too, and the truth of the matter is I'm so lonely and empty that I'll take your contract and whatever time limit you want to put on it."

He should push her away, but he found his hand running up to hers, to hold her against him. "It can't work."

"Maybe not forever, but we can enjoy ourselves now. I know that night wasn't a big deal to you," she began.

Somehow it was easier to speak the truth when he wasn't looking at her. "I think about it all the time."

She sighed against him. "Then let's give each other closure. For a minute there I thought you were punishing me, but walking away is more about punishing yourself, isn't it?"

He wasn't sure he liked how easily she saw through him. "I don't deserve even a few weeks with you."

"Sign the contract with me, Nick. Show me this world you love and share it with me, and maybe I can stop being angry with you and angry with myself for not being able to keep you. And maybe you'll stop being angry with yourself, too. We can be kind to each other."

"This doesn't end in marriage, *dushka*. You deserve that, but I'm never going to be the kind of man you need. I'm not going to go home with you and let you introduce me at faculty teas. This is why I left the first time. I was selfish. I knew I couldn't be what you needed and I took you anyway."

Her arms tightened around him. "Then you owe me. You stole my virginity and no man since has been enough. So give me this couple of weeks to get you out of my system. I'm not going to cry at the end and beg you to stay with me. I'll live my life. But I do want this. I liked what we did up until you were a total ass. It was more erotic than anything I've done in my life and that includes that night with you. I want to explore this."

She was killing him. He turned and finally did what came naturally. He pulled her into his arms. "I did not mean to be a massive ass."

She chuckled against him as she squeezed him tight. "All right then. We're agreed. We're going to have fun and when it's over we're going to be good friends, you and I."

There were tears in her eyes as she tilted her head to look up at him.

"I missed you. God, how I missed you." She'd been a hole inside him and only now could he see it. For years she'd been a friend, maybe his only real friend. He'd ruined it all. "I don't want to hurt you."

"Good because I don't want to hurt you either," she replied, not seeming to care that she had tears streaming down her cheeks.

His cell phone buzzed. He knew who it was. "Damn it, it's Walter. I have to go."

She took a step back. "All right, then. I'll see you when you get back."

He leaned over and kissed her forehead. "You'll get ready for tonight. We'll go downstairs and explore a bit and, *dushka*, I promise to make up for being a massive coward ass. I'm sorry. Get dressed and find Charlotte and tell her I apologize and that she should dress you properly. I'll have Damon draw up a simple contract. You have full run of the building, but please be careful. I don't want you going out."

She leaned in again, cuddling against his chest. "I won't. And don't do that again. Don't make me feel small. I can handle a lot. If you had told me you were feeling too much, I would have backed off and given you some space, but I can't handle you making me feel small. I won't do it to you."

How often in his life had he felt small? So many times. "I promise."

His phone buzzed again and he groaned. He'd been so ready to run out of here and now he hated to leave her.

She stepped away. "Go. Do your job. I'm probably going to masturbate."

She should have railed at him, thrown things at him. There should have been a massive fight.

She'd shown him grace and kindness. She'd made him laugh.

"Do all you wish now, *dushka*." The idea that she might touch herself and think of him made his cock twitch again. No one in the world had ever made him feel as young as this woman. Like a horny teen. "Once I have you under contract, that pussy is going to belong to me. I'll take better care of it than I did this afternoon."

He leaned over and kissed her one more time before he turned and strode out.

He might not deserve her, but he was going to make sure she got everything she needed out of their contract. Beginning with him figuring out what kind of mess she was in.

Chapter Eight

"Ah, you're here."

Nick sighed as he walked into Walt's office. Office was a nominal word. It was more of a laboratory, complete with blacked out windows because apparently sunlight could ruin his experiments. Walt had taken a large part of the east wing's fourth floor and turned it into a large open office with everything from a massive refrigerator to store some of his experiments, to long, industrial-looking desks with a bunch of science stuff Nick had no idea what to do with.

Walter Bennett sat at a microscope wearing his normal uniform of jeans and a snarky T-shirt. This one proudly proclaimed that the sloth was his spirit animal. Which was insane because Walt had plenty of energy. He simply used it in a different way.

The Garden's mad professor.

"I'm here. What have you found out?" He couldn't keep the irritation out of his voice despite the fact that he'd already accepted this was for the best. If he'd stayed with Hayley, he would be in bed with her and they wouldn't have the contract they needed between them. He might utterly forget about everything but finding pleasure in her body, and this time around he was determined to give her more.

"Oh, you sound touchy. Did we interrupt something?" Kayla

walked around the massive medical fridge, carrying a couple of pairs of latex gloves.

Which given Kay's proclivities could mean anything, but she didn't play with Walt. Lately she'd been partnering with a Dom outside the group who played in The Garden, but it didn't seem serious.

Walt looked up, frowning. "I thought they were fighting."

"I told you, mate. That kind of fight usually ends up in ripped clothes and someone shoved against a wall. Hello, Nick." Brody Carter was sitting at his desk, the laptop light illuminating his face.

Walt shook his head, turning on his stool. "See, now you're reminding me of middle school."

"I'm not talking about bullies giving you a wedgie. Sex, Walt. They had sex," Brody explained with a long sigh. "You'll have to excuse him. His genius-level IQ sometimes misses the subtleties of life."

Like the big, brash Aussie knew anything about subtlety. "I think we should talk about whatever it is you've found. You're the ones who texted me. Numerous times."

Kayla's mouth dropped open and she handed Walt a pair of gloves. "Oh my god. You did have sex. Like now. Or at least you started to. Did we cock block you?"

"I'm betting we did by the look on his face." Brody sat back, winking Kayla's way. "And by we, I mean they. I was willing to wait a couple of hours for you to calm down after the riot this morning. Bad business. You know those women don't play and they stick together. You start trying to tie one down in a non-fun way and they will come after your balls."

"Yes, well, one would think since those women are all submissives that I would get some aid from their Doms." Not that he wanted to get into this, but damn, he'd been left out in the cold. None of the Doms around the table had spoken up for him. They'd allowed the women to spout some of the foulest language he'd ever heard. And Charlotte had made sure he felt comfortable by cursing him in his own language.

Walt pulled one of the gloves over his hand. "You won't find help from that group, man. And I wasn't about to get in Charlotte Taggart's way. She scares me. I heard Big Tag ask Damon about popcorn. Apparently they both find it amusing when the chicks start in on a man. Another man, at least."

Maybe now the women would stop treating him like a monster. "Well, they will all be happy to know that I've told Hayley she can go to the club. She has my permission so you can all calm down."

Kayla gave him a smile that he was smart enough to know had nothing to do with amusement. "How nice of you to allow the little woman in. Your permission. Wow. Are you going to let her out of your flat for dinner, too? Should I apply for permission to speak with her?"

He had to hold on to his patience. "I've given her run of the place as long as she doesn't go outside. I believe she's with Charlotte and Penny right now."

"All right. I'll back off." Kayla pulled gloves on as well, snapping them on her wrists. "Are you going to let her play? There's no reason to let her in if you're going to make her sit in a corner with her eyes closed. I can sponsor her if she wants to explore. I won't put her with anyone who isn't safe."

Oh, he needed to make a few things plain right now. "She won't play with anyone but her Dom. We're signing a contract this afternoon and I expect you to honor it."

"Pay up, Brody." This time Kayla's smile was vibrant and Nick knew he'd been had.

When had he forgotten Kayla's moves? There was never a situation she didn't put her cute nose in.

Brody's head fell back with a groan. "Bloody hell. I've gotta get some cash. I was sure I was going to win that one. Couldn't keep it in your pants for a full day, mate, could you?"

"How about you keep out of my business?" Somehow betting on a person's private life was far more fun when he wasn't the one in question. He was well aware that if this bet had been about someone else, he would have wanted in on the action. "Or should we talk about why you've dodged the doctor's calls?"

Brody went a nice shade of red. "Ain't been dodging her. I'm busy is all. Besides, she was only calling me because I was her contact here in Europe. She's got in touch with Damon now. He's making sure she's all right. I believe he called in Ten Smith to help her out."

"What happened between the two of you?" Kayla proved his earlier point about her nosiness.

"Don't ask." Walt frowned as he held up the necklace Hayley had been wearing earlier. "He won't talk about it."

Brody stood up, his hands on his hips. "Because nothing happened. Nothing at all. She's a nice lady. We got to be friends. That was all. I was her bloody bodyguard, not her lover. Unlike the rest of you, I don't mess around on the job. She was a pro, too. Not all of us screw our clients. Sorry, Nick. I'm sure yours is totally different."

"Well, I have known her for ten years," Nick allowed. "I have to admit I was surprised when the good doctor needed help and you didn't go to her. You seemed to be more than friends."

Brody had worked a longer-term op roughly six months before. He'd gone undercover with a doctor in Africa and Nick had seen them together at one point. They'd looked an awful lot like a couple. The perpetually flirty Aussie had been more serious since he'd come home. Nick had attributed it to what had happened with Owen and being around a group of traumatized men, but now he had to wonder.

"It isn't that I don't like her," Brody continued. "She's a good one, but I don't think it's smart to get involved in something that can only be long distance. I like my job. She likes hers. That's the end of it. And that problem she had got taken care of. Ten Smith was close by. He dealt with the problem she had with her deliveries and according to him, everything's been smooth sailing since. That was six months ago. She's called since then, but apparently not on business, according to Damon. Just wanted a chat. I think it's best we keep things professional. I had Damon tell her I wasn't available and wouldn't be in the future."

Kayla sat down next to Walter. "I think it's sad. I had them married off in my mind."

"Yeah, you and Mum, but then she marries me off to every eligible female she meets. Some completely ineligible ones, too. Says my biological clock is going to explode or something. I tried to tell her it didn't work that way for men, but she's determined to get some grandkids." Brody held up a hand. "How about we make a deal? I stop asking you about Hayley and you leave my love life alone. We'll go back to being real men and have a beer and talk about football."

"It's a deal." Though Brody's words were sinking in. He was in the same position. He wasn't sure he could be happy as some man who worked a nine to five in an office. He was old enough to know he needed this kind of work, and this place was perfect for him.

And Hayley had always known she wanted stability. She would want a husband who didn't run off across the globe chasing down corporate spies or missing heiresses. Her father had hauled her around looking for the next big score.

This was all the time he would have with her. He wasn't going to come in and out of her life. He didn't want that for her. When he walked away this time, it would be forever.

That's what you said last time, idiot. It'll be until the next time she calls and you run panting after her, and when she leaves you, it'll be a hundred times worse than anything Des could have done.

"What do you have?" He needed to focus on the case and not the future. Hadn't he learned to live in the now? It was all he really had, and the now was looking up if he could deal with his coworkers and their incessant need to get into his business.

"Start with Brody," Walt said. "This is going to take me a moment."

He was unthreading the gold chain as Kayla handed him what looked like a small pair of pliers. Nick turned to Brody, hoping Hayley hadn't gotten too attached to that necklace. He would find her another since it looked like Walt was about to damage this one.

Not a necklace. A collar. She would need a beautiful collar around her throat when they played at night and something more delicate for the daytime. Yes, he could already see a lovely gold necklace around her throat.

"What have you been working on?" He knew Owen and some of the lads downstairs had been going through surveillance tapes.

"First off, I read the letters Desiree sent to both of you. I checked them for prints but there's nothing on there that would help. Just Hayley and Des and a set that's registered to a man who works for the company that shipped everything back. I looked into them. Des apparently requested that her Tokyo home be packed up by a specific firm, oddly enough a British firm. They paid to have a team of two men fly all the way out there, pack up her stuff, and ship it. Why not save the money and use a local firm? That's what most people would do."

He could clear that up quickly. Des had been anything but ordinary. He glanced down at Brody's notes and nodded. "Her family used that firm for all their legal issues. They're expensive and private. They would have gone to great lengths to follow Desiree's instructions. It would explain why it's been so long. I don't buy that this part of her will was in some legal challenge. Des did not want these particular items out in the open until a specific time after her death."

"The question is why." Brody sat back down, crossing one leg over his opposite knee. "Look, I talked to Damon about the investigation into Des. Even if this was some kind of blackmail scheme gone wrong, why would she set things up not to play out until two years after her death? And why send it to Hayley? Everything else went to her mother or her sister."

He knew it well. He'd been the one to pack up all her London flat, carefully discarding or hiding away anything that could have compromised her family. Of course. "She sent it to Hayley and had it packed up in a particular way because she knew if I could I would have gone through it. She didn't want those boxes searched and possibly seized. Given the investigations into her activities, if something had been delivered to her relatives here in England, they would have been confiscated by MI5. No one would be watching Hayley. Not even the Agency. She and Des hadn't spoken in years. Hayley was off the radar."

"All right, I can buy that. Still, it seems like if she knew someone was after her, she would want the rest of us to know," Brody pointed out. "Like I said, I read that letter, mate. There was nothing in it at all except personal stuff. She did seem to think something could happen to her. The letter wasn't specifically about what should happen if she died. She knew she was under investigation. She was leaving and this letter was her good-bye to you both."

"I doubt that. If Desiree was going to run she would want backup." His gut clenched at the thought of what could have happened. She would have come to him, beautiful eyes in tears, and begged him not to leave her alone. She would have gently reminded him of all he owed her and suggested that this was the time that everything changed. When they were alone, she would surely change.

How had he been so foolish all these years?

"That's not the way it was written, mate." Brody considered him for a moment as though trying to figure him out. "I was surprised to find it unopened. You sure you don't want to read it?"

He felt his jaw tighten. That letter had been a snake waiting to bite him since the moment Hayley admitted she had it. "Not if it's all personal. Not now. I know someone needed to read it, but I can't yet. Was there anything in Hayley's letter?"

Brody put a hand on the envelope. It was sitting right there on his desk. "More of the same. Des cared about you both. She did tell Hayley that if anything ever happened to her and she was in trouble, she should come and find you."

"So we're pretty certain this is about Desiree," Kayla said. "I had to do some research into Hayley to make sure this wasn't something from her past."

"No one would want to hurt Hayley. She's done nothing. She's a college professor." This was about Desiree. He could feel it in his gut.

"No one's perfect, Nick," Kayla replied as she took the gold chain from Walter and set it aside. "It's precisely why I decided to look into her. She seems likable, but everyone's got something they want to hide."

"Yes, me. I would be the one wild thing she ever tried." He didn't like the thought of them looking into Hayley, treating her like…well, like a normal client. This was exactly what they should do. Look at all the angles with the understanding that the client could be lying to them. "She's not lying."

"She's also not telling the entire truth. Did you know she was engaged?" Kayla asked.

"No," he said carefully. She'd almost married? Two days ago if he'd been asked, a comfortable marriage to some nice man would have been exactly what he wanted for her. Now the thought made his muscles tense. Had she asked this man to marry her? Had she offered some bland man all her sweetness the way she had offered herself to him that night? "What do you know about the man? When was this?"

"Four years ago," Kayla replied. "I've got a file on him if you want to read it. He was a fellow grad student. Apparently it didn't get to the actual wedding planning stages. She broke things off after a few weeks."

"Do you know why they broke up?" Who would be stupid enough to let Hayley go? Besides himself, but then he'd had reasons.

"According to the police report she filed, she decided things weren't working out. That's what she told the officers."

"Police report?" He didn't like the sound of that. What was she hiding from him? He wasn't angry with her, but she would discover that after tonight, she would keep no secrets from him.

"Yeah, that's how I found out about the ex. According to the statement, they broke up and he made a scene in the middle of the restaurant they were in. The police were called out and everything was amicable after that for a while. Then about eighteen months later, he started stalking her. I know we still think this is about Des, but I'm going to poke into this guy and see what I can find."

There was his anger, and none of it was directed toward Hayley. He might have to take a trip to Seattle in the near future. "I'd like a name."

Kayla huffed, throwing her hands up. "And then he'll be dead and I can't poke anymore. Well, I could, but I would have to invite the boys in. They like to poke things."

He wasn't going to let her divert him. "I want a name."

"And I want peace in the world." She leaned against the counter nonchalantly. "Not really. That would be so boring. His name is in the file so I guess I can't hide it. Greg Hansen. Look, you can't go after him right now. Let me deal with it and later you can play the white knight. Like we said, it's probably about Des, but I'm going to be careful and look at everything."

"Where was he when her house exploded? Did the police talk to him? I want you to send everything you have on him to Ariel so she can get me a profile."

Kayla held a hand out. "I've already sent what I have to Ariel. And no, the police didn't talk to him because according to the police, it was all an accident. We know that's bullshit, but it does mean the police didn't exactly have to do a full investigation. Also, he's got a cousin on the force."

"So that could explain how it got covered up." He liked the idea of someone he could easily kill and fix the problem. Not easily kill. Well, easy for him, not for his victim. He would torture the asshole until he begged for death and then Nick would torture him some more. Big Tag complained that no one let him torture people anymore. Perhaps they could have a party of some sort. It could be fun.

"It's not the ex-fiancé, though I find the coincidence of him suddenly becoming a problem again after eighteen months of peace interesting. I'll have to think about that." Walt was speaking but his whole body was focused on his task. He held a thin wire in his hand

and he was pressing it down into the hole where the hook had held the chain. It appeared to bisect the small heart, leaving room for the chain and now Walter's delicate tool. "First off, maybe this kid has connections to the Seattle police force, but that doesn't explain how someone was waiting here for her. He has mob connections? Here in England and back in the States? I doubt that. No. This is all about whatever is on this beauty."

"What is it?" Nick watched as Walt carefully pulled the wire back out.

Walt leaned in, his lips curling up. "That is a microdot. Old-school steganography. Damn, Kay, we're going to need a bigger boat."

"He means I need to reset the microscope because it's smaller than we expected." Kayla moved to his left where she started fiddling with the gear.

There it was, a tiny piece of technology that proved beyond a shadow of a doubt that Des had been true to the end.

Even from the grave she found a way to fuck with him.

"Let's get started," he said with a sigh.

* * * *

Hayley glanced down the hallway and wondered where she'd made the wrong move. She was a hundred percent certain she'd passed the same potted plant twice now.

While The Garden below was a thing of unique beauty, this particular floor was a maze of doors and halls that all looked pretty much the same.

And the damn things weren't numbered. She'd been told Charlotte Taggart had set up in one of the open offices in the west wing. Teresa had merely explained that she should take the second right, then a left, and then it would be the third office on her right.

Or had that been the second left and then a right?

Maybe Nick had a point about her not wandering around.

"Hello. You must be the new girl."

151

She stopped in front of the open office. Finally, someone who might know where she was. It was almost eerily quiet. "Hi, I'm Hayley. I think I'm lost."

The man gave her a smile that would send most women to their knees. If she had to guess, she would put the man in front of her in his mid-thirties. He stood up from his desk and walked toward her. Blond hair. Piercing green eyes. His shoulders seemed to go on forever. "Being lost isn't the worst thing in the world. Sometimes being lost takes you right to the place where you need to be."

She couldn't help it. She found herself smiling. He was a delicious man, sunny and vibrant. Unfortunately, she liked the brooding and hulking glorious beast type. "Well, I need to be in the place where Charlotte Taggart is. Any idea where I'm going?"

He stepped closer. "Now, I do seem to recall a woman walking around here earlier today. Strawberry blonde hair?"

"Yes. She's one of the owners of this place. Have you never met her?"

He shook his head. "No idea, but then I don't remember a lot. Maybe. Probably not. I'll remember you though. I promise."

There was a long groan from somewhere inside the room and she heard a masculine voice. "Stop flirting with Nick's girl, Jax. We have other things to do today."

The man named Jax waved him off. "Don't mind Robert. He's always so serious. It's all about work with that man. I would much rather play. Why don't we look around a bit and see if we can find your friend?"

This must be one of the lost boys she'd been told about. "I'm afraid my...Dom wouldn't like that."

It was a weird word in her mouth, but she was going to get used to it.

Jax's face fell. "Damn it. I owe Owen five punches."

The other man in the room made a sudden appearance. She recognized Robert from the night before. He'd been the one to ask Ariel for her help. Now he was frowning at his friend. "I told you not

152

to bet with Owen anymore. He actually knew Nick from before. He was Nick's partner. If he says Nick's crazy about the girl, he's probably right."

Jax huffed and turned back to his desk. "Owen doesn't remember being his partner so he shouldn't have any better insight than the rest of us. And so much for listening to Brody. He thought Nick would hold out longer on account of sheer stubbornness."

"You know Ariel says we have instincts that nothing can erase. Owen knows Nick deep down," Robert explained before turning back to her. "I'm sorry, Ms. Dalton. I believe Charlotte and Ian took the office two doors down. Let me take you there."

She was about to thank the nice man when she caught sight of a massive white board. There was nothing odd about that sight given that she was currently in an investigative security company, with the exception of the fact that it was her life they appeared to be investigating.

She stepped into the room, moving around Robert. There were several photos of her, some of her parents, Des, and the rest of her family. Her stomach turned as she saw they even had a picture of Greg up with a line drawn to her and the word fiancé.

They were investigating her. Like she was a criminal.

Or like she was the client and they needed to know as much as they could about her, the logical part of her said. The illogical part wanted to pull those pictures down and shove them in the pretty boys' faces.

Did Nick know about this? Had he seen the wall of shame?

"How did you pull this together so quickly?" She was pleased with how calm her voice was. "You seem to be thorough if you've already heard the rumor that I slept with the chair of the history department in order to get my job."

It was hard not to tear up. There was a photo taken off the college's website of her boss. He was a genuinely nice man whose love of American history was inspiring. He was also likely on his way out, caught up in a battle for the department chair. The ivory tower had turned out to have as much backstabbing as the real world.

Robert stepped in front of the board. "We were given the task of looking into your background last night. We started making some calls. Discreetly, of course."

"What does that mean?" Was there a discreet way to call up her colleagues and ask for the dirt on her life?

"It means I called around as a reporter," Jax explained.

"What would a reporter want with me?" She was sure they'd reported the home explosion. She'd seen some news vans that day, but she'd refused to talk with anyone. She'd been far too shocked to deal with the press. "I understand they'd cover the story, but why would a reporter call up people I know? They had nothing to do with the house fire."

Jax looked to Robert as if asking for permission. Robert nodded and Jax continued. "You're the story now. It's only natural that reporters would start calling. It's an easy way to make people feel comfortable about talking."

"I didn't think there was much of a story. I thought they were calling it all a gas leak."

She watched as Robert's eyes tightened.

"I'll find out sooner or later," she promised.

Jax gave her a grin and pointed to his laptop. "You're kind of a big deal now."

"Big deal?" She moved to his desk, utterly ignoring the way he patted his lap to offer her a seat.

"Nick's going to kill you," Robert said to Jax with a long-suffering sigh.

"She's so pretty it might be worth it," Jax replied. "Also, you know how I love a dangerous woman."

She gasped as she caught sight of the headline on the Seattle news site he had pulled up on his screen.

College Professor Wanted For Questioning In Police Officer Death

She stared at the screen trying to understand what the hell had gone so fucking wrong with her life that she was now a suspect in a murder.

"Do you need a hug?" Jax asked. "Because every time I find out I killed someone I always need a hug. It happens more often than you would think. I keep telling my therapist I need some affection."

"Don't you pull that shit with Ariel, either, you horny bastard." Robert shut the laptop. "Ms. Dalton, would you like a bottle of water? Do you need to sit down? I can call Nick if you like."

"He wasn't dead. The police officer wasn't dead when I ran. He was trying to kill me, but he was alive." She could still remember the moment she'd realized he wasn't there to check on her. He'd had his gun in hand and she'd watched as he'd screwed on a silencer and eased off the safety before knocking on her door.

She'd then watched in horror as he'd kicked it in when she didn't answer.

But he'd been alive.

"According to reports we found this morning, Officer Keller was found dead inside the hotel room assigned to you," Robert explained. "He was shot in the chest twice. Took out both lungs."

She shook her head, confusion setting in. "No. That wasn't his name. Did they run a picture?"

Jax had the computer open again in a flash. "Here he is."

She looked at the picture of the police officer. It was his professional photo, showing a man in his middle years, beginning to gray at the temples. He stared out of the photo, wearing his pressed blue uniform.

She'd never seen that man in her life.

"That's not the man who came after me," she said, recognizing the edge in her voice. "He was younger. Damon told me earlier that they'd figured out the man who tried to kill me wasn't really a police officer. He was posing as one. Why would they kill an actual officer?"

"I can think of several reasons," Jax offered. "Officer Keller might have seen too much, might have interacted with the killer at an inopportune time. He might have recognized that the killer wasn't an officer and had plans to expose him."

"Or they need a way to put pressure on you," Robert pointed out. "They need a way to force you out in the open. They're counting on the fact that you'll want to clear your name."

"I do." She was going to have to talk to someone. "If I don't face this, they'll assume something worse. The police, that is. I need to give the police a description of the man who came after me. He's probably the one who killed the officer."

"Or he knows who did. It could have been a member of his crew, too. Don't forget that man who came after you in the alley by the hotel is linked to organized crime." Jax stood up and walked over to the white board. "See. It's on the board so it's true. And it's a bad idea to go to the Seattle PD until we figure out who's real and who's working for whoever hired this dude."

He pointed to a picture they'd blown up from one of the crime scene photos. It was grainy, but that was the man who'd shown up at her motel that night. Minus the devil horns someone had drawn on him. And she was fairly certain he hadn't been carrying a massive penis at the time. Someone had drawn a big dildo in his hand.

Robert sighed. "Please don't mind the juvenile pranks. My men are idiots, but they're actually quite good when it comes to investigating."

"It takes our minds off all the bad shit," Jax agreed. "Owen and Tucker are out there right now researching your family here in England. I didn't get to go on the field trip though. Apparently there's some kind of Interpol warning out about me and Sasha and Dante, and Damon won't let us go have fun. So see, we're in the same boat, sweetheart. Stuck in this place with nothing to do."

"What are you wanted for?"

"Nothing I remember doing," he admitted. He gave her a charming smile as he changed the subject. "You want to pass some time with me? Maybe Netflix and chill?"

"I'm really freaked out about all of this so the only way I want to pass time with you is going to be by shoving my foot into your crotch and seeing how far I push your dick into your body cavity," she said, staring at the wall. It wasn't the first time she'd been around a guy like Jax who didn't seem to want to take no for an answer. It was absolutely best to put firm boundaries out there.

"Damn, that's cold," Jax said. "All right, then. Good to know."

"Why do you need to talk to my aunt?" She could imagine how that was going to go.

"Because I'm not sure she's actually your aunt," Jax replied casually.

The hits kept on coming. "What is that supposed to mean?"

"Go carefully on this topic," Robert warned. "We're not sure of anything yet. This investigation is very new."

"Yeah, but this feels right to me. The truth is in the details. Am I correct in saying this branch of your family wasn't one you grew up with?" Jax asked. "From what I read you didn't actually meet them until you were what? Fourteen years old?"

"Yeah," she managed, her brain still reeling. "My dad first introduced me to my cousin Desiree in Las Vegas when I was fourteen. It was summer and after this mega fight, Mom agreed to let me go with him for a few weeks. I ended up staying with him for almost the whole summer. He was playing some tournament in Vegas when Des showed up."

Robert leaned against one of the desks. There appeared to be six of them, one for each of the "lads," as the others seemed to call them. "This was eleven years ago? So Des was working for MI6. From what I remember from her file, she joined up young. They liked her social connections."

And her beauty and charm. Des could get most men to do anything she wanted when she was on her game. God knew Hayley had watched her manipulate Nick. "She didn't talk about that to me, but I wasn't surprised to find out that's what she did. I never bought that she was someone's secretary."

"Interesting. So your father introduced you. How did he explain how he found the connection?" Jax had lost his himbo smoothness and now sounded like a competent agent.

"He'd been researching our ancestry. Lots of people do it these days. He found the connection to the Brooks family in England and reached out to them. I think it amused him that we were connected to such upper-crust people. He met the family in London after that and they kept in touch. Our grandfather was a Brooks and he emigrated from England after World War II. I wish he'd kept the documentation, but my father traveled light. He lived mostly out of a suitcase. It was the nature of his job."

"Which was playing poker." Robert was watching her with intelligent eyes.

She was well aware her father's choice of how he made his living wasn't the most respectable. "That was my dad. He tried playing on the circuit for a while, but he preferred the back rooms. Once they started taping the big events, he dropped off the circuit and basically hustled in ring games."

"You can make a lot of money on the circuit," Jax mused. "I looked into it today."

"Yeah, you apparently looked into a lot of things." It was hard to believe he'd done so much in the day since she'd walked in the door.

"Jax is a speed reader and he has eidetic memory. If he scans something, he can bring it back and recite it to you. He never forgets. Unless a crazy doctor fills him full of drugs that erase his mind," Robert said, a hint of a smile on his face. "We're hoping that never happens again. My point is, he acts like a horny teen most of the time, but he's got a genius-level IQ. There's nothing he can't learn and quickly. Well, except manners."

"Manners are meaningless." Jax crossed his muscled arms over his chest. "All I'm saying is a man like your father should have viewed the explosion of poker players as celebrities as a way to make even more money. I'm intrigued."

"Why does any of this matter?" She was tired of the seemingly endless speculation about her family. They'd been weird but they were hers. "My father was incredibly private and he was always in trouble with someone. None of it matters because he's dead. And this doesn't tell me why you think my aunt isn't my aunt."

"Because I pulled some records and your father's grandfather wasn't named Brooks. He was named Johannsen. He did emigrate, but not from England. He came over from Sweden before World War II. He enlisted and fought in the Pacific theater. He came home, married a woman named Belinda Wells, and they had a daughter who married Antony Dalton. That's your grandfather. You're Swedish and German. There's no British side to your father's family, although your mom's side is oddly close to the crown. Not like in line or anything, but on her side you're like fourth cousins with Wills and Harry."

Normally that would be the leading story, but now all she could think about was the fact that her father had lied to her. "Why would he tell me I was related to Des if I wasn't?"

Jax shook his head. "No idea, but again I'm intrigued."

"There could be any number of reasons why he would do it," Robert said carefully.

She knew what he meant. "Because he was a con man? Don't mince words with me. I know who my dad was."

He'd been a dick most of the time, and then he would stop pretending and actually be her freaking father and she would need him so much. Her dad had been there for her after the Nick debacle. He'd taken her with him to Monaco and for once he'd paid more attention to her than he had his gambling. Oh, he'd disappeared for a few days to play in an underground tournament, but he'd left her in the happy hands of the spa staff.

He'd been there when she'd cried. He'd told her she was better off without Nick. She'd almost believed him.

"Yeah, I think that's totally what he was saying," Jax agreed. "Your dad was trying to con the Brooks family. You know he had an arrest record across a couple of continents."

"Like I said, he got in trouble a lot. How quickly do you think I go from person of interest to main suspect?" The fact that her father had attempted to con an entire family was a side issue she would deal with later. She was going to lose her job. She'd already lost her house, and if the insurance company decided it wasn't a gas leak, she wouldn't be able to afford another one. No job. No home. Maybe facing jail time. Serious jail time for a crime she hadn't done.

"I'm going to update Damon in half an hour. We'll start working this from a legal standpoint, but you need to understand that there's no way we allow you to go back to the States until we figure out why this is happening," Robert said calmly. "If we let you walk in there now, there's every possibility that you end up getting arrested, and you're completely vulnerable in that jail cell."

"You think that's why they killed him?" The idea that a police officer had been killed in order to manipulate her into a vulnerable position made her fists clench. Who had he left behind? Did he have a wife and kids who were mourning him even now? "To force me to come in so they can kill me?"

"I don't think they want to kill you. At least not at first. I think they believe you know something," Robert replied.

"I don't know anything." It was how she truly felt. She no longer knew a damn thing.

Except for one amazing moment this afternoon she'd felt complete. When Nick had ordered her to her knees, she'd understood what she'd been missing before. It wasn't about giving over her soul to him. In that moment, she'd trusted him enough to forget about everything else. He'd then been a complete dick, but she was smarter than he was. He'd been a dick because he'd gotten scared.

Had he gotten scared the first time?

Since the moment she'd met Desiree, she'd compared herself and found herself wanting.

That had been a child's vision. She was a woman and it was time to recalibrate. It was time to look back at her own history.

Nick hadn't been a dick because he'd wanted to leave, because he'd had all he wanted and was done. He'd been a dick because of what his past had taught him.

Maybe she should look at more than her relationship with Nick through fresh eyes.

She needed to look at everything again. Some of what Ariel had said to her the day before whispered through her brain. Sometimes when a person lost everything it could be freeing. She was an academic, a lover of history, but every historian knew one thing. Those who forgot history were often doomed to repeat it. This was her history. She needed to let go of emotions attached to it and try to see it without all the baggage of having to live through it.

"I think sometimes my father used me as a shield," she said quietly.

"Because he got in trouble?" Robert asked.

"I think so. I heard about it in one-sided conversations." She needed to be honest with herself and with them. It was too important to cover up. Especially if he'd lied to her about their relationships. "He owed money to people and he did some favors for them. I'm not sure what. He was fairly good about keeping me out of it. I know he'd met Des before he introduced her to me. He said they'd been talking for a while before he met her in Vegas. Honestly, it's possible he met her when he was in Europe and he convinced her it would be fun to prank her family with horrible American relatives, but I'm still having a hard time with this. She seemed so genuine."

"Desiree was an excellent actress," a familiar voice said.

She winced because Nick was behind her and she wasn't in a place where she could turn around and run into his arms. She'd just found out her father had been lying to her. Lying to him.

Unless…

"Did you know she wasn't my cousin?" She wasn't sure what she would do if he said yes.

His hands cupped her shoulders. "I did not. If this is a lie, I was lied to as well, *dushka*. I'll look through the records and see what I can find."

Her skin warmed where he touched her. She didn't want him to have to deal with that. "Don't bother. Apparently Jax is some kind of genius and he remembers everything except all the crap he's done. He's going to remember that I have a quick knee to the crotch."

Those hands suddenly wound around her chest, drawing her back against his body. "Excuse me."

There was distracting him and then there was pointing a massive weapon and pulling the trigger. "Nothing, babe. Do you see my wall? I like all the lines to and from the people I'm either related to or who fucked me over. It's awesome. Also, has anyone told you I'm almost wanted for murder in Washington state? Do you know how awful that is? We're the serial killer capital of the world."

"No, I wasn't informed. I was busy with Walter discovering that Desiree left a message for us inside your necklace." Nick's voice had deepened. "Don't get excited that we're closing in on what she was hiding. The damn thing's in code. Walt didn't recognize it, but Penny is excellent with codes so she's going to take a look at it. Hopefully we'll know something in a few days."

So Des hadn't kept the necklace out of some affection. She should have known. "So I've been wearing the information we probably need?"

"I don't know. We can't be sure of anything and Penelope said she didn't recognize the code, so it could take her a while to break it," Nick replied. "In the meantime, I'm going to need a briefing on this new information. How far has the story gone?" Nick didn't move from behind her, but something about him got Robert moving.

"I can debrief you on everything we've discovered so far," Robert said, his hands on the keys of his laptop. "I'm also sending you the intel through the private server."

"Right now the story's local only," Jax explained. "They covered it on Seattle stations last night and the police are looking for her as a material witness and possible kidnapping victim. That can change quickly."

Robert straightened up. "I'm worried the nationals will pick up the story in a few hours. Given where America is right now, any murder of a police officer is going to be national news. When they flash her picture across the screen on CNN's morning news, they'll find people who've seen her."

"I was careful," she insisted.

"Keeping your head down and a cap over your hair won't cover those eyes." Jax looked her over with a sigh. "If I'd been sitting beside you on a long-haul flight, I would remember you. Someone will talk and soon."

"Whoever is behind this is using the press to do their dirty work." Nick's arms tightened, squeezing her close. "I'm going to fix this for you. Don't think otherwise. You're going to be fine, Hayley."

She could only pray he was right.

Chapter Nine

Nick pulled his boots on, the hum of the locker room surrounding him. The night was starting up, the men of The Garden getting ready to play.

All he could think about was the woman across the building in the other locker room.

Was she scared? Was he doing the right thing by not calling off tonight's session? After all the shit she'd been through earlier, how would she be able to focus? Hell, he wasn't sure he could.

Then there was the fact that if Penny was as good as everyone said she was, this could all be over in a matter of days. If Penny could decode the information from the microdot and figure out who was after Hayley, she could be back in Seattle, ready to rebuild her life by next week. He should want that for her. He should want her safe and happy. That was what he'd sacrificed for all those years ago.

He'd thought he would have longer with her.

"Any word on the code, mate?" Brody sank down on the bench beside him. He was already dressed for play, his big body covered in leather pants and a vest that showed off his muscular chest. The Aussie still wore his hair close cropped, as he had when he'd been in the SASR. The only time Nick had ever seen him with his hair longer had been those months in Africa. He'd claimed it was all part of his cover, but Nick had heard the doctor Brody had been protecting talk about how she loved his hair.

"No, and Penny's taking a break tonight." Damon had come to him an hour before explaining that he felt they needed a night together despite the new intelligence. Apparently their son had been particularly needy while they were in Loa Mali. The Knights, it seemed, needed a vacation from their vacation, and with childcare in place here, they could spend some quality time.

"Is that a good idea?" Brody asked. "I thought we were kind of racing the clock here. The news story went national a few hours ago."

Nick thought it was a spectacular idea, despite the fact that her face had been plastered all over American morning news programs. "I know the clock is ticking, but she's safe here and no one knows where she is. It's going to take a while. Des was good at hiding her secrets. I'm not going to ask Penny to give up her life to solve the puzzle. It's a job. She needs time off like the rest of us do."

"Ah," Brody said, his mouth curling up slightly.

"What is that supposed to mean?"

Brody held a hand up. "Hey, it means we should all take our time with this one. Wouldn't want to make any mistakes. That's all."

Nick leaned forward. Why was he so fucking defensive? Brody was his friend. Damon was his friend. Owen had been a brother to him. Walt and Kayla were like family and yet he pushed them all away. He was tired of it. "I don't want her to leave."

Brody's hand came out, whacking him on the shoulders. "Of course you don't. You need time with her."

"Are we talking about Hayley?" Owen popped out from behind the lockers.

Yes, the nosiness never ended here. "I was mentioning that I would be disappointed if Penny solved the puzzle too fast and the case was over. I enjoy spending time with Hayley. I've missed her."

Owen sat on his other side. He wore nothing but a towel, his hair wet from the showers. His chest was on display, scars from what the doctor's drugs had done to him still red. He'd had a reaction to the drug he'd been fed and it didn't seem to go away. "I think the lass should stay here for a bit. If that so called family of hers is any indication, she's not got a lot of support around her. Lady Brooks has a stick up her arse so far I bet she finds it hard to breathe. Not that she needs to since she looks a bit like a desiccated corpse. Woman's so skinny I could count her bones, except in the face where someone stuffed her full. I do not get that. A slender girl is one thing, but this woman can't eat properly. It's not natural."

There wasn't a lot that was natural about Desiree's mother. She'd started in on the plastic surgeries the first time she'd spotted a wrinkle and hadn't let up since. And she had a real problem with healthy women. More than once she'd called Desiree fat when she'd been gorgeous and curvy. "Did you find anything out beyond the fact that the whole family's horrible?"

"Well, they certainly hate you, brother. I found that out and quickly," Owen explained.

"Tell me something I don't know."

Owen leaned in. "All right, did you know that right before he died, Paul Dalton showed up here in England demanding to know where his part of Desiree's estate was?"

That was news. Hayley's father had thought she would leave him something in her will? "Lady Brooks told you that?"

"Ah, hell, no," Owen replied. "After she figured out we knew you, she kicked us out right fast, but the housekeeper told us to meet her at a coffee shop up the road and she gave us the information. Lady Brooks believed the Daltons were related to them. Desiree had proof. Now we know she faked it, but the real question is why. She really never told you?"

Yes, now he remembered why he'd always held himself back. The old familiar shame welled up inside him. "There were plenty of things she didn't tell me."

Had they looked at him like he was some pathetic chump all these years? Knowing that Damon had been investigating Desiree made him wonder how the team truly viewed him. Damon said he'd never thought Nick was a threat, but wasn't that almost worse? What did that make him? Desiree's pawn? A man with no real will of his own?

"It wasn't wrong to love her," Brody said quietly.

He'd been wondering about that very question lately. "She used me. She used all of us. Now I find out that she's probably using Hayley from beyond the grave. I was with her for years. I put up with all of it."

"That's the problem with people," Brody continued. "We're complex. It would be easier if we would just be one thing. Good. Bad. Why can't we pick a side and stick with it? But Des did do some good in her time. She saved my arse more than once. Don't forget that time she had to ride in and save Owen because she found out the woman he picked up at that conference we were working was actually a spy for a cartel. Poor Owen had already been drugged and that girl would have gotten all the security codes concerning the ambassador we were protecting if Des hadn't shown up."

"Was she pretty? Did I actually get to do the deed before she turned on me?" Owen asked, his eyes bright.

"You were tied up and drooling, you dumb arsehole," Brody shot back. "Des saved you. That's my point. She might have been selfish at her core, but she backed us all up. And I do believe she loved you, Nick. Oddly enough, no matter what she was doing with Hayley, I think she loved her, too."

"How can you say that? She lied to Hayley." All afternoon Hayley had been quiet, but he knew hearing that news had shaken her.

"Des lied to a lot of people about a lot of things," Brody continued. "But that doesn't mean she was lying when she said she loved you both. You were loyal to a woman who saved you when you needed saving. There's nothing wrong with that. There's nothing wrong with missing her, either. Hell, I miss Des. I don't mind saying it. The only thing that would be wrong is to let her affect the rest of your life. If you care about Hayley, you don't let Des get in between the two of you."

"I don't think it's Des that's getting in his head when it comes to Hayley," Owen piped up. "He doesn't think he's good enough for her."

Owen might have lost the memory of his past, but he did a good job reading his partner, damn it. "I think we live in two different worlds. You understand this, Brody. Isn't that why you wouldn't date the charming doctor?"

Brody stiffened, his shoulders going back. "I'm a soldier. What the hell do I have to give a bloody doctor? She fixes people. She literally puts people back together. The only thing I've ever been good at is taking them down. I think it's different with you and the girl. You're smarter than me, man. You worked intelligence. I've been a grunt all my life. Grew up in a backwater town where we had more crocs than people, if you know what I mean. She went to med school."

He wasn't sure how Brody didn't see the similarities. "I did go to university, but that doesn't mean Hayley and I would work out in the long run. She needs things I can't give her. She needs stability."

"You're one of the most stable men I ever met." Brody stood up. "You didn't give up on Des even when she hurt you. You're loyal to the end. I'd let you watch my back. More than that, I'd let you watch hers."

Nick didn't pretend to not know what Brody was talking about. He should have known all that "I'm a professional" talk had been bullshit. He'd sensed the tension between the two. If they hadn't slept together, they'd definitely wanted to. "Call her."

Brody shook his head. "Nah. She ain't for me. She deserves better."

"Okay, a Scot, an Aussie, and a Russian walk into a bar," a sarcastic voice said. Ian Taggart was standing next to Damon, both men already in their leathers.

"And?" Damon asked, one dark brow arched over his eyes.

"No and. It's not a joke. It's just a nightmare of mine," Taggart admitted. "Too many douchebag accents. What's wrong with you people? Learn to speak American."

Brody flipped him the bird, though there was a smile on his face as though Taggart's sarcasm was a welcome deflection of the tension from a moment before. "Bugger off, you useless cock."

Taggart pointed. "See. That's what I'm talking about. I don't know why you people are so concerned with bugs, and my cock is totally getting used tonight. Big time used."

Owen simply stood and dropped his towel, turning and giving Taggart a view of his naked backside. He slapped it. "Bite me arse, Tag."

"That's very *Braveheart* of you," Taggart admitted.

Owen turned with a smile on his face. "We know how to start a battle right."

Damon looked to Tag with a sad shake of his head. "This is why I need more budget. You send me all the insane ones."

"Yeah, that's easy to see. We'll get you the training money," Tag agreed. "Hell, I'd up your budget for the simple fact that I don't have to deal with that maniac. Much less the bad news I'm about to give you. I'm staying on for a week or so because we're about to have a visitor. Ezra Fain is asking for permission to come in and interview Robert, Tucker, and Dante."

Well, they knew the Agency would want to talk to some of the men. It was precisely why they were here in England and not somewhere in the States. Ezra Fain was a CIA operative with deep ties in the intelligence world. He'd also proven fairly easy to work with, as government men went. "Has he had any luck finding their identities?"

Tag leaned against the bank of luxurious lockers The Garden provided. "Not that he's told me, but if one of those boys turns out to be a lost operative, they'll play it close to the vest. Given we find ourselves with a client who's wanted on US soil, I thought we might pick his brain while he's here. A quid pro quo, so to speak. It's good to remind him that he owes us, too. That's what I wanted to talk to you about, Nick. Can I have a moment please?"

Damn. He didn't like the idea of exposing her to Fain. "I'll talk to him, but I think we shouldn't mention that she's actually here. I'll keep her close to me for a few days and out of his line of sight."

Brody whistled as he strode away. "You did not learn your lesson this morning, brother. See you out in the dungeon."

Owen followed behind him, turning toward the other bank of lockers, and Nick found himself alone with Damon and Tag.

"You're afraid Fain will call the cops?" Tag asked.

Nick shrugged. "You never know what an Agency man will do. I should know this. I worked in intelligence many years before I realized I was selling my soul for nothing. I've done things I shouldn't have because someone convinced me it was for my country. Fain worked his way up. He's a company man. I heard he's taking Ten Smith's place now."

"I wouldn't say that. Fain's too much of a lone wolf to move into Ten's place, but the Agency does see his value. He's a good contact and one I'd like to keep up with. We get into trouble enough that it helps to have someone on the inside we can call," Taggart explained. "Until such time as he proves he's an asshole, and then we'll deal with him."

"You inspire such confidence," Damon snarked.

"I'm not here to inspire confidence. I'm here to kick a little ass when it's needed," Tag allowed.

"I want your word that he won't attempt to turn her over to the authorities."

"You have it." Tag held out a hand. "And I'll see if I can get him to take a look at what we have. He knows about the investigation into Desiree."

Damon pulled his cell phone out, frowning at the screen. "He's here. I'm going to let him in. Let's hope he can figure something out because Penelope's struggling with the code. I'll settle him in and be back. You know we should talk to him about his bloody timing."

"Seriously, Fain's not a bad guy," Taggart said as Damon walked away. "And if he fucks with you, punch him. It worked with Ten."

He had to talk to Hayley. Damn it. He was with Damon. Ezra Fain's timing was bad. "I'm going to change and take Hayley back upstairs. We need to talk about Fain. She'll be nervous."

"I know she's your sub for now and all, but I think that's a big mistake." Taggart straightened up.

"Why is it a mistake? I'm trying to think of her feelings and not my own. Do you think I don't want to play? This is the first chance I've had, and I don't know how many I'll get. So I don't understand how I'm making this mistake." He opened his locker, frustration pouring through his system.

"Because she's nervous, too, man. Look, you've been in the lifestyle for a long time, but you've never really had a submissive. I liked Des. I know she did some criminal shit, but so did my sister-in-law. I won't even go into some of the shit my wife's done. It was hard to forgive her, but I'm glad I did. My advice to you is to forgive Des and forgive yourself for not realizing she wasn't actually submissive. She played at it to get what she needed, but you never truly got what you needed out of the exchange. This is your chance. Charlie thinks Hayley is submissive and that means you need to figure this shit out and fast. I'm going to give you a clue. Not playing with her tonight will be a mistake."

"You don't think she'll be upset when I tell her there's a CIA agent here?" Nick asked.

Taggart seemed to give the question some thought before he answered. "She might be. Or she might trust that you'll take care of her. Either way, she's not talking to Fain until tomorrow, so why ruin tonight? She's a newbie. They get some weird ideas in their heads. She might think you changed your mind and man, nothing you say after that will change hers. She'll think you don't want her and it'll always be there between you. More to the point, she needs a night where she's your main priority. Not the case. Not her future safety. Her. Her body. Her mind. Her soul. Give her the peace she needs to get through tomorrow."

171

The peace she needed. Could he give that to her? Taggart was right about one thing. He'd never had a true sub of his own. Des might have worn his collar from time to time when it pleased her to do so, but she'd never needed him to find her peace.

"I haven't worked with her enough to know how to give her this." He hated feeling vulnerable, but wasn't she worth perhaps making an idiot of himself in front of Taggart if it meant she got what she needed? He realized in that moment that giving to her, knowing she had comfort and pleasure because of him was important, so much more important than his own pleasure.

"Start slow," Taggart advised. "If this were a training setting I would tell you to explore the world with her, but that's not what this is. She's not coming to the club trying to find a place to belong. She's here for you and there's nothing wrong with that. People come to the lifestyle for many reasons. She wants to explore what a relationship with you would be like. Show her. Show her how beautiful you think she is. Show her how open you want to be with her. Show her how giving up control to you in one specific place can free you both. And if you jar her a little, well, that's just pushing boundaries. I think you should push her intimacy boundaries in the beginning. Figure out if she likes the dungeon or not, if she likes the open sexuality of this place or if she needs privacy."

Explore. It was what they should do in the beginning, but Taggart was right. Their exploration should begin a bit differently. They needed to explore how far she wanted to go, whether or not she could be open and enjoy the kind of intimacy and sexuality he craved.

With her. It struck him suddenly that he wanted this openness, this closeness with her. Not some nameless, faceless sub. Hayley.

He needed to give her the experience that would leave her thinking about nothing beyond his next touch, their next kiss. He was treating this like a textbook, get-to-know-you-first play session with a submissive.

He needed to stop thinking about Dom and sub and traditional forms. He needed to let them be Nick and Hayley, and that meant breaking a few rules.

He stood up and opened his locker. He needed to change.

"What are you and Charlotte planning on doing this evening?" Nick asked. If there was one thing he knew about that couple, it was their love of exhibitionism. He could use that to introduce Hayley to some exotic play. Tomorrow would be soon enough to deal with the new problems they faced. Tonight he needed to exert some control. "Is there any way I can convince you to do it in the watch room?"

Taggart smiled. "See, now you're thinking, buddy. Let's have some fun."

* * * *

Hayley fought not to pull the thong from between her butt cheeks. Why couldn't cotton briefs be considered sexy? She thought they were sexy. Well, she thought they didn't give her a satiny wedgie.

And she could barely breathe in the corset Kayla and Ariel had stuffed her into.

All in all she wasn't feeling particularly sexy.

"I think you were right to go without the heels," Kayla said as she glanced around the dungeon. "If you're not used to them, you end up looking like a newborn colt kind of stumbling around everywhere."

"I'm with Hayley. I like the feel of the stone on my skin," Ariel said. "I wear heels all day. When I get down here I want to feel like a different person. I want to be comfortable. Being barefoot will help you get into your role."

"What will help me breathe?" Hayley asked.

Kayla ignored her, frowning Ariel's way. "That's easy for you to say. You and Charlotte can go barefoot because you're not five foot nothing. I got short girl problems."

Ariel grinned and hooked an arm around Kayla's waist, leaning in. "Well, my darling, if you were any taller, the rest of us would be in trouble. You'll have to settle for being a tiny, gorgeous badass."

Kayla sighed and leaned against her friend. "I suppose so."

Hayley watched them. They seemed like such different women, but it was obvious they shared something special.

Kayla looked over at her. "You're going to be okay, you know. This is fun. There's nothing to be nervous about."

She heard a loud shout and then a groan. What the hell was she doing? She wasn't this person. She wasn't the kind of person who did crazy sex stuff. Even the best sex she'd ever had had been with Nick, and it had been normal sex. He hadn't spanked her. He hadn't tied her up and it had been good. Great.

She was a college professor. She wore fussy business suits, not corsets that weren't at all historically accurate.

"I think she's going to run," Kayla whispered to Ariel.

Ariel put a hand on her hip. "Are you going to run? Is that why you didn't pick the heels?"

"That's pretty snarky for a shrink." Hayley pulled on the corset, trying to make it cover more of her boobs. She'd never considered them particularly large, but the corset worked wonders, drawing those suckers up and making them look big and round. "Aren't you supposed to be supportive?"

Ariel stepped away from Kay and opened her arms as though embracing the dungeon. "Ah, but I'm not a shrink here. Here, I'm a sub looking for some fun. That's the beauty of this place. You can be who you want. It's good to let go and explore without judgment or fear. And that *is* the shrink talking."

"Let loose," Kay advised. "Stop all the crap that's going through your head and do what you're supposed to do here."

"Not breathe and get a little scared by the noises? Is that normal?" There was a whooshing sound, followed by a hard crack that sounded a lot like someone was being whipped.

It was one thing to read about it in a book, a completely different thing to be here.

She didn't belong here.

"That's Teresa," Ariel explained with a wave of her hand. "She's playing around with a couple of the lads. Sasha is trying to get passed

174

to use the four footer without supervision and T is letting him practice on her. She's a pain slut so it's all cool. Trust me, we'll all get to see her welts tomorrow. She'll show 'em off."

Welts? She wasn't really into pain. Maybe she was going to run. And then she saw him.

Nick strode down one of the paths, and she realized that there were things in life she wanted more than her own dignity. Or her female parts took over, and they weren't as afraid of pain as the rest of her was.

He wore a dark suit, perfectly pressed, with a snowy white shirt and a deep red tie. The suit fit like it had been made for him, and it probably had. He wore expensive-looking dress shoes and gold gleamed at his cuffs. His hair was slicked back, showing off the glorious angles of his face. He looked like an incredibly hot mobster. Or a spy.

Or the man of her stupid, never-ending, optimistic dreams.

She forced herself to start thinking again with her brain. He wasn't dressed like the other men. They were all in fet wear of some kind. Kayla had explained that the Dominant aligning males would be in leather pants and vests and submissive men in much, much less. But fet wear was required in The Garden.

Were they leaving? Had he decided to do something else with his evening? Or had he come to the rational conclusion that she wasn't built for this world? He might have changed because he'd finally figured out she wasn't very sexual and now he would do something like offer to have dinner with her to kindly let her down.

Or something had happened. He looked ready for work.

Why did he have to look so sexy when he was working? And why the hell had she thought a dowdy college professor could keep his attention? He was a dangerous man, a man of action. He would be bored in her world.

He would get bored with her.

He hadn't seen her yet. She still had some time. Maybe dignity was going to win out. "I think I should go change. Tell him I'll be out

175

in a minute."

"Why would you change?" Kayla asked. She looked around and then waved Nick's way. "Hey, hot stuff, we're over here. Damn, you look good, buddy. Why don't you dress like that all the time?"

His lips curled up and she watched his eyes find her. "Because I would not wish to distract all the lovely ladies. How would you ever get any work done when I look like this? I only wish to distract one lady. This is for her."

Yep, there was the breathing problem again. He sucked all the air out of her lungs and at the same time made her mouth water.

She was so out of her league. "Should I go change?"

"Why would you change when you look so beautiful?" Nick reached out a hand to Ariel, who allowed him to bring it gallantly to his lips. He did the same with Kayla. "Ladies, you grace us all with your beauty. I thank you for helping my *dushka* into her beautiful clothes. She is as lovely as I imagined."

"You're welcome, Sir," Ariel said with a smile on her face.

Kayla gave him a little curtsy. "Always happy to help, Master Nikolai. But you should know, she's a nervous nelly tonight. I think the sound of the whip is disturbing her."

"It's fine. I'm okay with it." She proved her own words false as she winced when a loud crack emanated from deeper in the dungeon.

Ariel put a hand on her shoulder. "She might need to talk more, Sir. If you like, I can get changed and have a sit-down with her."

"That's sweet of you," he said, giving her a warm smile. "But it's not necessary. We're going to play privately tonight. I've set up an exhibition for her to watch. If she's comfortable with that, perhaps we can walk the dungeon tomorrow night. I'll keep her all to myself this evening, but I thank you for being concerned."

Ariel bowed her head. "Then she's in good hands." She looked back up and gave Kayla a wink. "Let's go cause some trouble. I promised Penny we would meet her in the lounge for a drink after we've all had our fun."

Kayla waved as she walked away with Ariel, leaving her all alone with the most beautiful man in the world.

"I'm trying to get used to it." She started to talk almost faster than her brain worked. "But maybe it's too much for me. I don't understand everything. You were different with Kayla than you usually are. They were different the minute you walked over here. And why are you dressed like that? I was told fet wear only. I would rather be in my jeans."

His hand came out, tilting her head up. "In here, we're not coworkers and the dynamic is different. In this place, they're submissives and they will be given all the respect and honor they're due. All submissives are beautiful here. They're accepted and honored for their service. They honored me for my service as a Dominant partner even though we've never once played together. They were kind to you and that earns my gratitude because you're important to me. I'm dressed like this because I think you'll respond to me like this. Authority doesn't come from a set of leathers. Arousal isn't assured because I'm wearing fet wear. Tell me something. Do you find me attractive like this? Do I seem powerful to you? In control?"

She looked at him, really looked at him. He used the words authority and control. What did they mean to her? Nick in a perfectly tailored suit looked like her every professor fantasy come to life. Those professors had been a sanctuary to a girl who'd moved at least twice a year and globetrotted during the summers. They'd been logic and surety in a world where nothing made sense.

She found Nick sexy on every level, but dressed like this was something different. It called to her on a base level. It was everything she wanted in a man. Cool. Calm. Collected.

In control.

"You look amazing and yes, something about you dressed like that calls to me."

His hand moved up, cupping her cheek. "Everyone's needs are different. I intend to fill yours. Do you trust me?"

Such a dangerous question but there was only one answer. "Yes."

"Then come with me and trust me to see to your pleasure.

177

There's nothing for you to worry about tonight but pleasing me. You will follow my directions and obey me. If you get scared or find something distasteful, you will tell me and we'll stop and discuss it. There will be no real discipline tonight, though I will have tasks for you to perform. Everything I ask of you is to create intimacy between us, to build the foundation of a relationship. Can you promise to be honest with me? I don't want lies to please me. I want honesty."

"I honestly hate this corset."

His lips curled up. "That wasn't a no. That was a plea to get naked as soon as we're alone."

The deep timbre of his voice was working its magic. "I can do that, Sir."

His hand fell away from her face, finding her own and tangling their fingers together. "Excellent. Then I think it's time we began."

Her heart pounded as she followed him down the path, toward whatever came next.

Chapter Ten

Hayley walked through the door Nick held open for her. "So we're going to be alone for the evening."

"Yes and no," he replied enigmatically.

He seemed determined to keep her on edge, but she couldn't force herself to turn back. She'd had that moment when insecurity had taken over, but now she discovered curiosity was far more pressing. She wanted…no…she needed to see where he was going to take her this evening. It was more than how hot he looked. It was about the press of his hand in hers, the warmth he imparted. It was about the way his shoulders had straightened as he'd walked her through the dungeon. As though he was proud to be there with her.

It suddenly didn't seem so bad to be wearing a lung-strangling corset as long as she was here with him. She'd even gotten a glimpse of Teresa on one of the X thingees. Her backside had red stripes on it, but she'd seemed relaxed.

Things were not always as they seemed. That was what she kept telling herself.

She stepped into the room with its low lighting and realized it was something of a bedroom. There was a bed in the back of the room covered with lush bedding. There were two nightstands and a plethora of plush pillows.

The night was looking up. Some straight-on sex might be happening in this room.

She turned and realized what he'd meant when he'd told her yes and no to the question *were they alone*. One side of the room was a massive window that looked into another room. She found herself in a decadent bedroom that stared right into another one. And it wasn't empty.

She stopped and stared as she watched Charlotte Taggart step into the center of the room completely naked.

That was a sight even a straight chick couldn't turn away from. Charlotte found a place on the carpet and sank gracefully down to her knees. Her strawberry blonde hair flowed around her gorgeous torso, curling around her nipples. She had beautiful breasts. Round and full and luscious, they led down to an hourglass waist and full hips. She was a fertility goddess complete with stretch marks that strangely did nothing to detract from her beauty. If Hayley looked at her objectively, Charlotte was slightly too large to be considered perfect, her breasts sagging a bit, fine lines around her eyes.

She was beautiful in a way commercial actresses with no flaws couldn't possibly be.

She was beautiful in a way Hayley could be. She was beautiful in a way no computer could perfect, no amount of lighting could make. That beauty was lit from the inside of Charlotte Taggart. It was love and confidence and life.

"Tell me what you're thinking."

He was behind her but not touching her yet, as though her answer would decide what he did next.

"She's lovely and amazing." Should it bother her? Should she not find another woman pretty? "I'm not aroused by her, but I am inspired. I wish I had her confidence."

The door behind Charlotte opened and her husband walked in, wearing his leathers. They looked right on him somehow. The same way the suit looked perfect on Nick.

Because they were different and yet the same. That was what Nick was trying to tell her. She could still be her. They could be them and still belong in this lifestyle.

"Do they know we're watching them?"

Ian Taggart stepped behind his wife, placing one big hand on her head. His whole body relaxed as though he needed the connection to her to be complete.

Nick moved beside Hayley, close but not touching. "Oh, yes. Ian knows who's watching. I set up this scene with him. Charlotte has only been told that another couple is watching. She can't see us. From her vantage point this window appears to be a large mirror. Exhibitionism is one of her kinks. She enjoys the idea that strangers are watching her, likely getting off while they do."

Taggart stroked his wife's hair, saying something to her.

"There's no sound?"

"I've left it off. I would prefer that you listen only to my voice. This is exploration, Hayley. The sex you've had up to this point has been mostly vanilla, and there's nothing wrong with that. If you would prefer, we can leave here and go back to my flat and get into bed."

She couldn't take her eyes off the couple in front of them. Taggart was saying something to his wife as he ran his hands over her body. Hayley watched the way Charlotte's nipples hardened, her skin flushing to a rosy pink. Whatever he was saying, she liked it.

Was it wrong to watch them if they liked to be watched?

"Would vanilla sex give you what you need?" It was odd to be standing next to him, the space between them electric with tension while they both stared straight ahead. Taggart had moved to the side of the room where there was a table with a number of items laid out. He selected a length of rope, pulling on it as though testing its strength.

"I can be content."

Contentment wasn't satisfaction. "But you need more."

He finally turned, placing a hand on her arm. "Hayley, it doesn't matter what I need if it doesn't please you as well. You're under the mistaken impression that the pleasure I derive has something to do with force. That's not true at all. I'll only enjoy the control if it's given with joy. I don't wish to stand above you and know I conquered by strength. I want you to enjoy what I do to you, to crave it. I want to train your body to accept the pleasure I can give it. Tell me. Does the thought of giving me control arouse you?"

"Yes, and I'm afraid of the impulse."

"Because so much of your life was spent out of control." He took a step back, easing out of the suit coat. "You moved around and your father was in and out of your life. I understand that. You need control and stability in your daily life. This is a different place. You saw how Ariel changed when she put on fet wear. She's a powerful, intelligent woman who does amazing work. There is nothing submissive about her or Kayla in their daily lives. This is how they relax. They find partners who can allow them to submit, partners whose needs dovetail with their own. Look at Charlotte."

Hayley turned away from the delicious sight of Nick, who looked lean and predatory in the dress shirt, tie, vest, and slacks. She looked back to the window and saw Charlotte had changed positions. She was still on her knees, but instead of her hands on her thighs, they were now over her head, the hands together and her breasts outthrust as her husband wound the rope around her torso.

"Why do you think she allows her husband to bind her like this?"

The answer was right there on Charlotte's face, and Hayley suddenly understood the point of this lesson. If she'd been asked the question without watching how peaceful and calm Charlotte appeared, Hayley likely would have said that Charlotte did it to please her husband. "She enjoys it. She enjoys giving over to him."

"Again, she's a powerful woman. She runs a powerful company. Ian leaves much of the day-to-day work to his wife. He doesn't see her as submissive outside of play. Not that there would be anything wrong with it. I know lovely women and men who choose to submit freely to their partners outside the bedroom. It's all about what works for the Dom and the sub. Is the scene in front of you arousing in any way?"

"Yes. It's very arousing."

"What is it doing to your body? Tell me. I like hearing the words from your mouth."

It seemed such an awkward thing to talk about, but then she was staring at a woman she knew, was becoming friends with, being tied up by her husband. "I'm feeling warm."

"Where?" He was so close, but he didn't touch her. He moved behind her. "Where do you feel warm, *dushka*?"

The sight in front of her wasn't the only thing arousing. His voice had gone to that rich, deep place where he no longer worried about the thickness of his accent. "All over my body."

His hands found her shoulders and he brushed her hair to one side. "That's not enough. I want to know where it affects you. Is it here?"

She shivered as he ran his nose along the shell of her ear. She could feel the heat of his breath, hear him breathing in her scent. In front of her, she could see Taggart's plan playing out. He wound the rope around and around, leaving his wife's breasts out, surrounded and supported by his ropes. On display for his eyes. Left vulnerable to his touch, to the play of his tongue and teeth, the tweak of his fingers.

"It's everywhere, Nicky. My breasts feel heavy. I can feel my nipples puckering."

He moved lower, his nose running over her neck. Somehow that trace of a touch sent an erotic shiver through her, a promise of things to come. "Where else?"

He knew where else, but he seemed determined to make her say it. To make her comfortable with the words, with her body. With him.

"I feel it deep inside. My pussy." That was probably the word he wanted and it didn't seem so awkward all of a sudden. For the first time that part of herself did feel like a pussy, a twitching, aching, needy pussy. "I'm getting wet. It feels good. It's been a long time since I got wet by watching someone or thinking about someone."

"What did you watch that made you hot?"

"Porn. When I have a couple of glasses of wine and I'm lonely, sometimes I'll go to one of those sites on the web." She didn't mention that she always looked for a dark-haired man, one she could think of as Nick.

"I like that. We could watch some together one night. I would enjoy sharing that with you." His fingertips brushed along her arms. "Who do you think about? You said sometimes you got wet thinking about someone. Was it your fiancé?"

She stiffened up. She hadn't exactly talked to him about the horrific mistake she'd made. "No, it wasn't him."

"Relax." Warm hands cupped her shoulders. "I was asking, not demanding. If you don't want to talk about him, we don't have to. I want to make sure you understand that you're safe with me. You will always be safe with me."

He didn't have to tell her that. She knew. Nick was an honorable man, the most honorable she'd ever met. He wouldn't hurt her. Not physically. She forced herself to relax, to watch the Taggarts' scene. It was trust and lust rolled up and played out in front of her.

"You know it's you, Nicky. Even when I had a boyfriend, it was always you in the back of my mind. I would close my eyes and see you." It was why every relationship was doomed from the start. No man could live up to him. Even after he'd broken her heart, she'd never truly let go of him. Never. She hoped this time she could.

"I think about you as well." He moved back. "I want you to tell me something. In all those fantasies of me, did you ever once see yourself in control?"

The truth flashed through her. A hundred fantasies she'd played out in her head over the years. Him coming back and begging her for forgiveness. Him telling her how much he needed her. Him saying he loved her.

But when it came time for the fantasy to move to sex, not once had she been in control. It was always Nick commanding, demanding.

"Never," she admitted.

"Then I think we can begin." He stepped back, his left hand going to his right wrist and twisting off the cufflink. "From now until we finish, you will listen to my commands. You will obey my commands. If you're frightened, you'll ask me to stop and we'll talk about what I'm doing and why I'm doing it, but this scene isn't about discipline so I don't expect to frighten you. This scene is about control and giving your body into mine. There's a hook above your head."

She glanced up and sure enough there was a hook she hadn't noticed before.

"It's adjustable so you'll be able to place both of your feet flat on the ground, but your hands will be tied overhead. You will face forward and watch the scene and we'll discuss what's going on."

She could do that. She wasn't sure what having her hands over her head would do besides hold her in place, but she was willing to try. "All right."

"Take off your clothes."

Oh, now she got it. He was going to make her vulnerable. She wouldn't be able to move and her body would be open to whatever he wanted to do to her.

Trust. Control. That was the point of this lesson. "I'll need help with the corset."

He stepped behind her and with a few swift moves of his hands had her out and taking her first deep breath in an hour.

"Take off the skirt and thong as well. We'll talk later about fet wear that makes you comfortable, that enhances your experience. For now, naked works. Keep your eyes forward. I'll tell you when I'm ready for you."

She pushed the skirt off and down her thighs and then dispensed with the thong as she stared at the scene playing out in front of her.

Charlotte's breasts were fully surrounded by her husband's rope, and he cupped them from behind as though offering the sight of them up to whoever was behind the mirror. Or as if saying, *these are beautiful and they belong to me.*

185

Charlotte stared at the mirror, a secretive smile on her face. Like the cat that had licked up all the cream and knew there would be more later. She merely had to wait.

Charlotte was older, had three children, and yet she was so very certain of herself. Was this one of the reasons why? "Do you think she finds confidence in submitting?"

She immediately wanted to call the question back. He hadn't told her he would do a Q & A. He'd told her to wait for him.

"I think she finds confidence inside herself and that began with accepting herself," he replied. "She accepts that sexual submission and having a dominant partner in the bedroom is something that works for her. She makes no apologies for it or how she lives her life. I believe that's the heart of Charlotte's confidence. The truth of the matter is I can tell you you're beautiful every day of your life but if you're not open to the message, the words will mean nothing."

She could hear him doing something but didn't look back. Only forward, where Taggart had a crop in his hand. He flicked it over his wife's breasts and her eyes widened, her mouth opening in a way that could only be a long, slow moan at the sensation.

Hayley took a deep breath because that had done something for her, too. She hadn't heard the sound of the crop hitting skin, only seen how it affected Charlotte. She liked it.

Would Hayley like it? If she opened herself to the experience, would she find a whole world inside herself she'd never known existed?

"You are beautiful, you know." He whispered the words behind her.

She didn't feel that way most of the time. She felt out of her league, but maybe that was her problem. She constantly compared herself to other women instead of finding her own unique beauty. Why would Nick lie to her about something like this?

He could have any woman he wanted, but he was here with her. He was picking her now and it was time to stop blaming herself for the past.

"I think you're beautiful, too."

"I'm glad to hear that." His hands skimmed her sides, the rope he held brushing over her skin. He was behind her, but his long arms easily worked the rope. He twisted it around her wrists, leaving a bit of space between them. She could feel his body against her backside, the buckle of his belt cool against her flesh.

But she was watching Charlotte and Taggart. Her every sense was stimulated. Her skin felt lit every time Nick touched her. Her mind flared as she watched Taggart use the crop on his wife.

Charlotte held herself still, her knees splayed wide as her husband wielded the crop. Everywhere he flicked, the skin turned hot and pink and Charlotte seemed to breathe easier. Her body would tense and the crop would come down and she would relax, as though the pain brought her to a higher place. Or the pain wasn't as bad as it seemed.

All that mattered was it worked. All that mattered was finding what worked with her and Nick. So she could be as happy and confident as Charlotte.

"Raise your arms for me." He whispered the command in her ear.

She brought her hands up, letting him lead her to the hook above her head. She took a long breath as he moved her into position, and she truly felt the vulnerable nature of where she was.

She was naked, every inch of her on display. With her hands over her head, her breasts were thrust out, her lower spine arched so her backside tilted.

She was primed for sex. Primed for sex with Nick.

"Tell me how you feel." Nick stepped in front of her, his shirtsleeves rolled up and his hair slightly messy. Like he'd run a frustrated hand through it. Like he couldn't help himself.

"Vulnerable." She closed her eyes and let her body talk. Her skin and nipples and pussy. What was she feeling? Her eyes had seen something lovely. Her ears had heard his words. How did the rest of her react? "Sexy. I feel like I'm sexy, Nicky."

She heard him sigh as he moved behind her, felt his hands on her

187

hips. "That's because you're sexy as fuck, Hayley. *Ty samaya krasivaya v mire.*"

She had no idea what he'd said, but she loved the way he said it.

"I'm going to look at you, to touch you in a way I've always wanted to touch you. Do you have any idea how long I've wanted you like this? Since that night when you knocked on my door and offered yourself to me. This was what I wanted to do to you that night, too." He started at her wrists, fingertips skimming over her arms down to her shoulders. "I wanted to truss you up and truly explore my prize. With my eyes and my hands."

She could feel his fingers moving over her back, soothing down her muscles, playing around the edges of her shoulder blades as though mapping the territory. Every touch made her skin tighten, begging for more, but she couldn't see him. She was forced to open her eyes and look forward.

Ian Taggart had shrugged out of his vest. Despite the fact that Nick was the only man she wanted, she couldn't help but admire how stunning he was, how gorgeous they were as a couple. He stood over his wife, staring down and saying something that sent a shudder through Charlotte's body.

All the while, Nick continued his long, slow survey of Hayley's body. He ran a single fingertip down her spine. All the way down, right to the curve of her ass.

She couldn't help but follow her instinct. She bowed toward him, her ass bumping against the fabric of his slacks.

He suddenly cupped her cheeks, his mouth against her ear. "Yes, we'll get to this eventually. We'll get to the part where I touch you in places you never imagined. There won't be any part of your body that you don't cede to me. You'll allow me everywhere. You'll crave my touch. The touch of my hand, my mouth and tongue, my cock. When I'm done, all I'll have to do is look at you the right way and your body will prime itself for me."

She felt primed right that moment. "Nick, I think I'm good. I get the object lesson. I like watching ridiculously gorgeous people having sex. I'm a pervert, too. We all are. So you should understand that I'm good to go."

"Are you? I don't know about that," he whispered in her ear. "And I haven't finished inspecting my new toy. Oh, look, apparently Charlotte's Master has decided to play with his toy. Do you think she can take that whole massive cock in her mouth?"

She gasped. Sure enough, Taggart had tossed off his leathers and boots and was standing in front of his submissive. They'd shifted, ensuring their audience wouldn't miss the sight. Charlotte was still on her knees, her breasts tight in the rope top he'd made for her.

Nick was right. That was one incredibly large penis. Cock. Penis was too technical a word. Like sex was technical. They weren't having sex. They were fucking.

She wanted to fuck, too.

Nick's hands moved around to cup her breasts. "See the way she licks it. Like it's her favorite treat. I loved how you sucked my cock, Hayley. I can feel your mouth on me. I can feel the heat of your tongue and the way your lips felt over my flesh. I'm watching them, but I feel you."

He rolled her nipples between his fingers and thumbs, sending waves of pure lust through her. It hadn't been like this the first time. She'd loved it and he'd brought her pleasure, but she'd been so conscious of him. She'd focused on him and pleasing him. He was forcing her to focus on her body, on every inch of skin he was bringing to vibrant life. She could feel the lust pounding through her, making her nipples ache, tugging at someplace deep in her pelvis.

While she watched Charlotte work her husband's cock, watched Taggart's hands in her hair, the way his body moved in time with his partner's, she realized there was no place for insecurity between them. There was only pleasure and love and affection. That was what sex should be. Two people who cared about each other exploring. It didn't have to be some grand love. It did have to be honest.

"I'm still crazy about you, Nicky."

His arms went around her, drawing her back against him. "I'm crazy about you, too. I've always been crazy about you, *dushka*. And now you're mine for however long we have. You should know that I plan to take excellent care of you."

"You could start now." She was dying.

"Such an impatient girl. Didn't I explain to you that I'm in control? You need to learn to obey me. I promised no discipline this time, but you should know I'm already thinking of how to punish you next time. Perhaps I'll place clamps on these pretty nipples. Do you know what that will do to you? They'll bite into you, but not so much you'll hate them." He found her nipples with his fingers again, rolling them and pinching in a way that made her squirm against him. "Yes, you can feel it, no?"

She would have told him she would hate the sensation, but as he tweaked her a shot of pure fire licked through her body.

"What are you doing to me?" It should hurt, but it didn't. It caused an ache, a restless need inside her.

"I'm getting you ready for me."

"I told you I'm ready, Nicky. I'm more ready than I've ever been in my life. Please." She was willing to beg him, anything to get off this hook, to get him inside her. She needed him in a way she hadn't thought possible.

"Are you? I can test that." He slid his hand down, moving slowly, maddeningly toward her core.

In front of her, Charlotte had worked her husband's cock deep. She swallowed him up, her head moving in a wicked rhythm.

"Let's see how ready you are." His hand slipped over her pussy.

She bit back a moan as he ran a finger over her clitoris. The simple touch of his hand had her sparked and ready. How long could he keep her waiting? He'd promised no real discipline, but now she realized he had different ways to torture her.

She also realized that if he'd asked how she would handle a spanking at that moment, she would have laid herself on his lap and let him. Anything so that he would give her what she needed.

He was in complete control and there wasn't anything wrong

with that because he wouldn't use it to hurt her.

Just to torment her. In the sweetest way.

"Oh, you do seem wet, *dushka*. Is all this lovely cream for me?"

"Yes. You know it is." She gasped as he began to rub gently with one hand while the other played with her breast.

"Let's play a game. I want to see if I can make you come before Taggart does. He looks like he's getting close, doesn't he?"

He did. Charlotte was working him over and every muscle in his body was tight and taut with desire. His hands were tangled in his wife's hair as he clearly took control of the situation. He fucked into her mouth with raw intent.

"Yes." It was a beautiful picture they made. Despite the fact that they were engaged in some filthy sex, their connection was easy to see. Even as he fucked into her mouth, his hands smoothed her hair and he was speaking to her, watching her as her eyes turned up to keep them connected.

"If you can hold off, you'll get a treat," Nick whispered against the nape of her neck. "If you come before he does, I win and I get a treat."

She wasn't sure she wanted to know what he would get. It might include more delays. Taggart looked so close. She could win this game of his. "I'll win."

"Oh, no you won't. I'll make sure of it because, my *dushka*, you are ready. You are so hot and wet and ready for me. Enjoy this because I'm going to love winning this bet."

She was pulled up against him, the feel of his suit rough against her skin. That wasn't the only thing she could feel. Something hard pressed against the small of her back, and she was pretty sure it wasn't his gun.

She could hold out. It wouldn't be long. The Taggarts were almost there. It was clear in the way the big guy moved, hard and fast, losing a bit of his rhythm.

She could win this bet. All she had to do was not give in to the desperate desire to fall over that crazy edge shimmering right in front of her.

Nick pressed down on her clitoris as his fingers delved deep, fucking up inside her. "Come for me, *dushka*. Come for me."

His thumb circled her clitoris and nothing mattered except the wild orgasm that flooded her system. It started low in her core and fanned out like a wildfire. She cried out as he kept up the pressure, sending her even higher.

Her head fell back and she heard him chuckle.

"I win."

Maybe he had, but damn, losing felt pretty good.

* * * *

Nick gently lifted her hands over the hook before drawing her up and into his arms. She felt so perfect, so right as she cuddled close to him.

She'd responded beautifully. So fucking beautifully. The session was going better than he'd imagined. Once she'd relaxed and made the decision to give this a try, she'd submitted with sweet perfection.

Every instinct he possessed told him to take her now. Fast and hard and not to stop until he came deep inside her.

He was going to ignore that instinct because he had more to gain than mere pleasure. He was going to show her how good it was to give up control to him.

"How is he doing that?" Her arms floated up around his neck. "I thought for sure he was about to finish."

He laughed, loving the fact that his little innocent was actively watching another couple have some fairly filthy sex and she felt comfortable enough to complain about the fact that the man had an enormous amount of stamina. It was time to confess. "He's famous for being able to go forever. When those two get going it can be hours before they come up for air."

"You set me up," she accused. "You con man. You think I don't know this set up? 'Come on. Let's play some poker. I'm horrible at it but we can go low stakes.' You look like you're going to lose, but then you pull out the winning card. Yeah, my father perfected that con."

"The stakes here weren't low at all. This was a high-stakes game and I made sure I would win." To his left Taggart had switched up positions, putting his lovely wife on her knees and fucking her from behind.

Yes, that seemed like a good idea.

But he had something to do before he got there. He had a point to make.

Taggart wasn't going to be the only one with excellent stamina this evening.

Pleasure was the key. Pleasing her in bed, proving to her that he could take care of her would bind them together, would make it more certain that she would turn to him when the bullets started to fly.

God, he didn't even want to think about that now. This wasn't the place for it. This was the place to forge those bonds they would need later on.

Tonight was about her and he was going to prove it.

He lowered her down to the bed and stepped back, looking over her body. Curvy and strong and so feminine it made his dick ache. It didn't matter if she believed him, the words had to be said. "You're so beautiful."

"You make me feel that way," she said, her eyes soft.

Yes, that was the look that haunted his dreams at night. That was the trusting look he'd worried he would never see again on her face, not aimed at him. "Tell me if you enjoyed watching the Taggarts."

"You know I did."

"Do you know why I wanted you to watch them?" His hands moved to the buttons of his vest without him thinking about it. As though his body knew what it needed and that was to be naked with her, to have nothing between them. Skin to skin for the first time in forever.

She brought one knee up, her body in a sexy repose he wouldn't have thought her capable of before. She stretched, thrusting her

193

breasts out and bringing her still bound hands over her head. She looked like she was posing for a pinup calendar, one he could stare at for hours. "You wanted to put me in a position where I had to admit I'm a sexual being. Far more sexual than I would have thought. You wanted me to understand that pain can bring pleasure when I'm aroused enough."

Partly. "I wanted you to understand that there shouldn't be any boundaries between lovers, not when they trust each other. There's nothing wrong or dirty or shameful about what we do when we're intimate as long as we both want it. Do you think there's anything wrong with the Taggarts enjoying being watched?"

Her head came up and her lips curled into a grin as she watched the other couple. "No. There's nothing wrong with it. They're beautiful together, and it's not merely about how lovely they are. There's a connection between them. They love each other."

"Very much, and that trust between the two of them means they can explore the limits of what makes them happy. I want to play with you. I want to find what brings you to a screaming climax. I want to be the man who shows you how hot you can be."

"I signed the contract, but now I know I honestly want this. I want to…what's the word you use? Play? I want to play with you. I'm not afraid anymore."

He unbuttoned his shirt. He wasn't going to need it for the next few hours. "I don't want you to be afraid of me. You have nothing to fear."

"I don't know about that." The new confidence in her was so sexy as she stared up at him, a gleam in her eyes. "I think I'm afraid of whatever torture you have planned for me next."

He tossed the shirt aside. "Torture can be sweet. I think you're going to find that out. What you call torture, I merely call taking my time. I'm going to take my time with you now. I gave you what you needed. I need more than an orgasm, though don't think for a second I won't have that from you."

"What do you need?"

"I'm going to know you this time. This time I'm not going to leave an inch of you untouched." What he didn't say was what he truly needed. To feel that connection with her. To know she was thinking only of him. He needed to know in the moment that she couldn't think of anything but what was happening between them. No future. No past. Just the long hours spent giving and receiving pleasure and comfort.

"Are you going to leave me tied up? Not that I mind. I like it, but I think I want to be able to touch you."

He wanted her hands on him, but not yet. "In good time. I told you, this is my game and we'll play by my rules. Luckily this whole room was built to play my games."

He reached for the rope that bound her hands together, easing her arms up. There was a hidden hook on the headboard, a clever setup that required the mere push of a finger to reveal the hook. Two, actually. One on either side of the headboard in case a Dom needed to tie up two submissives for a nice long torture session. He'd spent some wild nights here when Des had wanted something more kinky. He'd performed for her and whatever sub Des chose for the evening, tying them both up and topping them. But he wasn't going to point that out to Hayley.

She would be the only one for him. He would play to his heart's content, but only ever with her.

Hayley groaned as he hooked her into place. "You're killing me, Nick."

He frowned. "Is that what you call me when we're playing? In our next session, I'll give you a tweak to remind you."

"Sir." The word came out on a breathy sigh. "I'm supposed to call you Sir. I liked the tweaking thing earlier."

"That wasn't punishment. That was to show you that your body will react differently than you think when you're aroused."

"I understand. I was only saying I wouldn't mind it again. I also think I might be interested in the crop."

Another benefit of having her watch a couple as experienced as

195

the Taggarts. They could show her the joy of impact play and he didn't have to worry about her getting the wrong impression. Charlotte enjoyed a bit of a bite, but wasn't a masochist by any stretch. For her, the nip of the crop or the easy flick of the whip enhanced her pleasure. Like that tweak had done for his sweet sub.

"I'll take that into account. Spread your legs for me. Knees up and feet apart."

He loved the way her breath hitched right before she obeyed. She brought her knees up, feet flat on the bed and spread wide.

"Does this make you uncomfortable?" His cock was hard as a rock, but it was a pleasant sensation. It was easier to shove the need down as he watched her. She needed this, needed the dominance only he could give her. He was in a unique position to understand her, to bend his needs to meet her own. Talking was something that helped Hayley process. It always had. She needed to acknowledge her feelings aloud in order to accept them.

"It's awkward. Like a medical exam except without the paper gown thingee." She giggled a bit as she looked up at him. "But it's okay because you like it. You don't think it's awkward, do you?"

He ran his hand down her body, down to the mound of her pussy. He could see the way it glistened, arousal making her labia coral pink and swollen. Needy. Pouting and wanting attention.

He could give her that.

"It's not awkward at all. It's beautiful. I love seeing you spread out for me, waiting for my command, for my next action. Sometimes I'll blindfold you so you can't see. Later I'll put plugs in your ears so you can't hear, and I'll restrain your arms and legs. You won't have any idea what's going to happen but you'll lie there and wait because you'll know that whatever it is, it will make you scream out in pleasure."

"I trust you. What do you want me to do, Sir? Do you want me to beg? I don't mind. Please touch me again."

She was following his lead quite nicely. "You want me to touch you? With my hands?"

"Yes, please."

He brushed a hand over her pussy, covering the gorgeous flesh with his big palm. She'd followed his instructions and shaved the mound. It was perfectly bare, soft and lovely. He would have her keep it that way so he could always feel her soft skin against his hand and mouth and cock. "You're so warm and wet for me."

She thrust her hips up, rubbing against his hand.

He pulled back. "No. That is very bad girl. Bad girl will get a spanking later, but I begin to think you wish to push me. This is the behavior of a brat. Do you want to be a brat? Bratty girls wait longer for their orgasms."

She stilled beneath his touch, her whole body relaxing back into the bed as she seemed to catch on to the spirit of his play. She shook her head. "No, Sir. I don't want to be a brat. I want to be a good girl. I want to be Sir's good girl."

"Excellent. Then you must listen to Sir. You must do everything Sir tells you to do. I have much to show you, but I require a well-trained submissive. I want to know you'll obey me when we're on the dungeon floor. I want to be certain you will behave like the good girl I know you can be."

"You are touching all my feminist buttons," she said, her nose wrinkling.

When had she gotten so bloody adorable? He pressed down gently on the swollen nub of her clitoris and rotated. "I will happily support your feminist ideas outside of the dungeon, *dushka*. I will be the most modern of men except when it comes to two things. Sex and your protection. Then you will find me very much still in the cave. You understand?"

"Caveman in the bedroom. Got it. I can be me in the outside world and still be your submissive here."

"You can be both because both are a part of you," he explained, getting to his knees on the bed. Her body was laid out for him like a feast and he was suddenly so hungry for her. Why had he waited even this long? He should have been on top of her the minute she'd walked into his office. He should have locked the door and made it plain she wasn't leaving again.

God, was he thinking about trying to keep her? Was he thinking about making her an offer to stay with him even after the case was closed?

He moved between her legs, lowering himself to the bed. He felt her shiver, likely because she figured out what he was about to do.

"This is a part of you and there's nothing wrong with it. There's nothing wrong with wanting a man to eat you alive. There's nothing wrong with me wanting the taste of you on my tongue. It's all right because we care about each other. It's all right because there's nothing wrong with sex and exploring how far we want to take it."

He lowered his head and let himself breathe her in. She was peaches and cream and sweet, sweet sex.

"Again with the torture, Sir. This is the hard part. I want you to move faster. Please."

"No." He breathed over her. "We'll move at whatever pace I decide. I want to go slow. You've had your fun. Now it's my turn."

He heard her groan as he lightly dragged his tongue over her. She tasted perfect, exactly as he remembered her. He'd never gotten the taste of her out of his head, and some small part of him had prayed that he'd merely made it up in his mind, but her perfection was something he couldn't deny.

This was what he wanted. She was still under his tongue and he was in control. Surrounded by her. By the heat of her soft skin. By the sound of her moans. By the taste and smell of her. His world narrowed down to her and everything else fell away.

He laved her with his affection, running his tongue over her labia and clitoris, exploring the hot depths of her pussy. He speared her, fucking deep inside and drawing out all that sweet cream.

He couldn't get enough of her. He sucked and licked and laved until he felt her tighten up, her body ready to go off at any moment. One more stroke of his tongue and she would come all over his mouth. He would taste her orgasm, sucking it down like ambrosia.

But he couldn't wait. The time for waiting was done. He wanted her to come around his cock. He needed to bury himself inside her and know that she was with him.

All thoughts of turning her over and drawing her to her knees fled. He needed more. He needed to see her, to connect with her.

He pushed off the bed, fished the condom out of his pants pocket and shoved his slacks down. His cock bounced free, hard and ready for her. He stroked himself while he stared at her.

"Do you have any idea how much I want you?"

"I need you so much. You can't possibly want me more than I need you. God, I've been alone since that night. Even when I was with someone else, I longed for you."

He rolled the condom on, his whole body focused on her. "Look at me. Don't take your eyes off me."

He rubbed his cock over her, lubricating himself for penetration. She stared up at him, her eyes crystal clear and pleading.

He could give her what she wanted. He pressed against her core. Heat flared through his body as he thrust up and inside. She was tight, but so wet and ready. His whole body sparked as he began to fuck her.

"Yes," she whispered and her eyes started to close.

He thrust in deep, bringing their bodies so close. "No. You look at me. You let me watch you. Stay with me."

"I want to hold you."

"You don't have to. I'm here. Look at me. Keep contact. There's more than bodies involved in what we do, *dushka*. Give me your pleasure." He leaned over, holding himself inside her, and brought their mouths together. He kissed her, his tongue dancing against hers. "Give me everything."

He began to thrust, rotating his pelvis so he could grind against her clit. All the while, he held her eyes. He took in the sight of her pupils widening with pleasure and trust. She was looking up at him, utterly vulnerable to him, and he could see her every emotion play out on her face.

199

He gave it all back to her, holding nothing inside. He didn't try to hide his own pleasure, his need. She deserved to see every moment of it.

Her eyes flared, mouth coming open on a strangled scream as she tightened around him and came.

He let loose, pounding into her until he couldn't anymore, until his back bowed with the force of his orgasm. It sparked through his system and he could feel himself spilling into her.

He fell on her, giving her all his weight while he reveled in the way their bodies fit together. He rested his head on her chest, perfect lethargy pulsing through him.

He held her close and wondered how he would ever let her go.

Chapter Eleven

Hayley walked into the dining area well aware of the ridiculously bright smile on her face. She couldn't help it. The last several days had been nothing less than spectacular. Nick had taken some time off and they'd spent almost every second in bed together. Even when they hadn't been fucking like rabbits, they'd been curled up with each other, talking or watching movies. She'd worn very little clothing over those days, though she had ordered some spectacularly filthy undergarments online that should show up sometime today. Her Master had her sit naked on his lap as they'd found some lingerie he swore would make him salivate. Of course, talking about sexy underthings had led to him turning her around and ordering her to ride his cock.

She was pretty sure she glowed.

"Hey, stranger." Charlotte Taggart was sitting at the table with an actual stranger, a man with dark hair and brooding good looks. She had a bundled up baby resting in one arm and a mug of coffee in the other. "You haven't been around much. I saw Nick leaving earlier. He said you would probably stay in your room all day. He had that mysterious, so very Russian smile on his face when he said it. I wasn't expecting to get to see you today."

"Well, I…I…think he forgot that he doesn't drink coffee. He didn't bring me any this morning so here I am out of my cave." Awkward. Yep, this was awkward because the last time she'd seen Charlotte she'd been up against a wall taking her husband's enormous…yep, awkward. How did one handle this particular social interaction? She bet there wasn't a Miss Manners article on whether to send a thank you note to the woman who let you watch her have sex so you could figure out if you're a voyeur. It was a real oversight in Hayley's opinion.

Charlotte stared for a moment and then a brilliant smile crossed her face. "I wondered if that was you."

Hayley felt her cheeks go up in flames. She needed to work on her poker face. "I'm sorry. Like I said, I was just spending some time with Nick while Penny works on…well, my case."

She wasn't sure how much she was supposed to say around people she didn't know. She thought she'd met most of the team. So this new guy wasn't someone she'd start talking about her case to unless she knew it was all right.

And she certainly wasn't going to talk about her sex life. Her perverted, kinky, amazing sex life. Mr. Tall, Dark, and Piercing could be the janitor for all she knew.

A hot janitor who was wearing what looked like expensive clothing.

Charlotte's free hand played with her coffee cup. "I'm glad you're spending some quality time with Nick. He looked happy earlier. Hayley, this is Ezra. He's worked with us many times before. He's also a pretty fun guy for the most part, but don't tell him any of your secrets. He's a company man, if you know what I mean."

She didn't. It must be a security term. She would make sure to ask Nick what it meant, but for now she simply took the hand offered to her. "Hi, I'm Hayley. It's nice to meet you."

The dark-haired man took her hand in both of his. "Miss Dalton, it's a pleasure to meet you." He turned slightly to smile Charlotte's way. "This is your voyeur?"

Again she felt her whole body go what was probably a vibrant pink. She tried to pull back, but he held her hand tight. She did the only thing she could, turned to Charlotte with a frown. "I thought we weren't telling him secrets."

Charlotte waved that off. "Don't be silly. That's not a secret. That's a fun sex story. And I wasn't entirely sure it was you until you stammered and turned that lovely shade of mauve. And Ezra's been around the group long enough to know what we do."

He squeezed her hand and gave her a most charming smile. "It's some weird shit. Voyeurism is the kiddie end of the pool with these people. It's been a long time since I saw a member of the kink world blush like this. I'm so sorry if I embarrassed you. Please forgive me. Kinksters are usually open about their lives. It's one of the things I find so attractive about the lifestyle."

He seemed sincere, his voice and tone soothing. She found herself shaking her head. "I'm fine. It's no problem."

Charlotte watched their interplay with a smile on her face. Hayley was starting to realize that Charlotte Taggart viewed the world as something to constantly be amused at. "She's new, and see, there's pure proof that my instincts were right. Submissive. You gave her the sneaky Dom handshake, the one that lets her know how big and strong you are, and then came the apology that's really more of a flirtation. Well played, Ez. Unfortunately, she's spoken for and Nick is not going to share this one."

Ezra drew her hand up, kissing the back of it. "That's a shame. What's changed? Nikolai has never been a one-woman man. And I am sorry if I embarrassed you, though if you found the apology charming, there's no harm in that. You're not wearing his collar yet. There's still plenty of time for you to make up your mind."

She pulled her hand away because if there was one thing she'd learned about the whole power exchange thingee, it was that Nick wouldn't like another dude kissing her hand. Maybe that wasn't exactly about the power exchange thing. Maybe that was simply Nick.

"I'm perfectly happy with the Dom I have, thank you." She

turned on her heels and moved toward the object of this morning's affection. Coffee. Nick had left her high and dry. All he had in his apartment was vodka and water and tea. She needed to talk to him about a girl's need for some caffeine. They needed a coffeemaker.

Luckily, there were enough American types around this place that there was always a pot on.

Actually, if she was sprucing up his spartan apartment, she also might buy some accent pillows and comfy throws. Something to give the place a pop of color. Also things that felt good on naked skin since he seemed serious about no clothes when they were alone.

"Don't take it hard, Ez. I've heard Teresa was giving you the eye last night," Charlotte said, mirth plain in her voice. "And there's a host of subs in Dallas who sigh every time you walk in the dungeon."

"Tell them I miss them as well," he replied. "I have to admit I only took the class to annoy Case, but I find I rather like it."

"Yes, that's the only reason you took the class. It didn't have anything at all to do with work and keeping an eye on us," Charlotte chided and then groaned a bit. "Oh, baby boy, what have I been feeding you that you would smell like that?"

Hayley poured her coffee and turned around in time to see Charlotte carrying her son toward the door. Somehow she couldn't let the other woman leave thinking she was embarrassed about participating in what had happened the other night. She wasn't at all now that she thought about it. It had been one of the best nights of her life and not acknowledging that seemed wrong. "Did I thank you profusely for helping us out the other night?"

Charlotte smiled, the kind of smile that tended to light up whole rooms. Hayley kind of thought she was starting to smile like that, too. "No trouble. It was a good night for all of us. And don't go too far. Ian's out dealing with some business stuff with Damon but I got the report in this morning from Alex and Eve about what they found out about the fire."

"I can't go anywhere," she agreed. "The last time I checked I was pretty much…well, just know I'll be here. I was going to find Teresa to see if she needed any help. Idle hands and all."

If Nick was going to be working most of the day, she couldn't sit around the place. She needed something to do, a way to be productive.

"How about you meet me in the conference room in thirty minutes? I'm going to change him and see if I can get him down for a nap," Charlotte explained. "You remember where it is?"

How could she forget? A woman didn't tend to forget where she was the first time she was turned into a major player in a murder. "I'll be there. Thanks."

Charlotte left and Hayley turned back around to look for the sugar.

"So they're being careful with you? I worry because sometimes Nikolai can be reckless," Ezra said. "Sometimes he puts his own emotional needs in front of an operation. I would hate to see that happen to you."

So he was some kind of operative. He seemed to know Nick. "Nick is careful with me. He won't let me out of this building. It's lovely, but I'm getting a bit bored in here. I'm hoping the reason I'm staying blows over and I can relax. Maybe go out and see a show in the West End or go to a restaurant."

"Oh, I don't think that's going to happen anytime soon," he said smoothly. "Not when you're wanted for capital murder."

She felt the pit of her stomach drop about three feet. "I'm sorry, what?"

He moved to the counter and deftly opened one of the cabinets, bringing out a small sugar server. "One or two?"

Hayley put the coffee down. "What did you mean? Capital murder? The last I heard they were calling me a possible material witness."

He set the server down and faced her. "I meant that yesterday the Seattle police in conjunction with the FBI held a press conference and plastered your name and face all over the evening news. They found the gun used to kill the police officer and they've matched the prints to the ones you gave when you did your background check for the university."

What the hell was happening? Did Nick know? He'd been so casual this morning. He couldn't know. He would have told her. "I didn't touch a gun. I didn't have one, never owned one. There's no way they have my prints."

"Oh, there are so many ways they could have your prints. I assume you touched things while you were at the police station giving them the report."

She'd had a bottle of water and someone had kindly offered her some coffee when it had gotten late. "Of course. I wasn't trying to hide anything."

"I'm also assuming you touched things inside the motel room you were staying at. They could have staged a nice scene there."

She hadn't thought about that at all. She'd left everything behind when she'd run. And yes, there would be DNA evidence of her all over that room. She'd taken a shower and dried her hair. She'd lain in the bed for a while. How the hell was this happening to her?

"It's more than the physical evidence though. They've got you set up nicely. They also have an eyewitness," he claimed calmly. "Someone who puts you fleeing from the scene of the crime. I believe they have video. Did you happen to run past a bank?"

She hadn't thought about it at the time. She'd been far too busy running from the man who'd come to kill her. Later, she'd been more circumspect. She'd done everything her father had taught her to do when they were in casinos and he didn't want to get thrown out by a floor boss he'd crossed. But she hadn't been thinking about keeping her head down in that moment. "I was running from a man who was dressed as a cop. He was trying to kill me, not the other way around."

"Ah, that explains it." He leaned there casually, as if they were talking about the weather and not the potential end of life as she knew it. "It also explains why Nikolai has kept you under wraps for days. I don't suppose he let you turn on the television, did he?"

"We watched some movies."

"But no news." Ezra managed to make it sound like an accusation.

She had to shake her head. "That doesn't mean he knew."

"He knew. I told him myself."

She tried to act like those words hadn't been a kick in the gut. She was starting to think the man in front of her was a bit on the dangerous side. "Who are you and how do you know so much about my case?"

His expression didn't change a bit. He didn't have a problem with his poker face. "I told you. I'm Ezra Fain. I work with McKay-Taggart from time to time. I know about your case because I make it a habit to keep my ear to the ground."

"Who do you work for most of the time?" She had a nasty feeling she wasn't going to like the answer.

His lips curled up in a lopsided smile she was sure most women found completely irresistible. "Now you're asking the right question. I work for the CIA."

Somehow she didn't think he was talking about some desk job. The man in front of her wouldn't do anything as ordinary as push papers around. He was like Nick. He would be dangerous under the right circumstances. The question was, were the circumstances right at this moment? She took a step back, coming up against the table. "Why are you really here?"

He held out a hand. "Hey, I'm not here to drag you back to the States. Not at all. I don't work that way. I was curious because of your relationship with Nikolai. I'm actually here to work with a couple of the men. I'm nothing at all for you to worry about, though I do know a bit about what you're going through. Damon asked me to use my contacts to see if I heard anything at all about why a London crime family decided to greet you here in Chelsea."

She tried to tamp down the emotional reaction. If Nick had known, then he'd had a good reason not to tell her. He would come back and he would have an excellent explanation. Until then, she had to deal with the dude who seemed to have some information. "Do you know anything about why someone would try to frame me?"

Ezra thought about it for a moment. "Maybe you should talk to Nikolai."

Now he wanted to clam up? "It's my life and my case. I think I deserve to know."

"I happen to agree with you, but Nikolai and I have had a few run-ins. I don't want to cause trouble. I'm allowed in here because I've been helpful on a few missions, but I know damn well that Big Tag and Damon would cut me out in a heartbeat."

"What do you mean a few run-ins? I would think you would be on the same side."

"Well, sweetheart, at one point in time, he was basically a member of the KGB. He worked for Putin and he was a top agent. So no, we have not always been on the same side," Ezra pointed out. "I've been around for a while so I've known him for years. Ten or so. I also ran up against him when he and his girlfriend would run jobs."

She wasn't sure what that meant, but it sounded bad. "They didn't run jobs. That makes it sound criminal. They worked here. They were operatives."

Ezra looked at her like she was a naïve child. "Oh, they ran plenty of jobs and many of them would be considered criminal, though they were awfully good at covering their tracks. They needed cash to do what they did. Taking down sixteen members of the Russian mafia is no easy trick. It took cash and a whole lot of bullets."

What the hell was he talking about? "Nick worked intelligence. If he took down a mafia family, he did it to save people."

"He'd left his government job by then." He shook his head. "Look, I'm not here to cause trouble between you and Nikolai. I'm sorry. I'm running my mouth off when I shouldn't. I did find out a few things, but it's still early. I know that there's some talk on the Dark Web about someone in the States offering cash for anyone who can bring you in. The good news is they seem to want you alive."

That didn't make her feel better. "Why?"

"They didn't talk about that," he admitted. "And like I said, it's what I like to call a whisper. A couple of people asking about it, but I haven't seen anything from the person offering the cash. I'm listening in on the people asking about it. Honestly, that could be Adam Miles or it could be an assassin. I'm sure Big Tag put Adam and Chelsea Weston on the Dark Web to find out what they can. I'll run it past Big Tag when he gets back, but I think it's worth exploring. If I get an okay from Damon, I'll talk to a friend of mine and we'll try to see if she can find out if there's a contract out on you."

"I don't know anything." It seemed utterly surreal that someone out there thought she was so important they were willing to pay to have her kidnapped. "They can bring me in but they'll be disappointed."

"Sometimes we know more than we think," he said enigmatically. "That's one lesson I've learned in my years in the field. Don't discount yourself. You're the critical piece of this puzzle."

"No, whatever information is on the microdot they found in my necklace is the critical piece."

"Well, we can't know that until Penny figures out the code, can we? I suppose until then you'll stay here with Nikolai watching over you."

How long would that take? "That's the plan. Now more than ever. I can't step outside without some security camera catching me. If they decide to bring Interpol in, everyone will be looking for me."

"Don't doubt that they're already looking for you, sweetheart. But there's always a way if you know the right tricks," he replied. "Do you want to get a new cup? That one's probably cold by now."

Her coffee. She'd forgotten it. Now she couldn't even think about putting something in her stomach. "No, I think I'll pass this morning. I've got to go meet Charlotte in a few minutes."

He stepped up, putting a hand on her shoulder. "It's going to be all right. They'll figure this out. Please be careful. Nikolai has some unappealing contacts that I would watch out for. But you'll be safe as long as you stay here. This is a good group."

"Why do you call him Nikolai? Everyone else calls him Nick." It kind of unnerved her.

"I don't ever want to forget who he really is. He is Nikolai Markovic, a true Russian son. It's good to remember where people come from so you'll know where they are likely to go." He took a step back. "I've got to go down and have an interview with a crazy dude I'm fairly certain used to be Hungarian intelligence. I'll be around for a while. If you need anything, you should know I'm here to help."

"Why would you help me?" She wasn't sure what the CIA had to do with her case and she wasn't foolish enough to think this man helped anyone out of the kindness of his heart.

He stopped at the door. "Like I said, I like it here. Again, if you need anything at all, you know where to find me." He started to turn and then stopped. "I'm having to stay in the dorms, just so you know. I'm on a cot in a room with those idiots because I'm dedicated to figuring out who those boys are. So if you want to save me, feel free. I have no idea how they manage to make the whole room smell like feet."

He walked out and Hayley stared after him wondering what she would be forced to do next.

* * * *

Nick tamped down his frustration as he turned the car down Pretoria Road. At this time of day it wasn't crowded, but there were always people on the streets. Some of whom would as soon shoot him than speak to him. He took a deep breath and tried not to scream or vent his anger on the poor steering wheel. It wasn't the Mercedes's fault that he was forced to go back into the lion's den.

The morning had not gone well. He'd taken a chance and blown it. He was fairly certain he would be in for a hell of a lecture when he got home.

Now he was here in Little Russia about to do what might end up being one of the stupidest things he'd ever done. And given his track record, that was saying something.

"Well, you got to look at it as a funny story to tell." Brody was stuffed into the seat beside him. "You know when you think of it, it's kind of a joke, mate. A Russian and an Aussie walk into British intelligence and suddenly everyone's bloody stupid."

This morning's first mission had been a complete failure. He'd gotten absolutely nothing out of his contacts at MI6. Since Nigel Crowe had retired, even Damon's contacts had dried up considerably. Or no one was willing to talk to him in particular. He hadn't gotten past the lobby. According to the one agent who'd been willing to come down, Hayley Dalton's case was purely a matter for US law enforcement. They weren't sticking their necks out for someone with no deep connections.

Or they remembered Nick's connections to Des, who'd been this close to being arrested by her former coworkers.

"I should have waited. I should have sent Damon or better yet Penny. I got impatient and it cost us." It cost her. It cost Hayley. Penny had offered to call a few people, but he wanted the information now. Ever since the moment he'd realized whoever was after Hayley had put out an international call for her, he'd been in a state of pure panic.

Someone was willing to pay half a million dollars for Hayley. God only knew what they would do with her when they had her. Likely she would end up being so much bloody trouble they would murder her.

He had to do anything he could to keep her safe.

Not that his intelligence-gathering mission was going well. He'd come up with nothing and wasted a whole morning. Now he had to go to a place he'd sworn he never would again. And he'd forgotten her coffee. He needed to buy a bloody coffeemaker so he didn't have to go foraging every morning.

She also needed more clothes and hangers so she could use the closet. And a dresser of her own, since he only had a tiny one. Maybe he should switch to a larger one and she could have half of it. There was something satisfying about the thought of his clothes next to hers.

What was he thinking? He was driving into a place where there were people who wanted to murder him and he was redecorating in his head. It was an excellent way to get himself killed.

"Deep breath, mate. It's all going to be fine," Brody said. "The restaurant's up ahead, right? Nothing to be worried about. I got your back."

"I have to tell her today." Nick's hands tightened on the steering wheel. He'd spent two days trying to keep the news from her. He wasn't being honest with himself. He'd spent two days trying to pretend that it wasn't really happening.

Someone was serious about taking Hayley and they were no closer to finding out why. Penny had been working with the code for days, but hadn't come up with a reliable cipher. It didn't correspond to any she knew and that meant one thing. Des herself, or whomever she'd meant to get the message to, had devised it.

Codes were funny things. Anyone could create one. He'd used several in his days as an intelligence operative. Letters of the alphabet would correspond to symbols, numbers, or even other letters. It would appear to be nonsense to the uninformed. However, if one had the cipher, it would be easy to match up the code and read the message.

Whoever had coded this message had used more than one alphabet, tons of symbols, and even bloody emojis. It was exactly like Des to have slipped the smiling poop icon into her code.

He had to face facts. It could take Penny months to figure out a working cipher. Des had been damn good at her job.

He had to do something. He couldn't keep Hayley locked up forever, though it was tempting.

"She's going to be scared, but I don't know why telling her is such a problem," Brody replied. "She needs to know so she can be vigilant."

"So you wouldn't have any problem telling the doctor that someone wants her dead?"

Brody sighed. "Course I would, but I'd tell her and fast because I wouldn't want her to do something that could get her killed. Luckily I don't have to worry about that. Steph's practically a saint. No one would want to hurt her. She does too much for the people around her."

"Yes, well, Hayley is a history professor. Not exactly a high-risk job," Nick pointed out. "All I'm saying is it's hard to say these things to a woman you care about. I don't want to hurt her, but you're right. I have to tell her."

"Good news is you can also tell her that she's safe." Brody sat back, though the smile on his face had been replaced with a broody look. "At least she's the kind of woman who'll listen to reason. She'll keep herself safe because she's not some crazy Joan of Arc martyr who thinks she has to save the whole world."

Ah, so there was more to the story. "I thought you said she was safe."

Brody stared out the front window, a stony look on his face. "I said no one wanted to kill her. I didn't say she didn't make a habit of shoving her body in front of bullets from time to time. She's got it in her head that everyone deserves saving, and if her chance happens to come during some military skirmish, then logic be damned."

Brody had lost a brother during battle. It would be difficult for him to deal with a woman he cared about putting herself in danger. In this particular case, he had to agree that he had the easier time of it. Hayley would be reasonable.

"I'm sorry to hear that. Though she sounds like a hell of a woman, I can understand how it would be rough to have to watch her put herself on the line. Though we're about to do the same thing."

"Not the same at all. We're not risking our necks for some rebel soldier who'll probably shoot her the next time he sees her. And this is going to be easy. That's it, right?" Brody pointed to the nondescript restaurant half a block away.

"Yes, but we won't actually go in. There's a small garage up ahead," Nick explained. "We'll have to park there if we want to get in. There's the restaurant. The garage entrance is beside it. It shouldn't be full now. We'll see if they even let us in."

He stopped the car at the light, his anxiety already rising. This was not a world he wanted to venture back into.

"So what's the likelihood of us getting in and out without someone trying to kill you?" Brody asked the question in a perfectly calm voice. Like they weren't about to walk into a den of vipers.

"The man who owns this place isn't an enemy, but then again I wouldn't call him a friend. I did him a favor and he owes me." The light changed and he moved forward. "I sent him a message. He'll meet us in the garage if he chooses to meet us at all. I would not be welcome in the restaurant. I'm not welcome in Little Russia at all."

"Good to know." Brody shifted and his Ruger made an appearance. He started to watch the street.

"We're all right in the car. Damon tints the windows so we should be relatively safe. I could drop you off back at The Garden. I should have done that. I'm not thinking straight."

That's exactly what he should do. There was no reason to risk Brody. The Aussie had insisted on going with him when he'd left this morning, but that was when they'd been going to MI6 headquarters. No one was going to attack them there. Walking into the stronghold of the *Bratva* in London was a completely different thing.

"Don't you bloody dare." Brody pointed forward. "You keep going. Ain't no way I'm letting you walk in there without backup. Who do you think I am? Owen can't do this anymore so you need to learn to rely on me. Hell, I look forward to it. With Walt as my partner I spend way too much time in stinky labs. Why does the science stuff always smell so bad?"

He turned to Brody. "Don't risk yourself for me."

"All right, I'll sit back and watch 'em gut you then. But I'm not going back to The Garden. I need a bit of entertainment."

Nick sighed. "Please be careful."

"Always am. Who are we meeting?"

"His name is Boris Sokolov. He is a *shestyorka* to the Lebedev syndicate." Not everyone knew the inner structure of *Bratva* families.

And Brody definitely didn't speak Russian. "Uhm, he's like an associate to the organization."

"So he provides the brotherhood with information but he doesn't tend to be involved in their actual crimes."

Then again, Damon tended to force his operatives to learn as much as possible.

"Yes. He will give information he gathers to the *brigadier* he reports to," Nick explained. "The *brigadier* runs a section of the syndicate's businesses. Boris owns this place. This is where much business is done, so he always has intelligence. I helped his brother back in Moscow. This is me calling in a favor, but he won't be happy about it."

Especially given how he'd helped the man's brother.

He turned and stopped in front of the garage entrance. The gates were open at this time of day, but the guard stepped out. He wasn't dressed in any kind of uniform, but there was no doubt in Nick's mind who he was. He was the gatekeeper and he would be heavily armed.

"I'm here to see Boris."

The man stared at him for a moment and then slowly nodded at him.

Nick drove into the garage.

"Not much on talking, eh?" Brody asked.

"He won't talk for fear someone will record him. He doesn't speak to people like me at all. It's good sign that he didn't wave a weapon our way. It means this might be friendlier than we thought."

"Or it might be a trap," Brody pointed out.

Yes, that was a possibility. "I have to take that chance. If anyone is going to have his ear to the ground, it's Boris. It's not only *Bratva* that runs in and out of this place. Many independent contractors come here looking for work or information about work."

Surely someone knew something about the mysterious person out to get Hayley.

He moved from the bright light of day into the gloom of the garage. It consisted of two stories, the first reserved for guests, but

Nick knew he wouldn't be considered a guest. Business would be handled on the second floor. He drove right past the empty spaces and up the ramp that would lead him to the section devoted to Boris's staff.

At least there wasn't a question of where Boris wanted him. The big man stood at the back of the garage, his form shadowed. Nick pulled the car into a slot across from Boris, easing into the forward-facing position. He wasn't about to turn his back on anyone in this place. He'd learned that lesson.

"I've got you, mate. This ain't nothing but a piece of piss job. Easy in. Easy out." Brody nodded his way. "You tell me what you need."

"Just be ready for anything." Nick opened the door and stepped out. "*Privyet*, Boris. *Kak dela?*"

Boris frowned his way. He was dressed for work in a T-shirt that bore the name of his restaurant and jeans, a half apron around his waist as though he'd walked out of the kitchens and wasn't happy to have been called away from his job. "I'm fine. It's surprising to know you still speak our language since you spend so much time with foreigners. I thought you would only be speaking the Queen's English now that you work for her."

"I don't work for the Queen. I work for a private business." This was one of the problems he had anytime he moved back into this world. He got called a traitor. When he tried to work with MI6, he was met with resistance because he'd once been SVR.

Sometimes he wondered if he belonged anywhere at all.

Except he'd felt perfectly comfortable for the last two days, locked away from the world with Hayley. He'd fit in with her.

Boris's face wrinkled into a pointed sneer. "You work for Damon Knight. That means you work for Queen. Worse than that, you work for US president through that Taggart bastard."

Nick stood his ground. It wasn't going to be the last time he dealt with this kind of anger. "I'm not going to apologize to you. I've come for information. You owe me after what happened in Moscow. Your

216

brother is alive because I saved him."

"Yes, while killing everyone else. Believe me, everyone remembers you. We tell story often. You're the villain, by the way. In Moscow they call you *palach*."

Butcher. Yes, he'd heard they called him that. He'd earned the name. What would Hayley think of having the Butcher in her bed? "That part of my life is over. It was vengeance and now it's done. No one needs to fear me as long as they stay out of my way. Surely you can understand."

Boris nodded slowly. "Bloody vengeance. Yes, I understand this. I also understand that a man must always pay his debts."

Something about the way Boris said those last words made Nick's hopes leap. "You found information?"

"Yes," Boris replied. "I actually heard something about this yesterday evening. Someone in the States put out word that there would be much money paid if the American girl was brought in alive. Half a million in American dollars. None if she's dead, but they do not care if she is damaged in transit."

Nick felt his hands fist at his sides. Whoever was behind this had given free rein to a bunch of criminals to rape Hayley, to do anything they liked to her as long as she was given over alive.

Perhaps his time as the Butcher wasn't over.

"I would like to know who placed the hit on the American woman." He was well aware that the words were ground out of his mouth between clenched teeth.

Boris waved a big hand dismissively. "This I do not know. I was not contacted directly by buyer. I know several men who were, but they will not tell you who buyer is. You should know this. They're all professionals."

No one was that professional. Everyone broke at some point. Or had a price at which their professionalism could be bought. "Was Martin Donaldson on that list?"

He needed to know if Boris's information tied back into his own. Donaldson had been the man in the alley. Had he been one of the men now after Hayley due to the mysterious job offer?

Boris's eyes flared. "The one from Islington? I hear rumor he didn't make it back home a few nights back."

This wasn't an exchange. He had no intention of giving anything away that he didn't have to. "I only know that my people tell me he was following the woman at one point."

"We all know who the woman is, Nikolai," Boris said with a frown. "There's no point in playing this ridiculous game. She has connections to the bitch goddess, and everyone knows that she would run straight to the goddess's whipping boy. She runs to you and you are hiding her. This is why they have all come to London."

Well, he'd known someone had figured out the connection between Desiree and Hayley. Though now even that was mysterious. How many criminals had made their way to London? How many were waiting for him to make a mistake so they could take her? "I need names."

Boris's eyes closed briefly. "I need promise that this will pay my debt. I will owe you nothing after I give you these names and you will never darken my door again."

It was the best offer he was going to get. He was grateful that he'd had mercy on Boris's brother, despite the fact that he'd been working with the syndicate that had killed his sister. He'd granted mercy to the men who had not taken their oaths at the time. That one decision might help him to save Hayley. "You'll never see me again. Not in this capacity. I can't promise my firm won't come after you one day if you pose a threat."

"Understood, but never let it be said I did not pay my debts." He held out a piece of paper. "These are the names of two people I know received the job request and the information about the American girl."

Nick took the envelope. It wasn't the end of the road, but it was a place to start. It would give him something to do, a path to walk down while he waited for Penny. And he'd gotten valuable information. They knew Hayley was in England. It might be time to figure out how to move her.

They could go someplace off the grid. Somewhere quiet. He would go with her, watching over her every step of the way.

"*Spasibo*, Boris." It was one more thing closed and done. Boris was the last person who owed him anything from those bloody days. The last person who owed Nick. There were still a few who believed Nick owed them. Owed them his blood and his pain and his life.

And that was something to consider when he thought about convincing Hayley to stay with him. There would always be someone coming after him and that meant potentially coming after her. She would be his weak spot and the smartest of his enemies would use her against him. None of it mattered at this point because she was in more danger without him than with him. For now he could keep her without guilt.

Everything would change once he made sure she was safe again.

"Good day, Boris." He turned, satisfied that at least he hadn't gotten Brody killed. The Aussie was standing behind him wearing a grim expression. He'd stood back, as though he was Nick's enforcer and not his partner in this venture. He was excellent in the field.

It was time to take the names he had in his hand back to The Garden, study them and then figure out a plan of action.

Though mostly the plan of action would be hunting down these bastards and torturing them until they talked.

All in all, not a bad plan.

"Are you ready?" He started toward the car but stopped when he realized they weren't alone. Three men were walking up the ramp, each holding a gun.

He whipped back around to Boris.

The big man shrugged. "You're not the only one I owe. Good luck, Nikolai."

He heard Brody curse right before the bullets started to fly.

Chapter Twelve

Nick's heart started to pound in his chest as he heard the door behind him slam closed and then the heavy thud of a lock falling into place.

They were trapped.

That bastard had played him and quickly, too. But then Nick had walked into the one place in the country where such a double cross could be put together in the course of an hour.

Nick put his hands up. The only thing he had going for him was the fact that the men in front of him would want to torture him for a while. A long while. "Let my friend go and you won't get any trouble from me."

He heard Brody huff beside him, but ignored it.

"Ah, Markovic. As if we'd do anything you asked of us. My employer would prefer I bring you in, but he did not specify how many pieces would be acceptable. I think many. It is difficult to ship bodies in a single package these days," said the biggest of the men. He was dressed in all black, a cap on his head. He was a beast of a man and he wasn't alone. He was flanked by two other men, both with guns in hand.

Nick didn't recognize them but there was no doubt the trio had been sent from someone back in Russia. He'd killed the men responsible for his sister's death, but he hadn't done what Desiree had implored him to do. He hadn't scorched the earth. He hadn't found it in himself to destroy their families, to ensure no one was left who would want vengeance on him.

At the time, he'd almost welcomed the thought that one day one of the children or relatives left behind would come for him. Life had seemed cheap and inconsequential then. He'd done his duty and been at peace with the consequences.

He wanted to be back in bed with Hayley, touching her, laughing with her.

Life seemed far more precious now.

"I could come with you willingly or I could cause an enormous amount of trouble. It's your choice." Yes, he'd figured out too late how precious life was and he couldn't cost Brody his. "All you have to do is let my friend drive out of here. He has nothing to do with what happened all those years ago and killing him will bring hell down on your heads. He works for Damon Knight. Do you know who that is?"

"What are you trying to do?" Brody's voice was a harsh grind.

The big guy ignored him. "I know the name. You work for him, too. Killing one or two of his men won't make much of a difference."

"Ah, but he only hired me because he was trying to catch my girlfriend. He doesn't care about me. He was working for the government to bring her in. My friend here is a true war hero, and killing him will bring many of his friends after you. The Taggarts will come after you." He was willing to use any and all information if it got Brody out of this fucking death trap. "Perhaps even the Denisovitch syndicate."

That got all three to stop and a long moment passed. They knew the names. It was plain in the way they paled. He could still salvage part of this cursed day.

"I ain't going," Brody said under his breath.

"You will." He looked over at Brody. "You understand what they will do?"

He could hear the tension in his own voice.

Brody didn't look his way. His Ruger was up and aimed somewhere in between the two on his right. He was coiled and ready to strike.

He was going to die. He was too big a target and there was nowhere for them to go.

Unless…

"Perhaps we can make deal," the big Russian said. Nick could see the tats creeping up his neck. He would be covered in them, each one detailing the crimes he'd done in the name of the Brothers. "I don't want trouble. Well, I don't want more trouble than I can handle. You put down your guns, come with us, and we leave friend behind."

They would likely shoot Brody as they were leaving but he had to believe that Brody was smart enough to avoid them. The other asshole knew the odds. Three on two when everyone was trained wasn't that great. He had to wonder if Boris had told them he would be all alone and vulnerable.

Still, he couldn't take the chance.

"I've got a gun in a holster at my back," he said. "Do you want me to hand it over or would you like to disarm me yourself?"

He was reckless. He shouldn't have come here but pride had driven him, and now it would cost not only him but Hayley, since the damn names were in his pocket. He actually trusted that those names were real. Boris was a man who did pay back his debts, even when he found it distasteful to do so. He would have found it incredibly amusing to manage to pay back two debts at once and nullify any advantage Nick would have gotten from it.

If he'd waited and sent Damon in his stead, had thought for two seconds about protecting himself, he wouldn't be in this situation. He wouldn't be leaving her alone. It wasn't his own life he gave a damn about. It was the one he could have had with her.

It struck him quite forcefully that his sister would have loved Hayley. Would his sister be happy with the vengeance he'd sought? It hadn't brought her back, hadn't stopped other women from dying. It had merely brought suffering to other people and brought him here. His vengeance had cost him Hayley the first time around, and now it would cost him again.

"Stand there. Do not to move." The leader nodded toward the smallest of the men, who began to walk toward Nick.

He kept his eyes on the man walking toward him. "Please tell Hayley that I'm sorry."

"Sorry that you're such a pessimistic arsehole? What is it about you Russians that makes you so bloody dour? You know it makes me happy my normal partner's an American," Brody shot back. "Walt always knows that if you want to get out of a situation, someone's got to bend over and take one for the team. Walt never questions, just does what has to be done."

Shit. He should have known Brody wouldn't let them take him without a fight. Bending over and taking one for the team was Brody's lovely way of saying he was about to move and Nick better be ready. Bringing in Walt's name told him to duck. It was Walt's highest order in the field. Walt ducked; Brody dealt with the bad guys. Walt's genius-level IQ and his innate understanding of both physics and geometry made it possible for him to accurately describe the path any bullet would take. His lack of fine motor skills, however, made it impossible for him to hit the side of a building, so he dove away from the bullets.

Brody was telling him if he wasn't willing to fight then get out of his way.

Fuck.

The minute Brody moved, Nick ran, sprinting across the garage so they weren't close together. Two targets were harder to hit than one. Brody would be smart enough to duck behind the car, he hoped.

He heard cursing and then shouts in Russian to kill them both.

Nick dove for the car beside him as the world exploded in gunfire. He felt heat lash his side, but he rolled to his left. He hit the tire, the smell of rubber telling him he could stop. He ignored the pain in his side and pulled his gun, flicking the safety off.

He flattened himself against the car and took stock.

The garage had gone deadly silent.

Shit. Was Brody dead? Had the big dumbass gotten himself riddled with bullets?

"Only two left, mate."

The sound of that thick Aussie accent echoing against the concrete was the best thing Nick had ever heard. Brody was somewhere to his right, but Nick would bet he was close to the Benz. Nick was huddled against some kind of sedan, though the car on his other side was a smart car and wouldn't offer much protection at all. The bad guys would simply lift it up and use the thing as a weapon against him if he gave them a chance.

Where was everyone else?

He could see some of the floor, but the car was low to the ground. Good and bad. He couldn't see much further than a few feet but then to see him, one of them would have to get low to the ground.

"This won't work, Markovic. You do nothing but seal your friend's fate," a dark voice said. "Find them."

He heard the sound of shoes thudding against the concrete. Apparently Brody was hiding on the other side of the lot and now they were both being hunted.

But sometimes the prey had a better vantage point. Nick could see under the car, a small stretch of visibility that might give him the advantage. As the steps came closer, a pair of black boots came into view.

Five more steps and he might be able to see Nick over the car in front of him. The bloody tiny smart car. If this was happening in an American parking garage, he would be surrounded by massive trucks and SUVs, not shoved in between two tiny cars that had to be powered by hamster wheels.

Calm. He had to stay calm. He'd spent the majority of the last year working easy assignments, assignments where no one shot at him. He'd brought down corporate spies, and they didn't usually try to murder the man coming after them. He'd gotten soft and comfortable.

He took a deep breath and let a nice chill settle over him. He had to reclaim the predator he'd been before finding his home here in London. All that mattered in the next few moments was to take down the other men. Any way he could.

Nick went still, his firing arm out and flat against the concrete. Normally that would be a bad thing, but he intended to use it to his advantage. He knew exactly what he would do if he were in the same position. He would use that car as a shield and pick off the man on the floor. It was an easy, simple way to solve the problem, and the risk would seem minimal.

It wasn't going to work out that way for the other man.

"I've called in backup, Nikolai," a dark voice said. "They will be here in seconds and they will be annoyed because you pulled them away from their lunches. All you do now is make this harder on yourself and your friend. Perhaps we will bring him along, too. The boys like to have their fun, no?"

He was sure there was a crew on its way down right this second. They would enter from the same door Boris had fled through. They would be at Brody's back, and Nick wasn't sure how safe his partner's hiding spot was.

Time once again was not on his side.

Nick stayed calm, stayed still, his eyes on that thin strip of visibility between the concrete and the car's undercarriage. Those black boots began moving again, easing their way toward the car.

Closer. A little closer.

"We will have some fun games with your friend and take you in alive," the leader was saying. "You will not enjoy your trip back to Russia. Once we're there, my boss will take you apart as you did his son."

Shit. He didn't want to think about it. Couldn't right now. He certainly wasn't going to point out that whatever aging mobster had sent these men his way should understand that his son had ripped apart a beautiful young woman who'd had her whole life ahead of her. His son had been a monster, and a monster had come for him.

It was the awful, painful circle of life in the *Bratva*.

"You had to keep the bloody keys, did ya?" Brody blasted across the garage.

His shout was followed by gunfire.

So Brody was at the car. Excellent.

He couldn't panic, couldn't lose his shot or they would do exactly what that asshole had said they would do. Kill Brody and take him in for long hours of torture, and not the fun type.

He let the world slow, stopped thinking about anything but getting the perfect shot.

The boots moved closer.

One more step.

"*Ty proigral*," the man in the black boots said from above.

Nick didn't look up, merely stared forward and fired straight into the asshole's ankles. Once and then another a few centimeters to the left. He heard a shot go wild overhead and then the inevitable happened. The man cursed and fell, his ruined ankles unable to hold up his weight. The man's body dropped like a rock, his head banging against the concrete.

The minute he hit the ground, Nick fired again, this time hitting him square in the head.

He would not get up again.

Nick flipped onto his back in time to catch the boss racing up. He didn't bother to keep a car between them, merely ran until he was standing right in front of Nick. From his place on the concrete, Nick fired and the other man's shoulder flew back. Adrenaline coursed through Nick's body, giving him energy and focus.

Nick fired again, but the big bull managed to stay on his feet. Somehow he managed to raise his weapon and aim at Nick.

Pain lashed at Nick's side, but he managed to roll to his left before his assailant fired again.

Nick looked up, ready to fire until he ran out of bullets or until too many hit him.

Win or die. It was all him now.

The other man moved in.

And then his opponent's body went flying as the Benz plowed into him. One minute the boss had been standing there, ready to end him, and the next there was a sickening crunch and then the sound of something hitting the opposite wall. The squealing of tires echoed through the garage. The passenger door crashed open and Brody stared at him.

"What are you waiting on, mate? Get in."

Nick forced himself to move. His left arm was bleeding, but he couldn't stop for a bandage. Every muscle in his body ached as he rolled over to get to his feet. He banged a knee against the concrete and reached for the open door.

Behind him a door slammed open and he could hear a smattering of Russian curse words. He jammed himself into the passenger seat and managed to pull the door closed just as the rear windshield shattered into a million pieces.

Brody hit the gas, flying past parked cars and concrete columns. Nick rolled down his window, the smell of burning rubber crashing into him.

They weren't out of here yet, and he was sure the sound of a gunfight hadn't gone unnoticed by the guard downstairs. Still, he couldn't help but turn to Brody. "I thought you needed the keys."

Brody faced straight ahead, his lips quirking up. "Had a bit of an interesting youth. Decided to stop waiting on your lazy arse. What else was I supposed to do when you're taking a nap somewhere? Hang on."

Nick slammed back against the seat as Brody made an insane turn down to the lower level. The back half of the car fishtailed and Nick braced himself. "It wasn't exactly a nap."

"So you say. You all right? You look a bit bloody," Brody said. "Where did you get hit?"

"It's not bad. I think I got grazed in the beginning." He was fairly certain it wasn't bad. He could move all his limbs. That was a good thing because it looked like he was going to need his right arm.

Up ahead, light filtered in from the street, but Nick could see the gate being lowered and the guard stepping out with a gun in his hand.

Brody cursed and hit the gas.

It would be close. The guard fired, but it went wild. He stood his ground in front of the gate. Nick leaned out and started firing.

Fuck. They weren't going to make it. He fired again, trying to get the guard out of the way. Any hesitation might make the difference between getting out of this garage and crashing into the gate. They would be sitting ducks for whoever marched down that ramp.

The guard jumped back and there was the terrible sound of metal scraping across the roof. Brody turned onto the street and raced through the red light, putting distance between them and the men running after them.

He took his first deep breath since the whole fucking thing had started.

Nick slumped against the door. He was getting too old for this shit.

Brody turned on the next street, grinning wildly. "Damon's going to kill us, you know."

Yes, Damon wouldn't be the only one.

* * * *

Hayley slipped into the chair beside Charlotte and looked over at the elephant in the room. The super-hot, might-still-drag-her-back-to-Seattle-in-handcuffs elephant. Besides Charlotte, Ezra Fain was the only other person there. "What's he doing here?"

Charlotte turned her way, her eyes widening slightly.

Probably because she'd sounded like a brat. Still, she had a right to know. "You said I shouldn't spill secrets to him. I didn't get what you meant when you told me he was a company man. That was because he's with the CIA, right? Well, I already talked too much. And he doesn't like Nick."

He'd made that plain.

Charlotte placed her laptop in front of her. "He's here because I need his authorization to look at some video. Adam read about it in one of the public reports and thinks it could be helpful, but hacking the Seattle PD will take some time and there's a certain amount of risk we can avoid because of the access Ezra has. I made the decision to bring him in instead of exposing Adam to a risk we don't have to take. He takes plenty of them all on his own."

"Why would he have access to the Seattle PD? He's CIA. He isn't supposed to work on domestic soil."

"I have a lot of connections, Hayley. And if you think I don't keep an eye on what happens in the States, too, then you don't understand the nature of my job. I can leave if you like. I'll get Charlotte what she needs and then leave the two of you alone," he offered.

Charlotte looked her way. "I don't know what the two of you talked about while I was gone, but Ezra's smart and he's read the files. Normally I would wait and let Damon deal with this, but he and Ian got pulled into a meeting with some government bigwig about a security consultation for some royals and they won't be back until late. Penny's up to her ears in code, Ariel's in session, and Kayla is out working a case she's been following for two months. And Brody went out with Nick. It's me and Ezra or just me, and believe me, Ezra has more experience. If this were about either assassinating a rival mobster or convincing two cranky toddlers to go to bed, I would be your girl. I'm strictly behind a desk at this point. I run the company so my husband can shoot things."

She hadn't meant to be rude. "I'm sorry. I understand. I'm touchy since I found out about the warrants out for my arrest."

Charlotte opened the laptop. "You just found out about that? Why didn't Nick tell you?"

That was such a good question. "I don't know, but I do want to be updated now."

She'd had a wonderful several days where she hadn't been forced to think about the fact that her life was in ruins. It was time to wake up again.

Charlotte started working over her keyboard. "All right, I talked to Alex and Eve. They're the two Dallas operatives we sent up to Seattle to see if we could find anything out. They went to the police and told them Eve was your cousin on your mother's side. We got next to nothing out of the police. They are definitely treating you like someone they believe killed a police officer."

"That sounds bad." Maybe she didn't want an update. Maybe she wanted to go back to that moment she rolled out of bed. She shouldn't have left the apartment. This was what Nick had been trying to keep from her. Not the information but the sinking feeling that everything was going to hell.

"They didn't tell Eve anything at all. They aren't going to break rank when it comes to a fallen fellow officer," Charlotte explained. "And I understand that. So I'm going to send in a friend of ours. She's a reporter and she's going to see what she can find out about our mystery officer who isn't on the rolls."

"One of the important things to do in a case like this is to manipulate the media." Ezra sat back, looking calm and collected as he talked about playing chess on an international level. "Whoever is behind this knows what they're doing. He or she has put you in a position where no police officer is going to help you. I'm not saying they would actively harm you. Not at all, but your shot at getting one to listen to you before they shove you in a jail cell is gone."

"And once I'm in a cell, I'm a sitting duck," Hayley surmised.

"More than likely." Ezra crossed one long leg over his knee and continued. "Which is why I'm advising that we do a bit of manipulation of our own. We send in a bona fide reporter to start asking questions. There's nothing the press likes better than a good conspiracy theory. In this case, it's all true. We send in our reporter, show some of the pictures of our would-be kidnapper around, and shake some things up. See what falls out of the tree."

It sounded like an interesting idea, but she couldn't stand the

230

thought of someone else getting hurt over her. "What happens if one of these people comes after the reporter? They killed a police officer to set me up. They won't hesitate to kill a reporter."

"This reporter is quite good at taking care of herself," Charlotte explained. "She's my sister-in-law and her husband will be with her every step of the way. Not much gets past Case, so don't worry about it. I couldn't get Mia to give it up if I wanted to. She smells a story."

"I don't want her hurt."

"She'll do almost all the work remotely. The good news about journalism today is they don't need boots on the ground for something like this," Charlotte continued. "Mia can make her inquiries and shake things up from her comfortable and safe condo in Dallas."

That made her feel a bit better. "All right. So you think if these people feel threatened by Mia's questions, they might make a mistake."

Ezra glanced at Charlotte's laptop as she turned it to him.

He touched a few keys and shifted it back her way before speaking. "Yes, we're trying to draw them out one way or another. We're still working this from the criminal angle, too. We'll be talking to contacts in both the intelligence community and some in the criminal underground."

"I'm worried that's what Nick's doing today." Charlotte's face was grim as she worked over the keyboard.

"What do you mean? You think Nick's out talking to criminals?" That would explain why he wouldn't tell her anything about what he was doing except that he had some errands to run.

"He's probably talking to his *Bratva* connections," Ezra replied.

Charlotte looked up. "He wouldn't do that. We discussed this. I can handle that part with far more ease than he can. It might take me a few days, but I already called my cousin. He agreed to put out some feelers."

Something deeper was going on than a mere argument about how to move forward. Charlotte didn't appear angry that Nick might be going against her advice. She looked worried.

"Why would you be the better person to deal with the Russian mob? I know Nick has some ties. He would have met them when he worked intelligence."

Charlotte's lips were tight, her whole body tense as she replied. "My cousin is an active member of the *Bratva*. He's the *pakhan* of the Denisovitch syndicate. That's like a godfather. He should be able to get us some intelligence, but he has to be careful about how he does it so it could be a few days, maybe even weeks."

A derisive chuckle huffed from Ezra's mouth. "And that's why Nikolai is out there right now doing something stupid."

Charlotte shot Ezra a look that could have peeled paint off a wall. "You don't know that."

"Ping his phone," Ezra challenged. "What do you want to bet me that he's somewhere in Little Russia?"

Hayley wasn't sure exactly what was going on, but it scared her. "Why would it be bad for Nick to do the same thing you asked your cousin to do? Please don't sugarcoat it. Tell me the truth."

"The trouble is Nikolai is reckless and he won't be careful the way Charlotte's cousin will be. Then, of course, there's also the fact that Charlotte's cousin didn't brutally assassinate an entire syndicate." Each word out of the CIA agent's mouth felt like a bullet peppering her flesh. "Charlotte's cousin doesn't have a bunch of mobsters who would want to kill him on sight."

"Well, I wouldn't say Dusan is a saint, but he isn't reckless." Charlotte's voice had gone slightly hoarse, as though she was struggling to keep it down. "As for Nick, that's his story to tell and I won't let you take that from him. I trust him. Ian and Damon trust him. If you have a problem with that, the door is that way and I don't expect to see you again."

"You think I'll walk away from those men downstairs? We have no idea what kind of assets they could be," Ezra argued.

Charlotte leaned over. "I think you are trying to find the weak link and break the chain so you can do what men like you always do—manipulate us, use us as assets. I am not the weak link, Ezra. If you push me further, you'll find exactly how not weak this link is."

Ezra's hand came up. "Fair enough. And it's not all about using you. I will admit that I don't trust that man. You didn't go up against Nikolai the Russian operative. He's dangerous and he could be dangerous to your client." He stood up, shoving his chair back. "And if you think he didn't have anything to do with the games Desiree played, you're high. Everyone in our world knew that Nikolai was her enforcer. He was her muscle, doing her dirty work. You think I didn't see that firsthand? I did. And I saw what he did to that syndicate. There's a reason the syndicate calls him *palach*. And Des did things you don't even know about. Classified things that hurt our country. If she hadn't died, your Nikolai would have discovered how much fun rendition can be. Don't make me the villain here. Now you have your approval. You're in the system and there won't be any blowback. I'll go down and continue to try to figure out if those men you're keeping here have families that are looking for them. You know I've put my ass on the line for you. For all of you, and don't make that out to be something I did because I was currying favor from anyone."

Charlotte had lost her hard stare, softening as she looked up at him. "I know that, Ezra. We will have to agree to disagree on Nick."

He nodded tightly. "I'll be downstairs. Let me know if you're kicking me out."

"Stay away from Nick and we won't have to," Charlotte said, turning back to her computer. The door closed and she took a deep breath. "Damn it."

"What was he talking about?"

Charlotte was silent for a moment. "I think you should talk to Nick."

"I understand that Nick didn't mention the charges against me because he was trying to protect me. I'm not unreasonable. I care deeply about him, so if I was in his position I might do the same. But I would be wrong. I can forgive him for being emotional, but he is underestimating me. Ezra is right. I'm your client. What do I not know?"

233

Charlotte growled a little, but gave in. "Desiree was under investigation when she died."

"Yes, I figured that out. I assume it was bad."

"She was info gathering."

"What does that mean?" Hayley asked.

"It means she used her job and connections to gather information and then used that information to either manipulate people she wanted to or to make money."

"She blackmailed people?" There was no other way to interpret what Charlotte had said.

"She wasn't perfect. Not even close, but she was one of us and I don't believe what Ezra believes. I don't think Nick helped her in the worst moments. Damon hired Nick with Ian's support. He's still a part of the team and we all back him. I understand that Ezra has a different view, but we know Nick. We trust Nick. He's not the same animal as Des, though I'll be honest, I understood Des."

Thank god. "Explain her to me."

Charlotte thought for a moment before she turned to Hayley. "She needed freedom. I get that. She was raised in an oddly repressive regime and she needed to stick the finger to the world. I had a similar upbringing, though a bit more on the violent end. You learn to care about nothing and no one but your own survival. I was saved because I met this man I loved with my whole heart and he became my world. Nothing meant more to me than making Ian Taggart proud of me."

She felt her heart sink. "So it was like that with Nick and Des?"

"No. Nick always knew who Des was. Ezra says Nick is being reckless, but he's actually quite careful. He was reckless once before because he was emotional, and he has to tell you that tale. Now he's reckless for you. Because he found you. Because you're the one he wants to make proud. That's what Ezra doesn't understand. What he can't understand because he's never felt it. I like Ezra, but he's got some of the intolerance of youth. I know he's thirty-three, but he's never once been in love and that means he doesn't understand that we do crazy things when we love someone, things that can't be explained with logic, that are meaningless to those who don't know what it means to care more about a person than ourselves. Ezra's great love is his country, and one day a woman will come along and she'll make him question everything, and that will be the moment he understands Nick."

Hayley wasn't sure she understood. Not entirely. "What does that word mean? The one Ezra used. Pal...something."

Charlotte sighed. "It's all a part of his life that Nick needs to tell you about. Sweetie, do you want a real chance with him? If he's some crazy-hot sexual adventure you're having to take your mind off what's going on in your life, tell me now. I'll open the file and give you full access. If you think you could love him, give him the chance to tell you in his own time. I know it's hard, but if you could love him, honor him. Let him tell you. Trust him. I didn't and it cost me years of my life."

Years. Hadn't the years already gone by in a way she hated? Did she love Nick? It felt like it. She couldn't not think about him. She compared every man to him.

Should she trust him with this, too? "All right. I'll talk to him about it later, but are you sure about the CIA guy?"

"He's been one of our truest allies. I have to tell Ian that I had a badass argument with the dude who saved his brother. Ezra was crucial to the mission that saved Ian's youngest brother and I just faced off with him. I did that because I do believe in Nick. So I need you to trust me when I say Ezra's a good man. He's got a different viewpoint and we have to tolerate it because he was right. He backed us up when it could have cost him. And he gave me access to something that could hurt him if it was found out that he handed this video over."

So the secret life of spies was a bit of a soap opera. There was so much about Nick that she didn't understand, so much hidden history. "If he did go to Little Russia, would that be dangerous?"

"It could be," Charlotte replied. "But Nick is smart and you have to place some faith in him. Okay, here's the bit Adam thinks might be helpful."

She shoved the argument with Ezra Fain aside. She had to focus on the evidence he'd gotten them. "What am I looking at?"

Charlotte shifted so Hayley could move in closer. "This is from a security camera at the gas station a block from your house. The reason the police found it interesting is that they caught a man jumping over a fence from your neighborhood and then walking by the station. He didn't walk in and they've already made sure it wasn't the homeowner taking a shortcut. Apparently the home was empty at that time of day and they did not have a dog in the yard. This house is in the same position as yours, one block over. Its yard backs up to the lot behind the gas station. As luck would have it, the manager had recently placed a security camera to watch over the back lot. They had some kids screwing around with the car wash a few weeks before."

She felt a shiver go through her. "So your guy thinks this might be the man who blew up my house?"

"Well, he wants to check into it," Charlotte allowed. "The timing is roughly twenty minutes before your house exploded. Okay, here it comes. You probably don't know who this is, but at least we'll have a place to start."

She was confused about one thing. "If the police have this video, why did they decide it was a gas leak?"

"Ah, well, that's changed now, too," Charlotte admitted. "Now the police are saying you probably paid this man to destroy your house so you could collect the insurance. According to a couple of sources, you were deeply in debt."

It kept getting worse. "That's not true."

"I'm afraid it is now. Whoever is setting you up is also good at identity theft. So the narrative is that the fallen police officer found evidence, confronted you, and you killed him and ran. I think it's utterly ridiculous, but the press around Seattle seems to be buying it. You're the *It* girl of the moment. I think they want to keep the pressure on you by keeping your picture out there."

It was mind-boggling. She stared at the screen. It showed a black and white scene. She could see the entrance to the car wash and the paved drive that led to it on the right side of the screen. The neighborhood backed up to a small field. After a moment of absolutely nothing happening, she saw a man begin to haul himself over a fence in the distance. He seemed to struggle for a few seconds, his body shaking a bit. He finally threw one leg over and then the other before lowering himself down to the ground below.

Who the hell was that? Some criminal who'd been paid to do a job? Some dude taking a shortcut to get to the train station? He brushed himself off. He seemed to be wearing jeans and a lightweight jacket, his head covered in a baseball cap.

He started to jog across the field, his head down.

"Come on, look up," Charlotte pleaded with the screen. "I can't use facial rec if I don't have a face."

He sped up as he came closer and then his head turned suddenly as though he'd heard something in the distance, something that startled him.

That was the moment his face turned up and Hayley's world upended.

Charlotte clapped her hands right after she stopped the video, the man's face frozen on the screen. "Gotcha." She turned to Hayley. "Now we can put that mug through facial recognition and hopefully we'll find a name."

But Hayley didn't need a name. She knew the name. She'd been certain she would never see him again because he'd died.

"There's no need. That's my father."

Chapter Thirteen

Nick winced as Walt pulled the thread through his upper bicep. It took everything he had not to shout out. He should have downed half a bottle of vodka before letting Walt sew him up. "Someone gives you medical degree? I would place large bet that you do not sew up these people."

The stitches were worse than the bullet that had grazed him. Unfortunately, the graze had been more of a deep cut. Walt had told him to go to hospital, but upon seeing the Benz had agreed that perhaps Nick should stay in for the rest of the day. They'd been damn lucky the police hadn't pulled them over.

Walt tied off the stitch and cut the thread. "I mentioned that it's been a good long time since I did an ER rotation. I was more of a researcher before I came here. And my specialty was emerging viral threats. If you ever get a hemorrhagic fever, I can totally tell you all about the DNA structure of the virus that's going to kill you. And these sutures are perfect, thank you very much. You won't even have much of a scar."

The experience was scarring enough. "I'm sure I'll have more after Damon sees the Benz." But at least he had those names to investigate. If he still had a job after this. "Do you know if Hayley's been informed of my minor injury?"

He was already trying to figure out a way to downplay the situation. Of course he was also thinking about the fact that there were still people out there who wanted to hurt him. How many of them were left? Years had gone by and he'd felt relatively safe, but his past was coming back to haunt him at the worst possible time.

Just as he was beginning to think about a future.

"Do I even need to explain how bloody fucking wrong what you did this afternoon is?" Damon Knight strode into the room, Taggart hard on his heels.

"I told you, man. Those Euro cars are too easy to damage. You need to buy American SUVs. They're like tanks. Even Adam can't wreck one and he's a horrible driver. I'm pretty sure he spends more time looking in the mirror to make sure his hair is still douchey than he does paying attention to the road."

Damon ignored Taggart entirely. He was far too focused on Nick. "Are you trying to get me to fire you? Because I could have you out of here in a few hours, and we all know what will happen if you hit the streets of London at this point. You'll be dead or in jail within an hour now that you've prodded the sleeping dragon."

Brody stood up, facing their boss. "Hey, he wasn't out partying, you know. He was trying to find information that will help us with Hayley's case. And we got it."

Damon's face had turned a nice shade of red that let Nick know he'd fucked up at a high level. "I can fire you, too, Brody. You're supposed to be the voice of reason."

"Said no man about an Aussie ever," Taggart quipped and then held up his hands. "Sorry. Sarcasm is my default mode." Even Taggart seemed to understand that Damon wasn't in the mood to joke. "You know we've got insurance on that Benz."

"And how do I explain that away? I don't have a bloody police report," Damon shot back. "All I've got is a call from an old friend in Scotland Yard asking about a shootout in a Pretoria Street garage.

They've got CCTV footage of a vehicle fleeing the scene. Guess who's driving, and quite poorly, might I add?"

A frown creased Brody's face. "I thought it was pretty good myself. And that car handles beautifully."

"Do you understand that you're wanted for questioning by London police?" Damon asked, his voice tight. "I'm going to have to make a million calls and use favors I would rather have kept in my pocket in order to get you out of this."

"It wasn't Brody's fault." It looked like he was going to have to save the Aussie twice, though he wasn't sure Brody would be smart enough to let Nick take the punishment this time either. "He went with me this morning when we were headed to MI6 to meet with some contacts. He had no idea I was planning to go into Little Russia."

"He wasn't planning on going to Little Russia. We got bugger all from MI6 and he realized the only way we were getting shite was him putting himself on the line. He wasn't being selfish. Quite the opposite," Brody argued. "And it ain't like the Russians are going to file a police report. No one down there's going to talk to the authorities and the whole thing will go away. You know it, Damon."

Yep. Brody was going to fight him to the end. The same way Owen would have during the year they'd been partners. Desiree would have agreed with him. Des would have let him take the blame so he could spare her. She always did. It had been a revelation the first time he'd fucked up and Owen had tried to shield him.

He rather thought Hayley would be more like Owen and Brody.

"I was selfish," he admitted. "I should have dropped Brody back off and gone in myself."

Brody's eyes rolled. "And then you would be dead, brother."

"You shouldn't have gone in at all," Damon shot back. "Why do you think I send you on assignments that keep you as far from that world as possible? Do you even know what I have to juggle to bloody well keep you all alive? MSS wants to murder Kayla. I have to constantly watch to ensure they don't know where she is. Walt is legally dead. If anyone finds out about him an entire international conspiracy will unravel and Taggart and I will be in legal hell. Then there's you."

Brody held up a hand. "I'm very unwelcome in a few bars in Melbourne. Been told I'll be shot if I show up again."

"This is serious, Brody." Damon stood in front of him, his gray eyes narrowed. "There are people out there who would love to see you dead. It's my job to ensure that you stay alive and you're making that difficult for me. Let me make this plain. You are not allowed in that part of London. If I discover you've tried to make contact with any member of the *Bratva* again, I'll decide you're too stupid to live and kill you myself. Do I make myself clear?"

He'd never seen Damon so pissed off. Somehow he couldn't work up his former alpha male outrage at authority. Damon gave a shit. This was how it came out. "Yes, sir. It's clear."

"Excellent. I'm going to talk to my wife. We'll have a debrief in an hour. I want to know everything that happened this afternoon, and you will not leave a single detail out. Brody, I'll take your debrief in written form. I'll expect at least four pages. Single spaced."

Brody groaned as Damon walked out. "Now see, that right there is torture. The man knows me well. It's an easy debrief. We went. We got shot at. We got away. How do I make that into four bloody pages?"

"The man has had a rough couple of years," Taggart said with a sigh. "He really is trying to keep you all alive, and it's not an easy job. He lost Des and no matter what she was involved in, understand that she was a part of his team and he feels that loss. He blames himself for what happened with Owen. I put all the weight of dealing with the lost boys on his head because it was easier to bring them here than to smuggle them back to the States. Damon's got a lot on his plate right now so give him a break."

Nick shook his head. "Owen wasn't his fault. Owen was my fault. He was my partner. I should have seen what was going on. I should have stopped it."

241

"What is with the Euro drama?" Taggart huffed, a deeply annoyed sound. "Let it go. All of it. None of you can do your jobs if you sit around plagued with guilt. It's not manly. Owen made a choice. So did Des. We mourn them. We miss them. Well, I don't miss Owen because he's actually still here, but you get my meaning. So now that Damon's hissy fit is over, let me have one of my own. Do you have a fucking death wish, Markovic?"

"I was trying to get the names of some of the men who have been sent after Hayley. The best place to find a criminal is in an establishment run by criminals." He shouldn't have to explain this. "I wish I could have gone into the Tesco on the corner and gotten the information. It wasn't for sale there."

Taggart stood over him like a drill sergeant over a lazy recruit. "And it didn't occur to you that someone else could walk in there and get the information and not be nearly brutally murdered? Charlie and I could have done it. Charlie's roots run deep in that group, and not a one of those fuckers wants to go up against her cousin."

He had thought about it, but he'd underestimated the danger. "I'll be honest with you. The owner owed me a favor. I called it in. It's been years since someone tried to kill me, despite what Damon says. I walk the streets of London quite nicely. I thought it was the fastest way to get the information we need. I thought I could get in and get out quickly. I didn't think they could make a plan to attack me. I only gave Boris an hour before I am on his doorstep."

"Which should show you how badly some people out there want you dead," Taggart pronounced gravely.

Yes, he got that.

"If it helps at all, I think you're down to one man," a new voice said. "The rest have either died off or moved on. I think you're dealing with the father of one of your victims. He owns a bar in Moscow that caters to the *Bratva*. He's close to Boris, which is precisely why Boris offered you up and made the deal so quickly."

Damn. Ezra Fain. He'd hoped to avoid the CIA agent until he went back to wherever it was he'd come from. It wasn't good to know that Fain apparently kept a close watch on him, but he did know who the man was talking about and it made sense. "Yes, I believe Yuri Gregorov is still offering an enormous amount of money for anyone who is willing to take me apart. I didn't realize it was known here in England. I didn't know he had such close ties with Boris."

Fain grinned as he walked in. It was really more of a smartass smirk. "Oh, it's known almost everywhere. I do believe he's got wanted posters in many of the *Bratva's* hangouts. Which is why it was truly reckless of you to walk into one."

"We didn't walk in and order a bloody drink," Brody protested. "The bastard we went to see stabbed us in the back. Well, he sent in some people to shoot us in the front. I'm right and sorry we've caused Damon trouble with the authorities, but I ain't going to apologize for what we did."

"Did you hear the part about Charlie and me being able to get the same job done with no dead bodies?" Taggart asked.

"You don't know that." Brody waved him off. "Could have been even worse."

He didn't want to get into an argument. "I should have waited. I understand that."

"You were reckless." Fain leaned against one of the empty desks. "It's not terribly surprising. You're always reckless. It's why you should rethink your relationship with the woman you're guarding. I'm not sure why you think it's professional to screw the woman you're supposed to be protecting."

"None of my guys would have found a woman if I outlawed that," Taggart threw in.

Fain paced a bit. "Fine, has anyone considered the fact that being around Markovic puts Hayley Dalton in more danger than she's already in, and that's a significant amount?"

"She's safe here," Taggart pronounced. "This is a very secure location."

"She can't stay here for the rest of her life." Fain leaned against one of the desks.

Taggart pointed toward the back of the office. "I don't know why. Walt did."

"Hey, I go out." Walt frowned. "Every now and then. But why would I want to leave? Damon provides me with all the equipment I need and a brand new PS4. We have a massive screen with super comfy chairs. We don't need to go anywhere. Going places is overrated."

But it wouldn't be for Hayley. Still, he wasn't sure what her other options were at this point. "I was given two names to investigate. According to Boris, these two have talked to whoever put the job out on Hayley."

Fain snorted. "You mean the man who sold you out? You trust him to give you real names?"

"He owed me a debt. He would not shirk his debt, but he would use it in order to pay off another debt or to make some money." How was he going to explain this to Hayley? Why was he even trying to figure out a way to explain it? He should tell her the truth. She needed to know how dangerous it was to be around him.

"I might have to have a talk with good old Boris," Taggart said with a frown.

"You have more problems than Markovic's fan base. There's been some movement on your girl's case." Fain crossed over to Taggart. "I helped your wife with some tricky politics earlier today. I got her into Seattle PD's case files."

"You found something?" Perhaps one thing had gone right today.

"Yes, but I think you should see it for yourself. I'd like to get a look at those names," Fain continued. "I'm getting worried this is something I should insert myself into."

"Why?" The last thing he wanted was the CIA involved.

"I'm concerned about the level of cover-up involved in this," Fain admitted.

Taggart nodded. "As am I. This involves not only manipulation of the police and local government, but also the media. Whoever is behind this is smart and connected and very subtle, since we haven't heard a whisper. Alex and Eve spoke to some of Hayley's neighbors and friends. They all said the same thing. They said they didn't believe that she could be involved with anything criminal, and yet when I watched the interviews they did with local news, they were edited to make Hayley look like an outsider with possible issues."

"What are you talking about?" Nick had to catch up. It appeared a lot had happened while he was distracting Hayley.

"Charlie got the raw footage of the interviews. Like I said, they show almost exclusively positive comments about Hayley, but when the interviews were edited they focused on negatives," Taggart explained. "Like one of her students talked about how everyone made fun of Professor Dalton for her need to use her own chalk. She would carry it around with her because she'd found a brand she claimed wrote better and got less chalk on her clothes. When it was edited, they didn't mention the why, merely that she wouldn't touch other chalk and how weird and suspicious that was. The reporter talked about Hayley's mental issues and then made her seem OCD by using the student's words in a manner they weren't meant to be."

"I saw that video, too." Fain stood beside Taggart. "It was an elegant piece of manipulation. It's the kind of thing I would do if I wanted to put a target in a corner and leave them with no way out. Someone wants Hayley hurting and they're doing a magnificent job of it. When whoever this is brings her in, they'll offer a deal."

"*Give us what we want and we can get your life back,*" Taggart continued. "Look at what they managed to do. They can undo it. It's simple."

"They won't undo it." Now that he thought about it, he knew the play well. He'd used the play against his country's enemies. "What does the CIA know? Because you're right. This feels bigger than we thought and because it happened on US soil and the institutions being manipulated are US institutions, I have to wonder if you might know something and you being here at precisely the right time is more than coincidence."

He didn't believe in coincidence.

Fain's face went blank. "I told you why I came and I've been trying to be helpful. If you want to give me those names, I'll tell you what I can. And if I was here for nefarious reasons, I wouldn't be sleeping on some cot in the basement. I would have come with a unit of my own and full permission of the prime minister and taken Miss Dalton, and there would have been nothing you could do about it."

"Ask Tennessee how that worked out for him," Taggart said, his voice low.

Fain's lips quirked up in a smirk. "Yes, I'm not Tennessee Smith, and you should remember that."

"Believe me, I will," Taggart promised. "And you should understand that I'm not some CIA crony who goes by a rule book. I left because there was zero room for loyalty there. Nick, no matter what he says, this is your op. Damon can yell all he likes, but it's bluster. He's not going to fire you. He would have done the same thing had it been Penny's life on the line, and he knows that deep down. So what you choose to do with the information you have is all up to you. Brody, you did a damn fine job keeping your partner alive while he followed his dick around."

"His dick is very sentimental, boss," Brody replied.

Taggart nodded his way. "Allowances must be made and I think the Benz works better as a convertible anyway. Nick, it's up to you. You can give Fain the names or I can run them myself."

The man was such an ass half the time and then he proved why so many brilliant operatives chose to follow him, why he was so respected. Why his employees loved him.

"What would you do, boss?" He would give his boss the respect he deserved.

"I would give it to both of us," Taggart returned. "I would use every resource I had, and if Fain turns out to be doing something he shouldn't, I would get ready to punish him like the naughty boy he is. CIA agent or not."

Nick stared at the CIA guy. "I know you think I shouldn't be the one protecting her, but I intend to do everything I can to do my duty.

She's important to me. If I discover you're actively trying to harm her, you'll find out why they call me *palach*."

"You have my word that I have no intention to hurt Hayley Dalton." Ezra Fain put a hand over his heart. "I mean that as an American and my mother's son. It's as much of an oath as I can possibly give you."

He had to take all the help he could get. "Brody?"

The minute they'd walked in, he'd written down the names four times and passed them to Brody. He wasn't about to lose those names. Brody had taken the notes, promising to pass them around so they could figure out the problem. The Aussie pulled out two of the papers, passing them to both Taggart and Fain.

"And I'll help him," Brody said to Fain. "In case you think about crossing him. I don't care what your agenda is. He's on my team and I never neglect my duty to back up a teammate."

"I'll die if I betray anyone here. Yes, I do get that." Fain opened the page, his eyes reading the names there. "These are both known assassins."

"Yes," Taggart agreed. "I find it interesting that he gave you the names of a Ukranian assassin and an Irish contractor. He managed to not give you a Russian name."

"Like I said, Boris walks a fine line. I only asked for a few names I could meet with and ask a few questions of," Nick pointed out.

Fain chuckled. "Yes, you'll ask a few polite questions. I'll check my contacts, but I bet both of these men are here in England as we speak. They've gotten word that she's here. They'll all be waiting for that moment when she steps out of The Garden. Or they're planning on how to smoke her out."

"What does that mean?" a familiar feminine voice asked.

Nick winced. Damn it. Hayley was standing in the doorway, her eyes wide. "It means you're safe here for now."

She was standing beside Charlotte, both women staring in at the men. "That's not what he said. He said they would try to smoke me out. Like a damn badger. I'm not completely ignorant, you know.

How would they do it?"

"Hayley, there's no reason to worry. Come here." He gestured her forward. Damn but she looked good. She looked like home and comfort and stability all rolled into one gorgeous woman package.

She moved quickly to get to him and was in his arms in a moment. He tried not to wince as she held him tight.

It didn't work.

Hayley stepped back. "What's wrong? Did I hurt you?"

Before he could explain, Fain spoke up. "He got shot. It probably hurt pretty bad. He got stitched up a few minutes ago."

Hayley's eyes had gone wide. "Shot?"

Bastard. "It was nothing."

"You got shot?" Hayley turned to him. "While you were working on my case?"

He couldn't let her think that, even though it was true. "I miscalculated the danger of where I went this morning. It won't happen again, but I did get a good lead."

Charlotte put her hands on her hips. "Tell me you didn't go into Little Russia."

"Why would that be a bad thing?" Hayley asked.

"I left Russia and denounced my ties to the government, but even when I was with the SVR, I came up against some members of the *Bratva*. They can be dangerous and they have long memories." Maybe that would be enough for her.

Fain huffed. "That's all you're going to tell her?"

Taggart shot Fain a frigid stare. "That's between Nick and Hayley. You stay out of it."

Fain put his hands up. "Hey, it's your company. I'm going to make some calls and see what I can run down. Charlotte, you should definitely go over what you found out this afternoon. I've got some feelers out in Macau as well. I'll let you know if they find anything out about Dalton's accident."

"Dalton?" Nick was confused. "You think this has something to do with Hayley's father's death?"

If something Desiree had gotten into had caused Paul Dalton's death, how would Hayley forgive him? It was likely something he'd helped Des with at one point in time or another. He would find his fingerprints somewhere in the mess.

Would she be able to forgive him?

Hayley looked away, but not before he'd seen the way her eyes had gone dull. "My father isn't dead, Nicky. My father is the one who blew up my house."

He reached for her, bringing her in close. It looked like he wasn't the only one who'd had a shitty day. She stood in his arms, but he could feel how stiff her body was. She was in shock and no small amount of pain. He glanced at the clock. They still had an hour before the debrief.

He shoved aside all the questions he had. The case could wait for a while. She needed him.

It was time to show her what he could really do for her.

* * * *

Hayley felt like a walking zombie. Her feet shuffled but she didn't feel connected to them. Her brain was working on a base level, but all she could see was that grainy black and white footage of her father walking away from her house right before he'd blown it up.

But then of course she'd also discovered that he'd been lying to her most of her life. Her father and Desiree had been up to something. Had they laughed at the stupid child she'd been? She'd been fooled by them both.

Was she being fooled by Nick, too?

Why wouldn't her hands stop shaking?

"Did you know my father wasn't dead?"

He stopped in front of the door to his place. After she'd made her announcement, Nick had put a hand on the small of her back and led her away from the office. He'd told everyone they would be at the afternoon meeting, but that she needed some time.

Time to do what? Time to realize that her whole life had been one long lie? She'd gotten that. Now she needed to know how deep the lies went.

He loomed over her, his eyes staring straight into hers. "I had no idea your father wasn't dead. While we're at it, I didn't know he and Des lied about your familial relationship. She lied to me about that as well. She never called you anything but cousin. However, you should know that whatever is at the bottom of this, I probably had a hand in. I did Desiree's dirty work in the beginning and often didn't care to figure out exactly what I was doing. I did it because I owed Des and I rarely thought about the future. So you should know that I probably am a part of this. I played a part in this and you have to be ready for that."

"I'm not ready for anything." Except to scream. To run. God, she wanted to run until she couldn't anymore, until her legs didn't work, until she had to stop and breathe.

It was so much.

Her father wasn't dead. He was somewhere out there and he apparently wished her ill.

He was working with the same men who wanted to take her in and question her about god only knew what.

And now Nick had been shot and the CIA guy kept talking about something Nick was keeping from her.

She put a hand up between them. She knew at least one thing he'd definitely kept from her. "Did you or did you not know that the Seattle PD shifted from looking for me as a witness to accusing me of being a murderer?"

A long sigh passed through him. "Let's go inside, Hayley."

No. It was time to take a step back and not only from Nick. She couldn't let go of the idea that there was someone out there waiting and watching for the time to strike. If they knew where she was, why wouldn't they come after her here? There were babies in this building. There were people with lives and families who could get hurt.

Nick would have kept that information from her. He wouldn't have allowed her to make the choice she needed to make.

It made her antsy. What else was he hiding for her own good?

He swiped his card over the door and it opened. "I said come inside, Hayley."

She shook her head. "No. I'm going to go talk to the Taggarts."

She would figure out a better way. There had to be one, one that didn't involve someone storming in and hurting innocent people. She wasn't going to be a martyr and walk out and let them take her.

Though at least then it would be over and she would understand.

The impulse was right there. At least she would understand what had gone wrong in her life. She would know why her father had lied. She would know why the people she loved kept betraying her.

It would be awful, but it would be over and she wouldn't have hurt anyone else.

She started to walk toward the elevator but a rough hand gripped her wrist, stopping her progress.

"I said get inside, Hayley." His voice had gone dark.

For a second that voice worked on her. Her body softened and she turned, the hours and hours they'd spent in bed working on her. He'd done what he'd said he would do. He'd trained her body to respond to the mere sound of his voice, to know somewhere deep down that no matter how hard they fought he could give her more pleasure than she'd ever imagined. She started to follow him.

And stopped when she remembered that he was a big part of the problem. She planted her feet. "Fuck you, Nick."

His jaw tightened, but he held on to her. "I deserve that. I'll take it if that's what you need."

"I need you to let me go."

"So you can talk to the Taggarts?" He stared at her as though he could see through her skin and down to her soul.

"It doesn't matter. It's my choice."

"Not right now it isn't. And if it's the choice I think you're contemplating, then it might never be yours to make. Tell me you're not thinking about walking outside and finishing this."

She couldn't because it had been there in her head. She knew it was stupid, but the idea had brushed across her brain, warming her in the oddest way. All the pain would be done. All the uncertainty. Since her mother had died, she'd been essentially alone.

These people weren't alone. They had families and each other. They didn't deserve to be smoked out. Not for her. She'd never managed to find a group of people who could love her. It was easy to blame that on her circumstances, but at some point she had to question whether or not she was lovable, whether or not she deserved what these people had. From the stories she'd heard, she understood that despite the fact that they weren't blood related, they functioned as a family. They backed each other up even when they shouldn't.

She'd never had that with anyone other than her mother, and even her mom had sold her out to her father. It was something she could see so clearly now that she was on the other side of the truth. Her mom had let her go with her dad despite the fact that she knew what he was doing. He was using an innocent girl as cover for whatever the hell he did with his life beyond risk it all on the turn of a card.

What the loss of her house hadn't done, her father's truth had. She was broken and wasn't sure she could be repaired. She'd been made small and likely would always remain so.

"I'm leaving here." There was no need to take everyone else out. "I'm not going to risk the people in this building."

He sighed, an irritated sound. "Yes, this is why I withheld the information from you. I knew exactly what you would do. You aren't going anywhere except into our flat."

"It's yours. Not mine." She didn't have a freaking home anymore. According to what she'd learned earlier today, she didn't even have a name. Not one that the world didn't hate. She was being called a murderer. There was speculation that she was something of a whore.

It was a dark, nasty cloud swirling in her gut and she couldn't get it out. *Never let them see you sweat. Never let them know what you feel. Don't ever let your guard down, baby girl. That's when they get you.*

Her father's words.

She needed to scream, but it was stuck in her throat.

Nick softened slightly. "Come inside and we'll talk this through, *dushka.*"

She didn't want to talk. She wanted to fight and hard. She wanted to hit someone and make him hurt and bleed. It was wrong, but the rage that sat inside her, normally bubbling softly, had the flame turned up to high. It was boiling over.

She pulled against him again, twisting her arm. "Fuck you, Nick. Let me go."

His grip tightened, still not hurting her though. As if she was the soft, fluffy girl and he didn't need to use even a half effort to contain her. "No. I'll take you to Damon or Ian if that's truly your wish, but they won't allow you to leave this building either. Stop behaving like a child and get inside so we can talk this through."

"I don't want to fucking talk to you."

"Fine. We don't have to talk at all. We'll resolve your problem in another manner. You will walk inside and pull down your pants and then you'll feel the flat of my hand on your ass until you cry out all the tension you can't seem to find words for."

She hated the fact that he could see through her. What she didn't hate was the shiver the idea of submitting to him sent through her body.

Like a predator sensing weakness, he moved in for the kill. "Then let me take your mind off everything for an hour. We have a little time before we have to be back with the group. Give me this time to help you relax. Show me some trust and let me make you feel good."

Probably a bad idea. She still had so many questions. Questions about him. "I can't. I can't pretend that everything's all right. My father is alive. He's a liar. You're a liar, too. You didn't tell me."

"Guess what, my darling? I would do it again if this is the way you behave when we hit a small snag in our plans. I distracted you because you have no idea how to handle any of this. I will not allow you to sacrifice yourself in some idiotic plan." He leaned over. "And

I'm done pretending that you're in charge of this. You've proven you can't be."

He let her wrist go but before she could even think about walking away, he'd hooked an arm under her knees and hauled her up. He lifted her like she weighed nothing. Nick strode through the door, kicking it closed behind him.

"What do you think you're doing?" She was worried he knew exactly what he was doing and that her body was about to betray her.

Or would it be a betrayal? Was her body merely taking over when her mind couldn't find a way to cope?

"You have two choices once I put you down. You can sit on the couch and wait for the meeting with the group or you can take your clothes off and we can work through some of this tension between us."

"Because sex is going to solve everything." She knew damn well it wouldn't solve a thing. But it might give her a few moments of peace. Did she deserve that?

"Do you think that talking will do it?" Nick shot back. "Because it doesn't seem like you're capable of saying anything at all mature right now."

Did he have to be such an ass? "It's not immature to give a damn about the people around me. There are kids here. Have you thought about that even once? What happens if these people decide to toss a bomb at the building to see if I'll run outside? How would you feel if you were the reason one of those kids got hurt or even died?"

"Your choice." He moved into the middle of his sparse living room. "The couch or the bedroom. If I sense you getting off the couch for any reason, I'll tie you up and you can attend the debrief with rope around your wrists and ankles. It's your choice. We can work through this in a pleasurable way or I'll make us some tea and we'll sit in silence until you can say something that makes sense."

She went stubbornly silent. He wanted to be an asshole? She could be a bitch.

A hollow feeling opened in the pit of her stomach. She didn't want to feel this way. She didn't want to choose between silence and rage and walking outside in a suicidal attempt to find some peace.

"*Dushka*, it doesn't have to be this way. You're upset and hurting and I understand that. I know this place you're in and it's terrible. You've been betrayed by people you loved. You need a place to put all those nasty emotions roiling through you. If you want to punch me, do it. I'll take it. If you need to scream at me, I'll take everything you have to give me if it will help. I would rather work it out another way, but I won't allow you to hurt yourself. I wouldn't do it as a bodyguard and I won't do it as your lover. So I can be the bodyguard and protect you that way. I can be your friend and allow you to spit bile my way until you get it all out. Or I can be your lover and I can give you what you need."

He was right about one thing. There was something nasty bubbling up. Anger. Despair. A desperate need to make someone pay for how she was feeling. "What the fuck do you know about what I need?"

"I told you I've been where you are. I've felt what you are feeling right now. You want to know why those mobsters took a shot at me today? Because after they murdered my sister, I tore through them. The man who sent assassins today? I killed his son because his son tore my sweet sister apart. That was how I dealt with what you're feeling right now. You have to find a place to put your rage or it will kill you."

Some of the fight went out of her. "Nicky…"

He shook his head. "Not now. I can't talk about her now. I have to concentrate on you. I know you're afraid, but you…you're the last link to a part of my life that's important to me. You're important to me. I'm feeling this, too. Make your choice. Bodyguard or lover."

Was he feeling the same desperate panic that had lodged in her bones?

If he truly cared about her, maybe he did. If he loved her, even a little, maybe he was hurting, too. They did have things to work out, but being held in his arms eased some of the pressure already.

255

"Lover."

He eased her down, though he kept his hands on her. His head moved in, brushing his lips against hers. "We will talk. Later. For now, you will take off your clothes. You will offer your body to me and I will accept."

A shiver went through her and her hands came up to his chest, feeling the heat of his body through the shirt he wore. He'd promised that he would be able to get her hot with words alone and he'd come through on that one. Her nipples had peaked and she could feel warmth pooling deep inside her body. "Yes."

His eyes went hot. "Yes? That is all I get?"

"Yes, Sir." The panic was still there, the hurt and betrayal, but they were all being drowned out by need. Need to touch him. Need to submit.

Need to give over because she might find a place where she didn't have to be strong. A place where she only had to concentrate on him.

"Then you know what I want." He stood there, his hands on his hips.

Her hands went to the buttons of her shirt, as though they knew to obey that dark voice even before her mind had processed it. She slipped the shirt off and tossed it over the chair before working on the clasp of her bra.

Yes. This was what she needed. This was better than spitting bile and vitriol. This was better than arguing over things that neither one of them could fix.

He stared at her, his eyes catching her own, and she felt drawn into him. She wasn't sure how or why this one man could do this to her, but she couldn't fight it. Didn't even want to. It felt too good to let him take over.

"Yes, that's what I need." His jaw had gone tight as her breasts bounced free. "I need you naked and willing. It doesn't work if you don't want me as much as I want you."

"I don't know much right now. Everything is upside down," she admitted. "The one thing I do know is that I want you."

She wouldn't be able to keep him. At this point, she wasn't sure she would be alive tomorrow. Despite everything he'd said, there would come a point that she would have to make a decision between her comfort and the lives of others.

But he was right. They had the now.

She stripped off her jeans, dragging the undies with them. It was the first day she'd worn them. All the others since that first one, he'd kept her naked or in a robe. They'd found an oddly innocent wonderland in his sparse apartment where they didn't need clothes or the company of others.

She wished she could stay here forever. In this apartment. In this moment. When she was with him she was somehow larger than she was alone.

She dropped to her knees. How had she ever been afraid of this? Been ignorant of what this truly meant? Perhaps for some, submission was the deference of one person's hopes and needs, but for her it offered freedom. Not freedom from—though there was an element of that. Freedom from her own rigidity, from her worries and fears.

But what truly called to her was the freedom that submission offered. This was what Ariel and Kayla had talked about. Freedom to be someone she'd thought she shouldn't be. Freedom to explore parts of herself long buried. Freedom to indulge.

She took a deep breath and listened to her body for once. She let it flow over her, the way the air cooled her skin, the way her hair felt as it brushed her shoulders, how straight her spine could be.

This was freedom to enjoy her body, to love it. No one had ever encouraged her to love her body, but now it seemed an essential part of coming to terms with herself.

"Yes, this is what I want for you." Nick put a hand on her head. "It's about more than sex, *dushka*, though never think that's far from my mind. This is about connection. When we've fought or one of us has had an awful day, we reset it all by finding this place together. Your calm is bringing about my own. Do you know how long I waited for this?"

"Since she died, I would suspect." Even thinking of her…of Desiree…didn't pierce her the way it had before. Des was gone and Hayley was here.

His hand fisted in her hair, forcing her to look up at him. "She never brought me peace."

Hayley understood. "She was too exciting for that."

He shook his head. "I'm older than you and while you might be so much smarter, I am wiser in this. Do not discount the need for peace. What you might call love, I call passion. It's hot and it rages and it doesn't fill a man. This…what we have right here and right now…this fills me. This completes me in a way I've never been complete before. Throw out your notions of wild passion. Give me peace, Hayley. Give me joy."

She couldn't help the tears that pierced her eyes. It had occurred to her that the days they'd spent together had been a way to keep her from learning the truth and being troublesome. What if she was wrong? What if she'd been wrong all along? "I thought you would get bored with me."

His face softened as he stared down at her. "Never. The last few days have been the best of my life. Never forget that. Never forget the gift you have given me. Now let me give you one of my own. Stay here. Don't move. I want you to close your eyes and think about what I'm going to do to you. Let images roll through your brain. You're not to open your eyes again until I tell you to. If I catch you, there will be punishment, but you know you can handle that as well now."

Because the spankings he'd given her were more about pleasure than real discipline. She'd been hesitant at first, but like all the experiences Nick had given her so far, she'd come away from it with a smile on her face.

"Yes, Sir." She closed her eyes and let the darkness sink in as the sound of his shoes against the hardwood thudded through the space.

She tried to concentrate on feeling her body, but the anxiety of the day beat at the gates of her mind.

Deep breath. There wasn't a place for that here. This was the place for her and Nick, and no anxiety or fear was going to ruin it.

What would he do to her? What was he doing in the back of the apartment? She thought he'd gone back to the bedroom, likely to the closet where he kept a leather bag he called his kit. It contained all manner of sexy toys. He'd taken them out one by one and showed her a few nights before. He'd tied her up and forced her to look at each one as he explained what they did and how he would use them on her. He'd shown her nipple clamps with little teeth that would bite into her tender flesh and floggers with soft falls that would thud against her skin. He'd demonstrated the way a violet wand could crackle over her and how good a vibrator could feel when someone else was wielding it.

What would her life be like after Nick? If she had any life at all? Would she ever find another man who cared enough to spend hours exploring her body, showing her how deeply connected to another person she could be?

If she survived this, would it matter if she couldn't be with Nick? She might bring him peace, but was that enough to sustain them?

No one stayed. Not for long. Not unless they needed her for something.

How long would Nick stay? Or allow her to stay? What exactly would she do here in England? Somehow she couldn't see him happily going to faculty parties and enjoying quiet nights in front of the television while she worked on grading papers.

If she could find a job. If she could clear her name.

What had she worked for? Why had she worked so hard to find someplace to settle down only to discover that a house was nothing but a house when she was all alone inside it? She'd reacted to a nomadic lifestyle by buying a bland and colorless place and then walling herself up inside it so no one could touch her.

So no one could think to love her. It had seemed safe at the time, but felt so hollow now.

She would be empty and hollow again, but this time she would realize it. This time she would feel the ache of it.

"You're crying."

She lowered her head, but didn't open her eyes. "I'm sorry."

A warm hand tilted her chin up. "No, this is part of what I want. You need this. You need to cry."

She shook her head. Somehow it was easier to talk to him with her eyes closed. "No. I'm not supposed to cry. It's a weakness."

"And who told you this?"

"My father."

"He's a liar. There is no weakness in your tears." Fingertips brushed against her cheeks, wiping away the evidence. "There's only strength. You weep. You release. You move forward. I want your tears. I want all of you. You will give them to me."

She breathed in. "I'm fine, Nicky. I want what you promised me. I want to feel good."

"I never promised this. I promised to give you what you need. I think you do not realize how much you need this. Lean forward and get on your hands and knees."

She couldn't help it. Her eyes came open. "I'm sorry I cried. I don't like to do it."

His mouth tightened, lips forming a straight line. "Did I ask you what you liked? I did not. I gave you an order that I believe will lead to your comfort and pleasure. If you do not wish to follow orders, say your safe word and be done."

"I don't want to cry."

"Then don't."

"But you're going to make me, aren't you?"

"I'm going to give you a reason to. If you don't, it's going to sit inside you. It's going to eat away at your soul. Get the poison out. Unless you would prefer my way. I can help you to execute your father. I can allow you to watch while I make him sorry he ever lies to you. Or you could weep and let yourself feel the hurt so you can allow yourself to begin to heal. Pain like this is a festering wound. If you attend it, it can heal. If you ignore it, this sore grows until it leaks through your whole body and mind and warps you in ways you can't imagine."

"Like it warped you?"

He nodded slowly. "Yes, like it warps me. I am only now beginning to think I can be someone different. Someone better."

"Would you really kill him for me?"

"Yes. If you ask this of me, I would."

But she could see the shame in his eyes. How much had he done for Desiree? What had she asked of him? How much of his soul had he given away to stay close to her? He would do it because he thought it was all he had to give. Was that why D/s was so important to him? So he would have something besides brute force to give to a woman? She hated the fact that she'd put that look in his eyes. Reaching up, she caught his hand in hers.

"I would never ask that of you, Nicky. Never. I don't want that for you and I don't want it for me, either. I'm sorry I mentioned it." It was that nasty part of her, the part that needed to know he would give her what he'd given Des. Damn, but she didn't like that part of herself.

"You opened your eyes," he said quietly, but a bit of the tension in his shoulders had fled. "I believe I specifically ordered you not to."

She had to remember that he needed this as much as she did. She kept praying that he would care about her, but every time he showed that he did, she retreated to someplace selfish.

He needed her trust. Probably more than he needed her love. But then she knew that words could mean different things to different people. Love could be a difficult word for some. Actions were more important. He was here with her. He could easily have locked her away. This wasn't merely about sex for Nick. She could feel it.

"You did, Sir, and I broke that promise I made to obey you." She let go of his hand and leaned forward, dropping to her hands and knees and allowing her ass to tilt up and into the air. It was easy to make herself physically vulnerable with him. The trust she had in this place was implicit. It was time to give him the emotional trust he needed.

They were both damaged. Her by her childhood and him by so many things he wouldn't talk about. Could she find some small healing for them both?

"I won't fight it, Sir," she promised.

A long sigh came from Nick as he dropped to his knees beside her. It was a satisfied sound. He ran a hand over her back and down to her ass, spreading warmth wherever he touched her. "There is nothing weak about you. Crying won't change that fact. It will make you stronger. Only a weak person can't feel emotion."

She didn't want to feel this emotion, but he seemed to need it. She closed her eyes again and tried to find that place she'd found at the beginning of the session. Peace. Tranquility.

A sharp crack hit her ears and then she felt the pain. It smacked along the fleshy part of her ass.

He slapped her ass again, fire licking through her.

This was not the playful smack from before. This was a full-on, her-ass-was-on-fire spanking and she couldn't help but gasp at the sensation. She gritted her teeth against it and squeezed her eyes to keep them closed. Maybe if she pretended it wasn't happening she could get through it.

Her whole body shifted with the next smack and she bit back a cry.

"Don't pull away from me. Don't try to hide from this. We can get through this, *dushka*. We can do it together."

Another swift smack. Every instinct told her to suck it up, to not let him know how much it hurt. He could fuck himself. She wasn't giving him what he wanted.

"This can't work if you won't give an inch." He smacked her again, this time holding his hand against her flesh after. "Tell me if it hurts."

"Of course it fucking hurts, Nicky." Did he think she was an idiot? Or was he the one who needed advice? "Getting hit hard hurts."

"So does being lied to." Another smack. "So does being used."

She gasped at the pain of the next slap. It jarred through her, but it was more than simple pain. A thousand memories seemed to rush in, memories of her father, memories of Desiree.

Liars. They couldn't hurt her.

"It hurts to lose your home, your life, your name."

He kept talking, but she was busy building a wall. A wall against her father and her fake cousin. All the lies they'd told. All the times they'd used her, and what had any of it meant? Con artists.

The chaos in her head suddenly fell away and she was a child again.

She'd gotten lost in a smoky casino, lost and looking for her father. She'd known how angry he would be that she'd managed to lock herself out of their hotel room. She would have waited by the door, but she was in only her nightgown and a man had tried to get her to come with him. She'd run and gotten caught by a massive security guard who'd called her father. She'd sat in the cold room waiting for his fury only to be wrapped up in his arms, squeezed so tight.

I'm so sorry, baby. Are you all right? Please tell me you're okay.
She'd been so relieved and felt so loved.

A hundred memories flooded through her. Memories of the days he took off to share amusement parks with her. Nights when they watched movies and ate room service fries. How he'd taken care of her that time she'd been so sick.

He'd loved her. He'd worried about her. Why had he abandoned her?

Nick smacked her again and she felt the dam shake. A gasp shot from her mouth and her body shuddered from the pain. Not the physical. Her spine shook as though taking the weight of some horrible trauma.

Heartache and loss. She'd loved them all. Her mother, who had tried her best. Her father, the charming rogue. And Des. Desiree, the first woman outside of her mother to attempt to build her up. She'd loved her, too.

If anything happens, run to him, love. I took him from you once. You won't understand but it was in your best interest at the time. I always meant to give him back to you. I was simply selfish and kept him for a while longer. You see, you're the only two people I ever loved.

Another hard hit and she couldn't stop the sob that welled inside her.

"Yes." Nick's voice came out in a harsh grind. "Yes, love. That's what you need. Give over. It hurts. Let the pain flow through you. Like a river rushing out. Let it leave."

The next smack brought a scream from her mouth, a primal sound of agony that had nothing to do with the physical.

Why? Why had they done this to her? Why was it happening? She couldn't see at all, the world blurred by the emotion pouring through her.

She sobbed, unable to hold out a second longer. Once the dam had broken, there was no holding back the flood. Her body sagged, the will that held it up washed away. Before she could hit the floor, strong arms dragged her up and she found herself held tight against Nick's body.

"Hold on to me, *dushka*. Let me help you through. Cry all you like. I'm here," he whispered into her ear.

He started to talk to her, but it was all in Russian. Soothing words that she didn't understand. It didn't matter because she knew what he was saying. He was offering her comfort, affection. He was offering his love in the only way he knew how.

She clung to him, allowing herself the relief of tears. He held her, rocking her in his arms while she cried.

Slowly, so slowly, she began to come back to the world. She could feel the fabric of his suit against her skin, feel the warmth of his breath. The pain had leached away, but the residue would remain. It didn't hurt as much as it had, and an almost grateful acceptance flowed over her as though the very cessation of heartache was pleasure in and of itself.

But she needed more.

She craved intimacy with him. Sitting in his lap and crying had fed her soul, but her body needed him, too. She was well aware she probably looked like hell, but it didn't matter. All that mattered was showing him how much he was needed. She tilted her head up, bringing her mouth close to his.

"Please." The words came out as a breathy plea. "I need you."

He didn't hesitate. His mouth came down on hers and the hold he had on her body went from comforting to passionate in the space of a breath. As his lips moved over hers, she could feel the hard length of his erection. His back was against the couch, bearing the brunt of their collective weight and leaving his hands free to roam across her naked flesh.

His tongue played with hers, a silken slide. His palms flattened on her skin and proceeded to explore, warming her everywhere he touched. Shoulders, chest, breasts. He smoothed his hands over her, leaving nothing untouched.

She let her knees fall open, needing his touch at her core.

"I need you more than you can know, *dushka*." He licked at her lips before kissing his way to her neck as his hand moved down her belly. "What you gave me...I'll never forget it."

She finally understood what he'd wanted from her. He'd wanted her to open up to him, to give him what she'd never given anyone else. Her pain. He'd offered to take some of it as his own, to lessen the burden. She needed to offer him something of her own, something more than her pain. "Take me, Sir. Take what I have. Take my body and my warmth and affection. Take me."

His tongue traced the shell of her ear. "No. Not this time. I want you to take me. I want you to ride my cock and look in my eyes while you do it. Know that my body is yours. Only yours."

The idea sent a thrill through her, and though she was tired from the crying, her body suddenly leapt back to life. Hers. All hers. It was everything she'd ever wanted and nothing she'd allowed herself to hope for.

His hand fell away, but that was all right because he'd given her permission. Permission to take charge for once, to be in control of their intimacy. It wasn't something he would do often. She knew that instinctively, but today he was giving her back a measure of control because she'd allowed herself to be out of it.

His gift.

She shifted, turning her body so she had access to his. Hayley straddled her big, gorgeous Russian. He was beautifully disheveled, with his normally tamed dark hair all rumpled and curling over his forehead. Like something Michelangelo would have sculpted. His jawline was perfectly straight and those lips were something she'd never been able to forget. She stared at him, trying to remember him as he was in this moment, so long after she could pull the memory from her head and play it over and over again. A movie she wouldn't forget.

"I think you're so beautiful, Nicky." She cupped his face, letting her thumb trace over the curves of those glorious lips.

"No one has ever called me beautiful before, but I'll take it from you." His hands slid from her hips to her waist. "What are you going to do with me?"

She knew what she would eventually do with him, but first she needed to touch him. She worked the buttons of his shirt, pulling it free from his slacks and belt so she could put her hands on him.

His whole body reacted to her touch. She felt a shudder go through him and his pelvis pressed up against her. Nothing could make her feel as sexy as that erection pressed to her ass. Even when her ass was sore and achy. She ran her fingertips over his chest, reveling in every hard muscle she found there.

"I'm going to ride you, but first I get to touch you. I love touching you. I feel so free with you." She hadn't imagined she could ever sit on top of a clothed man and feel so comfortable with her own body.

With herself. It was more than her body that she was suddenly at ease with.

Something deep inside had loosened up. Something had come unsprung, and she felt lighter for it. Braver. Bigger than she'd been before.

"You are free," he replied. "There is nothing you can't do or say with me. No boundaries but the ones we make together. You can explore anything you wish to with me."

She leaned over, running her nose along his neck and breathing in his clean, masculine scent. She dragged her tongue over his skin. Yes, she could explore him. "What were you going to do to me before I cried?"

His hands gripped the cheeks of her ass. "I was going to torture you, of course. I was going to move you up to a larger plug and watch you wiggle and squirm, the same way you will when I finally work my cock into your ass."

For the last few days he'd been playing with her there. It had been odd at first and then merely one more part of their intimacy. He'd told her nothing would be forbidden, that it would all come down to what pleased her or didn't. After the initial shock, she'd found she liked the intimacy that came with giving over to him. The feel of the plug inside her had sent her into a deeply submissive state.

She couldn't help but rub herself against him. Like a cat in heat. That was what he did to her. He took her from the depths of despair to something like peace, and straight on to lust. He was everything. No matter what he did, he made her feel everything to a degree she never had before. "And what if I say no?"

His hands parted the cheeks of her ass, exposing her. "You won't say no. You'll want me there. You'll beg me. You'll say, 'please, Nicky. Please to take me there. Please to leave no part of me untouched with your cock.'"

God, when his accent thickened, so did her lust. There was something about how he lost control of his accent when he was fucking her that heated her blood, as though the words that came out of his mouth in those moments weren't measured or planned. They were for her, straight from his heart. Or his cock. She didn't care in that moment. She wanted them both.

"Yes, I'll say that. I'll give you all the dirty words you want." Because those words, those acts weren't dirty when it came to him.

"I want more than words, *dushka*. I want you taking my cock deep inside. Please. Don't make me wait forever."

She loved the fact that he couldn't handle the same torture he loved to dish out. Unfortunately, she didn't want to wait forever either. She couldn't wait. She moved down, her fingers finding the buckle of his belt and releasing it.

"Fuck, yes," Nick groaned as she pulled back his slacks and boxers and released his cock.

She caught that monster and stroked him, loving the way he pulsed in her hand and the drop of pearly fluid that seeped from the head. It was too tempting to pass up. She leaned over and licked off the pre-come. Salty and clean, she loved his taste.

She also loved the deep shudder that went through him and the way his balls drew up.

"Get the condom. It's to your left."

She licked him again.

"Please, dushka."

Now he was the one begging. She licked him one last time before reaching for the condom. Her body was desperate. She needed him far too much to keep him hanging on. She tore open the package and slid the condom on, her hands shaking with need. She straddled him, dragging her core against his erection until he was poised at her pussy.

She balanced her hands on his broad shoulders and sighed in pure pleasure as she lowered herself down. Her head fell back and she concentrated on the way he felt as she took him deep. His hands were back on her ass. Even the ache in her backside was nothing more than another sensation to be had, another way she was connected to him.

She opened her eyes and looked down at her lover. Hers. So beautiful. He was staring at the place where they were connected, watching her take his cock. A shiver went through her as she felt the tip of his finger rim her asshole.

"Yes." His voice was a low growl. "You're so wet, it's gotten back here, too. This is a taste of what I'll do here."

She hissed at the sensation. Jagged pleasure jarred her from the dreamy state she'd found as Nick's finger played at her asshole. It stopped her in her tracks and forced her to focus again.

"Don't stop," Nick ordered.

That finger circled around and around. With shaky breath, she moved her hips again, gasping when she felt him slip inside the ring of her ass. She couldn't help but clench around him.

"Relax." His free hand guided her hips. Up and down and a little back. Enough that she found herself fucking both his big cock and that intriguing finger. "Let it happen. Let me in. Don't fight it. Think about how deep I am inside you."

So deep. It felt like he was everywhere. She'd never given this to another man and that felt right and good. Only Nick. She found a rhythm that took him deeper. Up and down and back, the jangled sensation of having her ass fucked gave way to pleasure. It was hot and stretched and she needed more. She wanted more than that solitary finger and she knew she would do everything he'd said she would. She would beg him for his cock, present herself in any way that pleased him.

But for now all that mattered was the fact that they were together, that he was so deep inside her, connecting them, making them more than they were when they were apart. There was no feeling of being small, not when she was with him. When she was with him and not questioning every moment of their relationship, she was sure everything would be all right.

She let go and fucked him, riding him rough and hard. He was hers and she treated him that way. Her man, her lover. Hers to please and love and take comfort from.

More. She needed more. She wanted him as deep as he could go.

His hand tightened on her hip and he twisted up, hitting that perfect place deep inside her. That place that made her back bow and a strangled scream of pleasure come from her throat.

The orgasm bloomed from deep inside. It spiraled up and suffused her with heat and energy. Nick's finger slipped out and she suddenly found herself on her back, the carpet cradling her as he fucked her hard. He'd lost all semblance of control and hammered inside her. She watched as his beautiful face contorted and his body stiffened.

He fell on top of her, giving her his weight. She didn't mind. She loved the feeling of being surrounded by him. He kissed her cheek and neck and murmured soft words she couldn't quite understand. It didn't matter. She could feel the affection pouring off of him.

"We should take a shower." He finally switched back to English, but his actions betrayed the words as he sighed and settled against her.

She wrapped her arms around him and wished the moment didn't have to end.

Chapter Fourteen

Nick sat back and stared at the pictures on the wall. It showed two men, the two men he'd nearly died trying to get the names of. They were ghostly images on the wall, seemingly insubstantial, but Nick knew the truth. Those two men were real and they were only two of many. Two of the many criminals who were looking for Hayley.

The conference room was dark, the only illumination the light from the projector. This meeting was being kept to a minimum with only Damon and the Taggarts attending, besides himself and Hayley. Everyone else was working busily, proving that no matter how desperate the situation seemed, life did go on.

Even when it felt like it might come to an end.

"You'll find all the information Ian and I were able to compile on these two in the folder in front of you," Damon was saying. His boss was big on reports but Nick didn't need to read facts and figures to know what these men were capable of.

Anything. They would do anything for the money they were being promised, and they would enjoy the job. They would enjoy hurting someone as sweet and innocent as Hayley. They would enjoy making her cower and scream and twisting her life into something terrible.

A soft hand covered his and he was brought back to the moment.

"As you can see, these are both serious players in the criminal world. They have deep connections," Damon continued.

Hayley leaned against him, her eyes on Damon. Even while she focused on the meeting, she was reaching out to him, giving him comfort, as though she knew how tense he'd gotten.

"O'Malley is known to be the go-to guy when it comes to stealthy assassinations." Damon stared down at the reports he'd handed out at the beginning of the meeting. "I don't know of him personally, but Ezra came through in this case."

Naturally Ezra Fain had to be a part of the discussion, despite the fact that he was two floors down asking Dante the same questions over and over again. Fain had been in the break room when Nick had escorted Hayley from their flat. He'd been standing there like he'd been waiting for another shot at talking to her. He'd given her a soft smile when she'd walked in the room and offered to get her some tea.

Nick had offered to punch him in the face.

"O'Malley works privately, but according to Ezra's Interpol sources, he's also worked for some of the world's larger syndicates," Damon continued. "They go to him when they want the appearance of keeping their hands clean. He's considered smart, but a bit on the reckless side. He likes to gamble and he's known to have a roving eye for the ladies."

"Our Ukrainian contestant is known for being a bit more circumspect." Taggart took over the conversation. "And he's also known for his cruelty. Wanted in five different countries for everything from murder and rape to arson. He enjoys his job. Where O'Malley snipes from a distance, this guy prefers to play with his prey before he kills it. He's an expert in torture."

"And we've also identified three other known criminals who've surfaced here in England in the last few days." Damon sent him a pointed look. "I got that from some friends at MI6. The same ones who tossed you out because you shouldn't have been there in the first place, you impatient bastard. I'm trying to run those men down as well. I've got names and some intelligence. Brody should know where they're staying in a few hours."

Of course he would. Nick's gut twisted. Damon was right—he was an impatient bastard and this time it could cost Hayley. It was good to know he'd nearly been murdered for something Damon had gotten with a phone call. "Are they in the same vein as the other two? Professional? European?"

"I've got a couple of Americans, and one of my sources thinks the call possibly went wide," Damon replied, his voice grave.

"So they're running the gamut. They aren't targeting a specific type of expert to bring her in. We could be looking for anyone." It was his worst-case scenario. He wanted a small list of professionals because they would be predictable. They would know how to play the game and what the rules were.

"It tells me they're desperate and we have to watch our backs because we can't be certain how they'll come after her," Damon concluded. "All we can be certain of is that they will. Walt was able to figure out that they both left their home countries the day after Hayley showed up on our doorstep. They traveled with false passports, but Walt believes he's got them tracked properly down. Whoever this is, they want to act quickly. Which is precisely why we're going to do the same. Both men are here in London, so obviously someone knows where you've gone. I have to believe at least some of them know you're not merely in London, but here at The Garden. The element of surprise is no longer ours to claim."

It was Hayley's turn to tense. She sat upright, no longer touching him at all. "So they'll come here for me."

It was hard to believe that a mere hour ago she'd been purring in his arms. After they'd made love, he'd taken her to the shower and spent forever touching her and washing her. He'd even loved the way she'd fussed over him and forced him to bandage the hell out of the tiny wound on his arm because it wasn't supposed to get wet. Only when she was certain it was waterproof would she let him in the shower.

She'd been happy and relaxed when he was done. He'd been the same until they'd had to leave their nest and come back to the real world. Now he was facing all the issues that came between them once again.

Nick moved his chair closer to hers, leaning in so he could whisper. "Calm down. Listen to what they're saying. These men are professionals. If they thought you were in danger here and now, they would have moved you out."

Her jaw tightened and she kept her eyes on the wall across from them, as though trying to memorize the faces of the men who would come for her. "It's not me I'm worried about."

Yes, he had to deal with her martyr complex. He'd managed to get her to cry earlier and it seemed to have drained some of the sorrow from her, but he wasn't sure how to handle her guilt. If he hadn't made the moves he had earlier, she might have gone to the Taggarts and tried to get moved out of The Garden. The trouble was he wasn't certain she would invite him along. It wouldn't be out of her character to protect him. It was utterly ridiculous, but she would try.

She was different from any other woman he'd ever been involved with and he wasn't sure how to handle her.

He wasn't sure he deserved her at all.

"I've given this some thought." He needed to concentrate on getting the information they required. The only two leads they had were the men on the wall, and that meant breaking at least one of them.

A brow rose over Taggart's left eye. "Have you? Because I heard you were doing something else."

He couldn't help but roll his eyes. Everyone here was a sarcastic teen, especially Taggart, and everyone knew damn well what he'd done with his free hours. "I can think about more than one thing."

Charlotte leaned forward. "Ignore him. It's the only way to stay sane. What did you have in mind?"

"I know I'd like to have a personal chat with them. I think we need to find at least one of them and have a sit-down." He couldn't say what he meant. Not with Hayley in the room. He meant he would like to bring them in and torture them until they gave up the names of whoever was trying to hire them. "We can't take out every man they send to bring her in. We need to know who's behind this. Someone has to go out and bring back a target. How much intel do you think they have on the team?"

Hayley turned back to look at him. "You can't go out there again. They definitely know who you are. They already shot you once."

"That was an entirely different matter." And one he was going to have to weigh when it came time for her to go. If they were still serious about hurting him, she would be the easiest way. She was safe inside this place, but in the outside world he was a danger to her.

"Nick's right. That was about something that happened a long time ago. As to his question, if I've done my job properly they shouldn't know much about any of us," Damon replied. "I don't exactly advertise and there's no website with our biographies. I shudder to think of it. I suppose if someone got their hands on a list of our clients, they could question them and find out a few things."

"If we sent Kay in to seduce O'Malley, how much danger would she be in?" The minute he'd heard the Irishman was a bit reckless and liked the ladies, he'd known which route to take with him. Kay was smart and deadly, and he hadn't met a man yet who could resist her sunny charm. She could lure him in, slip something into his drink, and haul her prey home.

"You can't send Kay in to deal with an assassin," Hayley protested. "She could get hurt. If this guy is as dangerous as you say he is, how can you even think about sending her in?"

Yes, this was what he was worried about. "Because she's far more dangerous than O'Malley. I would do it myself, but I fear I'm not his type."

She still shook her head. "I can't ask her to put herself on the line like that. There has to be another way."

275

He began to protest, but Taggart held a hand up. Excellent. Perhaps Big Tag could explain that this was a ridiculous argument.

"She's right, Nick. We can't send in Kay."

Frustration made his hands fist. "Of course we can. She would be the first one to volunteer."

"Already sent her out after the Ukrainian," Taggart admitted. "She did volunteer for that one. Apparently she's in a shitty mood and really wants a fight. Something about a cliffhanger she wasn't expecting. She takes her novel reading damn seriously. It was either let her go after a nasty assassin or some chick named Zanetti was going to get Miseried. So it's going to have to be Charlie."

Charlotte beamed, excitement plain in her eyes. "Yes. It's been so long since I got to seduce a dumbass into thinking I would actually sleep with him. Can I rough him up a little? Please?"

Taggart smiled his wife's way, his affection clear to everyone. "You always look so sexy when you're working, baby. We're going to take this asshole down and then I'm going to put baby number four in you."

"Yes to the raucous sex, no to the baby," Charlotte shot back, but it was clear her mind was on the job to come. "Once we figure out where O'Malley's drinking tonight, I'll go in and when we go back to my room for some fun, well, that's when he finds out he's gotta deal with Ian. I love the look of fear in a man's eyes. It does something for me."

It seemed like a perfect plan to Nick.

Hayley stood up. "No. No. I don't think you should put yourself in that kind of danger. You have three kids."

Charlotte frowned. "Yes, I do. I don't think they would be good at this though."

"Yeah, they're totally not right for the job," Taggart concurred. "See, when we say he's into women, we mean adult ones. Ones with boobs. Charlie's boobs are spectacular. Very distracting. I should know. I've been on the wrong side of those boobs and they win every time. Now if I wanted to blow something up, my twins are there. I mean it. They can destroy some shit, if you know what I'm talking about."

Charlotte's head shook. "Seth is useless at this point. He pretty much just eats and poops and looks super cute. But I have a feeling one day he's going to be really good. His hand-eye coordination is incredible."

"You'll have to forgive them." Damon sat back, seemingly amused. "They're trying to build a whole team simply from their offspring. I keep telling them they'll have the muscle, but the brains might have to come from somewhere else."

Taggart shot him the finger.

Hayley sniffled, looking around like she couldn't believe how the others were behaving. "Don't joke about this. I'm serious. Charlotte could get hurt."

Charlotte gave Hayley a beatific smile. "I could get hurt driving home from work. I could get hurt falling down. This is my job, sweetie. I'm excited. I'm usually behind a desk now, but I can still take down one Irish dude who almost certainly will have too much to drink. And Ian's my backup."

"Trust me, I'm not going to let anyone hurt my wife, but she should be allowed to have a little fun." Ian sounded softer than usual. "This is what we do and who we are. Sit back and don't worry. We'll get to the bottom of this."

"It's why you came here in the first place," Charlotte pointed out.

"Nah, she came here to get in Nikolai's panties." Taggart smirked in his big old sarcastic asshole way. "Getting out of hot water is a side project, but we can handle it."

His wife sighed. "You have no discretion at all." She turned to Hayley. "Come on, sweetie. Why don't you come upstairs with me and we'll talk some more. I'll tell you some of my Russian mob stories and you'll feel better about letting me have some fun tonight. I think I'll go raid Kay's closet. She's got some killer hooker heels. Rule number one. Always let them think you're for sale."

He wasn't sure he wanted Hayley to learn that particular lesson.

"Perhaps she should stay here with me."

"I was actually hoping we could talk to you alone." There was a gravity to Damon's voice that let him know whatever he was about to say wasn't something Hayley should be part of.

Fuck. What had they found out that would scare her more than she already was? He nodded and stood up. "Go with Charlotte. She'll convince you it's okay. There's nothing to worry about as long as we stick together and play it safe."

The look on her face told him he hadn't exactly inspired confidence. "All right, Nick. Thank you all for the update. I know I'm not exactly a normal client, but I appreciate everything you're doing for me."

Damon nodded her way. "You're the best kind of client. Most of the time we work for corporations. It's hard to give a damn about a corporation. And Penelope believes she's close to figuring out the code. It shouldn't be long before we have some real information about what they think you know."

"That would be good." Hayley sent Nick a half smile. "I'll see you later."

She walked out with Charlotte and he wished that smile had been her normal, natural smile. The one she gave him when they were in bed together. The one that seemed to light up the world. The door closed behind her and he felt the loss. "Does Penny really think she's close?"

"Yes, she does." Damon closed one folder and dragged out another from the pile in front of him. It looked like his boss had been busy in the few hours they'd been apart. "Des was a tricky one, as you all know. Penelope believes the majority of what's on the drive is junk, but there are a few places where she mentions numbers. She thinks this is all about the numbers on the drive. It's her use of directional words in the reports and notes she stored on the drive that tipped her off. She uses south and east in places where they don't particularly fit speech patterns."

He sighed. "Yes, I don't know why I didn't think of this. You're looking for longitude and latitude, but she wouldn't have made it so easy. It's likely all jumbled up. Des loved a puzzle. Get me a list of potential sites and I'll tell you which ones mean something to me."

"Absolutely," Damon replied. "I'll also let you know when we bring in one of our targets."

He felt his eyes narrow. "As well you should."

Taggart's elbows hit the table and he leaned forward. "You will not be running the interview, Nick."

"This is my case."

"No, this is your girl and you're incapable of being reasonable and rational," Taggart pointed out. "I'll let you in on anything at all you want to know concerning the case, but after what happened this afternoon, you're benched."

He wasn't sure what a bench had to do with anything, but then he didn't always understand American idioms. He did understand that they were cutting him out. That was a phrase he knew. "No. This is my case. I know I fucked up this afternoon, but I'm not going to allow myself to be cut out."

Damon's spine straightened, his glare becoming steely. "You will do as you're ordered to do, or have you forgotten that you're an employee here?"

Taggart put a hand out, stopping Damon's dressing down. "Do you think I don't know where you're sitting right now? I do, Nick. I have sat in that same place where I should have been cool and calm about protecting a client. That client was my wife and that means she can never be a client because that woman is half my soul. The much better half. I was a dumbass at the time and I told everyone that I didn't love her so I could handle the case myself. I ended up strangling and damn near killing a witness whose cooperation we needed quite badly. I ended up hurting her because I chose to play the operative when I should have been her man. I should have allowed someone else to run point while I did my job to protect her and love her and be her rock. Don't make the same mistake I made. Let us handle the intelligence portion of this operation and you handle

Hayley. Because intelligence is not your strong point right now."

Well, at least he'd snuck in the words "right now." Nick's stomach threatened to roll. Was he truly this obvious? "I do care for the girl and we do have a physical relationship."

A frustrated huff came from Damon's mouth. "Bloody hell, admit you're in love with her. It goes so much more smoothly if you simply lie down in front of the steamroller and allow it to smash you. You can run all you like, but it will still catch up to you. And while we're handing out advice, tell her you love her. Even if it makes you a bit ill in the beginning. Women take those three words quite seriously and when you dodge them, they get their knickers in a twist. A good, firm 'I love you' will untwist the knickers and get them on the floor where they should be."

"Also, if you tell Charlie I mentioned that I was wrong, I'll murder you. I take a strict and hard line on rewriting history," Taggart explained. "As far as our kids will ever know, Daddy was a saint who welcomed their mother back from the dead with open arms and a loving heart. Though I probably will tell them about the time I strangled that Russian dude. He turned the coolest shade of blue."

There were a few things that they didn't understand. "Like I said, I care about her and I have for a long time. I want what's best for her. Do you honestly believe that the Butcher is going to settle down with a history professor and raise nice children? No. This is not life for me."

"Dude, I don't know if you noticed, but your history professor is totally wanted for murdering a cop," Taggart pointed out.

"This she did not do."

Taggart's shoulders rolled. Even his body seemed sarcastic. "I was merely pointing out that there's an upside to everything. She lost her job and it's going to be a long road to get that back. She's a wanted criminal, so the Butcher's looking better and better to her. That's all I'm saying."

"Nikolai, we all know why you did what you did." Damon was demonstrably more reasonable than his partner. "We know what they did to your sister."

Hayley didn't know. Hayley didn't understand the extent of his revenge or the consequences it had on them in the past and the future. "Still, there will always be threats to me. It's no way for her to live."

"Yes, that's what I wanted to talk to you about," Taggart said, turning serious. "It seems that old man in Moscow has reupped his efforts to take you out, and a few more have crawled out of the woodwork. Do you recognize any of these names?"

Taggart slid a file folder his way. He opened it and realized it contained a list of horrors. Five men he'd hurt in some way and who were vowing revenge even after all these years.

"According to my sources in Russia, all these men have at one point in time either attempted to kill you themselves or put out a hit on you," Taggart continued, his voice as calm as if he was speaking of the weather. "I would suspect once the news gets out that Boris and his men have made another attempt, they'll try harder."

He'd kept a low profile here in England the last few years. He'd worked all over Europe and in the States very quietly. He'd stayed away from any known *Bratva* hangouts until earlier today. Years of work undone in a single reckless moment.

"I know all these names and yes, they will come after me if they can pin down my location." Nick closed the folder, his soul sinking. "They will come for me and for anyone who is close to me."

He hadn't thought about the far-reaching ramifications of his actions. He'd only thought about Hayley. His whole team could be under fire because of him. If those men knew how much his teammates meant to him, they would each be targets in a game of revenge. They had hard enough jobs as it was. They didn't need to dodge Russian assassins. "I should go."

"Where?" Damon asked.

He should go back home and choose his path. He could continue down the road and take out the men who were trying to kill him, leave their wives widows and their children with vengeance in their hearts. They would come for him one day, too, when they were old enough.

Or he could walk into a bar in Moscow, order his favorite vodka, and wait for the inevitable to happen.

When he thought about it, he'd always been on this path. Ever since the day he'd chosen revenge over Hayley. He'd made the choice and now he had to live with it. He'd chosen blood and it was time to pay for it.

"It doesn't matter where." He closed the folder. "All that matters is I've become a burden to this group. I cannot do my job properly and my situation will hamper my fellow operatives' function as well."

"Dude, way to distance." Taggart sat back as though eager to watch the show playing out in front of him. "Told you he would go right for martyrdom. You Euros are so predictable. Too much Shakespeare and crap, I say."

"You think I should stay and allow my team members to take punishment meant for me?" He shook his head and stood up. "No, I will remain as long as it takes to ensure a smooth transition for Hayley, and then I will leave and deal with the consequences of my actions."

"Or you could sit back down and discuss with your team how to handle the situation," Damon replied. "You have options. You're not alone in this, although I know it suits you to think so."

"It doesn't suit me." But he wasn't sure how to think anything else. "And I don't see a proper way out of this that wouldn't cost more than I would be willing to pay."

"Charlotte and I would like to open talks with her cousin," Taggart explained. "We feel these men could be persuaded to drop their pursuit of you if Dusan stepped in. They all have deep ties and Dusan can use those ties to make them see that killing you isn't going to solve anything."

And then he would be indebted to another mobster, this time the head of a syndicate. "No. I won't get back into that world."

"Not even if it means getting out from under it?" Taggart asked. "Not even if it means getting your girl and being safe?"

"But she wouldn't be safe. You play at the edge of this world.

I'm sure that Dusan Denisovitch seems like a tamed tiger because he is the cousin of your wife, but I assure you he has teeth and he will use them. He will want things from me. Favors. Things I no longer do for men like him."

He couldn't go back to that life. It would destroy him as surely as losing Hayley was going to. At least this way he will have kept what little soul he had left.

"It doesn't have to be like that," Damon insisted. "Why don't you sit down and listen? Denisovitch is close to Charlotte. He's oddly attached to his family."

But there were no family ties with him. Dusan would tell Charlotte what she wanted to hear, but one day he would come for his payment from Nick. "I said no. Respect this. I'll talk to Brody. He should handle Hayley from here on out. I trust him and I know he'll protect her with his life."

"You're going to give up?" Damon was staring at him like he'd grown two heads.

"I'm going to do the right thing." They couldn't understand. Neither of the men in front of him had ever fucked up the way he had. They would never face something like this.

"How is what you're doing different from Hayley?" Taggart asked. "You shut her down when she was so worried about Charlie or one of us getting hurt. I suspect it was a conversation you might have had more than once this afternoon. I saw how upset she was earlier. I thought you might have to talk her into staying rather than throwing herself out into the storm to save the others. Yet you're willing to do the same extremely stupid thing."

"It's not the same at all. Hayley is innocent. Hayley hasn't done a damn thing to deserve the pain that's coming her way. I did. I made the choice and I knew what could happen. Here it is and I'm not going to back away from the consequences, certainly not when doing so could end up harming a woman I care about."

"Oh, I think you're planning on hurting her anyway," Damon replied. "Even before all of this went down. Or were you planning on asking her to stay with you?"

He found refuge in logic. "You know she's only been here for a few days. I would think I could have at least a week to decide if I should marry her. You move fast, Damon."

Taggart held up a hand. "I did. I married my Charlie within a few weeks of meeting her. Here's a key though. Keep eyes on her. Sometimes wives are slippery things and they get away."

Damon ignored him. "Do you think I don't know who she is? She's the one woman in years who actually threatened to come between you and Desiree. Des talked about her one night. I never mentioned it because it felt like she was bragging about the fact that she'd managed to get you to walk away from a woman you genuinely loved to be with her. It was Hayley she was talking about, am I right?"

Shame threatened to wash over him. She'd gloated about that? "I was going to run away with her. With Hayley. Des and I had broken things off. She showed up and she had all the information I needed to get the men who'd killed my sister. I made my choice then. My mistake this time around was getting into bed with her again. It was selfish. Yes, I'm going to hurt her again. I can't seem to not hurt her. Tell me you'll take care of her."

"And if I won't?" Damon sat back, awaiting his answer.

He wasn't playing this game. He turned to Taggart. "You owe me. I lost Des on a mission for you. For your brother. If you won't pay Theo's debt, I'll call him."

"Is everything a debt to you, Nikolai?" Taggart sounded more serious than he'd ever heard him. There was a sickening sympathy in the other man's eyes. "You know the world doesn't have to be a ledger sheet where you tally up your life by what you owe and who owes you. It can be something more. Damon is trying to help you."

He hated the way he felt. Stupid and small. Ridiculous. "Will you or will you not honor the debt you owe me?"

"I will take care of Hayley because she deserves taking care of, because I would never leave a woman alone in this situation."

Taggart's words were measured, but there was no way to mistake the disappointment in them.

He had to take that as a win. "Excellent. I'm going to talk to Brody. He can handle her here in England. If you take her back to the States, I would prefer you select your best bodyguard for her. I can send you the money."

Taggart held up a hand. "No. Like you said, I do owe you and I'll make certain she's taken care of. Besides, my best bodyguard is a six-foot, five-inch Cajun."

Yes, Nick had met the man before. He was a smooth-talking ladies' man, but he was excellent at his job. He would also try to do his job from the other side of Hayley's bed if he got the chance. Bastard. Taggart couldn't assign one of the married guards?

What was he doing? Once he walked away he wouldn't have any influence at all on her. He wouldn't be the one to guide her. Hell, she would curse his name because he would be the asshole who'd used her and walked away twice.

He wouldn't be here if she needed help again. He wouldn't see this through to ensure she had a good life because he would be dead, having paid his final debt.

Or would he have? What did he owe Hayley?

"Nikolai, you don't have to decide this today," Damon said softly. "Why don't you take a few days and think this over. Don't be reckless with her. I know you think you're keeping her safe, but she's all right here and everyone on this team wants you to stay. We'll all have your back. That's not something to throw away lightly."

"Talk to Charlie when she gets back from her date." Taggart closed his folder and started to get up. "Ask her what she thinks her cousin is going to want from you and if it's worth the risk to try to get your life back."

"How can you do it? How can you send Charlotte out there like that? Put her in danger? I'm not trying to be insulting. I'm trying to understand how it doesn't eat you up inside."

Taggart grinned, a youthful expression. "Oh, I do it because I

trust that woman with my everything. I do it because she's worth the
risk. I didn't fall in love with her because she was a safe bet. I fell
because she was the single most incredible woman I've ever met.
Hayley's never going to want to work an undercover mission for fun.
She's not that girl, but that's okay. Figure out why you fell for her and
then trust her instincts. If she wants to stay with you, trust that she's
smart enough to know what's best for her."

"But it's not best for her." That was what he couldn't understand.

"Sometimes our wives are far smarter than we are." Damon stood
up as well. "They understand that our life is only possible if we're
together, that what we become when we love someone else is worth
fighting for. It's worth dying for if it comes to it. Talk to Charlotte.
Spend more time with Hayley and when you're ready, talk to her, too.
Make this decision together."

They nodded and walked out and Nick was left devastated and
completely unsure of what to do.

He couldn't stay. He couldn't put her in harm's way. They were
wrong.

Weren't they?

He slumped into his chair, weary beyond measure. How could he
possibly do what Taggart asked him to do? He couldn't be in some
mobster's pocket.

Fuck but he missed Owen. Owen used to be his sounding board.
Well, when he thought to talk about something. Mostly Owen had
been the one to realize when Nick was falling into what he used to
call bloody Russian ennui. Owen had been the one to sit and drink
with him after Des died. They hadn't talked, but Owen hadn't allowed
him to be alone.

Owen hadn't come to him when his mum and sister had been
threatened. Owen hadn't trusted him. That said something.

Hell, he missed Des. She'd been a righteous bitch and yet
somehow she'd also been his best friend for years. Selfish and
manipulative, and sometimes she'd given him the best advice of his
life.

Of course, Des would remind him that Hayley didn't belong in their world. She would point out that Hayley would likely die in their world.

The door came open, unwelcome light spilling in right before a shadow filled the space. Big, broad shoulders nearly touched either side of the doorway and then he heard a familiar brogue.

"Hello, Mr. Markovic. Have you seen Mr. Knight? I have the report he asked about."

As though he'd conjured the man, Owen was here. "They left a few moments ago. You should probably be able to find them upstairs either in Damon's office or in his flat."

The shadow nodded and turned to go. He managed a step away and then turned. "You all right, mate?"

"I'm fine. I'm getting some work in."

"In the dark?" Owen stepped inside, leaving the door half open, but he didn't move to turn on the light.

"I was thinking." He'd been ordered to think. Thinking wasn't working for him. "About the case, of course."

Owen sank down into the chair beside him. "Of course. Darkness is good for thinking. Good for brooding, too. Nothing like a good brood in the dark."

"Was there something you needed?" Why was he still here? Didn't he have a job to do?

"Just seemed to be working for you." If Owen heard the irritation in his tone, he didn't show it. He sighed and sat back. "You're right. It's nice in here. Quiet. The other lads can be a bit loud and they're all antsy since the CIA guy showed up."

So Fain was busy causing trouble everywhere. Good to know. "What's he doing? You have to know Damon won't allow him to abuse you. He's explained to Fain that no drugs will be allowed or weird therapies. Your memories either come back or they don't."

"Nah, Fain's not a bad guy. He's trying to make connections, but the others get anxious about it."

"But not you."

"I know who I was. The rest don't, so it's rather like having a carrot dangled in front of a starving donkey. They try to chase the bloody thing but it's just out of reach and they end up tired and cranky. Punching each other only helps for so long. Those lads need women. I'm going to talk to Robert about bringing in some professionals."

That would be a fun business deduction.

Fuck, he was going to miss this place.

"Have you thought about leaving?" Nick had often wondered. "You do know who you are. You have a home back in Edinburgh. Why not go?"

"An empty home and no memories of it. Damon took me up there to see if anything would jog me memory. I walked around this place and it was a bit surreal. Do you have any idea what it's like to see pictures of yourself and you're smiling and the person in the picture looks like he's the happiest man in the world, and you can't remember a damn thing about it? I know I did something terrible because I was trying to save my mum and sister and I can't remember their names. When they showed me photos, they were strangers to me. No. This is me home now. In that way, I'm like the rest of them. This is the only place I know."

Sometimes Nick wondered what it would be like to forget. To forget all his mistakes, all the bad choices he'd made, the evil deeds he'd done. To be new and fresh. Could he have been with Hayley then? If he'd been the one to take that hit and Owen the one left standing? Would he have been worthy of Hayley then?

"One of the things I saw when Damon took me to the house I used to live in was a picture of us," Owen continued. "We were standing outside and we were dressed in suits. I wonder why we were in those suits?"

Or perhaps Nick would merely find that his sins were still out there lurking and he was utterly blind. Not that this particular picture was a sin of Owen's. It hadn't been. "You took me home with you for Christmas the year Desiree died. Your mother insisted on taking a picture of us before we went to church that morning."

He'd been sad and alone and Owen's family had welcomed him and made what could have been a dreadful time into something survivable.

A long breath sighed from Owen and he took a moment before speaking again. "What was Mum like? I look at her picture and I don't know who she is. I don't know what kind of food she liked or if she was happy. She's nothing but a face in a photo next to mine. I don't recognize that smiling bloke either."

He'd only met Owen's mother a few times, but he'd picked up on her character. "She was a strong woman. Your father left when you were young and she had to raise you and Hannah on her own. She worked in a laundry for years, rough work but she managed to save enough to buy that house. She was proud of it. She made a nice beef stew and cooked a goose every Christmas, from what you told me. She loved you, Owen. That's all you have to know."

Katja had loved him. Should that have been enough? Would she have been pleased with his bloody vengeance and what it cost him? Now, sitting here in the dark with a bleak future ahead, he somehow doubted it. Had he honored his sister or his own rage?

"Do you hate me now, Nick?"

His heart twisted because it was one of the first times Owen had used his Christian name rather than being formal. "No. I don't hate you. I might have done the same thing in your place. I just…"

"What?"

"I have a question, but I'm asking the wrong man."

"Ask anyway. Ariel says I'm still somewhere in here. She says my impulses likely haven't changed. Ask me and I'll try to give you the answer he would have."

This question had been an ache in his soul for months. "I would love to be able to ask you why. Why didn't you come to me? We were partners. I would have helped you in any way I could have."

"And then you would have been in danger, too. Or I was too scared at the thought of losing them to think straight. I guess there are some people in the world we can't risk losing because they hold such dear pieces of our souls. It wasn't that I didn't trust you. I feel it even now. I can look at you and know somehow that we were friends. Aye, I trusted you, but I didn't trust the world not to fall apart if I lost them. It did, you know. It all came crumbling down no matter what I did. I know that deep down too."

Nick was silent for a moment, Owen's words sinking in. "I think I have to leave for the same reasons."

"Because of what happened this afternoon? With the brotherhood?"

So the story was making the rounds even on the lower levels. "Yes. There are some men after me and the only possible way out will put me in a position I promised to never be in. I can't risk Hayley's life. She deserves more."

She deserved a good life.

Did she deserve the chance to decide on what that good life should consist of? Taggart was wrong. Charlotte was built for this world and Hayley wasn't. It was why he'd left with Desiree in the first place. He'd known she was more suited as a partner, a lover. Des had been born to fit into his dangerous world and he'd lost her, too.

"You're going to leave? The company?" Owen asked.

"Yes." It was for the best. He would take a few days, but he was fairly certain that this was the only path he could take. He needed those few days to figure out a way to explain it all to Hayley, but he also needed to put his plans for her in place. He had some money and he would use it to ensure she had something to fall back on when everything was over, and she could go back to her normal, safe life.

"I don't think that's such a good idea," Owen argued. "Why would you leave your family? That's what we are. I figured that out. We're not like other people. We mostly don't have anywhere else to go. Kay's got parents but she's worried MSS would hurt them. Ariel has a mom but she doesn't see her much. Brody's the same way. We're all we've got in the end. Why would you give that up?"

"To protect them. Like you said, some things are too precious to risk."

"But they're always at risk. Every second of every day. If you walk away, how will you be there to protect her? Do you honestly believe you can trust another man to do your job? I think if I could talk to the me I was, I would call him out as a bloody idiot. I would smack him for being so afraid and not trusting his family to take care of him." In the darkness, Owen took a shaky breath. "I think if I had, they might be alive. Or at the very least I might remember them."

Nick stood, the air too thick around him. He needed to breathe. He needed to remind himself that this was the right choice. The only choice.

"I never belonged here in the first place. I came here for Des and she's gone. I should have left then. I've been hanging on to something that isn't truly mine." He moved toward the door, resolute. He stopped when Owen remained sitting. Guilt plagued him. He was leaving Owen, too. "Do you want me to get Ariel?"

In the low light, Owen turned and shook his head. "Nah. Like I said, it's good to have a nice brood every now and then. I think I'll sit for a bit and make up stories in my head. If I pretend hard enough, I can trick myself into thinking they're memories."

Nick turned and walked out before Owen would have the chance to see how emotional he was.

Sometimes memories were all a man had.

* * * *

Hayley stared down at the cup in her hand, the silence around her punishing.

It left her far too alone with her own thoughts and they were turning seriously dark.

Nick had almost been killed earlier today. He could still be killed and all because of some dark force she didn't understand.

It made her depressed, but another emotion was starting to bubble up over the fear and sadness and anxiety.

Now that she'd had time to think about it, to begin to process, she was starting to get pissed.

"Do you mind if I join you?" Ezra Fain stepped into the room, pulling a messenger bag off his shoulder and settling it over the chair across from her.

"Sure." She put her hands around her own mug.

The handsome CIA guy smiled as he strode over to the coffeemaker. "Excellent. I spent my whole day with lunatics. Seriously, whatever that crazy doctor put in her drugs to turn those men into mindless servants turned them a bit loony. Or she picked the crazy ones on purpose. The world may never know since I don't think a single one of them is getting their memories back. No matter what Ariel thinks."

She knew she should go, but she had to wonder about him. Everyone else was so quick to tell her that everything would be all right and she should simply stick close to Nick. That was all she had to do to ensure a positive outcome. Charlotte Taggart had been relentlessly upbeat, but Hayley kind of thought she could use a second opinion.

Should she get one from a man who didn't like Nick?

Maybe it was time to be bolder. She'd played the mouse a lot lately. She forgave herself for it because it was kind of hard to deal with her house blowing up and the world collapsing.

But when she thought about it, she'd actually done a fairly good job. She'd managed to get herself here in one piece. She'd brought along a valuable clue. Sure, she'd done it by accident, but she'd done it.

She'd faced up to her fears and sexual hang-ups. Why had she allowed Charlotte to deflect her every probing question with a breezy "let us handle it and don't worry about it"? And a surprising amount of nudity. The hours she'd spent with Charlotte had been spent making her over. There had been lots of wardrobe changes and playing with her babies while she tried to make sure her perfect boobs were evenly placed.

It had been a pleasant way to spend the afternoon, but she wasn't any closer to real answers about her case or her relationship with Nick. He didn't want to talk about his past, but it was affecting them. No one else would gossip either. The team had closed ranks around Nick and she understood that. This team was Nick's family.

Maybe Ezra Fain would talk.

He sat down in front of her, a mug in his hand and a weary expression on his face. "Are you all right? I hear the gang is going to try a retrieval op. Hopefully they'll have something for you soon."

"Do you honestly believe they'll be able to clear my name?"

"Yes, given time," he said after a moment's hesitation. "They're a good group. They know what they're doing. If Ian Taggart says he'll find a way to clear your name, he will. It could take a bit of time, but he'll do it."

There was something about the way he said it that made her pause. "You think there's a better way."

"I think you need to follow your instincts," he hedged.

She had to laugh at that thought, but it was a bitter sound. "I don't have instincts. I almost had tenure, but no instincts. I think I've proven that by being the world's biggest doormat."

"I wouldn't say that. A woman will do a lot for a man she's attracted to," he replied.

She felt herself flush. He would go right there. "I wasn't talking about Nick. I was talking about Des and my father."

"Ah, well, Desiree and your father were well trained. They were adept at the art of deception and obfuscation. You can't blame yourself for losing that particular game. They were professionals. So is Nikolai. That's why I would advise caution when it comes to him. I know you're involved and it feels like love, but he's got a bad history."

Ah, there it was, that opening she'd been waiting for. "What do you mean by bad history? Why do you hate him? Not that it will change the way I feel about him, but I'm curious."

"I find it refreshing that after everything you've been through, you can still trust a man like him. It gives me hope for the future. All right, all cards on the table, I don't like Nikolai because he spent far too much time on the other side from me. It's like having to welcome a rival football player to your team, one who liked to play dirty and who hurt people you cared about and now you're expected to make nice because you're both on the same side."

"He worked for his country the same way you work for yours." She wasn't buying into that argument. "Everyone thinks they're the hero, Mr. Fain. I assure you no one taught Nick about American freedom and how much more right the American way is while he was growing up. He was educated to think we were the bad guys. When he understood what he was doing, he walked away. I think that says something about him."

"He walked away because his sister was killed and he couldn't handle the fact that he was nothing more than a cog in the machine." Fain's voice had gone a bit dark. "You say we all want to believe we're the hero, but I don't think you understand what that word means to me. It's certainly not some James Bond level of satisfaction. I work in the shadows and I understand that if I screw up, I'll be on my own. I understand that if I do my job perfectly, there will be a desk job at the end and a piece of crap government pension, and no one will ever know my real name. If I do my job well, but not perfectly, I'll be a star carved into the wall at Langley that no one really thinks about because all those stars are is a reminder of what happens the instant you fuck up. Nick wanted to be special. His sister was an operative and he expected the world to stop when she died. He didn't like the operation they'd been working and expected everything to change because he said so. He wasn't cut out for this work."

He seemed a little cold. "Wow, you must never have lost anyone because it does feel like the world should stop."

"Oh, you have no idea what I've lost in my lifetime. I've mourned and wept and felt like I lost pieces of my soul. Do you know what I never once did? I never once started a mob war. He and Desiree slashed their way through an entire syndicate to get revenge for his Katja. That's why they call him the Butcher."

A chill went through her, but deep down she'd always known what Nick was capable of. He was a man who would love deeply, and he would go dark if that love was taken from him. Like Des had been. She'd accepted that about him long ago. "She was his sister."

"And I lost my brother. He died serving our country. I didn't start a land war to avenge him. I honored him in ways most people can't understand." Fain placed the coffee mug down slowly, as though he needed the moment to gain control of himself. "I believe in justice, not revenge. I will do a lot to get that justice, but I certainly wouldn't start a war that could have blown up the streets of Moscow."

"Could have?"

"All it would have taken was one mistake, killing the wrong person, and you get full-on mob warfare," Fain continued. "If there had been any question about who was doing the killing, if the syndicate thought for a single second it was another syndicate, you get dead bodies everywhere. You get kids in the streets getting cut down because they're in the wrong place at the wrong time."

"But that didn't happen. So that means Nick let them know he was the one involved." And that had gotten him shot today. A minor injury, but she knew how close he'd come. If he'd moved at the wrong time, it would have been his chest that bullet hit.

"He announced he was going to do it. The fucker walked into a bar in Moscow and tacked up a list of the men he was going to kill and took credit before it happened."

Yes, that sounded like her Nicky. "So he knew what he was doing and went in and performed a surgical strike, to use a military term."

"And surgical strikes sometimes go wrong," Fain replied. "Sometimes, despite our best efforts, we still do damage we don't mean to do."

"That's life. We try our best to mitigate the damages but we make mistakes and people get hurt." She stopped, a thought racing through her head. Dates were important. Events and their outcomes were tantamount to explaining history. It was what she did every day.

She broke down the whys and hows of history, placing them in their proper settings—the dates and places where events happened.

Had she examined her own history? She'd known Nick's sister had died, but not the hows and whys. She knew Nick had met Des sometime after.

"When did this happen? When did he go after the men who killed his sister?"

Fain frowned for a moment. "It was roughly five years ago. I remember it because I was working in Eastern Europe at the time. It was roughly mid-summer."

Tears sparked behind her eyes, but she took a long, slow breath to banish them. She'd sought the mysteries of history all her life but never contemplated her own. She'd accepted that Des had crooked her perfectly manicured finger and Nick had gone panting after her. She'd accepted the fact that she was his second choice and when his first had walked back in, she'd lost.

What if it hadn't been about Desiree but what she'd offered him? When they'd gone to sleep, cuddled up together, he'd been happy. She'd felt it in her bones. There had been no reluctance in him that night, not until he'd walked back in from seeing Desiree.

Had she been so deep into her own misery that she hadn't seen what was truly happening? Had he thought she wouldn't want him if he went after the men who killed his sister? Or had he been too worried she would get caught in the crossfire.

Something slid into place, some piece of herself that had been wedged and jangled. It had been an ache she'd had for so long it had become a part of her.

She'd been right to go to him that night. She'd been right to offer him her love. He'd been wrong to turn her down, to not give her the option of choosing her own path. He'd seen her as soft, sweet Hayley who couldn't handle the world around her, but she wasn't that person.

She was smart and capable and it was past time for her to start taking back her life. It began with asking the right questions and using her damn brain.

"Are you all right?" Fain asked.

Ezra Fain had an agenda. She needed to figure out if she could use his agenda to further her own. Nick and his colleagues had their own way of looking at this case, but she thought she should come at it from a different angle.

"I'm just realizing that things are not always as they seem," she said, not willing to go into her romantic life with Fain. "You're wrong about Nick, but it's not my job to change your mind. You said something earlier and it's only now resonating with me. I do this thing where I get depressed and unfocused. I've done it since I was a kid and it's time to stop. So many pieces of the puzzle are there, but I've been far too wrapped up in myself to take a look at them. You said Desiree and my father had been trained in deception."

His head shook. "No, I'm certain I said Desiree had been. MI6 has an excellent training program."

But that wasn't what he'd said. "No, you mentioned my father."

"Well, he was a poker player. There's an enormous amount of deception in that particular game."

And there was some going on right now. Ezra Fain had a tell. At least she thought he did. One of the things her father had taught her was how almost everyone had mannerisms they used when they bluffed or lied. Whether it was in the eyes or in the minute tics of the body, there was almost always something in normal people that would tip off the observant to a lie. A sociopath was another story, but Fain wasn't devoid of humanity. When he'd replied both times to her questions, his hand had tightened around his mug. Why hadn't she seen it before? Because she'd been worried about whether or not Nick could love her. Silly girl.

"I don't think that's what you meant."

His face went a careful blank, and he removed his hand from the mug as though sensing he was giving something away. "All right, what did I mean?"

Ah, the deflective question. "I suppose I can't presume to know what's in your head, Mr. Fain."

297

"I prefer Ezra."

If that made him more comfortable. It occurred to her suddenly that she was playing a game and Ezra Fain was a master. Life was poker, her father had taught her. It was all about placing careful bets, for the most part, and following your gut when the time came. The master player never played his or her hand. The master played the other players. Her father had kept journals on the players he regularly found himself up against, detailing the hands they'd played and the observations he'd made.

"All right, Ezra. What would you do if you were in my shoes? Would you sit here and wait for your boyfriend to solve the problem for you?"

He relaxed a bit, as though happy she'd switched topics. "I would be unable to. I'm more of a man of action. I would take a look at everything I know and try to complete the puzzle. I think they're taking the wrong tactic. They're acting as though you're off the board, as if you're incidental to the puzzle at hand."

"Like the messenger instead of a player. I happened to be the person Desiree sent her crap to."

"Yes. The question is why. Why, of all the people she knows in this world, would she send it to you? Why not Nikolai?"

"I can answer that one. She knew if she sent it here, whoever she's trying to hide it from would find out. Nicky's the obvious choice and so are her parents. So why…" The answer hit her and she closed her eyes because she'd been so stupid not to see it. "My father was still alive when Des set this up. Well, he hadn't faked his death at that point. She couldn't have known he would. She arranged to have it sent to me because I'm the easiest way to get to him. Dad lived out of his suitcase. He had an apartment in Vegas for a while, but she couldn't be certain he would keep it. I was her best bet for him to get it."

"Yes." His lips tugged up and even Hayley had to admit the man was gorgeous when he smiled. "I believe you're right. I believe you were the conduit to your father. Take it further. Question it all and you'll find the answer to part of this puzzle."

"I already know one of the answers. They're looking in the wrong place." Her mind was whirling. "They shouldn't be looking for some random assassin who can't know much. They should be looking for my father. He knows everything. What if he didn't blow up my house to hurt me? What if he did it to protect me?"

"That's an intriguing question, isn't it?"

"What do you know that you're not telling me? It wasn't coincidence that you showed up the night after I came here."

"They aren't giving you enough credit," Fain said softly. "Underestimating someone isn't usually Taggart's flaw. I chalk it up to all those kids. They've made him soft. You're right. I didn't really come here because I had a lead on Dante's past, though it is certainly something I'm working on."

"You came here to talk to me."

"I came here to try to convince you to leave with me and find your father. I've been looking for him and I've got a line on where he might be."

"Where?"

His face went blank again. "I can't tell you that unless you agree to come with me. Even then, I won't tell you until we're on the plane. I know your first impulse is going to be to run to Nick and the rest and try to get them to force it out of me, but I won't break and all you'll do is ruin a decent working relationship."

There was only one reason why he wouldn't tell her, and so much of her life fell into place. "Did my father work for the CIA?"

It explained why he'd known and worked with Desiree Brooks, why they would have lied about their relationship. As a poker player, no one would question him moving around the world. He could easily move from Vegas to London to Macau and Hong Kong. Anywhere there was a game. And those games tended to take place in expensive hotels and cities where power players stayed.

"I don't know what you're talking about." His eyes were steady on hers. "And I won't give anything away. I know you caught me lying about what I'd said earlier. Maybe I'm getting soft, too, but I won't bend on this."

Because he considered it a matter of national security and Ezra Fain believed in his job.

"You want me to leave here and go looking for my father?"

Fain leaned in, his face relaxed again as that smile of his turned seductive. Though he was smart enough to know not all seductions were about sex. No, he tempted her with something else entirely. "That's exactly what I want you to do. We can sneak away and every one of those criminals they sent after you will think you're still here. Or we can walk out in full view and I'll still lose those bastards. It's up to you, but once we're out in the field you'll be my partner. I'll need your intelligence and your knowledge of your father and Desiree to finish this thing. I think in this case two people are truly better than a group. We can work smarter and faster and you'll draw him out. If you stay here, you're the princess in the tower. You'll sit here and watch as they do the work. Isn't it time you took your fate into your own hands?"

For a moment it was like she was sitting with a super-charming Mephistopheles. He was right. The impulse was there to take all this into her own hands. But then she wouldn't truly be doing that, would she? She would be exchanging one bodyguard for a perhaps less restrictive one.

And one she wasn't in love with.

"I have to talk to Nick."

His head shook sharply. "I told you I can't work with McKay-Taggart on this case. If they come to me for answers, I'm going to disappoint them. I don't want to have to tell them you're lying, but I have to protect this relationship. And I definitely have to protect my country and my agency."

She wasn't offended at all. She kind of found him fascinating. He was the kind of man she would love to write about, the ones who had a hand in history but never took credit. "I'm not going to mention this meeting, though I am certainly going to talk to Nick about finding my father. I think you're right. That explosion happened during my office hours, and those are plainly stated on the website and in every syllabi I've ever handed to a student. It would take a stupid man to not bother to check if I would be home. My father wasn't a stupid man. He didn't intend to kill me, but he intended to make someone think that I'd lost everything."

"Unfortunately, whoever is after you decided you were more valuable than whatever happened to be in your house," Fain pointed out as he stood and stretched. He picked up his bag again. "Sure I can't convince you to come with me?"

"I love Nick. This is my last chance with him and I have to try." There was one thing she was confused about. "Why not take me? Or blackmail me? You could have told me the people who are after me will come here and hurt Nick or the rest of the group. Or the kids. I would have gone with you."

Fain's eyes widened. "If I were in trouble and needed a place to hide out, I would come here. This is one of the safest places I know, and unless they want to send a missile into the building, they aren't getting in. I don't like to lie if I don't have to. You'll be safe here and Taggart isn't going to allow his wife and children to get caught in the crossfire. They'll find another way to get to you eventually. It will probably be your father, and that's not blackmail. That's the truth. I'm heading out in the morning and I'm going to look for him. Besides, a blackmailed partner tends to be one I can't trust. I only wanted you to come along if you believed in the mission. You have another way, and I'll honor that. If I see your father, I'll tell him hello for you."

"Tell him I'm going to kick his ass." She would take lessons and everything.

He winked her way, turned and started to walk out. He stopped at the door. "Oh. And when you talk to Nikolai, you might ask him what he's doing. I heard him arranging for Brody to watch after you while he's gone. I wasn't aware he was going anywhere. It looks like he might have a lead. I don't know how the two of you work, but I wouldn't let him cut me out of my own case. Unless you know what he's doing."

Now it was time for a poker face of her own, though she could feel her body heating. Nick was going somewhere? He'd said he would stay with her, protect her. She wasn't going to freak out, though, and she wasn't going to present less than a united front. "Sure. I'm okay with it. He'll only be gone for a day or two. I don't need a guard if I'm in here anyway. I guess he's being overprotective."

Ezra stared at her in a way that let her know she wasn't fooling him. "Good to know. If you ever need me, Big Tag knows how to get in touch. Good luck."

She watched as what might be her best bet walked out of the room. It didn't matter. She'd gone all in with Nick. It looked like it was time to show her cards and see who had the winning hand.

Chapter Fifteen

Nick opened the door to his flat and wondered if he was doing the right thing. Brody had called him a foolish bastard, but then admitted he was one himself and that he understood. Brody was the only one on his side, the only one who got that he needed to protect Hayley above all other considerations, even his wants and needs.

God, he was going to miss her.

He closed the door behind him, grateful for the darkness of the room. He took a long breath. He was going to miss her so damn much. Not that he would likely live long. Once he got to Moscow, he didn't give himself more than a few weeks, but at least then it would be over and she would be safe. He would pay for his sins and she would have a long, full life ahead of her.

He had another couple of days with her. His flight to Moscow was scheduled for the day after tomorrow. He would put off telling her anything until the moment he had to because he was a selfish bastard who wanted every single minute with her he could have.

The light switched on and he realized he wasn't alone. Hayley was standing in the kitchen.

Even in jeans and a T-shirt, her hair pulled back in a ponytail, she took his breath away. "Hello, *dushka*. How was your day with

Charlotte?"

There. His voice was calm and even. He didn't sound like a man who was about to rip his soul out of his body and shove it into Purgatory. He could do this. One last mission and it was all for her.

"It was fun. She's an amazing woman. I like how her husband values her opinion and trusts in her abilities. They make a good team. I suspect they're out there right now stalking their prey like a lion and his lioness," she said, her lips curling into a smile.

"That's a rather apt analogy." He didn't want to talk about the Taggarts. He wanted to spend every moment they had left with her in his arms. "Come here. Greet me properly."

She started to move around the bar but stopped, her shoulders squaring as she turned to him again. "I think we should talk before we play."

He didn't want to talk. He undid his necktie with a twist of his hand. "You can talk to me naked."

He was sure she wanted an update on the case, but that would merely frustrate her.

"Are you leaving me here?"

He stilled. "What do you mean?"

"I mean I heard a rumor that you talked to Brody about guarding me while you're gone."

Bloody fucking rumor mill. He wasn't sure who she'd heard this rumor from, but he would have a long talk with whoever it was. "It's nothing for you to worry about."

"I want to go with you. If it's about my case, I think I should go along. I need to be more involved. I have a few theories that we haven't considered yet."

He needed to put a stop to this line of thinking and quickly. He crossed the distance between them and put his hands on her shoulders. "You have to know I can't allow you to step foot outside this building until everything is cleared up."

Her jaw tightened, forming a stubborn line. "That could take months. I can't stop living my life for months, Nick."

"You can if it means having a life at all at the end of this. That's all that matters to me. That you survive this and have a good life."

"That's what I'm trying to do. Look, I know up until now I've been terrified out of my mind, but it's time to start thinking. Like I said, I have a few theories I want to talk over with you, but first I want to know where you're going and why I can't go with you. Don't give me the 'I'll be murdered the second I leave the grounds' thing. I've thought that through, too. We take private transportation everywhere we can. Once I'm out of London, it will be much harder to track me. I talked to the boys downstairs and they said getting me good ID isn't going to be a problem. Charlotte thinks she can alter my appearance by cutting my hair and using wigs and makeup and colored contacts. It's all very *Mission: Impossible*. I'm kind of excited by it. What do you say, baby? Want to play spy with me?"

The grin on her face was the absolute sexiest thing he'd ever seen in his life. There was a spark in her eyes he hadn't seen since that night before he'd left her behind. Had he killed that spark with his rejection? He rather thought not. It had been lying dormant while she worked to build something and was coming out now because she was getting her confidence back, feeling her power.

He was going to have to kill that spark. He had to if he wanted to save her.

Nick pulled away. "No, you won't be playing the spy. You're going to stay here and be safe while my team fixes the problem for you. You will not be allowed to leave."

"You can't keep me prisoner here, Nick. I want to go with you. I think I'm the key to all of this."

He shook his head. "I know you wish to believe that but this is nothing more than some scheme Desiree cooked up. You'll find there's money behind it. You were nothing but her pawn and if you think for a second that you can beat her at her own game, you're wrong. Even dead, she's still a powerful player."

She stared at him for a moment and he could see her eyes shining in the low light, but she didn't shed a tear. "She's still the queen, isn't she?"

"If we're referencing chess, then yes. She is and the only way for you to win is to not play at all." Weariness stole over him. How many years had he played these games? He was bad at them. It was hard to believe that once he'd been good, once he'd been excited by them because he'd believed in the cause.

"Tell me why you left me that night."

All thoughts of spending a final few days with her fled. If she was taking them down this road, then it was going to be the end. He couldn't give her false hope. "I told you. I wasn't the man for you then. I was with Des and it was better that way."

"Was it because of what happened to your sister?"

Who the hell had she been talking to? "That's none of your business, Hayley. If you don't want to play tonight, I think I'll go down to the club for a drink."

Her hands moved to her hips as she squared off with him. "I know why you left that night. You went to Russia and you took out the men who hurt your sister."

Anger started to bubble up. "Who killed my sister."

"Yes." She softened, moving toward him again. "You avenged her death. Did you think I wouldn't understand that? Did you think I wouldn't wait for you? I would have. I would have gone with you. I know I couldn't have helped you like Desiree did, but I could have been there for you."

The idea turned his stomach. She was being so naïve. "Would you have washed the blood out of my clothes after I slit a throat?"

"Yes."

"Would you have been there to help me toss bodies into their shallow graves?"

"If you needed me to, then yes."

He shook his head. "You have no idea what my life was like then. It was blood and pain and death and yes, there was some wicked joy in all of it. I enjoyed my work. It was no place for a woman like you."

"A woman like me? I'm not sure what you mean by that."

"It doesn't matter in the end." The rage he'd felt fled like air from a popped balloon. "All that matters is that you're safe."

"Safe isn't a life, Nick. You say that word like it's the most important thing in the world, but it's not. It's more important that I live a life, and I can see now that I haven't been. I thought I could find myself by burying my nose in a bunch of books, but I lost more than I ever found. I buried myself away because you didn't love me. How stupid was that? We have a second chance, Nicky, and I want to take it, but if you say no this time, I won't bury my head in work again. I won't stop living because you can't love me. I'll be brave this time. I'll move on."

He couldn't quite meet her eyes. "Good. I want you to. You need to find the right man."

"Because you're not the right man or because I'm not the right woman for you?"

It hurt but he needed to do it. It was all for her, so she could be happy. "I had the right woman for me. She died. Everyone else is a pale imitation."

Her skin blanched, but she remained steady. "You're lying."

He forced himself to look straight at her. "I'm not. Do you honestly believe you can compare to Desiree? She was stunning and sexy and there wasn't a thing she couldn't do to a man. You're a naïve girl. I took you that night because Desiree and I had fought. She came to me and brought me a gift. That was our way."

"She brought you the information about the men who killed your sister."

He was worried she saw things too clearly. He needed to give her something else to think about. "Yes, and then she helped me kill them. Do you know what we did after we would take care of one of those scum bags?"

"I can only imagine."

"I doubt you have the imagination for the sex we had after killing. Sometimes we didn't even wash off the blood before we would go at it." He clutched the chair in front of him, needing something between them. It was all a lie. For months afterward, he hadn't touched Desiree. They'd worked together and formed their odd friendship. It was only after he'd realized he could never have Hayley again that he started sleeping with Des. No, after his jobs in Moscow, he would throw up or drink until he could pass out. "That's the kind of man you've welcomed into your bed, *dushka*."

"I'm going to give you one more chance. If you're so afraid of losing me that you need me to stay here, I'll do it. It goes against my every instinct, but I'll do it as long as you stay with me. We can monitor the investigation from here, but I want to be fully in the loop." She said the words in a shaky tone, like she was trying so desperately to hang on to her composure.

He couldn't let her hang on to him. "I'm leaving the team. I'm also leaving London. I will not be taking you with me. Brody is going to be your guard from now on. You'll obey him and stay here until Damon decides it's all right for you to leave."

"Leaving London?"

He nodded. "Yes, I'm going home. I'm tired of this life. I only came here for Desiree and now she's gone."

She faced him, her hands in frustrated fists at her sides. "Stop it. Stop saying her name like she can shield you from me. I'm not an idiot, Nikolai. I know what this is about. I get it. You got scared today and you think if you stay with me I'll get caught up in your damage, but I'm okay with that. I'm willing to take that chance because I love you. I've always loved you."

The words hit him like bullets. It was everything he'd ever wanted and nothing he could have. He backed up. "No. I'm not doing this with you. I don't love you. I can't. I'm sorry if I made you feel like I could, but it was nothing more than sex. I believe I explained to you that this wouldn't last."

"You also told me I brought you peace."

The only truth he'd given her. Now it would be one more lie. "Peace is boring. I need more. I need excitement. I need passion, and I don't feel that for you."

"Only Des."

"Yes."

She sighed and now the tears fell. Only a few before she wiped them away. "Because Des was the love of your life."

"Yes."

"Your eyes flare when you lie," she said quietly. "They always have. I even remember you doing it that night, but I didn't take it for the tell it is. Don't play poker, Nicky. You're bad at it."

"I'm not lying." But even as he said the words he realized he'd done exactly what she'd said. "It doesn't matter, Hayley. I'm leaving and it's for your own good."

"This is not about my good. This is about your fear. Don't do this to us. Couples face things together. They take the risk. Anything could happen. I get that it's dangerous out there for me right now, but it doesn't help to break us up."

It wouldn't do any good to point out to her that she was in more danger with him than she was without him.

"I'm leaving, Hayley. It's already set and nothing you do or say is going to change my mind. We aren't a couple and we never were."

"Then what was all that bullshit about being your sub? About having a connection between us?"

"A lie to get between your legs again," he replied.

She rolled her eyes, an expression of pure disgust. "Try again, because I still don't believe you. The one thing I do believe is that Desiree did get the best of you. She got the Nick who was bold and brave. She got the Nick who walked into a Moscow bar and posted a sign telling everyone that he was coming after them so no one was mistakenly accused. That's the Nicky I fell in love with. This one in front of me is a shell of his former self. That Nicky could have been my man."

It was his cue to leave, but not without making a few things plain. "I'll stay downstairs tonight. In the morning, I'll pick up what I need. Feel free to stay here. I won't need the flat. This is your home until the case is solved. Brody will be by in the morning. Listen to him."

He reached the door and opened it, understanding this would be the last time he would see her. He turned and took her in again, wanting to memorize every inch of her. She was standing in the middle of his living room, her arms crossed over her chest and a frown on her face, and she was still the most stunning woman he'd ever seen.

"Do you honestly believe you can dump me like this and I'll behave like a good girl? If you think that for an instant, then I've given a poor account of myself."

Something about the way she was standing, the glint in her eyes, made him stop. Yeah, she wanted to challenge him? He could go a few rounds. He could prove to her who her Master was.

He didn't have that right anymore.

"I think you're going to do as you're told."

"And how are you going to stop me? You'll be somewhere in Russia."

"I have my ways." He had Brody, but what exactly could Brody do if she decided to walk out? They couldn't keep her tied up. Could they? He would do it for her own good, but what would Damon think? He might still have more work to do. "You will not be allowed to leave. I'll come back in the morning when you're more rational."

"Oh, I'm crazy now? You know, I get that you're scared, but you're doing a damn fine job of pissing me off. You want to talk? You want to show me the error of my ways? Stay here. Fight with me. Don't run off like a fucking coward."

"Don't you curse at me." She was pushing his every button and he found himself stalking back into the room so he could tower over her. Anger rushed through him. Anger at her for challenging him, anger at the fucking world for not being what he needed it to be. Anger at himself for putting them both in this position where they couldn't be together. It cracked through him, looking for a vent.

He could think of a good one. He could get her on her back, get his mouth on her, and then she wouldn't be spouting curses at him.

"Then stop being a coward and sit your ass down and talk to me," she continued. "Be the man I know you can be. Give me what you gave her—the bold lover, the one who doesn't stop, who never gives up."

It made him still in his tracks. That bold Nick, the one who hadn't stopped…he was also the one who lost the women he cared about. He was the one who'd lost his sister and who hadn't protected Des.

He couldn't do this with her. Not now. "Stay here. Don't you dare leave this room. Like I said, I'll be back in the morning. We'll talk more then. You'll see you're being very foolish. You're acting like a child and it's past time for you to grow up. Think about that tonight and hopefully you'll see I'm right."

Even when he heard her call his name, he didn't turn this time. He closed the door behind him and then damn near ran to the lift.

What the hell had happened? She'd said she loved him, had always loved him. It made his heart swell and then break because he couldn't give her what she deserved. He couldn't be the Nicky he'd been because his past was right here, threatening them all.

Unless he took up Taggart on his offer.

He needed a drink. He needed to think. It went against everything inside of him to be beholden to a gangster.

But would that be worse than never seeing Hayley again? Never holding her again?

Was he going to leave her to some nameless, faceless man? Who knew what that man might do to her? Maybe he would love her or maybe he would hurt her, cheat on her, and make her life an unmitigated hell.

The lift door opened and Brody was standing there. His eyes widened as he took in Nick.

"Brother, you look like you could use a drink."

"I think I might be making a terrible mistake." He could feel it deep in his gut.

Brody held the lift door open for him. "Come on then. We'll talk

311

it out over a pint or five. If you love Hayley, maybe you should think about staying."

"What happened to you telling me I was doing the right thing?"

"That was before I saw that look on your face, mate."

Nick stepped into the lift, his whole soul dragging. No matter what happened, he wouldn't be the same again.

* * * *

Hayley finished stuffing the last of her measly possessions in the backpack she'd found at the back of Nick's closet. Not that it had been hard to find. The man owned next to nothing. His whole flat was spartan, as though he couldn't stand to have anything extra, nothing more than what was required to survive.

Nick was a man who cut loose all the extra weight, and she'd been deemed unnecessary.

She stood up and took a deep breath. No. That wasn't what he was doing. That was her insecurity talking and she was done listening. Nick was being a martyr and she hadn't been able to talk him out of it. She had two choices in front of her. She could weep and moan and sit back, waiting for someone else to save her.

Or she could do what she'd told him she would do. She could move on and find something good for herself, starting with finding her father and getting to the bottom of the mess he'd undoubtedly had a hand in creating.

She'd made her play, put all her cards out on the table, and she'd lost. She'd meant what she'd said. Maybe she'd been harsh, but it was true. She wanted the Nick who would fight for her, who would hold her hand until the end and never let go because wherever she went, that was where he would be. She would have been that kind of a partner to him, but he didn't want that. He wanted a good girl who stayed in her place and didn't cause him trouble.

She needed to cause a whole lot of trouble.

But that meant getting the hell out of England, and there was only one way that was happening.

She glanced at herself in the mirror, the image stopping her in her tracks.

Who was she? She'd considered herself a bit mousy all her life, but when she looked back with a critical eye, she saw something else. She'd been dragged across the globe, never staying in one place for too long. It had made it difficult for her to form strong friendships, but it had also made her resilient. How many other college kids could have moved to a city where they hadn't known anyone and made it all work with very little help? Her mother had been gone at that point and her father only showed up from time to time. After the debacle of her twentieth year and the complete end of her relationship with Des and Nick, she'd been on her own.

And she'd made it work.

She'd built a home and a life for herself. She could do it again, but this time she wouldn't hide away, wouldn't lose herself completely in her work. This time she would understand that Nick had closed a door and he wouldn't reopen it. This time she would move on because he'd shown her that she needed love and affection and she was worthy of it.

She touched the heart at her throat. Walt had given her back the red and gold Venetian glass heart after putting it back together. He had what he needed, he'd told her. At the time, she'd tossed the damn thing on the dresser, promising herself she'd throw it out when she was ready. And yet she'd found herself putting it on before she'd packed.

That heart was a piece of her, acknowledgment of her history. She wasn't broken by the past. She was made strong by it. Sometimes moving forward was the decision a person could make.

The woman in the mirror was deserving of more than she'd given herself. It was time to stop doubting and start living.

If she survived the next few days.

God, she was going to miss him. It was right there, the impulse to go downstairs, find him and beg him to change his mind.

Hayley picked up the backpack. She had to ignore that impulse because she was out of time. She was certain no one would hold her prisoner here, but she could also see all the ways they could force her to stay of her own free will. Namely they could smile, open the door, and wish her well. Oh, she was fairly certain that if she started out the door she would find someone dragging her back in, so it was best to do things her own way.

As Ezra had said, a reluctant partner wasn't one she could trust.

Could she trust Fain? She was betting a whole lot that she could.

She settled the backpack on her shoulder and made her way to the door.

Damn it. She pulled the backpack off her shoulders. How would she explain it if someone caught her walking around the halls? It would be easy to say she was heading down to the kitchen to grab a sandwich or something, but these weren't unobservant people. These were the best of the best and they would wonder why she needed a backpack to get a sandwich.

Fuck a duck, she was going to have to do what she'd done before. She was going to start again with absolutely nothing but the clothes on her back.

She stashed the backpack with a sigh before going back to the door, opening it and heading out to the hallway. She could hear the heavy thud of music drifting up from down below. She took the risk, edging to the railing and glancing down. From this high, mostly she could see green plants and the ghostly illumination of lights from below, but she did catch a glimpse of Brody Carter striding down a path, two bottles in his hand.

At least Nick had something to do tonight.

Would he miss her? Or would he be so angry that she'd defied him, he went back home without a backward glance? Either way it was the last time she would see him.

God, she hoped he found someone who could make him happy, someone he could love enough to take the risk on.

She turned and found the stairs, jogging down, careful to listen for the sounds of anyone who might be hanging around at this time of night. Charlotte and Ian were on their mission. The rest were likely playing in the dungeon. She prayed Ezra Fain had taken the night off, prepping for his early morning flight.

She eased into the hallway, breezing past the cameras. She had complete run of the building and she'd been down on this floor several times. No one had come running to stop her.

The key, her father had taught her all those years ago, was to act like you belonged. *People see what they want to see, what they think is normal. Give that to them and most won't look past the surface.*

At the time she'd thought he was teaching her about poker. Now she realized he'd been teaching her about his life, the way he lived.

The hall was quiet, her footsteps the only sound with the exception of the music in the distance. She eased up to the room where the CIA agent was supposed to be and knocked quietly.

What the hell was she going to do if he was somewhere in the dungeon? She couldn't go into The Garden in street clothes, and Nick would spot her in fet wear. Someone would certainly ask him why his sub was running around looking for Ezra Fain.

She couldn't simply sit here either. Her mind was racing, going through all the scenarios, when the door opened and a sleepy-eyed Fain was standing there wearing nothing but a pair of pajama bottoms that hung low on his hips. The dude worked out. Hard.

He'd been frowning as the door opened, but a smile spread across his handsome face as he took her in. "You ready then? Come inside. My lovely roommates are all out in the dungeon for the night so it's safe for us to talk."

She nodded, entering the room and trying to ignore the ache in her heart. "I don't have any ID. Hell, I don't have any clothes."

"Don't worry about it. I'll have everything waiting for us when we get to where we're going," he assured her as he closed the door. "And ID isn't a problem. I've got a team who can have proper papers waiting for us before we get to the airport. A private one. No Heathrow for us. We're going to Rio in style." He seemed much more awake now.

"Rio?"

"It's where I believe your father went after he left Seattle."

So she was going to Brazil. She'd never been to Brazil, likely because of the country's strict laws on gambling. There were no glittering casinos her father could work to gain some quick cash. Luckily, she knew how her dad operated. He might not have been there before, but he would find the illegal games. She simply had to figure out who to ask. Of course, there was another issue, a far more pressing one. "But how are we going to get out? I'm pretty sure Nick left instructions that I wasn't supposed to leave."

The small smile became a full-fledged, arrogant, only-a-little-sexy smirk. Okay, she wasn't dead. It was a lot sexy, but she was swearing off spies for a while. "Leave that to me. Give me ten minutes and we're out of here, partner."

She watched as he disappeared into what had to be the bathroom. As she found a place to sit and wait, she tried to forget that she'd seen the last of her Nicky.

Chapter Sixteen

"Wake up, buddy. It's time to rise and shine and face the consequences of your many poor choices from last night, some more unexpected than others."

Nick heard the wretchedly sarcastic voice, but he tried to ignore it. It was so much nicer to stay in his happy place. He was with Hayley and she cuddled up against him, her dark hair spread over his chest while she slept. She was warm, her silky flesh a blanket for him to curl up against.

Ya tebya lyublyu, dushka, he whispered to her. Softly, so he didn't wake her. She needed her sleep. He'd been rough with her the night before, but he'd needed her so badly.

"I think you should take over, Damon. He says he loves me and called me some Russian thing. I get it. I'm super hot and I'm not offended at all, but if he grabs my balls, we're going to have a problem."

"Ian, I have no idea how your wife puts up with you," a familiar voice said. "Nikolai, wake up. We have a problem."

He blinked, pain slamming into his brain in an instant. The room was far too bright, the sounds too loud.

"Yeah, there you go. That's what happens when you drink a fifth of vodka." Taggart stood over him, his hand on his hips and a smile on his face that could only be described as judgmental. "Imagine how your liver feels."

Fuck. Where was he? The last thing he remembered was opening the vodka bottle after Brody had gone to bed. He'd tried to get Nick to sleep on his couch, but Nick had other things to do. Like pass out.

His back spasmed and he forced himself to sit up. He was in the kitchen, leaning over one of the tables, his body bent in two. And there was something on his head. He swatted it away.

"Sorry, apparently Kay thought you needed a hat. She made one out of a napkin and decorated you during breakfast this morning. I can't believe you managed to sleep through that," Damon explained. "You're lucky I got in here before the lads did or I fear it could have been much worse. Can you stomach some tea?"

"Coffee, please." He needed something strong. Super strong.

Who would get Hayley's coffee? He hadn't managed to get a coffeemaker delivered so she would wake up to bottled water and some energy drinks. She liked coffee in the morning. A shot of cream with two sugars. When he would pass the mug to her, she would wrap her hands around it and breathe in the scent, her whole face lighting up.

Had she come down here to get a cup and seen him laid out in all his misery? Had she found him so pathetic that she was happy he was leaving soon?

Was he leaving?

He scrubbed a hand through his hair. Last night while he drank, he'd thought about all the ways his plan could go wrong. There were a million and one horrible scenarios, and in every case there was a simple solution.

Hayley could get free of all this nonsense. She could live out her life alone and never find love again.

Hayley could get free and she could marry an unworthy man, one who couldn't love her the way Nick did. One who could abuse her, and she would have no family or friends to defend her because Nick would be dead in a back alley.

The case could go to hell and she would be stuck here. She would be stubborn and with no one to watch her, she would be careless and thrown in jail or taken by the men looking for her.

He could go on and on with the horrors that plagued him, but during the night he'd realized there was a simple solution that fixed them all.

He stayed with her and made sure nothing bad happened.

"I want to talk to Denisovitch. I need him to fix my situation." The words felt heavy in his mouth, but he forced them out. "I'll do what he asks of me, but I would like to know what he will want in advance."

Not that it would change his mind. He simply wanted to be prepared for what would come. He was going to do this. He would do it for her. He would do it for them.

As for her fitting into his world, maybe it was time he stopped treating her like a china doll to protect and started looking at her as a partner. They would sit down and figure it out.

The woman who had greeted him the night before had been a woman who knew damn well what she wanted, a woman who could handle herself.

A woman who might kick his ass.

Maybe she would see how much pain he was in and take pity on him.

"Now you decide this?" Taggart asked with a shake of his head. "You've got horrible timing, but I can tell you what that son of a bitch is going to want. He's going to want use of my house on Loa Mali. He's got this girl, some sort of Russian supermodel, and he's trying to impress her. He thinks he can do it if he has rights to come and go at my gloriously beautiful beach house. Do you know how I got that beach house? Blood. Blood and death and sweat and tears. The tears came from the king who gave it to me for saving his life. He's a sentimental guy. I swear to god if that Russian smokes in my beach house and makes it smell like a cheap bar, it's your ass I'm coming after."

Nick shook his head and then realized that was a terrible idea. Still, he forced himself to look up at Taggart. "The favor is from you?"

"Yeah. Dusan loves this shit. He's all about making deals and having everyone look at him like he's some power broker. He likes all that political stuff. He also loves calling in favors."

Nick sent Taggart a glare that most men would back down from. It was the same stare he used on men he was going to murder horribly. "Why the hell didn't you tell me the favor was from you and not me?"

"I can be a total dick sometimes," Taggart admitted.

"Finally, something out of your mouth I can agree with one hundred percent." Damon set a mug of coffee in front of Nick. He also placed a bottle of aspirin in his grasp. "Take two of those as well and then report down to Walt. He's going to treat you with IV fluids. I need you on your feet. I know you think you should leave…"

He cut that off quickly. "I'm not going anywhere. I was being a fool. I'm needed here."

He swallowed two of the pills, the coffee burning its way down his throat. It didn't matter. He needed to wash away the sins of the night before. It was time to get back to work. She needed him.

"Damn straight, brother," Taggart agreed. "It's all gone to hell. The mission last night ended up with me murdering the target. Kayla brought hers in but he's not talking."

Despite the pain, he managed to frown up at Taggart. "You killed him?"

Taggart slumped into his chair with a long sigh. "Apparently he's got a high tolerance for liquor. Way higher than yours, and he's a damn fine actor. Was. He played drunk, but when he got Charlie out of the bar, he suddenly had complete control again. He put his freaking hand on my wife's ass and rubbed himself against her. I'm the only one allowed to do that. I intervened and there was a knife and yeah, we might have fought over it and I might have gutted the dude. Charlie already yelled at me. I ruined our perfect night by murdering someone. You have no idea how loud that woman can yell."

Damon shook his head. "Yes, well, I'm the one who had to clean things up. Next time please make it less messy. The Ukrainian is being stubborn. He insists all he had communications wise was a series of e-mails. We've got Adam working on it, but it could take time. So now I have a Ukrainian who could use a bath in the basement, a rather wretchedly large bill from a cleaner, and a security guard who's in worse shape than you. We'll be lucky if he doesn't sue. I promise if he does, I'm sending that bloody bill straight to the Agency. What kind of roofies are they using these days? Giles is still mumbling in his sleep about biscuits and no one taking his."

"Someone drugged Giles?" Giles was the night guard on the parking garage. He allowed cars in or out. The night before he would have been waiting up to greet the Taggarts and Kayla and her guest. "Why would someone drug Giles?"

The answer hit him and suddenly it didn't matter that the room was spinning. He was on his feet and moving toward the stairs. Someone had gotten in and taken Hayley. That was the only reason anyone would have drugged the guard. His heart was pounding in his chest and there was zero question about his sobriety at this point. He was hyper aware of everything around him.

"Nick, it's not what you think." Damon was running behind him.

He stopped because it was obvious that someone had screwed up. He turned on his boss and his...other boss. "Where is Hayley?"

"No idea," Taggart said. "But dude, she's really good with a hypodermic needle. Like shockingly good. Even Charlie thinks she could learn a thing or two from your girl."

He felt off balance again. "What is that supposed to mean? Is she here or not? She's supposed to be in my flat. She's supposed to be protected. You promised you would watch after her."

Was she here or not? His gut threatened to churn as he stood there.

Damon stepped up. "There's been a development. Apparently Hayley has decided she no longer needs our protection."

He shook his head. "She wouldn't leave on her own. She's not stupid. She knows how dangerous it is out there. Someone took her. I want to see all the surveillance videos. I want to know every single person who even walked close to the building yesterday evening. We have facial recognition. I'll find the bastard and if he's laid a hand on her, I swear to god, I'll hang him with his own entrails."

Taggart's face lit up. "I knew you were cool. Entrails are the only way to go. Old school. I love it. But we don't need facial recognition. She left with Ezra."

He stopped, his whole body stilling to the point that he was happy his freaking heart continued beating. "Excuse me?"

He couldn't have heard them right.

Damon put a hand on the railing, his weariness clear. "She and Ezra left last night at roughly one in the morning. They took the car Ezra arrived in and we've tracked them to a private airfield. He had a private jet waiting for them and they took off at two-thirty. I've been told their flight plan is classified, which means whatever flight plan I can get my hands on is certainly a total lie."

Ezra Fain had kidnapped his woman. "Where did he take her?"

Damon shook his head, his mouth flattening out in clear frustration. "You're not listening to me. He didn't take her anywhere. I looked at the security tapes myself. Hayley is the one responsible for my guard taking an extra long nap. She even high-fived Fain after he caught Giles when he passed out. Lucky for him they left him in a comfortable position or he would be looking at some serious back problems."

They were missing the point. "Do I look like I care about the state of Giles's spinal cord? Where is Hayley?"

"Dude, you look seriously crazy right now. I get it. Your girl took off with the hot, horny CIA guy," Taggart pointed out. "But it's not Damon's fault. Honestly, they didn't need to roofie poor Giles. We

322

can't keep her here. It's like kidnapping and shit. I'm sorry that you told her you were staying and she left anyway. That's gotta hurt."

Nick suddenly found the floor endlessly entertaining. Well, easier to look at. "We had a fight."

"So you had a fight and you told her what?" Damon asked. "I'm surprised you didn't know that she'd left. I assumed that was why you went on a bender."

"I told her I was leaving London and that she needed to remain here. I broke off our relationship. She did not take it well." He could still see her standing there, tears in her eyes from the second time he'd ripped her heart out.

"I think she took it all right. You dumped her. She got a new boyfriend and he's got a private jet."

He might kill Taggart. "Where did they go?"

Damon sent Taggart a stare that actually had the man backing down. "Leave him be for a moment, please. We need him sane and cooperative." He turned back to Nick. "Penelope believes she's pared the code on the microdot down to three possible groupings. I need you focused. You're the one who can tell us if any of the locations make sense."

"I have to find Hayley." And Ezra Fain. Yes, he was going to have a long talk with Ezra Fain.

"Track down the location of whatever it is these guys want and I suspect that's where you'll find Hayley," Taggart replied, serious for once. "I'm fairly certain Ezra knew exactly where he wanted to go the minute he set foot in The Garden. He's got a plan and he needed Hayley to make it work."

"I'm going to kill him. He's going to understand why they call me Butcher."

"You can't kill Fain. He didn't force her to leave with him. That will be made plain when you see the surveillance tapes." Damon turned and looked out over the garden below. "He's smart, that one. He prefers to use seduction over force. And he knows we're in a bad position. We need his contacts on too many cases to truly freeze him out."

"Seduction?"

"Now who's poking the bear?" Taggart asked. "When his voice goes low like that and he actually sounds like a real scary Russian crazy person, that's when we calm him back down. We don't know that she's fucking Fain. Probably not. Maybe. Some women would view him as a good candidate for a revenge fuck. You know what I'm talking about. It's when you dump a chick and she finds another dude to rub your nose in it with. Preferably one with his own jet. But probably not. Maybe Fain doesn't even like chicks. I don't know. I don't watch him."

"Yes, you're excellent at this," Damon said with a sad shake of his head. "Nikolai, I expect you downstairs to meet with Walt and fix your physical issues. We convene in two hours and we'll decide where to go from there. I'm going to pair everyone up and send you all to the three locations Penelope has discovered, with you going to the one of your choice, the one you decide is the closest to where Desiree would have hidden something."

It struck him suddenly that Damon could be out. Hayley had gone and it wasn't like she was paying for Damon's incredibly expensive services. She'd left and apparently gone on her own. It made sense for Damon to step back.

"Why are you doing this?"

Damon looked out again, over the small space that was his kingdom. "I'm doing it because you're part of my family, Nikolai. Because I was once exactly where you are and I thought I was alone. A very important person taught me that family doesn't have to be blood. Family is what we make of it. Family is the people you choose and once you've chosen, when your silly family member falls, you pick him up. You weren't going to be allowed to leave, Nikolai. I already had Walt steal your passport and you'll find your bank accounts shut down. In the event that didn't stop you, Brody was going to lock you up until such time as I dealt with the matter. We had a meeting yesterday after you announced your plans. We're all in agreement."

He had to force himself to take a deep breath, the emotion of the moment threatening to overwhelm him.

Somehow, even though he'd been on the team for years, he'd always considered himself an outsider. He was someone they took on because he and Des had been a package deal, someone to be tolerated, but not truly one of them.

He felt his jaw tighten at the idea of Kay and Brody, Walt and Owen and the lads all coming together to decide how best to deal with him.

He wasn't a fool. There might be some stubborn asses out there who would see that as meddling, as troublesome, but he remembered what it meant to be cared about. He remembered how his sister would poke and prod at him, how his parents would shove their noses into his business.

"I will not leave, Damon. This is my promise to you. My promise to my family." His vow. "I will go see Walt and meet you at the proper time. And I thank you for taking care of this for me."

"Of course." Damon turned and nodded shortly.

Taggart leaned in. "You know I'm the one who taught him all that family shit."

"I was talking about my wife, you wanker," Damon shot back and then the slightest smile creased his face. "Perhaps you had a small part in it. Nothing more."

Nick left them arguing like an old married couple. He started toward the lift with purpose.

He was a man with a mission and now he realized he'd always had a team behind him.

Two hours later, Nick looked over the three locations Penelope had managed to pluck from the code on the microdot. The whole team was around the conference table, each one studying the information packets they'd been given on the locations.

A location in Hong Kong's Wan Chai district.

An office building in the Upper West Side of Manhattan.

An apartment building in Rio de Janeiro.

"I can verify that she and I stayed in apartments in Hong Kong and Rio. She kept a place in the Ipanema district there. We went to Manhattan many times. She had a place there in Greenwich Village, but I'm almost certain it was left to her mother in her will," Nick explained. He felt perfectly focused thanks to some hydration therapy.

"It was." Penelope sat next to her husband at the head of the table. "I checked, but that wasn't the location I found in the code. The longitude and latitude pinpoints an office building. I ran a list of all the business who have rented there for the last ten years. Do any of them look familiar?"

He glanced down and one name bounced out at him. "Yes, this one. The legal firm. Her family used them for their American business interests."

"So she could have left something with them," Kayla concluded.

"Possibly." He didn't think so though. It wasn't Desiree's style. The New York law firm was one selected years and years before by her grandfather. They'd handled the family's American investments since shortly after World War II. "The law firm she employed to handle her own assets was much more in line with the way she tended to work. They were very small, very exclusive. A roster of around thirty clients, most of them involved in criminal activities on some level. We certainly need to check this out, but it's the least interesting of the three to me."

"All right, I'll send someone up to check it out," Taggart said. "I've got a Brit on my team. He can pose as her relative. I'm sure Simon and Chelsea would like some time in the city on the firm."

Kayla held up a hand. "I'll handle Hong Kong. I know it well and I'm the only one who speaks the languages."

"You're also the only one wanted by MSS," Damon pointed out. For years Kay had been a double agent, spying on China's intelligence agencies.

Nick shook his head. "No, absolutely not. You can come with me to Brazil."

"Why Brazil?" Damon asked.

"Because Des was happy there." He wasn't sure why, but Rio stood out to him. His instincts told him to go there. He remembered the sunny apartment she kept that overlooked the beach. When they had time or when she was weary, she would ask him to take her to Rio. She would walk up and down the beach and shop and pretend she was normal. She kept a whole drawer of scandalously small bikinis and she would lie on the beach and soak up the sun.

Penny frowned as she pulled up something on her computer. "According to this, the Ipanema flat was included in her will. It was left to her family and they sold it off quickly. I can't find anything about a Hong Kong flat."

"She sold it," Nick explained. "Right before she died, she sold off some of her property. Working for a living hurt her bottom line. Once we signed on here, I didn't want to have anything to do with her side businesses. She'd settled down a bit and when she needed cash, she sold property."

"I hate to be the bearer of bad news, Nick, but she hadn't stopped her side businesses." Damon closed the folder in front of him. "According to my investigation, her finances picked up in the year before her death. To the tune of three million pounds."

"Do you have financial records?" He let the betrayal wash off him. He had other things to consider and he was done allowing Des to turn him into a whiny wanker, as Damon would call him. "How were the deposits made? In small amounts? From what bank?"

"I'll send you a copy and you can read it all on the plane. Are you sure you want to go to Rio knowing the apartment was sold?" Damon asked.

"If it was important she wouldn't have stashed it where she stayed. She would have found another place. I want Rio." It was there in his gut. If he had to choose, he chose Rio.

He prayed that was where he would find Hayley, too.

"All right." Damon stood up. "Kay, you're heading out with Nick. Brody, take Owen with you to Hong Kong and make sure you don't lose him."

Brody nodded. "Will do."

"Everyone check in when you get to the destination. Nick, take the company jet. Brody, have Teresa make arrangements for you. Go in as tourists. I don't want to tip anyone off. We have too many enemies in that part of the world." Damon nodded and was off. "Taggart and I will work with our Ukrainian friend to see what else we can get out of him."

"Make it fast, though. I've got to get back to Dallas in a few days or my whole office will implode." Taggart eased out of his chair. "And maybe we can let Charlie torture the dude in the basement for a while. It might make up for last night. I'm still in the doghouse, man, and British doghouses are worse than American. Your couch sucks."

They were arguing as they stepped outside the conference room.

"I'll go pack. Rio, fun." Kay winked his way before she practically skipped out of the room.

Brody looked at him across the conference table. "Are you sure?"

"That I want Hayley?" He'd never been surer of anything in his life. "Yes. I love her. I'm not sure that she'll greet me with open arms, though. She might tell me to leave."

"What will you do then?"

"I don't know."

Brody sighed and slapped an envelope on the table as he stood. "Maybe this will help. It's time for you to read this, mate. I know you think you've put all this behind you, but it's obvious to me you haven't. You think I don't remember what you were like before Desiree died? You like to pretend that you've always been this brooding, but you used to be quite dashing. You used to take life by the bollocks and swing on the damn things like Tarzan. You think pretending you didn't love Des is helping, but it's not. It's putting a wall up between you and a woman you could love even more. Forgive yourself for making the wrong choice."

He stared at the letter and couldn't help but call Brody out. If he had problems, then so did Brody. "And you? I know Stephanie called again and asked for you. Are you going to call her back?"

"She's just being sweet. She's deserves far more than a grunt with nothing but a basic education. I left her a message, one I think she'll hear. I guess in the end it's better for her to hate me than to let me ruin her life, you know."

"I think our women are smarter than we give them credit for. They know their minds." He hoped Brody hadn't done something stupid.

Like he'd done.

"Well, Steph hasn't seen much, not in any romantic fashion. She's quite innocent in that way. It's over and that's all there is to it. Be safe, brother." Brody turned and walked out the door.

And Nick was left with that letter he'd been avoiding.

Desiree certainly hadn't known she would die. She had no psychic powers, so that meant one thing and one thing only.

She'd been ready to play him for a fool again.

He slid the letter out and immediately recognized her handwriting. How many years had he wasted? How much of his soul had he put into that woman?

Dearest Nicky,

How do I say good-bye to you? I thought in the beginning that you would be nice to have around, a big strong loyal man to do the heavy lifting for me. It's why I saved you that day. I'd certainly done my homework on you. The MI6 analysts had a code name for you. The Siberian Husky. Not because you look like one, but for your dogged loyalty and moral standards. There were bets on you around the office. Which one would win. Your loyalty to your country or your morality, once you truly figured out what was going on. I knew when I saw you that your battle had been fought and you would look for a new loyalty. I decided to make you loyal to me, to make you my faithful pet.

The funny thing is how attached we get to pets.

I love you, Nicky. As much as I can love anything, you're it for me. You should know that all these years I've struggled to keep some necessary distance from you because I can't be one more woman who follows her heart. My heart is a flawed and faulty thing. It's better for me to love myself. I'm likely the only one who truly can. If you knew half of what I've done, you would put a bullet through my heart and I can't end that way.

It's been difficult keeping you out of the more unsavory portions of my life. Working for McKay-Taggart was exactly the distraction I needed, but now the thing that allowed me to keep you is what pushes me away. Damn Damon. He was always smarter than I gave him credit for. I've come to believe he's investigating me and it's time to disappear. We've got one more mission together. As I write this I'm preparing to go back to England where I'll hop on a plane to the Caribbean and meet you one last time. I'm hoping since we're helping out Tennessee Smith that perhaps I'll get some credit points and Damon won't expend too much energy coming after me.

I finally have my big haul. I won't bore you with the details, but I caught a massive fish. A great white whale the likes I never thought to net. I fully intend to bleed him dry. I've got something that will keep me comfortable for the rest of my life. I wish I could spend it with you, but alas, I fear you were always meant for her.

If there's one thing I regret, it's the last few years. I can feel that you miss her, but I worry that something broke inside you when we took out the syndicate. You're darker than before, my love. That spark you had in the beginning is dimmed and I only see it again when I mention her name. I find it important to think of you as happy, as the wild, amazing man I fell for.

So this is my gift to you. I'm taking my freedom and giving you back yours. You followed me for years out of loyalty and affection and the deep belief that you didn't deserve better. I've always known I was a sort of punishment for your sins. It's time to stop.

She's in Seattle and she's alone. I've watched her from afar for years because I love her, too. Not because she's my blood. I love her for who she is. For who I might have been. She's worked hard and she thinks she has everything she wants out of life, but she needs you. She needs the you you used to be. Go after her and sweep her off her feet. Show her that merely having a house you go to every night doesn't make a home.

You were my home for so very long.

Try not to hate me. You know Desiree is a lovely name for a girl. Perhaps that's too much to ask, but know that somewhere I am out here living it up and wishing you both well.

And darling, if anything should happen to me, know that I am careful as always and thinking of you. Isn't that the key to everything? You have my heart and she has yours. I think that is fitting.

Love,
Des

He slumped back, his whole being focused on that letter. He'd made Brody read it in case Des had said anything important. Unfortunately, Brody didn't know her the way Nick had.

Des had told him everything he needed to know to solve the mystery she'd left behind.

She'd left a key.

Unfortunately, it was currently around Hayley's neck and she was still the target.

Nick hustled, his soul somehow lighter than it had been before. He almost ran into Penelope and Charlotte in his haste. The two women were rushing into the conference room, both looking a bit flustered, but in a way that had a smile on both their faces.

"Nick, I'm so glad we caught you," Penelope began. "This just came in. You see, I had a thought about the private airfield. Ezra Fain doesn't run his own team. He's a solitary operative. That means he tends to be on his own when it comes to getting places, and his per

331

diem won't cover a private jet."

"Ah, but Ezra has friends in high places," Charlotte continued. "When we realized he wasn't heading for Heathrow, I decided to check on where the 4L Software jet was."

He shook his head, not quite understanding. "Why would a software company send him a jet? Wait. Isn't your sister-in-law a member of the family who runs the company?"

Charlotte nodded. "Mia's married to Case, but at one point in time she needed a bodyguard to follow her all over the world while she was working. Mia always says she owes that bodyguard because he saved her several times. In return, she allows him to use the jet when he needs it. Guess who that bodyguard was?"

His heart started to race the tiniest bit. If they could track that plane, he could find Hayley. "Ezra Fain. And was there a private jet owned by 4L in London last night?"

Penelope's smile was a mile wide. "It was and I got the flight plan. They're going to Rio."

Everything slid into place. His instincts weren't wrong. He simply hadn't thought to use them in forever.

It was time to get his girl, time to start over again, and this time he intended to get it all right.

He just had to save her first.

* * * *

Hayley yawned and forced herself to sit up. The bed was way too comfy for an airplane.

Of course, the fact that the airplane had a bed at all had kind of blown her mind, but then it wasn't like they were flying commercial.

"Morning, sunshine."

She turned over, clutching the blanket against her chest. It wasn't like she was naked or anything. She was in a perfectly respectable T-shirt that managed to hit her knees. Ezra had offered her one of his to sleep in. It felt wrong, but she didn't have much of a choice. Luckily he claimed that when they got to the place they were staying at in

Brazil, there would be plenty of choices for her.

He strode in, looking like a man who hadn't stayed up all night. She wasn't sure how he wasn't rumpled and managed to be so alert after a night of flying. Not that he'd been the one doing the flying. There was a pilot for that, but Hayley had made it plain that while she was in this with him, she wasn't looking for a new lover. If Ezra had slept, it had been in his chair in the main cabin.

Of course this morning he was all sexy smiles, and he looked ready to try again.

"I'm not feeling sunny, Mr. Fain."

He placed a mug of coffee on the nightstand table and proceeded to sit on the edge of the bed. "Well, you look adorable. And it's Ezra."

She gripped the coffee in her hands, loving how warm the mug was. "I thought we agreed that you would stop hitting on me."

"I'm not hitting on you. I'm being charming. It's the way I am. I would be spectacularly bad at my job if I couldn't make anyone like me. It's the reason most operatives fail, you know. It's one thing to know how to blow up a building. It's entirely another to be able to convince someone else to do it for you."

Like she'd blown up her relationship with Nick.

No. She wasn't taking credit for that. He'd been the asshole who decided she wasn't smart enough to make up her own mind. He was the one who had made it plain there was nothing for her in London.

She already missed him.

She took a drink of the coffee. It tasted a whole lot like heaven. Whoever Fain's billionaire friend was, he knew his java. "How far out are we?"

"We'll be landing in an hour and a half. I have a friend meeting us at the private airfield with our luggage, and she's got everything we'll need to change up your appearance. She's a whiz with wigs and makeup. After we finish, it'll take about an hour to get to the hotel, and we need to talk about that."

She felt her eyes narrow. "If this involves anything but us having

333

two separate rooms, we definitely need to talk."

He pulled out a shiny gold ring. "Now why would I want to be apart from my wife?" He held up a hand as though to stop the argument he knew was coming. "Think about this. They're looking for a woman on her own. They're not looking for a couple. This is what we call cover in the business. We have the honeymoon suite at one of the nicest hotels in Ipanema, across from the beach. Also, I'm not letting you out of my sight. I take your safety personally. You're doing me a huge favor and you're going to be alive at the end of all of this. I've already got some colleagues working on how to get your life back."

She had to admit, they did need a cover story. Those men had found her in London quickly. She didn't want the same to happen here. "Why Ipanema? Is it because of a girl?"

She couldn't help herself.

Ezra laughed, the sound deep and yes, awfully charming. "Isn't it always about a girl? This time that girl's name is Desiree and she used to own an apartment a block from our hotel. It's also the district where my intelligence puts your father."

Her father. She had a million questions that would be followed by a hearty smack in the face. Yeah, that would feel good. "So you tracked him to Rio?"

He placed the ring on the nightstand and leaned back. He looked perfectly comfortable lounging around on a strange woman's bed. But then he probably did that a lot. "I tracked a man traveling from Seattle on a passport with an alias your father used back in the nineties. He took a ride sharing service to SeaTac. I might or might not monitor those. I find these new ride shares incredibly useful. In order to be safe, you have to share information or have a credit card on file. Many people upload photo ID so the driver knows who they are. So much lovely information. It was harder to track people when we all used cash."

Her father had been careful about cash. That meant Ezra was likely right. "If he's using plastic it's because he's out of cash, and that means I should be able to find him. But why go to Rio? There's no gambling in Rio, no easy-to-find poker games. It would have been smarter for him to head to Vegas or to go to Asia. There's practically a game on every corner there."

"I believe that what he ultimately wants is in Rio," Fain said. "And you know as well as I do that he can find a game if he needs to. The question is can you."

It had been a while, but she remembered how it all worked. "I think I can. I can certainly figure out where to look once we get there. So now that I've blown up my life and we're partners, are you going to tell me what this is really about?"

That was the moment he lost his charm and his face went blank. "I'm not sure what you mean."

She set down the mug and sat up because this was not happening. "What was my father working on when he decided it was time to punch out? To fake his own death."

"I knew what you were saying. Your father wasn't an operative, per se. He was an asset. Do you understand the difference?"

She was a student of history. Of course she did. She'd done her class on military history. "So you're saying you used him, but he wasn't exactly on the payroll."

"Oh, I paid him, but he wasn't a trained operative. Your father was caught in a sting operation thirty years ago for passing off secrets to the Chinese government," Ezra explained. "I've read all his files and even the agent who brought him in was uncertain if he actually knew what he was doing. It didn't matter. It was high treason. He was brought in and offered a deal due to the nature of his job."

"He traveled often and to some countries that would be of interest to the Agency," she surmised. "He had an awfully good cover. He could go anywhere there was a poker game, and often times he would come into contact with powerful people."

"Gambling is an excellent way to pass materials back and forth," Ezra agreed. "Casinos tend to be crowded and no one would question a man like your father coming in and out at odd times. He worked quite well for a few years and then something happened."

She could guess what that was. "He met Des."

"Desiree Brooks. She was the problem child of MI6. A brilliant operative who did more good for the Western world than anyone will know. Unfortunately, she also liked to skim a bit from the top, or bottom, as it was. She used her position to gain information that she then used to blackmail various members of political, social, and business organizations. It was a game to her and she liked to win. She saw both an opportunity and a kindred spirit in your father."

Thus a partnership and a million lies were formed. "Does this have something to do with her blackmail schemes?"

His jaw tightened but before she could call him on it, he was shaking his head. "I believe so. I believe that Des and your father decided to blackmail the wrong person. Des died, one of the world's crazy coincidences, but I think your father attempted to keep the business going. In my opinion, he faked his death when he realized he'd bitten off more than he could chew, as they would say in my neck of the woods. He decided he couldn't handle the fallout without Des and he faked his death. All hell broke loose when the contents of that apartment got delivered to you."

She had to let him know where she stood. "I spent a lot of time with Des, but she never talked about that part of her life. If you're looking for me to have some great secret, you're out of luck. Des and I talked about a lot of things. She was incredibly interested in history and we had some great debates, but not once did she explain her blackmailing business to me."

"I would be surprised if she had. She was known for being fairly careful. It was why MI6 couldn't catch her in any meaningful criminal activity. Or your father."

"But you believe they were blackmailing people. Powerful people." People who didn't mind killing to protect their secrets. "Any idea who they might be?"

"Given that whoever this is was able to manipulate the police the way they did, I suspect we're dealing with a US government official.

Someone of very high rank. Or someone with access to a government official."

"Is that why the CIA is involved?"

"Your father is why we're involved. He has information he took with him to his fake grave, and I want that intelligence."

A shiver went through her at the chill in Ezra's voice. He was a charming man. So charming that she sometimes forgot there was a predator under his smiles and polite ways. "Are you going to kill my father?"

"I'm going to talk to him." The chill was gone, replaced with an easy smile. "Hayley, this is nothing for you to worry about. I understand why he did what he did, but I need that intelligence. I'm sure he has it. I'm sure he'll use it to get himself out of his situation. He's a big boy. He knows what he's doing."

He'd known what he was doing all along. He'd lied to her and dragged her around the globe. He'd used her as cover, too.

And he'd loved her.

It was so hard to accept the limitations of others, hard to still find a way to forgive.

Should she have stayed and fought it out with Nick? No. He'd made himself plain, and not for the first time. Nick loved her, too, but it wasn't enough.

It never seemed to be enough. It was always the wrong time.

"I need you to promise me that you'll see this through." She watched Ezra, taking in his every minute expression. Now that she was back to practicing the long unused art her father had taught her, her instincts were coming back to life. "Or do you intend to use me to find my father and then leave me in the cold?"

He sat up straight, all charm gone, and he leaned toward her. "I do not leave my partners behind. I do not make vows lightly."

"You're in the business of subterfuge and you made an excellent case for why you were better at it than Nick."

"This case is important to me. The intelligence your father possesses was delivered to him via an operative in Northern Africa.

About ten years ago someone gave the enemy classified information on black ops teams and their missions that ended with ten American lives being lost and several important missions being scrubbed. We lost a team of soldiers who were attempting to liberate fourteen schoolgirls who had been taken by a Jihadist group. It should have been a simple mission. Someone betrayed them. Your father has the name of the man who sold out those soldiers. I want that name, Hayley. I've waited years to look at that name."

The air seemed chillier than before. "This feels personal."

"One of the men killed was named Ezra Fain."

She had to shake her head. "What?"

"He was my half brother. I use his name to remind me every single day what I am working for. I use it because he's the one who should be alive. He was the best man I knew and I need to ensure that whoever did this to him pays for his crime. I'm not going on a solo mission of vengeance. I am going to do my job as my brother would have wanted me to and know that he would never have left a man behind. You're safe with me, Hayley."

She believed him. "I'm sorry about your brother."

Ezra took a long breath and glanced at the window. In that moment he seemed so weary, she had to wonder if she was getting a look at the actual man inside all those masks.

"I'm sorry about a lot of things, Hayley," he said as he stood up. "I've got a mountain of regrets. Everyone in this business has them. You will not be one of them, I promise you that." He seemed to shake off the pain and he smiled again, sliding right back into his easy-going persona. "You know as part of our cover we should do some romantic, honeymoon type things. People who honeymoon in Rio aren't going there to play golf or read by the pool. I'm quite a good dancer. I think we should samba in Rio. Hide in plain sight, that's what I say. They won't expect that."

She had to laugh. One day some woman was going to have to deal with all that. It was not going to be her. "I think I'll pass on the dancing. We're going to be a boring newly married couple."

He pointed a finger her way. "I'll change your mind in the end. Get ready. We're about to start. You'll see. We're going to have some fun. Every day is another adventure."

He strode out of the room and she sat back, wishing she was having that adventure with another man.

Chapter Seventeen

Nick adjusted his sunglasses because he couldn't possibly be seeing what he was seeing. The sun was high in the sky and maybe it was all an optical illusion. There were so many people on the beach that it was probable the woman he was following wasn't Hayley.

For four days he and Kayla had been attempting to track down Hayley and Fain. After they'd gotten into Rio, Nick had found a hotel along the beach close to where Desiree's old apartment building stood. If Fain had known to go to Rio, he'd obviously walked in the doors of The Garden with information he'd chosen not to share. And under false pretenses. He'd been there to get a shot at Hayley. Fain had known she was the key, though it was apparent he didn't know that "key" was meant literally. Or they simply hadn't figured out where Des had stashed what she wanted them to find.

Much of his time had been spent walking around the Ipanema district with Kayla, quietly asking shopkeepers and waiters if they'd seen a couple fitting Hayley and Fain's descriptions. Oh, they'd been casual about it, convincing the people they were talking to that they'd merely met the couple their first night here and hit it off, but somehow the gentleman had left his keys behind in a cab they'd shared and Nick was trying to return them.

So far nothing. Not until he walked out on the beach and saw her.

"That is quite a crowd," Kay said as she joined him. "I heard it's worse a little ways down the beach. There's some sort of gathering going on with an outdoor concert."

"Yes, they were warming up a few moments ago." He'd heard the thud of a bass guitar from far away. It looked like the woman he thought was Hayley and her companion were moving in that direction.

Kayla wore an emerald green bikini and something she called a cover-up that didn't do a good job of covering much. Her toned body was on display, but looking at her was like looking at a sister. Her long, dark hair flowed down her back and she adjusted her sun hat. "I nearly got mowed down by a kid on a bike. He was fast and he didn't care that an incredibly beautiful woman was in his way. I liked him. We should recruit him."

Nick started forward, his feet hitting the sand. "It's Sunday. The street is closed to cars. Everyone will be out, walking, rollerblading, biking. This place is a zoo on Sundays. Naturally that's when I find her."

Because he was fooling himself. That self-possessed woman walking ahead of him was Hayley. That sexy-as-hell-and-knew-it woman was his.

Kayla didn't seem to sink into the sand the same way he did. She easily kept up with him. "You found her? I was right? That was her on the surveillance camera?"

They'd gone through hours and hours of hacked security camera feeds from the various hotels around the district. Finally, the night before they'd hit what Kayla called pay dirt. She'd managed to catch a man and a woman leaving one of the more expensive hotels right across from the beach. They'd been dressed for a day in the water. The man's head had been down the entire time, but at one point someone must have said something to the woman and she'd looked up. She'd been wearing a blonde wig and it looked like she'd used some kind of tanning agent on her skin, but he knew those eyes and the stubborn tilt of her chin.

They'd spent the night before hanging out in the lobby and trying to figure out what name Fain would use. All to no avail, so he was watching the beach, hoping they would go out once more.

All this time he'd had nightmares about her being kept a virtual captive, forced to hide in some dingy motel, surrounded by people she couldn't understand. He'd wondered if she was hungry or cold.

Nope. She was stunning. She looked happy as she sipped on a cocktail and strolled down the number nine beach, her free hand in that soon-to-be dead CIA agent's. He shouldn't have worried about her finding a decent meal. It was apparent she'd been dining at the finest places in Rio and staying in an expensive hotel. Food and shelter had been taken care of. Clothing, on the other hand, appeared to be optional.

She was barely dressed.

"Where is she?" Kay scanned the beachfront. "Oh, there she is. Wow. That's so cute. I almost bought that one but I decided three hundred dollars for a few inches of fabric was a bit much when I live in London. Not a lot of bikini wearing around the palace, if you know what I mean."

Hayley was dressed in a bright blue, could-barely-be-called-even-underwear style swimsuit. "Does she not know her own size? That's at least a size too small."

"Oh, I doubt Hayley would have picked that out," Kay said as they moved parallel to the other couple. They stayed back a bit, neither having to tell the other one to stay out of sight. "She's far too shy, though she looks hot in it. If I had to bet, I would say Fain picked that sucker out for her."

"It barely covers her nipples," he growled. Fain had been paying for her clothes, and he hadn't skimped, it seemed. Except when it came to actual fabric. Fain likely hadn't presented her with plain jeans and cotton shirts and utilitarian underwear. No, Fain had selected a color that set off her skin and made it glow. He'd bought her the filmy cover-up she'd been wearing in yesterday's security video, the one that skimmed her every curve and plunged down to her waist, showing off the sides of her breasts.

"It shows less than mine," Kay complained.

He stopped and frowned her way. "That's not an excuse. And honestly, I think you should cover up, too. Men are looking at you."

"That's kind of the point," she replied with a frown. "And I'm sure that's what Fain's doing. The key is to keep eyes on the ladies so you boys can do what you need to do. You know if you want to be the beefcake, I can handle the physical stuff. We can get you a Speedo and oil those muscles up."

He got her point, but that didn't mean he had to like it. Sure enough as they walked through the crowd, many a masculine head turned to take in the sight of Hayley's backside, the outline of her suit clear through the gauzy cover-up. "I'll keep things the way they are."

"Where do you think they're going? It doesn't seem like they're roaming."

"He wants everyone to think that's what he's doing." Nick slowed his pace as they moved further on the beach and away from the iconic white lifeguard station with its big blue *9* on the side denoting that this was *Posto 9*.

As they walked along, following a fair distance behind, the music was starting up again.

Hayley and Fain continued their walk. They were moving toward the west where the Dois Irmãos mountains dominated the skyline. It was romantic. It was sexy. Fain glanced around and then brought Hayley's hand up to his lips.

It was going to be a nice place to bury Fain.

"You know you have crazy eyes right now," Kay pointed out. "Chill. She's not exactly as good at this as he is. See how awkward she is with him? I would make a big bet that they're not sharing a bed."

The thought nearly made him see red, but he needed to see something else. Reason. His jealousy wasn't going to win her back. "I wouldn't be able to blame her if she did. I was leaving her."

"That is a mature attitude to take." Kay praised him as they passed a group of scantily dressed men and women playing volleyball.

Fain had been trying to get her to fit in. In this crowd, Hayley wearing a one-piece would have stood out. The beach was full of skin. Brazil wasn't known for its uptight dress code.

"I understand that I hurt her and I have much to make up for."

Kay gave him a brilliant smile. "See, you need to keep that tone when we finally talk to them. You sound like an actual rational man."

He never said he would be rational with Fain. Only Hayley. "I'm still going to beat the shit out of that CIA agent."

"And reason flees," Kay said on a sigh.

He *was* being reasonable, when he really thought about it. "Fain took advantage of her. He took her from someplace where she was safe and brought her into danger. For this alone, I will dismember him. Have you found that place I asked you to look for?"

He couldn't see her eyes. They were hidden behind gold sunglasses, but he was fairly certain they were rolling in disdain.

"No, I did not find a place where we could buy a barrel of acid to drop Ezra in."

They'd had this argument already. He'd even talked to the boss about it. "Taggart said it was a perfectly reasonable expense and I should save the receipt."

"You're going to do what all reasonable, rational men would do in this circumstance. You're going to punch him in his pretty-boy face and then we're going to figure out how much they know. But only after we find out if they're meeting someone. I don't think we should have this reunion in public."

Kay was absolutely correct. He already had plans for their reunion and none of it could be done in public. "I'm having our baggage taken to their hotel. We're moving into the suite next to theirs. That took a bit of cash, but it will all be worth it. I'll make my move soon."

It had taken a lot of cash because fucking Fain had her in the honeymoon suite. He better be sleeping on the couch or Nick wouldn't need the acid. He would simply drop the fucker off the roof of the building and let gravity do all the work.

"And what will I be doing while you're making this move of yours that will not have anything to do with a vat of acid?" Kay shifted as the beach started to become more crowded, with many of the people surrounding them moving toward the outdoor party.

"You'll be monitoring the situation and continuing to go over that list of names I gave you."

Kay groaned. "I hate the boring part of the job. I want to kill someone. Do you know how many storage places there are in Rio? Hundreds. Why are you so sure that what we're looking for is going to be at a bank or with a storage company?"

"Because Desiree believed in redundancy," Nick explained. "I told you it was all in the letter she sent me. If something happened to her, I was to remember that she was a careful woman. When Desiree and I first got together she taught me how she worked, how she gathered and protected the information and intelligence she retrieved for MI6. Specifically the intelligence she felt she couldn't send over a computer. She wasn't always able to immediately get it out so she would copy it and she would store it away in case she lost it. She kept small apartments in several key cities around the world and she always had a place where she stored important things when she wasn't around. It will be here."

"It's not in the name she used on the property."

"Be patient. You'll find it." Desiree could be tricky at times.

"While you're doing what?"

He felt his lips curl up. "Hayley."

"That's so unfair," she shot back.

"It's necessary. I'm not going to win her back by talking. I'm not good at it. I will blind her with pleasure. I will make her scream my name." Yes, he was feeling better just thinking about what he was planning on doing to her.

Kay stopped, a smile on her face. "Who are you? I like this Nick.

You're always so serious."

"I am perfectly serious about this. This will happen. I will not quit making love to her until she agrees to marry me. We can work everything else out at a later time. Perhaps after all the lovemaking, I won't feel the need to rip Fain limb from limb." He felt his eyes narrow as he watched the couple up ahead. "Though if his hand gets any closer to her ass, I will do it here and damn the mission."

"Someone's following them." Her smile didn't change at all, but Kay's voice went low. "Red Speedo. He totally shouldn't be wearing that."

He glanced to his left and saw the man Kayla was talking about. He was standing close to the tide rushing in, but he paid no attention to the water at his ankles. His face was turned toward Hayley as she walked toward a grouping of outdoor canopies where beachgoers were grilling and dancing. She seemed to be looking for a specific one.

There was something familiar about the man. He was older and had developed a nice paunch to his belly that hung over his Speedo. His shoulders were slumped and he'd lost the majority of his hair.

Still, there was something about the profile…

"Whoever they're meeting is somewhere in there." He watched as the man in the red Speedo started to trail after Hayley and Fain. "They're going to use the party to distract attention from what they're doing."

That was when he noticed Fain's head turn ever so slightly. Hayley was saying something, pointing toward a place in the distance. Fain glanced toward her, but his whole body had slightly stiffened, his shoulders straightening.

"Fain's caught the scent," he pointed out.

"Our's or Speedo's?" Kayla asked.

He shook his head because he couldn't be completely sure. "It doesn't matter. We need to get a bit closer. The good news is our new friend can't possibly be hiding a gun in that bathing suit."

"Agreed," Kayla replied with a nod of her head. "It looks like

Hayley found what she wanted. They're moving toward the tent with the red and yellow flag. The crowd's thick there. I think we can safely get closer."

It wouldn't have mattered. He was already moving in. She could hate him later, but he wasn't going to leave Hayley's safety to a CIA agent.

He wouldn't leave her safety to anyone. Ever again. She was his and he would be her lapdog in most things. He would make it his highest goal in life to see to her happiness, but when it came to her safety he would be by her side.

He couldn't keep her from the world. That was one thing he'd ruminated on for days. In some ways, he'd placed her on a pedestal, made her the opposite of Desiree.

The two women he'd loved. He accepted that now. Maybe he'd been a fool to love Des, but he had. He'd always known it was smarter to hold a part of himself away from Des, to compartmentalize her in ways. He'd gotten so used to doing that, he'd done the same to Hayley. He'd placed her in a box marked for his heart and his emotions and he'd covered it up when not in use. He couldn't do that anymore.

If he loved Hayley, he had to allow her into every centimeter of his soul. Even the rough parts.

"Shit. I don't think red undies is the only one," Kay whispered. "Do you see him?"

There was a man walking roughly ten feet behind Hayley. He was dressed in jeans and a T-shirt, the only man on the beach wearing a light jacket. Likely because he was hiding the gun he carried. The man moved in and out of the dancing crowd.

Up ahead, Hayley stopped and put her hand out to a younger man, who nodded and began speaking. They moved slightly out of the crowd, toward one of the tents.

It would be an excellent place to kill her.

"Hurry." The music was thumping from here. It was loud, a dance party on the beach. He had to practically shout to be heard over it.

If the jackass following Hayley was a professional, he would have a suppressor on that gun he was hiding. He would be able to shoot her in the head and no one would realize what had happened over the noise until they saw her fall. The assassin would then slip away and Hayley would be lost.

He pressed through the crowd, his heart starting to thud in his chest.

Kay put a hand on his arm. "Don't. Fain's got it."

He stopped as he realized she was right. Fain smoothly moved around, positioning himself behind the man. He had a big smile on his face as though greeting an old friend. He moved in and to the outside world it might have looked like Fain was hugging the other man.

Not slipping a stiletto between his ribs.

Fain moved the man back out of the dancing crowd, as though he needed help. Nick watched as he settled the man down, his back propped against one of the tent poles.

Fain managed to be back next to Hayley before she realized what was happening. She'd started to look around for him and there he was, smiling politely and taking her hand like he hadn't murdered someone mere seconds before.

"Oh, come on, Nick." Kay was shaking her head in clear appreciation. "Those were some slick *Weekend at Bernie's* moves. No one even knows the dude is dead. He looks like he's passed out drunk. There's barely any blood."

Because Fain had been smart enough to leave the knife in, hidden by the jacket the assassin was wearing.

The smooth operative hadn't even gotten his hands bloody. It had been a smart play, a sleight of hand. Like a brilliant cheat with an ace up his sleeve no one ever saw him retrieving.

An ace.

Nick turned, catching sight of the man in the Speedo. He was walking now, but he seemed to be moving toward the street.

"Watch them," he told Kayla. It was obvious Fain had this party covered. "I'm going after our bathing beauty. I know him. He's aged and gained some weight, but that's Hayley's father."

Desiree's partner, the one man who would know where all the secrets were buried. The one man who might be able to get Hayley out of this mess.

He didn't look back, trusted Kay to handle things. She was an excellent partner and beyond that, she was a member of his team and he could count on her.

It gave him the freedom to go after his prey.

He pushed through the crowd, looking for the edge. In the mere moments since they'd joined the concert, the mass of revelers seemed to have swelled. The band onstage was finishing up their first song and speaking to the crowd. Bodies bounced and danced around him, thickening the air and making it hard to move.

He caught a glimpse of Dalton. He'd pulled a red robe around his body and now walked with purpose toward Joana Angélica Street.

Nick had to be cautious. If he spooked the man, he could run, and Nick was too far away at this point if he managed to get into a cab.

Nick pushed his way through until he got to the edge of the crowd.

Where had he gone?

He caught sight of the red robe to his right, but the crowd was between them now. Dalton was moving in a way that would take him far out of sight of his daughter and Fain. He stopped and looked back as though trying to catch another glimpse.

Nick ran, his feet sinking in the sand. Why sand? He was used to running across any manner of horrific man-made material. Cobblestones. He was used to fucking cobblestones because he'd grown up in Europe. When people tried to chase a man down in Europe, he better be fast on his feet when it came to uneven roads.

There wasn't much sand in Moscow.

He worked his way parallel, trying to keep sight of the man through the dancing pit of humanity.

His heart racing, lungs starting to burn, he jogged up to the street.

Even here the crowd was steady and Kayla was right. The pedestrians were aggressive in getting to where they wanted to go. He jumped back as a kid on rollerblades nearly mowed him down.

Where had Dalton gone?

He glanced to his right and there he was, moving toward the row of hotels that faced the beach. His hand was up, as though calling to someone.

That was when Nick felt the press of metal at his back.

"Nice and easy, Mr. Markovic," a deep voice said. The man behind him had a thick New Jersey accent. "I was told if I could find you, I would find the girl. My partner's down there taking care of her right now. We'll have her in custody and you can be the means to show her how things will go if she doesn't give us the box."

Ah, he didn't realize his partner had been taken care of. Nor did he realize how poorly this was going to go for him. Unfortunately, he didn't have a handy concert around him. He could hardly take the man down here. "Are you completely mad? There's a cop six feet away. If you shoot me out here, your game is going to be over. Move with me toward that alley to the left. Do you see it?"

He could feel the hesitation coming off the other man. "Why would you willingly come with me?"

"If you knew to follow me, then you know I love the girl. I'll do whatever it takes to keep her alive. If you have her, I want to be with her. But if you call attention to us, that police officer will not only arrest you, he'll find out I'm here illegally and then I can't stay with her."

"Fine." His voice had gone tight, but he started to move the way Nick wanted him to.

"You want to tell me who you're working for? As a professional courtesy?" Nick walked toward the alleyway between the hotel Hayley was staying at and a small strip of restaurants. It was narrow and looked perfectly empty, but they had to make their way across the street first. He might as well build a rapport with the man before he killed him.

"It's a contract, nothing more. Absolutely nothing personal. Your girl apparently pissed off some bigwig. He wants something she stole from him and he's willing to pay big to get it."

"Yes, I heard he's upped the payment to two million." That was the amount Damon had finally gotten out of the Ukrainian before giving him up to MI6. He simply hadn't known anything about the man who was willing to pay. Whoever was coming for Hayley was careful and only acted through agents.

They made their way up the slight hill.

"Two million and all we have to do is find some box and hand it over."

"That simple? How will you know you've got the right box?"

"What do you mean? I assume your girl knows what she stole."

"Hayley had nothing to do with any of this. You're looking for her cousin, Desiree." He wasn't going to take the time to explain the myriad of lies surrounding that particular relationship. "She died. You're only after Hayley because Desiree left her some things in her will. She has no idea what you want of her. She's completely innocent."

Perhaps if the man could be made to see reason, he wouldn't end up like his friend.

"I doubt that. Anyway, we'll find out soon, won't we? Don't move. I'm going to text my partner and he'll bring the girl here." He pushed Nick into the quiet of the alley. "I think we're going to have some fun with her. See how innocent she is."

Or not. The moment he felt his adversary shift, he kicked back, not bothering to turn around. He caught the other man in his midsection, pivoted, and managed to bring his arm up, throwing off the shot that came from his Ruger.

It pinged against the wall and Nick brought his fist up, the impact jarring through him. Hardheaded bastard. The other man slammed back against the brick and his gun clattered to the pavement.

Before he could reach for it, Nick pulled his own and fired just as the man aimed. A neat hole formed in his forehead and he slumped

351

back.

Nick moved fast, checking the man's jacket. He lifted the wallet and cell phone and then hefted him into the rubbish bin, letting the lid slam down on him.

Fain wasn't the only one who could take out the trash.

He hurried out as a red pedicab blew past him.

Dalton rode in the seat, his eyes toward the beach.

Nick stared after it as it pedaled down the sidewalk, making its way through the throng.

Beaten by a kid on a bike. It had been that kind of day.

"Where the hell did you go?" Kayla stalked up to him. "Hayley and Fain passed that guy they were talking to an envelope and then made their way back to the hotel. I think it was cash. What are you doing all the way over here?"

"I had to kill a guy," he admitted. "But now we have the cell phone and wallet of one of the assassins. And his hotel key. I think we'll probably find a laptop and a way to communicate with whoever's stalking Hayley."

Her mouth dropped open. "You got to kill a dude. No fair. You've gotten to do all the fun stuff. I'm ordering a bottle of tequila and a shit ton of carbs."

She was complaining as she strode up to the hotel door.

Nick smiled because the fun stuff was about to begin.

* * * *

Hayley wished Ezra Fain believed in one-piece swimsuits. "You couldn't buy something that wasn't a thong? When we get into that poker room, I am going to be wearing something that covers my ass. If we get into that poker room."

She sipped her caipirinha and let her feet sink into the sand as they walked back toward the swanky hotel she'd been living in for days. She turned and glanced one last time, trying to memorize it. Ipanema Beach was stunning, with mountain views to the west and ridiculously clear blue water. She wanted it burned into her brain, and yet she still felt restless. The whole place was like something out of a dream, but she wasn't here with the one person she wanted to see.

She was basking in the sun while Nicky was somewhere in the chill of Moscow.

Still, she had to admit the day had gone off without a single hitch. There had been a weird moment when she'd thought Ezra had disappeared, but everything had turned out fine.

"I wanted you to fit in." Ezra slipped in beside her, his hand sliding along hers and tangling their fingers together as they walked past the pool. "You need to look like the trophy wife of a high-rolling player. We agreed you should look like you're comfortable being here."

"That was what I agreed to when I thought I would fit in by wearing a bathing suit. I don't think this covers enough. It's a thong and pasties," she complained. Though even as she said the words, she could look around the pool and see far more flesh on display. Women and men were soaking up the sun in super-skimpy swimwear, and no one seemed to be giving it a second thought. There were no scandalized gasps as she walked by.

"It's stunning and every man on that beach was looking at you and thinking how much he wants you. No one wondered what we were doing and absolutely no one saw me give that man the money to try to bribe our way in," Fain replied with a gracious smile. He glanced back at the beach as though trying to find something that had gone missing. "I don't think you realize how far we've gotten because you're a charming, attractive woman."

A waiter strode up to her, offering her another drink. She smiled and thanked him, gave him her glass, but didn't pick up a second drink. She was too nervous to relax. They would know in an hour or so if the bribe had been enough to get in.

They'd found two underground games so far. Ezra had lost a total of ten thousand dollars and they still weren't any closer to finding her father.

She had to believe that he would be at The Palace. That was the name given the underground game she'd learned about at one of the small venues they'd been to. Everyone who was anyone played at The Palace. It was rumored to be run by a European gangster who killed players who couldn't pay their bill at the end of the night. Not that she would be playing poker. She would be Ezra's arm candy as he played. She would be the one watching for any hint of her father.

She stopped and settled her cover-up around her waist. "Can we do room service tonight? I need to take a shower and do my hair before the game if you want me to be as charming as possible. I'm trying to be optimistic. Are you looking for someone?"

He was standing at the railing, his hands wound tight around the wrought iron as he stared across the street. "Yes, I'm almost certain we weren't alone out there. Someone was following us."

"Is that why you disappeared?"

He turned and gave her that ingratiating smile of his. He'd been working on her for days and she hadn't been fooled by a second of it.

If she wasn't still heartsick about Nick, she might have taken him up on his silent but continual offers to make their cover a bit more pleasurable. It was there in the way he held her hand, the way he took care of her even when the doors had closed and they no longer needed to keep up the cover.

But she couldn't. She knew one day she would have to with someone, but it wouldn't be Ezra Fain. She would have to do exactly what she'd told Nick she would—move on. It was simply too soon. How could she move on when she could still feel his hands on her body, still hear him whispering in her ear?

"I told you what happened. Poor guy had way too much to drink," Ezra explained, offering her his arm. "I had to help him find a place to sit down. Don't worry about that. I'm talking about something else entirely. I swear I saw a woman who looked a bit like Kayla in the crowd."

Her heart did a flip-floppy thing at the sound of the name. "Kayla from London?"

"Come on. Let's get up to our room so I can run a quick check to

354

see if we've been found. And absolutely we can order room service. Anything you like. Make me a list and I'll have it brought up. Starting with champagne. We should celebrate because getting this far is a miracle that wouldn't have happened without you. I have no idea how you found that game."

He was also quick with the compliments. Of course, sometimes those compliments were actually distractions. She let him lead her toward the elevator. "Why would Kayla be in town?"

"Because that is a nosy group of busybodies who don't know when to let a man do his job," he muttered under his breath. He pushed the button for the elevator and escorted her inside. "Also, Taggart was serious. He feels like he owes Desiree and he'll want to know that you're all right. It's my mistake that I didn't contact him. I need to suck it up and take the extremely sarcastic lecture I have coming to me. I'll deal with it. I was going to run some checks to see if I could verify that Kayla left London, but I think I'll act like an adult and call Taggart. Once he knows you're fine, he should let up. I'll explain the job to him."

She shook her head as the elevator began its ascent. "Why didn't you do that in the first place?"

"Because you never know how that group is going to react," he replied. "Taggart can be frustrating. Knight only seems less frustrating because he says all the same things with a British accent, and that makes him sound smarter than everyone else. Do you want me to ask him about Nikolai?"

Desperately. She wanted to know if he'd made it on his plane, if he'd found a place to stay in Moscow, if he was safe. If he missed her half as much as she missed him. But he'd made his choice and she had to follow through with hers. "No. I'm sure he's fine. Please let Mr. Taggart and Mr. Knight know that I'm perfectly safe and that we've had no complications at all. Which is surprising since I got a nice talking to by the concierge this morning."

The elevator opened and he exited. She knew what to do. Normally he would have held the door open for her, but Ezra had explained how they were going to work. He went in first. It might make him look impolite, but he was assessing threats and didn't want to make her a target, even in an empty hallway.

"What did he warn you about?" Ezra asked, pulling the key from the pocket of his very reasonable board shorts.

"Apparently there have been several bodies found in the last few days." The concierge had been horrified, explaining that this part of Rio was normally safe and the *policía* were distressed at the idea of a killer on the streets. All the victims had been foreigners, though there seemed to be problems with identifying them. "One of them was even found outside that restaurant we went to a few days ago. So we've been lucky we haven't gotten caught in that murder spree."

He smiled her way as he opened the door. "You know I would never let anything happen to you. Don't worry about it. We're perfectly safe here. And the room is undisturbed, so feel free to take your shower."

He had various ways to tell if someone had entered the room. Even after the maids did their jobs, he would run a check for bugs and carefully inspect every inch of the room, but if his markers were undisturbed, she could enter quickly.

"Tell the London group hello for me and that I apologize for leaving like I did," she said as she made her way to the bathroom. "I was under the impression that they would be upset, or maybe I was hoping Nick would come after me. It was immature of me and very ungrateful."

"Hey, it's his loss, you know." Ezra stood in the large living area, his phone in hand. "You're an amazing woman."

She was going to try to be. "Thank you, but I have to earn that. Starting tonight. We find my father, figure out what Desiree left us, and solve the puzzle. I'm ready to get my life back. And could you order something light, please? Unless the dress you got me tonight isn't tight."

One muscled shoulder shrugged. "It's Prada and it's perfect, and you like it when I order for you."

Only because she didn't read Portuguese and he seemed to know all the most decadent things to eat. "A salad with lean protein please."

If he had his way, he would stuff her with *picanha* and *pão de queijo*. The round cheesy bread things were going to be the death of her. And the *quindim*, a type of custard/cake that she was obsessed with now.

She would have to hit the gym when she got home.

Ezra pulled out his phone and his face fell.

"What?"

"The Palace is full tonight." He seemed to force a smile back on his face. "We'll try again next week. I'm sorry it's moving so slowly. We'll go back out tonight and perhaps if I lose another couple of thousand in one of the smaller games, I'll get a reputation as easy prey and we'll get in."

Her heart fell, but she forced herself to smile back. "All right, then."

She started the shower and shed her nearly not-there clothing and bit back a groan of frustration. She had to believe that Ezra was right and they were simply making them wait so they could get more cash out of them when the time came. Games like this were highly exclusive and the players would be vetted. Ezra promised her that their paperwork would hold up, it was simply a matter of time before they got into the game and before she could go home.

She could be home in a few weeks, but she wasn't sure what that word meant anymore. All the things she'd worked so hard for now seemed silly. Her job? She was tired of the constant competition, the backbiting.

Once this was done, what would she be going home to?

She stepped into the shower, the hot water hitting her skin and making her sigh. Maybe she would take some time off and get back to her first love. Research. She loved losing herself in a subject. It might be fun to study the history of the Agency and find the hidden stories behind the world's greatest spies. Ezra talked about how no one would ever know his story, but there were certainly things that had become declassified, interesting points of history that could say things about the world she lived in today.

She wished she could tell Nick's story, the one about the brave man who'd walked away from his job when he'd realized what he was being used to do. She would have to settle for other brave men.

Maybe by telling their stories, she could feel close to him, have some connection though there were miles between them.

Ten minutes later, she stepped out of the shower and went to work drying her hair. She wrapped herself in a robe and hoped dinner would be coming up soon.

When she was clean and dry and couldn't stand another second alone with her thoughts, she made her way through the bedroom with its magnificent bed.

And stopped in her tracks because there was something on her pillow that absolutely shouldn't be there. Hayley felt her jaw drop at the sight of that box of condoms sitting on her bed. That wasn't the only thing. There were sex toys laid out on her nightstand. She barely registered those as her anger rose.

Her nightstand. Not theirs. Ezra had been sleeping on the couch, though he did insist on messing up the other side of the bed so the maids wouldn't talk.

She picked up the box of extra-large, ribbed-for-her-pleasure condoms and turned because they were going to have a talk.

She strode into the room, feeling the heat of anger on her face. "Do you want to explain these? Exactly how are you planning on using these, Mr. Fain? Because if this was a hint..."

She gasped as she felt an arm go around her waist. Before she could scream, a big hand clapped down over her mouth. Panic flared through her system and she tried to kick back.

Someone was in her room. Someone had gotten to Ezra because she couldn't believe that man would hurt her like this. No. He'd opened the door to the wrong person and now she was going to find out the hard way exactly what those men coming after her wanted.

"Stop fighting me. I rather thought you were aware of the many uses of prophylactics," a familiar voice said. Deep and dark, that voice went straight to her pussy. "Let me explain. I will roll it over my erection and then I'll be free to fuck you in any way I wish. I believe you'll find I have a lot of wishes to fulfill when it comes to you, *dushka*. But first we're going to discuss your punishment."

She went still in his arms.

Nick was here. It looked like her trouble was just beginning.

Chapter Eighteen

Hayley relaxed and stopped fighting. There was no way she was fighting this man, though she did have some questions. "What are you doing here?"

His lips were close to her ear, the heat of his words nearly scorching her. "You're not where I left you, Hayley. I came to collect what belongs to me and to make it clear that you will not run from me again."

"Uh, I didn't run from you in the first place. You were leaving. I had nothing to stay for."

"That's not how I remember it. I remember explaining to you quite plainly that I needed some time to think and that you were to stay safely where I put you."

"That is revisionist history," she shot back.

"I've been told it's the only way to go. So we're going to have a long talk, you and I, and you will understand how this will go from now on, but first we should get this out of the way."

His hand moved up and suddenly her towel was on the ground, cool air caressing her skin. Her nipples peaked immediately and she tried to cover herself. "What are you doing? I need that back. We're not alone here. Oh, god. Where's Ezra?"

What had he done to Ezra? Nick could get dramatic at times. She blamed it on his Russianness. She had to hope he hadn't actually killed the CIA agent. She tried to reach for the towel. Nick had it in his hands before she could grab it.

"Mr. Fain is indisposed," he said as he tossed the towel away. "Don't worry about him. We've had a nice talk and he understands that I'm going to be your bodyguard from now on. He's got plenty to think about and he knows you're safe. I was far more courteous to him than he was to me. I wouldn't allow him to believe you're in danger."

"Well, why would we call you? You're the one who told me you were leaving. Aren't you supposed to be in Moscow by now?"

"I never left London. I wouldn't have. I came to my senses after a long night of contemplation, and do you know what I found?"

Did he think she was a complete idiot? That she would ignore what had happened that night simply because he walked in looking like the most gorgeous man she'd ever seen? Nope. She had some small amount of self-respect. "Probably the bottom of a vodka bottle? Do you think I don't know where you went? You ran off to the bar with Brody. The bar that happens to be attached to a lifestyle club where all the naked women roam."

He stood there in the middle of her suite, his lips curling up in a perfectly infuriating smile. "You sound like an aggrieved wife, *dushka*. While you look beautiful when you nag at me, I can't allow you to continue at this moment. We have other things to do. And we do need to talk about when it is appropriate to be naked. Right now is very appropriate. On the beach this afternoon was not."

She started to open her mouth because if he thought she was a nag now, he needed to wait and see what she could unleash on him once she had her clothes on. Before she could say a word, he had wrapped a big hand around her wrist and was pulling her forward.

"Nick, you can't walk back in my life like this." She started to tell him that they needed to sit down and talk. He sat down, but the next thing he did made Hayley believe he had little interest in talking.

He flipped her around and she found herself over his knee. He'd maneuvered her as easily as a doll and showed no sign of strain. Her belly was over his lap, her bare ass up in the air. "I can. I did."

His hand caressed her ass and she could feel her whole body begin to light up. Her heart might have missed him but the rest of her had gone into starvation mode, all her sexual instincts drying up the minute he rejected her. She'd felt numb for days, but now the heat between them roared back.

"Nikolai, you ended our relationship." She needed to say the words, to remind herself that her head and not her stupid heart or her suddenly active female parts were in charge.

"I did nothing of the kind." One hand cupped her ass and the other was at the small of her back, balancing and holding her. "We had a fight and I said things I shouldn't have said. I said them because I was afraid, not only for you but of you, of loving you. I cleared up the problems with my past. There's no one coming after me again. You're safe. I'm safe. Do you understand?"

He'd done that for her? It was everything she'd asked him to do. "You're safe?"

"I'm safe. But more importantly, you're safe. As for the other, I'm still afraid. But I figured out what I'm afraid of more. Not being with you. Not knowing where you are and who is taking care of you. Not having my arms around you. Be as angry as you like with me, Hayley, but don't deny us this. Tell me we can play."

Play? He wanted to play? Such a silly word. Being intimate with Nick didn't feel like play. It felt serious, but then that was how he would put it. He would frame it in his own language. Play was serious for Nick. The fact that he was here and not in Russia was serious for Nick.

But could she trust it?

For now it didn't matter because she wanted him too badly. She had a chance to get her hands on him again and she wasn't going to miss it. If she was going to leave at the end of this, she could have one more night with him.

One more crazy, kinky night.

"Do your worst, Nicky."

His hand left her for a moment and then she heard the hard smack as he spanked her. His hand came down again and again, sparking against her flesh and making her shiver and shake with sensation. Ten times he slapped her ass and then he stopped, one hand slipping between her legs and teasing at her pussy.

"I want you hot and wet for me."

She couldn't be any other way. "I already feel it."

He tested her, sliding a finger in to part her labia. "Yes, that's what I want."

She whimpered as his fingers receded after that minor play. She needed more. So much more.

"You are not to run away ever again." His hand rained down on her, but this time in an oddly soothing way. The pain was there, but something about the way he peppered the smacks spread heat through her system.

"You started it." She couldn't seem to help herself. Not that she should. He had started it.

The next one was rougher, but then his hand stilled as if he could hold the heat in. "I know I did, but I had my reasons. You had no reason to run except that I hurt you."

He needed to understand a few things. "No. I didn't run because you hurt me. I wasn't trying to be dramatic or to get your attention. I left because Ezra was willing to give me a say in how this investigation goes. He wasn't going to lock me up and force me to wait around when I can help."

The next smack proved her theory. This one hurt like hell in comparison. The rest had been a fun game, a way to connect. This one was all about business. She hissed a little and then found herself squirming because despite the pain, she was getting hot and wet.

"He put you in danger," Nick insisted. The smack sounded through the air, jarring her and forcing her to focus on the moment.

On the way she felt. On how every inch of her skin seemed open and willing to take his discipline.

She groaned when he spanked her again. When she shifted slightly, she could feel the thick length of his erection under her belly. "I'm in danger every minute of every day, but I'm not going to hide from it when I might be the only one who can solve the mystery. I'm not going to be some toy you pull out and play with and then lock up when you're done. I'm through hiding. If I get hurt, then at least I'll know I lived."

The hand on her backside smoothed across her skin. "You're precious to me. I can't lie to you. I want you safe, but I also want you happy. Can we agree that I have the right to…how would Taggart put this…I reserve the right to lose my shit when assassins are after the woman I love."

Hearing that word come out of his mouth did something to her heart, but she tried to let her head remain in control. Something had happened to change his mind, but then they'd been here before a couple of times. She didn't want to think about it. She could keep him for a while, could store up memories for that moment when he decided to leave again.

"You can lose your shit, Nicky, but I can't hide anymore."

She gasped as he flipped her over again, turning her neatly so she was in his lap, his arms supporting her. He stared down at her, his eyes serious. She couldn't help but soften under his gaze.

"You will hide nothing from me," he said, his voice low. "And I will not hide from you. You have to be patient with me. I've lost so many women I loved. Please be patient and I will try."

She wasn't sure she could ask more of him. Her heart ached because it was everything she'd ever wanted to hear and she wasn't at all sure she could trust it. He had lost and those losses had preyed on him for years. Those losses had driven them apart. Why would they be able to come together now? She didn't doubt the love she felt for him, only that it could last.

He cradled her as he stood up. "I know you're scared, *dushka*. I made you scared, but I won't do it again. This time I won't put anything above you. Not even my pride and my guilt. This time around you are the queen of my world."

She wanted so badly to believe him. Right now it didn't matter. She was going to live in the present. Her whole life had been about working for a future, and now she understood how quickly it could all go away. Today was the only time she truly had and she was going to make the most of it. She wasn't going to hold back. "Please make love to me, Nick."

Before Ezra came back and she was forced to deal with the problems that would come with the evening. Before she had to face her father.

His lips curled up in the softest look she'd ever seen cross his face. "This, I can do. You should know that I came prepared. You should also know that I intend to be your servant in this life. My world will revolve around your happiness. I will make you my partner in all things, and I won't ever again make a decision that affects us both without talking to you. We're in this life together. I only request one place where I am king."

He strode back into the bedroom, carrying her like she weighed nothing at all. She got a better look at the presents Nick had left for her. While she'd been in the shower, he'd turned her nightstand into a table for his toys. For the objects he would use to bring her enormous amounts of pleasure.

He set her on her feet at the end of the bed and she wondered when she'd gotten comfortable with her naked body. She liked being naked in front of him, enjoyed the vulnerability of being naked while he was fully clothed, loved how he towered over her. When had she begun to love the ache she felt in her cheeks?

She looked at him, trying to memorize every expression on his face, the way his eyes seemed to heat as they looked at her, the way his hair curled slightly around his ears because he'd let it get a tiny bit too long.

Hayley knew what he wanted and she wanted it, too. She'd thought perhaps she would never play again because she would never trust another man with her body the way she did Nick. She'd known she would never take another Dom. He was it for her, the only man she wanted taking control. The only man she would ever kneel for.

The carpet was soft as she dropped down in front of him, beginning the exchange of power that would connect them. She lowered her head and placed her hands palms up on her thighs. Submission in the bedroom was her gift to him, her gift to herself.

His hand came down on her head and she heard him sigh as though the connection somehow brought him real physical relief. "You have no idea how much I've missed this. How much I missed you. I know it's only been a few days, but it felt like forever. I don't want to be apart from you again, *dushka*."

She took a deep breath, fighting the emotion she felt. "I missed you, too."

Sometimes she felt like she'd spent most of her life missing him, longing for him. She wondered if she would ever be complete without him.

"Do you have any idea what I want to do to you?"

She had some thoughts on the matter. "Everything."

"That's a good answer. I want everything from you. I want there to be no walls between us." He tangled one hand in her hair and gently forced her to face him. The bite along her scalp sent a shiver down her spine. "I want you to stand up and lean over the bed. Palms on the mattress, legs apart, and I want that pretty ass in the air. You will keep your eyes forward. No peeking. Can you do that for me?"

She nodded, thoughts of what he was going to do to her swirling through her head. Part of the fun was not knowing exactly what he would do, but giving him permission to do it all. He helped her to stand and when she began to turn, his head swooped down, locking her in a kiss.

His tongue tangled with hers and she could feel his passion, his need. She gave him back her own. When he released her, she turned and did as he asked.

Nick walked across the room, heading over to the nightstand. She stared straight ahead, not turning to look and see what he was prepping.

A big hand slid over her back and down to her ass. "No, no. This won't do, *dushka*. I need your ass higher. You're going to have to do better."

There was a whooshing sound and then the crack of a crop on her ass. She hissed at the pain and then felt her pussy pulse. She had to bite back a groan. Hayley moved from her hands on the bed down to her elbows, her spine straight, placing her ass firmly in the air.

So vulnerable. He was standing behind her and he would have access to all her tender parts. He would be able to touch her, to spank her, to do anything he liked.

Now it seemed what he liked was using a crop to tease her.

The cool of the leather tip traced the curves of her ass.

"That's much better." Nick skimmed down the middle of her cheeks.

She squealed as he brought the crop up and laid a little slap to her pussy. One and then another.

"Yes." His voice had deepened, his accent so much thicker. "This is exactly as I wished. I want you open to my every touch. This belongs to me. This body is mine to discipline and pleasure and worship and adore."

"Then you should definitely do those last three."

He chuckled. "Yes, you hate the discipline. I can tell. I can smell your arousal from here."

She couldn't help that. It happened any time he was around, but he was also right. Her nipples felt heavy and she longed for him to touch her. Not in a soft, sweet way. No. She wanted the rough Dom with his tweaks and spanks, and that hard cock that would inevitably drive into her.

One last swat had her panting and then he placed the crop on the bed next to her.

"Don't make me pick it up again. If you do, we'll begin all over again and you'll be that much further from getting what you want. If I have to start over, you'll find I've brought along a nice ball gag that I won't hesitate to use. I'll tie you up and have my fun and it will be hours before I allow you to come."

She bit her bottom lip to keep from begging. Or saying something truly bratty because that was in there, too. She wasn't scared of the ball gag, but drool wasn't high on her list of sexy turn-ons.

"That's better." Nick put a hand on the small of her back, steadying her. "I want you to stay still. You can whimper and whine all you like. Make all the noise you need to, but don't move an inch or there will be punishment. This is going to be a bit chilly."

Hayley braced herself as Nick parted the cheeks of her ass, and then he was probing the sensitive rim of her asshole.

She had to catch her breath because she knew what came next. Sure enough, she felt the hard tip of a plug circle her rim.

"I want you to feel me everywhere tonight. I want you to know that I can take care of every single inch of your body. I'm going to take what's mine, and you won't ever be able to forget who you belong to." He rimmed her with the plug, the sensation sharp and ragged and oh-so sensual.

She could never forget. No matter how hard she tried, she knew he would still be there in her head and her heart the day she died. Belonging to Nick would only work if he belonged to her, too, and she worried that a part of him would always be somewhere else.

She forced that thought aside. All that mattered was tonight, and tonight she was his.

"Please, Nick. Please take what's yours. I'm yours. Every part of me."

He pressed the plug in, the hard tip breaching her and making her moan. He fucked her with the plug, taking her inch by delicious inch. Over and over, he worked his way in.

Hayley forced herself to relax, to let the plug take its place deep inside.

"Have I told you how beautiful you are?" Nick asked, his hands on her cheeks.

He was staring at her, looking at this intimate piece of her and finding her lovely. No one else would see this part of her. Not even herself. And yet she'd been stripped bare, her soul and body laid out for him to judge, and he found her beautiful.

She felt beautiful. For once in her life, she felt free. "You make me feel that way."

She felt him move, felt the soft press of lips on the small of her back. "I'll never let you down again. Give me a moment and then I'll worship you properly."

Something thudded behind her, but she held her place. Nick was moving. She heard the sounds of him washing up and kept her body perfectly still. It was an exercise in discipline that forced her to focus on the now. Patience was rewarded with attention and gratification. This was what he'd trained her to do. To wait for her pleasure, to delay it so it bloomed so much more vibrantly.

"Let me help you up." He was back and his hand came down, giving her balance so she could stand. "Don't lose the plug. I wouldn't want to have to start all over again."

With the spanking. He would start by spanking her and then bring in the crop and a larger plug. Sadist. This was how he kept her on the edge, focused on him and not random thoughts running through her head. She was here with him, and that was all that mattered.

He pulled her close and she could feel the heat of his skin. He'd taken off his jacket, gotten rid of his dress shirt and tie. All she could see was the smooth, glorious muscles of his chest. She brought her hands up, unable to stand so close and not touch him. She was sure some D/s couples worked on the idea of only touching with permission, but Nick's eyes closed in obvious pleasure as she ran her hands down his chest.

"I love it when your hands are on me. Don't ever stop touching me," he growled. "I always want your touch, your skin against mine. It's the only way I feel whole."

His mouth came down on hers again, taking her lips with a dominant strength that left her breathless.

His hands were everywhere, soothing over her back and down, cupping her ass and pulling her against him. She loved the feel of him. Chest to chest. Core to core. His tongue dancing with hers.

There was no space between them and soon he would be inside, connecting them fully, making them one.

He eased her down on the bed, supporting her and making it so simple to lie back and allow him to have control. When she felt the soft silk of the comforter at her back, he stood over her and stared down.

"You are so beautiful. I know I keep saying it, but I can't help myself."

She didn't want him to. She needed him. "You're beautiful to me, too. So lovely, Nicky."

His hands went to the button of his slacks. "I have no idea what you see in me, but I'm done arguing. I'm done martyring myself. I do it with you and I do it with my team, but never again. You're my family now. You and my people back in London. We can make this work."

The family he'd built. Stronger than blood. More resilient because it was chosen.

If only she could trust it. No family had been stable for her. No unmoving ground beneath her feet.

What would it feel like to completely trust someone? To know that no matter what came, she had someone who had her back, who thought of her before every other consideration.

A husband.

He kicked his slacks aside and walked to the end of the bed. He towered over her, his perfect body so lovely to her eyes. She could feel the hard press of the plug inside her. She could feel his gaze like a stroke to her skin.

"Take me. Take all of me," Hayley said, beseeching him to finish what he'd started.

She wanted him inside her every moment they had. No matter how many I love yous they said, she knew how they ended. How they always ended, and she wasn't going to lose a single minute with him. Not this time.

He tossed aside the last of his clothes and she could see how much he wanted. His cock stood proud against his belly. He stroked himself. "I will, but only if you take all of me. I was born to love you, Hayley. Nothing has worked until I realized what I was meant to do. Spread yourself. Open for me."

She moved her feet, giving him free access to her body.

He put a knee on the bed, joining her. He loomed over her, placing himself at her core before drawing out the condom. He stroked himself before settling it over his cock.

She reached out for him. "Please, Nicky."

He nodded and covered her body with his. "I'll never leave you again. I know I've made mistakes, but if you'll have me, I'll be yours forever. I want it all with you, Hayley. I want a life and family."

Tears blurred her eyes, but she couldn't find the will to say the words. She couldn't quite believe them. This was all they had. This moment.

He stopped, cupping her face and wiping away her tears. "Don't cry. I'll prove it to you. I'll show you. You be patient with me and I'll be patient with you. You don't have to believe today. Believe five years from now when I'm still by your side, when we're building something together. Until then, I don't need the words. I only need you to tell me I can stay."

She nodded, words too much for her.

He leaned over, bringing his mouth to hers as his hips flexed and she felt him start to thrust inside.

He kissed her as he locked their bodies together, connecting them in the sweetest way possible. Hayley wrapped her arms around him and there was nothing to do, no other worlds to worry about, no space to allow doubt to come between them. There was only Nikolai and this moment when their bodies mingled, when it felt like every inch of her was caressed and loved by him. He worshipped her with his mouth and tongue, with his hands and his cock.

The plug made her tight, so tight. It forced her to feel every inch and movement of his cock inside her. He found a rhythm, thrusting in and rotating so he ground on her clitoris while he plunged deep. Pulling out and dragging on the plug, stimulating every inch of her.

She held out as long as she could, desperately wanting for the moment to last. Wanting to stay here in this place and time, connected to him forever.

Nick thrust in hard and sent her over the edge. She clutched at him while calling out his name, lost in the feeling of being one with this man.

Nick seemed to lose control, fucking into her again and again, his body tightening, and then he fell forward, holding not an ounce of his weight off her, surrounding her with him.

I love you. The words were right there. They were stuck in her throat and she couldn't manage to say them. When she said them, that was when he would leave. That was when he always left.

Nick shifted, hauling her with him. "It's okay, Hayley. It's all right. Tell me I can stay. That's all I need, *dushka.*"

She clung to him, emotion threatening to overwhelm her. "Stay with me."

It was all she could give him for now.

* * * *

Nick wrapped the robe around Hayley after carefully drying her off. He kissed the top of her head and wished he had words that could fix what he'd done to her.

It was going to take time to convince her he wouldn't disappear, wouldn't choose some mission over her ever again. Making love to her had been life affirming for him, but he was worried it had done nothing but confuse her.

Still, she cuddled close to him, her arms wrapping around his waist. "I'm going to leave the hotel with a crazy water bill. That was my third shower of the day. I was out on the beach earlier and got sand everywhere."

He breathed her in, loving the fact that he could catch a hint of sex still clinging to her despite the thorough cleaning he'd given her. Of course, he'd needed to use his tongue on certain delicate parts of her body. And then he'd kind of shoved her lovingly against the side of the shower and made her scream again. "I know this. I watched you as you walked down the beach with Fain. I did not like the way he held your hand. It bothered me greatly, but I trust you."

He brought her hand up to his lips, kissing it before settling it over his heart. He trusted her implicitly. Fain, on the other hand, was a woman-stealing bastard who had gotten far less than he deserved.

"You were watching us? Don't try to distract me with those gorgeous puppy eyes." Even as she said the words, her free hand was holding him close.

He had no idea he had puppy eyes. He was fairly certain he'd been born with full-grown mutt eyes, but he would take what he could. "I have been frantic to find you. Kayla and I have been here since the day after you ran…very reasonably chose to relocate to South America."

He could be careful.

Her lips curved up in the most gorgeous smile. "More revisionist history?"

Seeing that light in her eyes made his heart soft. "If it makes you smile like that I'll revise all of it, Professor."

She groaned and leaned into him. "Please tell me how you found me. And where Ezra went. We've only got another three hours until we need to be downtown. We're playing in one of the smaller poker games."

He managed to not growl at the thought of anyone expecting her and Ezra as a couple. "I came to Brazil because of what Desiree left me in her letter."

Her head came up. "You read it?"

"Finally, and it was a good thing, too, because she told me what I needed to know in that letter, though no one else caught on to it." It was so much easier to think of Des now, to give her a place in his own personal history that didn't cut at him the way it used to. "Desiree had been planning on leaving after we returned from the Caribbean. She knew Damon was on to her plans and she had recently uncovered intelligence she believed would bring her enough money to live on quite grandly."

Her face fell and she took a step back. "She said she was leaving in her letter to me, too. Are you okay? Reading that had to hurt."

"It's all right. She was right to go. We weren't good for each other. We brought out all the bad parts. But she knew exactly who I would run to. She knew who brought out the best parts of me, who made me a better man. She told me I should be with you. She told me that I needed to teach you that a house doesn't make a home. Only love can. I know that makes me a sentimental fool, but I am. I forgot that for a long time. I forgot that the world can be so beautiful if we open our eyes and allow it in."

She sniffled and turned away, her shoulders moving as though she was taking a deep breath. "I don't know that I can talk about this right now. I'm willing to stay with you but I can't talk about the future now."

He moved in behind her. Patience. "All right. I will stop talking about the future, but you should understand that I love you very much in the now." He kissed the top of her head before moving on. He wasn't going to prompt her to say the words a second before she was willing to give them back to him. It would come. He had faith.

Having faith felt good. Having faith filled the hole inside him, the hole he'd ached with for years.

She reached for the comb on the vanity. "Why don't you tell me what Desiree said in her letter about this information we're supposed to find?"

"Sit." He pulled the chair out for her. Part of the decadent bathroom was a lovely silver mirrored vanity. He eased the comb from her hand. "Allow me. I love to brush my lover's hair. I have not for years because I thought I should be more manly. I don't have to be this way with you. I can be myself, and myself truly wants to take

374

care of you."

She glanced at him in the mirror. "If you were any more manly, you might explode with testosterone. I take it Des didn't like it."

He eased the comb through her hair. She'd used enough conditioner on it that the gorgeous silky stuff was already smooth. "Do you like it? That's all that matters now. And Desiree's letter basically allowed me to be certain of my instincts. I believe she kept a copy of whatever intelligence she had in her possession that allowed her to blackmail her victims. She would have kept it in a storage facility and she would have paid it up for many years. I believe one copy was in the belongings that were sent to you from Tokyo, though your father chose to blow those up."

"Or he stole it and then tried to cover his tracks," she replied. "I can't figure him out. One minute I'm sure he was trying to save me. The next minute I wonder why he wouldn't have found a way to contact me. I don't know how I feel about him."

Yes, he had to deal with her father as well. "He's here."

Her eyes caught his in the mirror. "I know. Ezra and I are trying to get invited to an underground casino. There's a high-stakes poker room there. I think that's where I'll find him, but we were told no tonight. Unfortunately, the game moves once a week and now we have to wait and try again."

Damn but he had bad news for her. "Your father was at the beach this afternoon. Hayley, he saw you. I don't think you have to go. I think he'll stay away now."

She paled. "Seriously? He was there and he…of course he didn't."

"I'll find him for you when this is through," Nick replied. "I'll make sure he gives you all the answers you need. This I promise you."

She shook her head. "I don't need anything from him, but Ezra does. Dad apparently faked his own death before he could hand off intelligence about whoever sold out Ezra's brother's unit. I also figured Dad would know where Des had hidden whatever she hid."

"I have Kayla working on it. She's looking for a storage place somewhat near where Desiree used to keep an apartment. How did Fain figure out he should go not only to Rio, but here in Ipanema?"

"He had intelligence that this was where my father had gone. Since this isn't a hotbed of gambling action, he couldn't have come here for cash. He came here for whatever Des was trying to leave him through me. I figured he would try to find a game since it seems like he's cash starved. I started asking questions and found out that there's an illegal casino that moves around the city every Sunday night. High rollers only. My father will be at that game. Or he would have if he hadn't seen me talking to the only man who can get a tourist in. Some spy I turned out to be."

He stroked her hair back. "That was Fain's job, though I don't blame him. He was far too busy killing the man who was about to assassinate you."

Her eyes went wide. "What?"

Had that fucker not bothered to mention that she'd nearly been murdered? "You had two stalkers. I took care of one of them. Fain killed the one in the light blue jacket. He did a good job. Left him looking like he was sleeping. I don't like to admit it, but he has some skill. I tossed mine in the rubbish bin outside the hotel."

She turned, her jaw hanging open. "He told me he'd helped that man."

"He did since I would have slit him open and played with his intestines, so yes, he does this man a great favor."

Hayley stood up suddenly. "Where is Ezra? I need to talk to him. He told me we were safe here, that no one had followed us."

Well, Nick had no intentions of making the same mistake. "Not at all. I've seen at least two, and contractors are like cockroaches. Where are two there are likely many more. We'll have to be careful. As of last night, the Dallas team was tracking ten known players, and six of them were either here in Rio or on their way."

"But I haven't seen anything. It's been so quiet around us. I've felt perfectly safe even though I've been told there's a crime wave going on. Tourists have been murdered."

He gave her a moment. She was a smart girl. All she had to do was connect a few dots…

"He's been taking them out behind my back, hasn't he? I knew that was blood on his shirt the other night. He tried to tell me it was ketchup, but we didn't have any on the table."

The idea that Fain had been spending such quiet, intimate time with Hayley made him wish he'd been rougher with the ass, but he was perfectly satisfied that she had no designs on the operative. He trusted her. "Oh, undoubtedly. If this upset you terribly, I could kill him for you. This would be my greatest honor and a true pleasure."

She stared at him like she'd never seen him before. It was good to know that he could surprise her. "You can't kill Ezra."

"I assure you it would be an easy job right now. He's tied up and helpless. One quick drag across his throat and the job is done." He glanced over at the shower. It was definitely big enough. "Though we should bring him in here. Much less mess. After he bleeds out we can stuff him in a suitcase. Kayla brought one that is large enough to handle him. How many pairs of shoes does one tiny woman need? I ask her this. She threatens to murder me with her Louboutins."

"What?"

He was surprised she didn't know this. He would have to buy her a pair. She would look lovely in them. "It's a type of shoe. Apparently because the soles are red, it is very expensive, but I swear I have seen the same shoes on Moscow strippers, though without the red. No one sees the bottoms of your shoes. Why is this important to women?"

Her face wrinkled up so sweetly. "I wasn't talking about the shoes. I know about the shoes. I was talking about the fact that you apparently tied up a CIA operative and left him somewhere."

"And gagged. Remember when I threatened to gag you? This was a bluff. I had already used the ball gag on Ezra. Do not worry. I'll buy a new one for you. We can buy one together. A whole new kit chosen just for you."

Hayley put a hand on her hip, her eyes taking on that steely gaze

377

that let him know she was completely serious about whatever she was going to say next. "Nicky, I need you to tell me where you stashed Ezra. Is he out in the hallway? Is he vulnerable? You admitted that there are professional criminals looking for us. Did you leave him out there to be murdered?"

She wasn't being any fun. "I told you, I will only murder him to please you. Otherwise, I was ordered by Damon not to pull him into many pieces, urinate on the pieces, and feed to alligators. Do they have alligators here or is it crocodiles? It doesn't matter. Any large reptile would have done the job. In any case, I did not do this. I was kind. I tossed him in the wardrobe. He's perfectly safe there."

She went completely still and he watched as her skin went a lovely, vibrant shade of pink. "The wardrobe in the bedroom where we recently had sex?"

She turned and strode out of the bathroom.

Nick followed her, feeling the need to correct certain parts of that statement. Words were important to her. He'd learned this. "Where we made beautiful love. Yes. I captured him, took him down, and then placed him in the wardrobe. See. He was safe. If something had happened, either Kayla or I would have rescued him, though he doesn't truly deserve it."

Hayley was standing in front of the wardrobe, staring at it like it was a snake about to bite her. "Kayla? How would Kayla have helped?"

The door to the outer room of the suite came open and there was his partner. He'd given her Ezra's key to the room and she'd been ensuring their safety when Nick was otherwise occupied. "Thank god. I thought you guys were going to fuck forever. Does anyone mind if I order the tapas? Like all of them. I'm starving and I bet Ezra could probably use a drink."

The wardrobe shook slightly.

Hayley turned to him. "How could you do that? He heard everything."

"That wasn't too hard," Kayla said. "You're incredibly

enthusiastic, but I kind of think that was part of Nick's point. I believe he wanted to prove to our friendly neighborhood CIA guy that you're his girl."

Nick stalked to the wardrobe. It was obvious his fun was over and it was time to get down to work. He opened the wardrobe and pointed at the man who was kind of squished into the bottom of it. Cool blue eyes looked up at him.

He stared down at Fain, pointing a finger at him. "You are never to mention this to Hayley. You heard nothing. You saw nothing. You do not even know that she has sex at all. She's a virgin to you."

Hayley groaned. "Could someone bring Broody Nick back? I miss him."

He started to turn to her, but suddenly he found himself jolting forward as Ezra's legs came out, kicking him squarely in the small of his back and sending him to his knees. How had the fucker gotten his ankles untied? There was no time to ponder that question as Ezra was on him in an instant. His hands were still tied, but that didn't seem to bother Fain. He wrapped them around Nick's neck and started to squeeze.

"Nick!" Hayley screamed.

Nick merely threw himself back, landing right on top of the CIA agent.

Kayla was leaning against the bed, not at all ready to jump into the fray. "You promised not to kill him."

He hadn't promised not to maim the man. He threw a quick elbow into Fain's gut and hopped up. As much as he would enjoy pummeling Fain, they had other things to discuss, and he might prove helpful.

He punched Fain square in his pretty-boy face. He wasn't going to be that helpful.

Fain made a sound Nick was sure would be quite threatening had it not been for the ball gag in his mouth.

"I promise not to punch you again if you'll calm down. You know damn well you deserved this. She is mine. She has chosen and I expect you to respect that. Now do you want me to get rid of the ball gag? Or should I let you do it? You'll have to tell me how you got your feet undone. I'm usually pretty good with knots." Now that he'd had several hours of truly filthy, beautiful sex with the woman he loved, he was feeling rather indulgent. "We can work together, you and I. I hear that you need the information to find the man who betrayed your brother. I promise I will help you find this. You help me clean up Hayley's problems, and I will be your partner in this. I vow this on the souls of my family. You will find a good helper in me."

It was the most sacred vow he could make. He needed Hayley to see that he was going to be different. He was going to be honorable. He was going to be a good man, the kind she would want as a husband.

Fain went still and then slowly nodded.

"I'll help you with that. Ball gags suck, man." Kayla expertly twisted the ball free. "You'll probably want to brush your teeth. Damn things taste like latex. I once had a really nice Dom get me a strawberry-flavored one. Unfortunately, it tasted like strawberry-flavored latex."

Nick quickly got his hands untied and then stepped back.

Fain merely wiped his mouth and massaged his jaw. "You're a bastard, Markovic. And I would have gotten out of the hand ties in another few minutes." He turned to Hayley. "And I'm not sorry at all about killing those fuckers. They were coming after you and I promised I would keep you safe."

"You lied about it," she shot back, coming to stand at Nick's side.

It was good to know his boundaries. She could handle murders, but he mustn't lie about them. He put an arm around her, drawing her close. "Yes, you see I told her about the murder I was forced to commit this afternoon."

Fain groaned. "I thought I recognized that guy at the beach. Yeah, he had a partner he always worked with."

"Not anymore," Nick replied. "His partner is now in the dumpster, and I hear we're going to a casino tonight."

"Yeah, we should probably talk about that." Fain put a hand out. "I'm sorry. I'm only trying to do my job, but I was never going to let her get hurt."

He shook the other man's hand. "And that is why you live."

Hayley sighed and pulled away. "I don't understand men at all. Kay, I think I'm the one who needs the drink. And food. I'm super hungry."

"Yeah, let's get all the tapas." Kay started to lead her out to the living room. "And hey, don't look so sad. We might get to murder someone tonight. We can't let the boys have all the fun."

Hayley groaned, but when she closed the door she was smiling.

He looked back at Fain. "We should put all our cards on the table. I know things you don't. I've thought this through quite carefully and I have a plan that might get Hayley out of this mess we find ourselves in without anyone firing another shot at her."

Fain nodded. "All right. I'm willing to listen, but you have to understand that I need her father alive."

"I would like to speak with him as well." Nick had been ruminating on the plan ever since that moment when he'd realized why a bunch of contractors had been sent after Hayley. Hayley herself was utterly useless except as a pawn, but that heart around her neck was everything.

Sometimes sacrifices had to be made to protect the queen.

"The truth is I wouldn't mind having some backup," Fain replied. "But you're still a bastard. You know you could have simply had a conversation with me."

What fun would that have been? But he merely nodded. He was in an agreeable mood.

There was a knock on the door and he barely managed to get there in time to keep Hayley from throwing it open.

Fain stood back and shook his head. "I've been trying to teach her. At least now she's your problem. The girl doesn't seem to understand how dangerous our situation is."

Hayley frowned his way.

Nick looked through the peephole in the door, his hand on the Ruger he had tucked into a holster on his belt. One man, dressed in a bellman's uniform. No visible weapon. The kid looked fairly young and completely at ease with his current job. As one of the maids walked behind him, his smile went douchebag lothario and he winked her way.

He stepped back and nodded to Fain, giving him the all clear.

He looked back at Hayley, who was quite calm even as Kay stood in front of her.

"I do take it seriously," she whispered to Nick as Fain greeted the man at the door. "Of course I would have taken it way more seriously if Ezra hadn't killed a bunch of people behind my back."

He was going to take every opportunity to show her the differences. He lifted her hand up, bringing it to his lips and kissing her fingers softly. "I will always murder them in front of you because I would never want you to feel left out."

Her jaw dropped again, but this time she laughed. "You're such a weirdo."

He would take it because she was smiling.

Ezra closed the door, locking it again. "It looks like a slot opened up for tonight. This is an invitation from the head of The Palace."

Hayley's hand tightened in his. "That's great."

Nick didn't think so. Fain's jaw was tight. "What's wrong?"

Fain held out the invitation. "It's for the four of us. This invitation requires that we bring our lovely friends."

There was a picture of the two of them attached. He and Kayla were walking together on the street in front of their hotel.

Things had just gotten more dangerous.

Chapter Nineteen

Hayley nodded to the man who stood in front of the nondescript metal door. It looked like any other office building in downtown Rio, though they weren't going through the main doors. They were in a quiet alley at the rear of the building, the darkness only held back by a single light above the doorway.

"You're sure?" Nick's hand was firmly in her own, their fingers tangled together.

It wasn't the first time he'd asked. And no, she wasn't sure. She was walking into a gangster's den, and a gangster no one could find any intelligence on except for the rumors of what happened when people crossed him. She turned her face up, giving him a serene smile. "I'm sure."

Because she knew if she didn't give him every indication that she was all right with her place, she would likely be the one tied up and gagged and left somewhere that Nick felt was "safe."

The only reason she was walking into The Palace was the fact that the invitation required all four of them to be there.

Were they walking into a trap? Almost certainly, but it wasn't something they could stay away from.

She felt completely out of place in the Prada dress Ezra had bought for her. Nick had been the one to zip her into the tight-fitting sheath, telling her the whole time how beautiful she was and how she would be safe because he would be watching out for her the whole time.

"She's going to be fine, but we should try to keep up our cover." Fain looked perfectly comfortable in his three-piece suit. His hair was slicked back, showing off his Hollywood-worthy face.

Nick's hand tightened on hers as though he was afraid she would get away. "If they know about Kayla and myself, then they know about your cover. There is no need for Hayley to not be at my side."

It was something else they'd endlessly discussed.

"Come on, handsome. I'll take care of you." Kayla looped her arm through Ezra's.

The invitation had informed Ms. Hayley Dalton that if she wanted to learn the truth, she would seek it at The Palace, but she wasn't to come alone. She was to bring her friends, and all were promised safe passage.

Apparently that was gangster speak for no one was going to be murdered tonight. Then again, gangsters didn't always tell the truth. Despite the fact that all three super spies had decided it was all right to take the chance, they were all armed to the teeth.

They stepped into the light and she couldn't help but notice the bulge at the guard's side. His jacket couldn't quite cover the gun he wore on his belt.

Was this what Nick felt every time he went on a mission? Did he feel this rush of excitement combined with a complete and abject horror?

Ezra gave the man with the gun a confident smile and said the words he was supposed to say. They were in Portuguese and were some sort of code word that would get them in the building. Her heart pounded in her chest as he opened that door and Nick led her through.

They followed behind Ezra, whose suit fit so much better than the guard's since there wasn't a hint of the arsenal he was wearing. And Kayla's stunning designer gown hid at least one gun and a couple of knives.

Nick's arm went around her waist as they entered the lobby, his gaze constantly moving around the area seeking threats. She took a moment to get a lay of the land. The lobby was decorated in a lush old-world feel, but she could hear the thumping of industrial music coming from behind heavy oak doors.

"Had I known Nick was going to be in charge of your jewelry, I would have selected another color," Fain complained, under his breath. "That necklace doesn't at all go with the dress."

"That necklace is one of the reasons we're here," Nick shot back. "Are you going to be an operative or is your next job going to be fashion designer?"

They'd snipped and sniped at each other all evening. It had driven her to shut both men out and spend her precious time with Kayla, who had done her hair and makeup and given her tips on how to handle anything physical.

But mostly she'd stared at herself in the mirror and realized that her time was rapidly running out and she had a decision to make.

Maybe the best way to handle things this time would be to walk out on him before he could do it to her. Nick would get bored or something would happen that would send him into protective mode and then he would push her away to keep her safe.

She reached up and touched the heart at her neck. Nick had inspected it earlier, the first time she'd taken the thing off since she'd gotten it back. It had been odd how she'd felt naked without it, and yet shouldn't that stupid heart be the symbol of betrayal? She'd given it to Des in love and friendship, and apparently Desiree had turned it into some kind of key that opened the door to her blackmailing business.

Had she done it as a joke?

Or out of some odd sentimentality. Desiree's letter to her...she could still see the delicate handwriting on the page. When she'd read it she'd heard Desiree's voice.

Your only problem, my dearest, your only true enemy is and always has been your insecurity. Find a way to beat it and the world will open up to you. Find a way to beat it and still remain your own sweet self and you can be his queen in a way I never, ever was. And he'll be yours in a way he was never mine. He'll be yours forever.

"Good evening. Would you care to make a donation tonight?" There was a well-dressed man who stood behind a desk right outside the casino doors.

Fain stepped up. Hayley noticed that Kayla moved to a place in front of Hayley while Nick stayed at her side.

Everyone had agreed that protecting her was their ultimate mission. All these people willing to step in front of a bullet for her. They had lives. They were all beautiful and strong and yet they were protecting her.

"We don't need to make a donation," Fain was saying. "We were invited by the management."

The concierge's face went a polite blank. "Ah, you're the boss's special guests. Yes, I'll have Mr. Jones escort you up."

Mr. Jones turned out to be a large man who looked like he ate raw meat on a daily basis, and not in a caged-lion kind of way. He was a dude who hunted down his supper. Mr. Jones was roughly six and a half feet tall, with pale skin and flinty eyes. He was carved from marble, cold and unmovable. "You'll need to leave any weapons you have with my team."

That was the moment she realized they were surrounded. The men in Mr. Jones's "team" had moved in silently, like stalking panthers.

Nick tugged her closer to his side. "I'm not giving up anything. Please tell your employer that this is not an acceptable way to greet his guests."

Fain had moved back, his hand going under his jacket as he and Kayla maneuvered so that they formed a sort of triangle with Nick, giving them visibility on all sides. "Yes, I think we'll find a more courteous host for the evening. And should you decide to attempt to force us to do something we don't want to do, you need to understand that Ian Taggart and Damon Knight have been informed of our whereabouts this evening and my personal employer has also been made aware of where I am and who I'm meeting with."

It was their only way to check the potential threat. The hope was whoever the boss turned out to be knew those names, knew who Fain actually worked for and didn't want to mess with them. Or the boss couldn't care less who they worked for and he would simply kill them all, take the necklace, and hope he could find the box it opened.

Mr. Jones touched his ear. "Yes, sir. Of course, sir." He nodded to his men. "The boss is certain this party isn't carrying weapons of any kind. I'll take them through and up to the office. The boss says they don't need more than a simple escort. You may all stand down."

The men around them seemed to shrink back into the shadows.

Hayley was able to breathe again.

"It's all right." Nick leaned over as they began to walk. "We have something to bargain with if we need to. I think he wants to talk. Know that I won't allow anything to happen to you. I love you, Hayley."

It damn near broke her heart. Those words were all she'd wanted to hear and they stuck in her throat when she wanted to say them back. Instead, she turned and walked after Ezra.

The doors slid open and she was assaulted by the sounds of the casino. How they managed to move this massive thing once a week, she had no idea. It was like walking into a completely different world.

The whole of the warehouse had been transformed into a sumptuous space. There was rich carpet at her feet and a chandelier hanging from the rafters. Hayley counted ten tables of various card games, each with what appeared to be luxurious chairs for the players. Cocktail waitresses worked the floor wearing little more than Hayley herself had worn at the beach. They had to work their uniforms while carrying a tray of drinks, balancing on stilettos, and keeping their hair and makeup flawless.

"It's all illusion," a feminine voice said.

Mr. Jones stopped in the middle of the floor and nodded to the woman. She was a stunning brunette with a killer figure. Hayley would have pegged her age at mid-thirties, but something about the way she held herself made her nudge the number up slightly.

Mr. Jones nodded. "Miss Helena."

She nodded back, the regal dismissal of a queen to one of her employees. She continued in her perfectly clipped posh British accent. "Mr. Jones. I thought I would come down and welcome our group. I've read so much about you in the last few days. Well, about the men at least. I've heard much about Miss Dalton for years." Her eyes narrowed on Kayla. "Nothing on you, dear. You seem to be quite the ghost."

Kayla gave her a hint of a smile. "Not at all. I'm merely here with my…friend." She put a hand on Fain's shoulder. "A working girl like me can never be too careful with her identity."

Helena's brow arched. "Somehow I doubt that. As an actual former working girl, I know a spy when I see one. Mr. Fain, Mr. Markovic, my employer would like to welcome you to The Palace."

Nick was watching the woman with suspicious eyes. "You look familiar to me."

Helena's lips tugged up slightly. "Because we've met once before, though I doubt you would remember. You only had eyes for my boss at the time."

"Desiree," Nick said. "Yes, now I remember. I met you in St. Petersburg. You brought Des intelligence about the head of one of the local syndicates."

"Yes, he was my lover at the time. A quite brutal man. I wasn't unhappy to see him go." She moved in, stepping close to Hayley. "I've had several jobs over the years. I think I like this one the best of all." She swept a hand out, gesturing to the room. "What you see here is mostly pure theater. We can have the entirety of The Palace torn down and stored in roughly twenty minutes. This particular station of ours is much larger than it looks. The walls appear painted, but they're actually clever draperies that go from above the lighting all the way to the floor. Lighting does much of our work for us. Keep the lights low and the illusion remains intact."

"Somehow I don't think twenty minutes is enough if the cops show up," Fain said, looking terribly unimpressed.

Helena shrugged one delicate shoulder. "I doubt they will since we have several politicians and high-up members of the force enjoying the evening with us tonight. You should know the first job of any good host is to find the best guests possible. But even if they did show up, we have plans and protocols. Never fear. Come with me. My employer is most eager to meet with you."

Hayley had a few questions. She looked up at Nick. "So you know her and she knows Des, and somehow she knows me."

Nick put a hand on the small of her back. "I met her briefly and now that I'm here, I can only guess what this place really is. I think they make more off women than the actual casino. The casino is merely the trappings and bright bow for the real work done here."

"Desiree always said you were a clever man, Nikolai." Helena headed for the back of the casino, marching in her sky-high heels.

"Somehow I doubt this," Nick replied, his expression turning grim. "I think she would have said I was a useful man, nothing more."

"She cared about you quite a bit. Enough to keep you out of her games," Helena remarked as they approached the back of the "room." It was clearly marked with a red velvet rope. "It was one of the things she made her girls promise. We were never to offer ourselves to you nor were we to discuss the business with you."

"The business being blackmail," Kayla explained. "Like I said, I've been around long enough to know what kind of a scam this is. What you really sell is high-class mistresses who can supply powerful men with sex and drugs in exchange for money and opportunity."

Hayley grasped the concept quickly. "Ah, the opportunity to collect information. Information you can sell or use as blackmail."

It confirmed everything Nick believed about how she'd ended up in this position. It was good to know that Des's legacy continued after her death. And she meant that as sarcastically as possible. It was so like Des to continue to fuck everything up even after she died.

Helena stopped in front of the massive man who guarded the door. "I prefer to think of it as we provide good service to our clientele. Anything more would be indiscreet to discuss. Now, if you'll join me, the boss would like to see you now. He's a busy man, of course. And a private one."

She nodded to the guard and he pulled open the door for them. It was more of a flap, a place in the curtain where two parts met. Now that she was close, she could see what Helena had been talking about. From a distance, with the soft lights and mood music setting the scene, the place had looked rich and decadent. Up close, it was nothing more than a façade, and one with pieces that were threadbare and worn.

Pay no attention to the man behind the curtain.

It was all smoke and mirrors and a perverted wizard. Was this what Desiree had hoped to become? The wizard of her own decadent Oz?

Helena allowed them to walk through. Ezra and Kayla stepped past the curtain and disappeared into darkness.

Helena stopped Hayley before she crossed the threshold. She looked down at her neck, right to the place where the red and gold heart sat. "That's a quaint piece of jewelry. I do believe I've seen it before. Desiree wore it a few times. I always thought it was odd. She was quite serious about her appearance and never wore less than the best, yet she wore that quite often. Did she leave it to you?"

Nick had told her not to lie. He'd explained that the necklace was bait of sorts. The necklace might be traded for Hayley's life if they got into a sticky situation. "Yes, though in truth, it was a gift from me to her. It was a silly thing. I was a teenager and I spent pretty much everything I had on it. Everything I had was about fifty dollars. I'm surprised to find out that she wore it when I wasn't around."

"Yes, it surprised me, too," Helena replied.

"Desiree was very private." Nick's voice had gone deep, his

accent coming out. Hayley had learned that happened when he was emotional or trying to be intimidating. "She would not show these pieces of herself to mere employee. This she would keep only for family. Hayley was family. I was family."

What was he doing? Beyond dropping his articles, he was deliberately provoking the woman. It made Hayley nervous as hell, but she had to trust that he knew what he was doing.

For a second Hayley was almost certain Helena's claws would come out, but the brunette merely smiled, her eyes cool as she gestured them through. "Well, I'm sure Hayley is family to many people. Family, in my opinion, is far overrated."

Hayley stepped through and realized that Helena had been playing with them all along. She'd been shown into the industrial portion of the warehouse. All was dark around them with the singular exception of a light illuminating a metal staircase that led to an upstairs office. Standing there at the bottom of the stairs was a man wearing a dapper suit and looking far more alive than he should have.

"Hello," her father said. "I see your taste in men hasn't changed, sweetheart."

"Hello, Dad." She gripped Nick's hand and prayed her father wasn't about to end them all.

* * * *

Nick didn't like the fact that there was a man at his back and two above him. For all he knew Helena had a gun on her, too. They were outnumbered and outgunned and had only the threat of extreme retribution to keep them safe.

He hated that he'd brought Hayley here, but there had been no choice. The only thing that brought him any comfort at all was the fact that Paul Dalton was staring at his daughter like a desperate man. He was definitely the same man he'd seen on the beach that day, and that made Nick wonder how long he'd been planning whatever the hell this was.

"You look beautiful, sweetheart." Dalton stepped forward and then stopped as though he wasn't sure of his welcome.

Hayley frowned his way. It was the frown that Nick knew meant trouble. "You look alive. That's a bit surprising."

"I can explain if you'll let me," her father said quietly. "Why don't we go up to my office? I'll have coffee brought up and we can talk for a while. I need you to see that everything I've done has been to protect you."

"Including blowing up my house?" Hayley asked.

He nodded. "I know it was shocking, but I had to do it. I thought I could keep you out of this. Please come upstairs with me and I'll tell you everything you want to know. Your friends can enjoy the casino. Helena will show them around."

Dalton held out a hand, but there was no chance at all that he was going to allow her to leave his side.

He stepped up beside Hayley, his hand finding hers again. "She goes nowhere without me."

"And he goes nowhere without us." Fain stepped into the light. "Hello, Paul."

Dalton sighed, a weary sound. "Hello…I hear you're going by your brother's name now, Beck. I suppose you should all come up. Let's end this game so we can all try to move on with our lives. Helena, could you please begin preparations? We'll need to move quickly. I think after tonight, we'll leave Rio for a while."

"Of course." She strode up to Dalton and laid a perfectly non-platonic kiss on her boss's cheek. "I'll take care of everything, darling. As I always do. And you were right. She's lovely. She looks a bit like you. I'll talk to our friends and then bring some coffee up myself. Do be careful. You know what the Russian is capable of."

"I don't think it's only Nick I have to worry about," Dalton said quietly. "But we've all agreed to a parley this evening."

Hayley laughed, but it was a bitter sound. "You are so clever, Dad. What a word to use. It brings your two worlds together. Parley in the pirate vernacular means giving an enemy the promise of safety while you negotiate, but if you spell it just a little different it means something in the poker world. I think you meant parlay. Is that what you've actually been doing? Placing bets and risking it all to parlay into the real treasure? How much is on the line?"

Dalton had paled a bit. "I suppose I hadn't thought about it that way, but yes, they both apply. And there's more on the line than you can imagine, my girl. Please, can we do this upstairs? I meant it. No harm will come to you. My men are merely here to guard the money from the casino and to protect my patrons. So much of my work is about illusion and creating a persona that protects and conceals who I really am."

"Dare I ask who you really are?" Hayley was staring at her father, pure stubborn will in her eyes.

"I'm a father who missed his daughter, a father who wishes he could go back and do it all over again." He turned to Nick. "Nikolai, I have a way to get her out of this forever. I can save her, but you have to make her listen to me."

"You want the key." He'd known the minute they'd been invited that the key would be his main bargaining chip. Hell, he'd set it up as bait.

Dalton stepped onto the first stair. "In private, please, Nick. You're all welcome, if that's what it takes to make Hayley feel safe."

Nick turned to Hayley, stepping in front of her so all she would be able to see was his face, his promises. He prayed she understood that he would honor them all. "*Dushka*, this is up to you. If you wish it, I will step back and allow Fain to do all our negotiating so you don't have to deal with him."

"He lied to me."

"Yes, he did." The words lay between them and he knew the subtext wasn't merely about her father. He needed to bring them to the forefront because there was more on the line than the next few moments. His whole future was there and suddenly he realized what happened between Dalton and Hayley would affect him. Perhaps deeply. "I've lied to you as well. I need you to know that I will not lie to you again. Never."

393

"He left me."

Again, his heart clenched at the vulnerability he heard in her words. He gripped her shoulders gently. "He did. And I did. And I need you to understand that I will never leave you again. Not until my soul leaves this body, and even then I will find a way to wait for you, to watch over you. I will do anything to bind us for all time because I will never love another woman. Not in this life or the next. My heart and soul are yours. So you make this decision and I will follow you."

"You think I should listen to him." Her hand had come up, brushing against his cheek, touching him as though she couldn't quite help herself. "You think I should listen to him so I'll listen to you. Because if he's not so bad, then maybe you aren't either. If he had a reason, maybe you did, too."

Such a smart woman. He wished she didn't see through him so easily. "I love you, Hayley. I can't imagine how he couldn't love you. He might have been a shit, but he's your father. Yes, I hope if you can forgive him, you'll find a way to forgive me. But it's up to you."

Slowly, she nodded and moved close to him, her hand seeking his. "I'll talk to him, but not without you, and Ezra gets his answers, too."

It wasn't an *I love you, too, Nicky*, but she was still with him. He started to lead her upstairs, Ezra and Kayla following behind. He couldn't help but turn to watch Helena walking away, her arm on Mr. Jones's shoulder as she leaned in and whispered to him.

"Did you take over the business when Desiree died? Is that why you faked your own death? So you could run the business after Des was gone?" The words were out of his mouth before the door had closed behind him.

Dalton leaned against the desk. There were pictures and office supplies scattered around. The pictures were of a happy family, certainly not Dalton's. It looked like he'd taken over the manager's desk for the evening. That would be his life, constantly in motion, always on the move.

It had been Nick's life for years. It had often been Hayley's.

Dalton gestured for them to sit. There were only two chairs. Ezra shook his head, preferring to stand, and Kayla stayed close to the door, so he settled Hayley in and then took the seat next to her. He got the feeling this was his show for now.

"Do you understand what I was doing during those years when you were growing up?" Dalton asked, his whole attention focused on Hayley.

"You worked for the CIA."

He nodded slowly. "And for some other friendly intelligence agencies. You have to understand that I got into some trouble when I was younger and working for them was the way I got out. I know you won't believe it, but I did it for you. I did it so I wouldn't have to go to jail and you wouldn't be left alone with your mother."

"My mother was a wonderful woman," Hayley shot back.

"Yes, and I loved her so much. I never loved anyone or anything the way I loved you and your mom. I wasn't a good man. I know she complained about me and she never told you, but I paid for almost everything. Those jobs of hers, she made nearly nothing. I had to stay out of jail so I could make sure you went to college, got to eat, had a roof over your head. I took you during your school breaks because your mom needed time off. That's a lie. I took you because I hated being away from you."

Hayley sat quietly, the silence lengthening.

He had to be the one to ask her questions. She couldn't do it on her own. She was too angry. "How did you meet Des? Was she your MI6 contact, the way Ezra was with the Agency?"

"Yes, like Bec…Ezra was," Dalton confirmed. "I met Des and we found we had some similar interests."

"Meaning you both liked to blackmail people?" Hayley asked.

Nick reached out, sliding his hand over hers. She seemed to calm a bit.

Dalton sat back, his eyes shrewd. "I met Desiree and unlike her CIA counterpart, I knew she was someone I could make a deal with. She was someone I could work with in a way I couldn't with Ezra."

"Tell me about what you set up with Desiree." Ezra stepped in, his arms crossed over his chest.

"Yes, I would like to hear it," Hayley said when her father waited too long to answer.

"Des and I set up a couple of long cons. I had access to some places it would have been hard for her to get into, certain games with power players that women weren't allowed to play in at the time. Because I had a name in that world, I grew close to some of the true high rollers. It gave Desiree some connections she wouldn't have had. She knew some lovely women and men who were willing to be a bit flexible when it came to making cash, and we started there. Gambling and liquor and drugs and sex. That was how we started making money. I'm not proud of what I did, Hayley."

"Excellent, because I'm not proud either." She pulled her hand away from Nick's, putting space between them again. "So you hired hookers to pillow talk with various and sundry politicians."

"And businessmen and actors and royalty. You have no idea how well we do in the Middle East," Dalton explained.

Hayley was staring at her father like she couldn't quite figure out if she recognized him. Nick could feel her pulling away from Dalton, from him. "So this was all about money. Desiree set this up and you decided to take it over, so you offed yourself to get away from Ezra and the Agency and kept the party going. Can you answer a question for me? How much is enough? If you make ten million, will that be enough? Twenty? When will you stop hurting other people and be content with what you have?"

Nick could answer that question for her. Unfortunately, he knew her father a bit too well when it came to this. "It's never enough for him, *dushka*, but he can't help that. It's a sickness. At least that's how Ariel would describe it. He can have all the money in his hands that he needs, but the truth is the money itself doesn't please him, doesn't make him feel alive."

Dalton seemed to age before his eyes, his shoulders slumping, eyes dimming. "Nick is right. I make the money, I gamble it away. I can't tell you how much I've made and lost in my lifetime. Millions. Tens of millions. I'm a little better now because running The Palace is one big bet. It gives me the adrenaline rush I need. But before too long, I'll have to find a game or a race and bet everything I have. Sometimes I win, but I always lose in the end. And this wasn't Desiree's idea. Believe it or not, Des really was getting out of the game. She had enough because of that one last play she made."

"Tell me about that op. It seems to me it's why we're here." Ezra spoke, his tone bland. "What do you know about it?"

Dalton sat back. "I know that I thought I had buried it, and that it will get my daughter killed if we don't do something about it."

"You cared so much you blew up my house," Hayley stated, her bitterness an almost palpable thing.

Nick was starting to see a pattern emerge. Hayley might be missing something because she couldn't see past her anger. "You did that because you were trying to throw them off the scent, weren't you? That's why it happened during office hours. You knew what Desiree had sent her."

"I didn't at first. I have a few people who owe me favors, and one of them is rather good with computers," Dalton began.

"So you have a hacker on the payroll." It would do him well to have one. A hacker could watch for everything from police activity concerning The Palace, to which high rollers might be coming into town and would need an invitation. A hacker would monitor the Dark Web for all kinds of activity. "When your hacker told you there was talk about Hayley, you knew you had to move."

"You could have given me a call." Hayley didn't seem like she was about to bend.

"I had to make it big. I didn't want to disrupt your life more than I had to." Dalton grimaced under the stare that came from his daughter's eyes. When Hayley wanted to, she could cut a man with that stare. "I know. I know. I might have gone over the top, but I didn't want anyone to think for a second that the information was in Hayley's hands. I worried I was going to be too late. I had to sneak away as it was. I don't trust anyone with my identity. I faked my death when I realized that whoever Desiree had blackmailed thought I was the only other person who knew."

"We figured she had it sent to me so I could get it to you," Hayley replied. "It was fate that Des died. She couldn't have known you would fake your own death. This was her way of ensuring someone would keep the business going."

Dalton shook his head. "I don't think so. I think she wanted you to have whatever was there. Desiree thought quite highly of you. I believe at first she liked the idea of having an American cousin to poke her relatives with, but she came to care for you quite deeply. I think it surprised her, too."

Ezra scrubbed a hand over his head as he paced across the office. "So you don't know anything. Is that what I'm supposed to believe? You don't know why someone is after what Des left behind. You don't know who is after it, and yet you felt strongly enough that you blew up your own daughter's home and sent her on the run."

"No, I'm not completely ignorant. I know it has something to do with a video she made years ago. Right before she died. She called me before she left for the Caribbean. She wanted to let me know she was leaving and might be out of touch for a while because she was expecting some kind of big payoff. She told me she'd finally done it."

He remembered her words. "She finally caught her whale."

Dalton pointed his way. "Exactly. That's what she said to me. She thought her boss was catching on to her and she'd decided to get out. I was surprised when she told me she wasn't taking you with her. She told me she was sending you back where you belonged."

He wanted so much to reach out to Hayley, but she'd stiffened at the words. He had to settle for continuing the dialogue. There would be time later when they were back in the hotel for him to beg and plead with her. To explain to her that he was done with the past and only interested in the future. "Desiree understood my feelings for Hayley, but none of this explains why you're here in Rio when everything I believe puts the information right here in the city."

"I believe that as well," Dalton affirmed. "I'm here in Rio because this was where Des and I were based. She had an apartment in Ipanema, but we had a home in the city. It served as a base of operations."

"You and Des?" Hayley asked the question in a soft voice, her skin flushing.

Dalton couldn't quite look his daughter in the eyes. "As much as any man was ever with Desiree. She was leaving me, too. The house was in one of my aliases so when I needed to hide, I came here. Also, I knew her habits. I've been trying to figure out where her storage is. I've combed through all the places I can think of. I believe one set was with the Tokyo apartment. I took care of that. The other is likely here. If I can find it and destroy it in a way that everyone understands it's gone, Hayley can get her life back. So far I haven't found it, but I will. I promise you, Hayley."

"Because we all know your promises mean something," Ezra spat out between clenched teeth. "I want what you owe me."

Dalton turned, looking every year of his age. "I lied to you. I told you I had the intel because I needed you off my back so I could do what I had to do. I never had it. Never got close to finding out who gave up your brother's unit. To tell you the truth, I didn't try. I was far too busy making money with Des."

Nick stood, putting himself between Ezra and Dalton. He couldn't have Ezra murdering Hayley's father. They still needed him. "Please calm down. I told you. When this is done, I am your partner in finding these men. For now, let's concentrate on saving Hayley. She's innocent in all of this."

"She is." Dalton had stood up. "Fain, if you'll help my daughter, I'll go quietly at the end of all of this. You can take me to prison and I won't give you any trouble at all. I'll even confess. I'm ready. I can't do this anymore. I can't when I know what kind of pain I've cost her."

Fain stepped back, nodding silently.

Nick turned to Hayley's father. Oddly, it didn't hurt that he'd been one more man Desiree had played around with. It didn't matter. He was thankful to the man because without him, Hayley wouldn't exist. Still, there was a price to be paid, and at least he felt somewhat certain that Dalton was ready to pay it. "Desiree did leave the information here and she guarded it with a key. I believe the reason everyone is after her is that Desiree's mark knows about her security system. They certainly do now that I've informed every mercenary on the Dark Web that the heart around Hayley's neck is the only thing that will unlock the security system Desiree put in place. Hayley, I need the necklace now."

She turned wide eyes his way, her hand going to the necklace around her throat. "I can't give this up."

He got to one knee in front of her. God, one day he hoped he would be giving her a piece of jewelry rather than taking one away. "Do you trust me? Hayley, I think I can get you out of this. I don't care about justice or revenge anymore. I only care that you're safe. Do you understand me? You mean more to me than anything. I would give my life and my soul if it meant you were alive and happy. Please trust me in this."

Dalton moved in, looking down at his daughter. "I think you should trust him, sweetheart. He sounds serious. I'm going to take that necklace and let everyone know that I'm the man who has it and I'm the only one who knows where it is. This is on me. Let it finish with me."

"After we hand over the necklace, Kayla and Ezra will put out the word on the Dark Web that we're out of this," Nick explained. "You and I will get on a plane back to London and you'll stay at The Garden until Ezra can get your name cleared."

"But those men or whoever...they ruined my name, my reputation," she said, a little stutter to her voice.

He put a hand over hers. "And I would love to kill everyone who had anything to do with it, but I've discovered there's a time to step back because you're more precious than any revenge. I love you, Hayley. You stood in front of me once and asked me to change my life to be with you. You asked me to walk away from everything I knew and you were right to do it. I was wrong. So I'm here now asking you to walk away with me, asking you to change my life again."

Tears shone in her eyes as she shook her head. "That's not fair."

"It's not and I know you think you should walk away from me, but you need to understand that I won't be far behind. I'll follow you and watch out for you. I'll always be there, making sure you're safe."

"Stalker," she said, but her lips curled up enough to make hope flare inside him. Her hands moved back and she undid the clasp of the necklace. She held it up to the light for a moment and then sighed and passed it to him. "I do trust you, but I have to think about the rest of it. I'll go back to The Garden with you. That's all I can promise."

It was all he could ask for now.

He stood back up. Now that he had her consent, he was ready to get her out of here as soon as possible. He wouldn't feel truly comfortable until they were safely behind the walls of The Garden. "We're going to walk back out into the casino and I need you holding that necklace."

Paul reached out a hand, taking the heart on its gold chain. "I have some cameras in the casino. I'll have my hacker leak the photos."

That would play into his plan, but he had already set a few things in motion. He looked to Ezra, who nodded. "Thank you. Photos will help, but we've got a couple of friends who are even now talking about the fact that the key has been transferred. Ezra is putting the same information out on certain intelligence lines we're certain these groups monitor. We believe within a few hours, the heat should be off Hayley, especially when she settles back in London and is completely out of the game."

Dalton pushed his chair in and started for the door. "Let's get her out of here then. Nikolai, please take care of her. She's been let down by most of the men in her life. Mostly by me. She needs someone who can put her first."

Nick held out a hand because no matter what this man had done, he was still Hayley's father and the moment felt sacred, the solemn promise of a husband to a father. That was what he would be one day. Hayley's husband. "All my life I look to find something I can give my whole heart to. I tried to give it to my country. I tried to give it to revenge and the ghosts that haunted me. All my life I wanted to belong to something bigger than myself, but now I only wish to belong to her. This I promise you. For the rest of my life I will put her first."

Dalton shook his hand, emotion plain in his eyes. Regret. Relief. "Thank you."

"Hey, we need to get out of here." Kayla's low voice broke through the quiet of the moment. "Someone's moving downstairs. Could be nothing, but I'd like to see the street now."

He trusted Kay's instincts. If she thought something was changing, then it was time to leave. He held out a hand and helped Hayley up, hating the fact that there were tears clinging to her cheeks. She was so far away from him in that moment, but he couldn't think about that. He had to get her home and then perhaps he could start trying to heal the wounds finding her father had caused. "Stay between me and Fain."

Ezra was already moving in. "Get down the stairs as quickly as we can. I don't like being stuck here."

"Kay, can you take our six?" There was no one else he would rather have at his back. Well, no one except Owen or Brody or Damon. His team. He trusted them. How long had they been there in the background, waiting for his ass to wake up and join them? He thought he'd lost his family, but he'd found another.

Perhaps that had been Desiree's gift to him.

Kay stood, holding the door open, her whole body taut with awareness as her eyes swept the floor. "We have three guards and Helena, who just came in. There're several more hovering at the door. I don't like it."

Dalton moved in after Fain. "I'm sure it's nothing more than a problem with the casino. My guards are well trained to take care of things quietly."

"Yes," Kay said. "The quiet bothers me, too."

That was when he realized the noise he'd heard earlier from the casino was gone. The place was almost eerily quiet.

They were in serious trouble. His time had run out.

Chapter Twenty

Hayley wasn't sure exactly what was happening but she knew it was bad. She could feel the tension rolling off the rest of them and it informed her own. Nick moved in front of her and Ezra behind. They kept close to her, so close it was hard to move. Nick stepped down cautiously, his head swinging as he glanced around the darkened room.

That was the problem. The light seemed to have shifted to the office. It was hard to see the reaches of the floor below, but then Helena had told her that everything here was theater.

It looked like Helena had set the scene for the final act.

Hayley wiped a hand over her eyes because tears had blurred her vision after the last few minutes.

Her father was alive and he had apologized, had said so many of the things she'd longed to hear all her life. Her father was a gangster who ran illegal casinos and sold information to be used in blackmail schemes. Her father had been Desiree's lover.

Nick loved her. Hayley, not Des. Nick loved Hayley. Nick was ready to put her first.

It was all a great big roiling pot of emotion and she couldn't focus on it.

They were in some kind of trouble. She forced herself to move along the stairs, emotional numbness settling in. She tried to force it back. Numb was easy and she didn't want that anymore. She wanted to feel. That was one thing she'd learned. It was okay to feel even if it was bad.

"What's wrong?" Hayley whispered the question because it seemed like the right thing to do. She wasn't going to hide behind them.

"Nothing, yet," Nick whispered back. "Stay close and keep your head down. We're going straight for the street. Once we're there, we stick to the shadows and go for any crowds we can find. Hayley, can you run in those heels?"

Nope. She would be horrible at it. She could sort of walk in the gorgeous things, but there was no way she could run. Luckily they were easy to kick off. She shed them and felt the metal stair beneath her as Nick hustled them down. "They're gone. I'm ready."

She would run even if she hit glass. She would run because Nick thought they should and she wasn't about to hold him back. They'd made a deal. She was his partner in life. She was in control of the throw pillows and how they spent cash. He was perfectly amenable to most of what she wanted to do. He was in control during sexy time and when the bullets started flying.

She was cool with that. It was a perfectly reasonable exchange. Why was she even fighting it?

"I don't think there's any reason to worry," her father was saying. "We have protocols to follow. We're an illegal business. We go quiet anytime the outer guards sense a police presence. If you'd actually been a guest of ours, you would have gone through a nice lecture on how we handle things like this. The first rule is that the casino goes utterly silent. We have to."

"I would rather be safe than sorry." Nick took the stairs quickly.

Hayley glanced behind her and noticed that Kayla was still standing at the top of the stairs. Was she not coming with them?

Everything was happening so fast and she couldn't quite keep up.

She knew she'd given away their only real bargaining chip since they hadn't been about to find the actual intelligence. That necklace was the next best thing. But Nick had a plan and she was following him.

Because she trusted him.

Because no matter what he'd done before, she loved him and always had. Why hadn't she told him? Why hadn't she given him the words back?

Nick hit the bottom of the stairs and started to lead her toward the curtain entrance they'd come through before. They'd almost made it when the flap opened and one of the big, black-suited guards stepped through, a shiny automatic in his hand.

Nick stopped, putting his body between hers and the gun. "We will be leaving now."

The man simply shook his head and nodded to someone behind them.

"I think we have a few things to work out before you leave us," a feminine voice said.

"Helena, what's going on here?" Her father moved out of the line they'd been in, taking a step toward his second in command. "Why aren't the guards at their posts?"

"Because I've put our protocols in place and had the casino evacuated," Helena stated calmly. "We've never actually had to do it. It worked quite nicely. We evacuated in under five minutes and made very little sound."

Her father looked back. "Nick, get her out of here. If she's taken in by the police, she'll be a sitting duck."

"I don't think the police are on their way," Nick said, his tone grave.

"Ah, see, I always thought you were far smarter than Des gave you credit for," Helena said, her heels clicking across the floor. "Although you are the one who walked in here carrying the key. Such a stupid man, but then I've made my living by being underestimated. I'll take the key now."

"What the hell is going on?" Her father held his ground even as he found himself surrounded by his own guards.

Helena laughed, a sinister sound. "Oh, Paul, you can't think they ever truly accepted you. You're weak and everyone knows it. I kept you around because of your connections, and you knew this world better than I. I've learned and now the guards all understand it's time for a coup. I find paying them a bit on the side helps to settle their loyalties. Where is the other girl?"

"Other girl?" her father asked.

"Yes, I can count. You walked in with two women and two men. I see Nikolai, your precious daughter, and the CIA agent. Where is the lovely Asian girl?"

"She's from California," Fain shot back.

"Semantics," Helena replied. "Where is she?"

Hayley glanced back and sure enough, Kayla wasn't where they'd left her. The stairs were empty. But she was almost certain Kay hadn't come down with them. "She went to the ladies' room."

Fain moved in behind her. She was surrounded by men with guns.

"Kay's serious about her makeup," Fain offered. "I'm sure she got lost or something. She's amazing eye candy, but she has no sense of direction."

Helena snorted, an oddly elegant sound. "I'm sure. I know a trained operative when I see one. You, go and do a sweep of the office. Be careful. She's pretty but deadly." Helena waved a hand at one of the guards with her and he promptly trotted up the stairs. "Now, I'll take the key and the girl."

Nick's gun came up and suddenly there were five or six guns pointed her way. Hayley found herself squished between Nick and Fain, but neither man could completely cover her. They were caught in a circle of guards, neatly flanked by Helena's men.

She held on to Nick's waist, terror starting to well inside her. She couldn't lose him like this. She couldn't lose him at all. Not when she'd finally found her way back to him.

"Hayley doesn't know anything," Nick said, his focus on Helena, but Hayley didn't doubt he knew what they were up against. "If you want to talk, you'll let her go and then I'll have a conversation with you. You know no one knew Desiree better than I did. You can have the key and me. Let my friend take her out of here and then I'll make sure you get what you want."

"No." Hayley opened her mouth to make her case, but Ezra threw an arm around her waist, pulling her back toward him.

"Keep quiet," Ezra whispered. "Let him do what he needs to do. Don't make this hard on him."

She wasn't going to make it hard. She was going to make it impossible for him to martyr himself. "I'll go with you if you let the rest of them leave unharmed."

"Don't listen to her," Nick insisted. "She knows absolutely nothing and she no longer has the key. She wouldn't know what to do with the damn thing even if she still had it. Your best bet to survive this is to let Hayley leave with Mr. Fain. Do you really want to deal with the Agency?"

Helena sighed as though she couldn't possibly care less. "I think the Agency will burn him. They don't care about their operatives. If he disappears, they'll hire another one just like him. And don't invoke your boss's name. I'm not afraid of them. I know how to avoid the real predators of this world. Besides, once I get that video, I won't have to work anymore."

"What kind of video?" Despite the horror of the situation, Hayley found herself curious.

Helena's lips curled up. "The kind that someone will pay an enormous amount of money to keep from leaking to the press. I happen to be one of the last people left on earth who actually knows what's on that video. There's only one other, and he'll be hearing from me soon. He's been looking for it for a very long time. He'll reward the woman who brings it to him."

"You know where it is?" She couldn't quite stop asking questions. Maybe she shouldn't. Kayla was somewhere. She wouldn't be hiding and she wouldn't have run and left them behind. Kay was up there and that meant she was planning something. Hayley might not know the woman as well as Nick, but she knew enough about his team to know they wouldn't ever leave one of their own behind.

So Kay needed time and space to work.

"Hayley, I need you to let me handle this," Nick said, his voice tight. "Please be quiet."

Unfortunately, she knew what Nick's only goal was. He wouldn't think about anyone else until he'd gotten Hayley out. Hayley had to think for the team, had to keep Helena talking to give them all some time.

Including her dad.

"I want to know. I think I deserve to know what's on that video because I'm the one who suffered the most," she shot back. "I want to know what I've been suffering for."

"Your backside's going to suffer," Nick said under his breath.

She was absolutely sure it would, if they survived this. She was certain at some point she would find herself over his knee, and he would take out some frustration on her ass before ripping off her clothes and taking her hard and fast in a desperate attempt to prove to himself she was still alive and safe.

He loved her. It was different this time. This time he'd chosen and he wouldn't go back. She could feel it. All she had to do was believe.

Believe in him. Believe in herself. Believe that she hadn't gone through all this hell to die in a random warehouse in Rio.

"You can see it for yourself," Helena said. "I'll take you to the storage center. I worked with Desiree for years. I know all her secrets. I knew her. The place might have moved, but the accounts did not. I figured out how she'd left her ultimate personal data. Silly, sentimental fool. That surprised me. The one thing she ever did that surprised me. She protected it with that stupid necklace. Come with me, Hayley. I'm interested in you. I'll show you."

She wasn't walking away and letting them kill her boys. And her girl. They were a team and Kayla wasn't ready to move or she already would have. "I want to see it. I want to know what Des had. She left it all to me. Did that bother you?"

It was a good bet that Helena had some sort of relationship with Des. Des hadn't done simple relationships. Des made everyone think they were special. She'd needed everyone to be obsessed with her or she hadn't trusted the person.

Helena lips curled up, but her eyes told the real tale. They were cold. "Not at all. You were her cousin. I understand family."

Ah, but she had some info poor Helena didn't have. "She wasn't any blood of mine. Tell her, Dad."

She saw the way her father's body went tight, his shoulders straightening out.

"I don't know what you're talking about, sweetheart," her father said. He turned toward her, his eyes widening in that way that let her know he was in.

They'd had a language no one else understood. Poker language. He'd trained her in it. When he looked at her like that, he understood the game. He would back her.

Her father had been a bastard, but he'd been hers. Her dad. He got her. He knew what she needed. He would aid her bluff.

Time. They needed time.

She stepped away from the men protecting her, putting her hands on her hips and a frown on her face. Sometimes distraction was the best bluff. "Oh, you don't know? Because I know. Do you think I'm that stupid, Dad? I figured out your con. You, ass. Why didn't you bring me in? Were you conning me, too?"

Her father brought his hand up, a righteous finger pointing her way. "I never once conned my own daughter. How dare you even accuse me."

"Step back." Nick moved in front of her.

Chaos. Sweet, sweet chaos. It was exactly what they needed. She could see it in Helena's eyes. They were tight, her body caving in on itself like she didn't know what to do. Everyone else was looking to her and she wasn't sure how to move forward.

Yes.

Helena didn't want to kill her so she made herself a big old target. She moved toward her father.

"You never conned me? Do you remember my childhood?" Staying out of Nick's and Fain's hold wasn't easy. Thank god she'd kicked off the heels. "You conned me every single time we met."

"I didn't con you ever, girl. You were my daughter and I treated you like gold." His face had gone a nice shade of red and Hayley had to wonder how much of it he meant and how much he wished were true. "Don't you dare talk about cons."

"My childhood was one long con," she accused. She could see the way Nick was easing up behind her. The guards had no idea what to do. They were glancing around, trying to figure out what Helena wanted them to do. "You lied about Des. You told me she was my cousin."

Sometimes truth was the best distraction.

Her father's face went grave. "Cons can go wrong. You need to remember that the con has a heart too, and sometimes the game gets confused. Life isn't black and white. It's so, so many shades of gray, baby girl. You were loved. I know you had trouble, but you were loved, and I wouldn't have stayed around someone who couldn't love you. Not anyone I would have brought you close to."

Hayley stopped, Desiree's own words coming back to her in a flood of revelation. She'd memorized that letter Des had written.

I never could help myself. I had to put my fingers in every single pie I could. I had to stir up trouble where there was none. It was one thing Nicky and I completely disagree on. He wants peace in his life and I think that sounds like the most boring thing ever. The only time I ever wonder if I'm missing something is when I'm with the two of you. Somehow time seems to slow down and the world seems like a softer place when you're in the room. Especially when Nick is there, too. Did you know in all my life, I never found anyone who made me so aware of what's missing inside me as you? That should have made me hate you, Hayley. Instead it made me love you. If...well, we both know

411

that wouldn't have worked, but that "if" has defined my life for some time now.

Tears suddenly blurred her eyes as she made the deep and certain revelation that somehow Desiree had loved her. Desiree had loved Nick. Though her heart had been twisted and scarred, she'd still loved them.

Her father had loved her.

Ariel had told her that love was stability. Maybe she'd had more stability than she'd thought. Maybe it was time to forgive herself for her insecurities. Maybe it was time to grab life and love and happiness with both hands and promise to never let go.

Out of the corner of her eye, she saw something move. In that instant, she chose. She chose to believe that it was Kayla in motion, that she would win.

And that she had things to say.

"I love you, Dad."

A loud crack split the world and Hayley watched as the first guard, the one nearest to her, went down easy. A second shot slammed through the room and then time seemed to speed up.

She heard Nick shout, but she was watching her father. His body stiffened, his spine going straight, and a red stripe bloomed on his chest.

He stared right at her and took a step toward her. "Hay…love you, girl."

Before she could reach him, she was tackled from behind. Nick pressed her against the floor as the bullets started to fly. He covered her, not exposing an inch of her skin. She couldn't breathe, couldn't see. What had happened to her father? She'd been so angry with him, but now she knew she could forgive him. She could move on.

"Stay down, *dushka*," he whispered in her ear.

And then his body jolted in a terrifying way. Once. Twice and then again.

"I love you, Hayley. Stay down. Don't move."

But she was starting to panic because something warm and wet ran onto her arm. Blood. Not hers. Precious blood. Nick's blood.

Please. Please. Please. She tried to force him off her. She could hear a war raging all around them, but he wouldn't move. He wouldn't leave her. He was dying above her and he wouldn't save himself.

He would give it all up before he would leave her.

Hayley felt a jolt and used every single bit of energy she had to shove Nick off her. She shouted and screamed and didn't give a single damn that all around her was death and blood and pain. Nick mattered. He didn't even know.

She felt something against her forehead. Something cold and metal.

"Don't move or I'll kill her." Helena was standing above her. "Come downstairs, bitch, or your friend is done. Same for you, asshole. Come out from wherever you are. I might be alone now, but I still have the upper hand."

So Erza had made a move. He'd gotten away and he and Kayla had taken out the others. None of it would matter if Nick died. Hayley could see the blood on his white dress shirt. She wasn't sure where the bullets had gone in, but one was definitely in his belly and another higher up. How much could his body take? How long would he survive?

He was so still.

She glanced to the side and saw what she hadn't before. Her father was on the ground, his eyes staring up, blood creasing his mouth. Her father. She'd mourned him before. She would have to again.

God, she couldn't mourn Nick.

She didn't have time and there was a gun to her head.

Nothing mattered if Nick didn't live. Risk. Des hadn't been afraid to take a risk. She'd been a badass bitch with more personality problems than Hayley could imagine, but sometimes love meant excusing those things in favor of the best qualities of another human being.

What would Des do?

She would fight to the fucking end. She would risk it all for the big play—to win what she loved.

Hayley threw her head forward and then back, catching Helena right in the pelvis and sending her foe reeling back.

Kay would take care of her.

Hayley leaned forward, hearing another volley of gunfire but not caring about anything except Nick. He was bleeding and she needed to stop it.

His eyes opened as the gunfire seemed to stop. "Love you, *dushka*."

She shook her head, tears streaming. This couldn't happen. Her whole soul revolted against the idea. "No. No. You don't get to leave me."

"Kayla, we need a bus and I'm going to have to get her out of here." Ezra had blood on his shirt, but he was calm. His eyes strayed to her father's body. So much regret was in that stare.

Kayla was on her cell phone, talking into it and asking for help. She hung up and walked in. "I've got a bus coming for him. Get her out of here. Interpol is looking for her. She can come to the hospital later, but this is going to be a crime scene. They'll check into all of us and I would rather make sure her cover is secure. Nick wouldn't want less."

Hayley shook her head. She wasn't leaving him. She dropped to her knees, trying to get her hands on him. "Nicky, baby, you have to hold on. I won't leave you. I love you. Do you hear me? I love you."

God, she wished she knew how to say it in Russian.

He couldn't seem to lift his head, but his eyes found hers. His clear, perfectly blue eyes. *"Ya lyublyu tebya."*

Ezra pulled her away, ignoring how hard she struggled against him. He rushed her out the door, but Hayley's heart stayed with Nick.

As Ezra carried her out into the night, she prayed it wasn't the last time she saw her love.

* * * *

414

One week later, Nick sighed and rubbed his cheek against Hayley's as she helped him into the conference room. He was so tired, his body aching, but none of it mattered because he was home. Finally. He'd spent the night before in his own bed, cuddled up to her.

Hayley was safe and all felt right with the world.

Ian Taggart looked up from his file. "Dude, you look like shit without a spleen. It's like you died."

He started to give boss number two his happy middle finger, but his girl got there first.

Hayley stared Taggart down. "If you don't have anything nice to say, take your ass somewhere else. Am I clear?"

Charlotte applauded along with Penny and Kay. He thought he heard one of them whisper something like "one of us."

Taggart frowned but then ruined it with a wink. "Your girl is mean, Nick."

His girl was perfect. So freaking perfect. He could still remember that moment when she'd looked down at him, her eyes crystal with tears, and he'd felt her love. She'd begged him not to leave her and he'd promised he wouldn't. He'd told her he loved her, but he'd promised himself he wouldn't die. Not on her. She needed him.

When he'd woken up in the hospital, she'd been there, asleep at his bedside, her hand holding his. His surgery had been touch and go, but he was going to be okay.

"I'll have to disagree with you, boss. My girl is quite nice." He smiled Taggart's way because he'd definitely softened toward the man. After all, it had been Ian who had introduced him to Ezra Fain, and that CIA agent had gotten Hayley out of The Palace before the authorities could nab her. Ezra had taken care of her while Kayla had explained things to the authorities. Ezra had convinced the ambassador to step in and help sort through the confusion. Ezra had been the reason Hayley could come to the hospital and see him through his recuperation. The Brazilian government now believed that Nick and Kay were private investigators attempting to find a missing person—Hayley's father. They'd gotten caught in a small gang war, and after promising to keep the story out of the press, the police were happy to let them all go. After all, they had given the police the chance to take down an infamously illegal gambling ring. It was all over the press and they were happy to look like heroes.

The man hadn't been home in two months, but here he was waiting for the debrief.

Hayley wouldn't let go of his hand. His sweet sub wasn't about to let her Master fall. He could have told her that she was his strength and nothing would stop him now. He allowed her to help him sit, though he felt stronger than he had in days. He felt good. He felt right.

"How are you feeling?" Damon sat at the head of the table. "You made the flight all right?"

He had because he'd had Hayley there with him the whole way, taking care of him, loving him. "It was perfect. Don't worry about me physically. The doctors took good care of me and I have an appointment to follow up. I intend to follow all their instructions. I'll be at a desk for about six weeks, but I'm going to recover and it's all thanks to Hayley and Kayla and Ezra."

He wouldn't call him Fain again. He would call him Ezra or brother. He wished Ezra was here, but he'd faded off like the ghost he was after ensuring Hayley was safe and that her life was given back to her.

Of course, Ezra had something else to deal with now. That damn video they'd found once they'd figured out where Des had hidden it. Ezra was dealing with a shitstorm, but one day he was sure the man would come back and they would have business to conclude.

Nick looked forward to the day.

"Well, I had a good time," Kay said. "I got to snipe like ten dudes. It was awesome. I probably should pay Damon for the pleasure."

Damon held up a hand, his lips curling in a smile. "I'll forego repayment. Sniping is just a happy benefit of your job. So tell me how you figured out where to find the tape. I got the debrief file, but I'd like to hear it from you, Nick."

He settled in and warmed as he felt Hayley's hand slide over his as she sat beside him. She was never far away now. He picked up her hand and brought it to his lips, promising her everything that would come once he was cleared to perform. Oh, he would be a very good boy. He would take care of himself because he had a higher purpose—taking care of her. He kept her hand in his as he turned back to his boss. "Hayley figured it out. After Ezra got her back to the hotel, she spent her time trying to decipher what Helena had told her."

Charlotte piped up. "I did the file on Helena. Fascinating woman. She was a low-level prostitute when Des came in contact with her. Her background was very lower class, but she managed to work her way up. She was the one who reached out to Paul Dalton and kept things going, though he was the one who added the rolling casino."

Hayley's hand squeezed his. She'd struggled with her father's death, but had also found some peace in knowing the man had loved her.

"How did that help you figure out where the video was being stored?" Damon asked.

"Helena told me that Desiree was sentimental," Hayley said. She held his hand close, seeming to gain strength from their connection. "We knew the coordinates hidden in the necklace pointed us to one place, one specific place. The problem was what lay there wasn't a storage shed. It was a warehouse."

"But three years before, it had been a storage shop," Nick continued. "They'd moved. We found them again, but Desiree hadn't rented a place from them."

"Sentiment," Hayley said quietly. "That was where I found it. I read the letter she'd left to me and the one she'd left to Nicky. She wouldn't have rented the place in her own name. The storage closet was in Hayley Markovic's name. It was where she saw the future heading." Hayley frowned. "Though she could have left us a better wedding present than a twelve-hour video of a gangster bragging about all his ties to politicians and businessmen to a hooker."

Nick saw nothing wrong with it. It had been a long video, spliced

417

together over the course of what seemed to be a year and a half, with the head of the largest mob family in the States. The man was known in the media as Johnny "Teflon" Bianchi for his never-ending ability to get out of legal trouble. Unfortunately, the guy liked to get coked up, and he spilled his guts to his favorite "girl." Who happened to be Helena. "It got you your life back, *dushka*. I'll take it."

Hayley was still shaking her head, having none of his arguments. "It was horrible. The sounds he made."

"Hey, Desiree knew what she was talking about when she said she'd landed a whale," Brody agreed. "Not only could she blackmail Bianchi, she could go after everyone he mentioned on that bloody tape. It was half the politicians in the Western world and some really rich blokes. No wonder he wanted the thing gone."

"So Desiree took Helena's tape?" Penny asked.

He'd sorted through all of this from his hospital bed. "Desiree paid Helena for information. Helena was one of a large network of women Desiree and Dalton sent power players to. From what I can tell, Desiree would set up and pay for the rooms. I don't think Helena knew she was being taped. She thought she controlled the information. Naturally, Des never left anything to chance. She had a safe created for the tape and it required the necklace to be in place when the code was punched in for it to open."

"Helena had been looking for that tape for years," Hayley explained. "I did some research on her and she'd made several trips around the globe to places where Des had lived. Somehow she'd managed to miss the Tokyo apartment, but she had a man watching the law firm. When she was informed where the contents were going, she called Bianchi and let him know what could be coming their way. Dad got to my place first, but Bianchi had someone planted in the Seattle PD. Helena also figured out that Rio was the most likely place for the secondary site. She knew where the tape was stored, but she didn't have the necklace. I was worried that we'd lost the necklace when we ran, but when I got back to the hotel, I found out that my man here is a sneaky one. He'd traded the real necklace for a fake. I didn't even know it."

"Well, I wasn't going to truly give up our best bargaining chip," he admitted. "The necklace is still available in several chain stores. I found one easily, though it wouldn't have worked. It needed the microchip installed for it to work. Walt put it back together at my request after we downloaded the intel. I should have told you, but I wanted your reaction to be real. It was the microdot and not the necklace that opened the safe."

She wrinkled her nose his way before continuing. "So I found the necklace with the microdot in Nicky's luggage. I figured out where the tape was being stored, and Ezra and I went down and opened it. I got the code in one try. Nicky's birthday. Des really was quite sentimental."

"Johnny Teflon is going down because of a college history professor," Ian said with a grin. "It's a good day."

Hayley had managed to make some connections between Bianchi and the Seattle police. He'd bought off a bad cop, and now that man was going to see justice, too. The federal prosecutors assigned to the case had a lot of work to do.

But all that mattered to him was that Hayley was safe and she loved him. They would work everything else out.

Including their future. For now they were staying at The Garden. Hayley was going to try her hand at something more than an academic paper. She'd decided it was time to write a history about the men and women who worked in the shadows. She was going to write about spies.

He was going to be her loving husband.

"Well, I for one am happy to put this behind us." Taggart closed his file. "I'm heading home tomorrow. It looks like we've got a new client. The king of Loa Mali is getting hitched, if you can believe that. We're handling security. I always thought he would marry the doctor who clears up all his STDs. I'm still in shock. Nick, if you need anything at all, please call me. And, dude, don't forget what I said about protection."

Charlotte stood up with her husband. "Protection is overrated. Be happy, you two. And don't forget to invite us to the wedding."

The meeting began to break up, with everyone shaking Nick's hand and welcoming him home. Hayley hugged everyone, spending long moments with Charlotte planning a trip to Dallas and asking for advice on wedding planning. They were having a real white wedding and they would take their time and get it right.

It didn't matter. In his heart he was already her husband.

Brody held out a hand. "Good to have you back, mate."

He felt for his friend. Now that he had Hayley at his side, he wanted the same for Brody. The big Aussie was wrong to think he wasn't good enough for the woman he so obviously had feelings for.

Nick shook his hand. "Good to be back. Even though I will miss my spleen. And a portion of my liver. I suspect I'm going to drink less now."

"Suspect so," Brody said, a sad smile on his face. "I guess I'll have Owen to keep me company. And the lads. They get quite funny when they're drinking."

"Call her," Nick urged. "Just to talk. Ask her how she's doing."

Brody shook his head. "Hurts too much. But I'm happy for you, mate. I'll see you around."

Brody strode away.

It was a problem he would need to work on. He was turning into a nosy busybody. It felt good.

Hayley was suddenly in front of him, holding out her hand to help him up. "We're going to the kitchen. Teresa set out a big buffet to welcome you home."

Of course she had. She was part of their happy family. Nick groaned a little as he stood. He might keep that up. He loved how Hayley fussed over him. "Let's go then. I find myself very hungry."

He let her lead him out. He was hungry again and for more than food. Hungry for her. For the life they would have. For the love they would share.

Life was good again.

* * * *

Dallas, TX
Three Months Later

Stephanie Gibson stood looking at the beautiful wrought iron and wood door. The house she was standing in front of was a stunning Mediterranean, proof that the family who lived here had it all together. They were living the American dream.

Stephanie found herself in the middle of a nightmare.

She could still hear the sound of guns, feel the press of steel against her throat. She'd felt so vulnerable, so small and weak.

I'll kill you myself if he don't live. Do you understand that, bitch? I'll make sure you don't spend another day on this earth if you can't save him, Doc.

She could still see all the blood. Her hands had been shaking and all she'd wanted was to have that man beside her, her big Aussie with kind eyes and a gentle heart. She'd longed for him in that moment in a way she'd never wanted anything before.

He wasn't hers. He'd made that very plain.

What was she doing?

Panic threatened to overtake her. Maybe not merely panic. There was plenty of guilt in there, too. She had no right to be here. Avery and Liam O'Donnell owed her nothing. Nothing. She was the one who owed everything to Avery and here she was standing on the woman's doorstep, perhaps bringing danger into their lives.

She couldn't do it. There had to be another way.

If only Brody would have answered her damn calls.

Tears pierced her eyes. She wanted to feel his arms around her again. When he'd held her, she'd felt safe for once in her damn life. When he'd made love to her, she'd felt clean and pure. How odd was it that sex could make her feel innocent, could wash away her sins.

It was over now. He'd made that clear with his months and months of silence. He was done with her. She'd been nothing but a job to him, and that last night had merely been a way for him to pass the time. He couldn't have felt what she'd felt. If he had, he wouldn't have been able to turn her away time and time again.

That night had been everything to her and he'd left her a voice mail asking her to never call him again. Because she was making a fool of herself.

God, he'd been the one to make a fool of her.

Maybe she should ring the doorbell and run. Everything that was important to her was right here on this porch, and she could trust Avery. Avery would take care of things.

Stephanie could run and face her fate and bring no one else into it. Maybe it was just the way it was supposed to end. There would be an odd sort of justice to it. Leaving Avery a child...

Before she could make a decision, the light came on and the door opened.

A big man stood in the doorway wearing nothing but a pair of pajama bottoms. Well, unless one considered the gun in his hand a form of clothing. Liam O'Donnell was likely never without one. "Stephanie? I thought that was you. The damn light's not bright enough on the security camera."

She wished she could shrink into the shadows, wished she'd never come up with this stupid plan, but after what had happened, she'd gotten on the plane to the second place she'd wanted to be. Her first instinct had been to go to London, to show up at Brody's office and plead for him to love her, to protect her.

To protect their son.

She'd promised herself after he'd told her never to call again that she wouldn't allow her baby to be raised by a man who would resent him. She'd promised she could do it alone.

She couldn't. She was going to get her son killed, and she couldn't allow it. "I have no right to be here, no right to ask you what I'm about to ask."

Liam's eyes went from surprised to concerned. She watched the moment he changed from interested friend to the head of his family. Thank god by some miracle of the universe this man considered her family.

It was only one of the acts of grace and love she'd received from his wife.

"Come inside." Liam flicked the safety to the gun in his hand on and eased it into the pocket of his pants. "I need to know everything. Were you followed?"

She reached down to pick up the car seat. So heavy.

"I'll get it." Liam reached for the handle and then the blanket covering her son fell away. Liam's eyes widened as he looked down at the baby. Her son had woken up and he was grinning that toothless baby smile that made her heart melt. Liam shook his head as he looked back to her. "Bloody hell. I'll kill him. I'll kill that big bastard meself. He thinks he's met dangerous animals down under. He ain't met the real me, yet. It's time to introduce meself."

Suddenly Avery was in the doorway, wrapping a robe around her body. She was soft and round and roughly seven months pregnant. "Steph? It's the middle of the night. What are you doing here? Is everything okay? Whoa."

Liam nodded. "Yes, love. Whoa. Get that Aussie bastard on the phone. Better yet, get me on a plane to London and I'll drag his arse all the way back here. I sent him to protect you, not to get you pregnant."

She'd forgotten how old-fashioned Liam could be. Besides, they didn't know the whole truth. "Please, Liam. I need help. Not because of the baby. Someone's trying to kill me."

Liam's shoulders straightened and he opened the door wider. "Get inside. Avery, love, I think we're going to need some tea. It's going to be a long night."

Avery reached out to hold Stephanie's hand. "Come inside. We'll work it out. You're safe now."

Stephanie looked down at her son, who grinned up at her. Nathan Avery Gibson was about to meet the godparents he hadn't known he had. Not that they knew she'd put them in her will. She had a lot to talk to them about. Her boy kicked his fat baby legs and reminded her that no matter how bad it got, she couldn't give up. Not ever.

"It's going to be okay," Avery said, tugging on her hand as Liam hauled the car seat up.

"How old is this kid?" Li complained. "He feels like a toddler."

"Two months," she replied. "He weighs fifteen pounds already."

"Bloody Aussie," Liam said, but he was already smiling down at her son. "Hey, boy, I'm your Uncle Li and I'm going to kick yer daddy's arse."

Liam walked inside and Avery closed the door behind them.

"Please," Stephanie pleaded. "Brody can't know. He doesn't want to know. He doesn't…he doesn't want me. I chose to have Nate. Nate's mine and no one else's."

Avery laughed at the thought. "Oh, dear, I'm afraid that boy belongs to all of us now. He's family, as you are. Come on. Let's figure this out. I'll make sure Li doesn't get on a plane tomorrow. Now, what kind of trouble are we in?"

We.

For the first time in weeks, Stephanie took a deep breath.

She was home. It was all she needed for now. Tomorrow would be another fresh hell.

Brody, Stephanie, and the whole McKay-Taggart family will return in *Love Another Day…*

Author's Note

I'm often asked by generous readers how they can help get the word out about a book they enjoyed. There are so many ways to help an author you like. Leave a review. If your e-reader allows you to lend a book to a friend, please share it. Go to Goodreads and connect with others. Recommend the books you love because stories are meant to be shared. Thank you so much for reading this book and for supporting all the authors you love!

Sign up for Lexi Blake's newsletter
and be entered to win a $25 gift certificate
to the bookseller of your choice.

Join us for news, fun, and exclusive content
including free short stories.

There's a new contest every month!

Go to www.LexiBlake.net to subscribe.

Love Another Day
Masters and Mercenaries 14
By Lexi Blake
Coming August 22, 2017

A man born to protect

After a major loss, Brody Carter found a home with the London office of McKay-Taggart. A former soldier, he believes his job is to take the bullets and follow orders. He's happy to take on the job of protecting Dr. Stephanie Gibson while the team uses her clinic in Sierra Leone to bring down an international criminal. What he never expected was that the young doctor would prove to be the woman of his dreams. She's beautiful, smart, and reckless. Over and over he watches her risk her life to save others. One night of pure passion leads him to realize that he can't risk his heart again. When the mission ends, Brody walks away, unwilling to lose another person he loves.

A woman driven to heal

Stephanie's tragic past taught her to live for today. Everything she's done in the last fifteen years has been to make up for her mistakes. Offering medical care in war-torn regions gives her the purpose she needs to carry on. When she meets her gorgeous Aussie protector, she knows she's in too deep, but nothing can stop her from falling head over heels in love. But after one amazing night together, Brody walks away and never looks back. Stephanie is left behind…but not alone.

A secret that will change both their lives

A year later, Stephanie runs afoul of an evil mercenary who vows to kill her for failing to save his son. She runs to the only people she trusts, Liam and Avery O'Donnell. She hasn't come alone and her secret will bring her former lover across the world to protect her. From Liberia to Dallas to Australia's outback, Brody will do whatever it takes to protect Stephanie from the man who wants to kill her, but it might be her own personal demons that could destroy them both.

Arranged: A Masters and Mercenaries Novella
Masters and Mercenaries 13.5
By Lexi Blake
Coming April 25, 2017

Kash Kamdar is the king of a peaceful but powerful island nation. As Loa Mali's sovereign, he is always in control, the final authority. Until his mother uses an ancient law to force her son into marriage. His prospective queen is a buttoned-up intellectual, nothing like Kash's usual party girl. Still, from the moment of their forced engagement, he can't stop thinking about her.

Dayita Samar comes from one of Loa Mali's most respected families. The Cambridge-educated scientist has dedicated her life to her country's future. But under her staid and calm exterior, Day hides a few sexy secrets of her own. She is willing to marry her king, but also agrees that they can circumvent the law. Just because they're married doesn't mean they have to change their lives. It certainly doesn't mean they have to fall in love.

After one wild weekend in Dallas, Kash discovers his bride-to-be is more than she seems. Engulfed in a changing world, Kash finds exciting new possibilities for himself. Could Day help him find respite from the crushing responsibility he's carried all his life? This fairy tale could have a happy ending, if only they can escape Kash's past…

* * * *

"Good lord, man, put on some clothes." Simon Weston stood and walked back to the coffee service. "Everyone else might have seen that, but I've been very careful not to."

Kash wasn't sure why Weston was such a prude. The man was known to be a member of Sanctum. It was a club in Dallas that catered to people in the BDSM lifestyle. One day he would go to this

428

club, but then all the submissives would want him and he would lose his friends.

He'd lost too many friends.

"My mother has overreacted. I'm sure she was terrified when she learned I was over here in America without a proper guard, but she certainly shouldn't have called McKay-Taggart to escort me home. I assure you I can find my way. You don't have to make the twenty-hour flight." Who had he brought with him? Yes, that lovely girl from the east side of the island with the pretty breasts was the flight attendant. He could spend some time with her.

"There are currently around two hundred members of the press outside waiting to get a statement from you."

Kash stopped. "Two hundred?"

"Give or take a few. That's why we're going to require a police escort." Weston continued on as though nothing was wrong. "I've got my man with a limo in the parking garage. We'll meet Jesse down there and Boomer will join us in the lift. The hotel has agreed to shut down one of the lifts so it only stops on this floor and the parking garage. Boomer will ensure no one gets through. Miami PD has offered an escort to the airport. You should hurry and shower. We don't have much time."

His head was reeling in a way that had absolutely nothing to do with the unholy amount of vodka he'd downed the night before. "Why is the fact that I had sex with three women news? Believe me, it happens all the time. Second, why would I need a bloody police escort? And what is a Boomer?"

"A Boomer is one of two new former Special Forces bodyguards your mother has hired until Jesse and I train a new group to protect the royal family since it's getting larger. I hope you have a very large refrigerator. Boomer eats constantly, and you should watch out for any erratic behavior. He's a nice lad, but he's been hit on the head more than anyone could imagine. However, he's a bit of a savant when it comes to marksmanship. No one cares that you had sex with three women last night because no one knows. I took care of that and your mother is not going to be happy about all the bribes I had to expense to accomplish that. You need a bloody police escort to get through the throngs of reporters, as I mentioned earlier. Now could you please put that thing away? My wife is meeting us at the airport. I would like to be able to tell her the amount of nudity I witnessed was minimal."

He was getting irritated. He tossed on last evening's slacks. If the Brit wanted to power play him, he could get with the game. It wasn't like he would allow them to come in and drag his ass home like he was some kind of wayward child. He was a king. "Don't bother to bring your wife. I'm sure she's lovely, but my mother has overstepped herself. I will choose my guard and I will select who will train them."

Weston checked his watch. "How soon can you be ready?"

"Have you heard a word I've said? I thank you for helping me out last night and keeping that tape from hitting the web, but I can manage from here."

Weston picked up the newspaper that had been delivered along with the coffee service. He tossed it Kash's way. "If you feel that way, I can certainly let Michael and Jesse know they should stick to Her Majesty's side and allow you to be brutally murdered if it comes to that."

"Mother already has guards." He clutched the newspaper. She'd had the same set of guards for years. She liked to call them her girls. Four women who'd served in the military and had been trained by…well, by McKay-Taggart. Had something happened? "Why is Mother so afraid she needs more guards?"

"Not for your mother," Weston replied casually. "It's for your future bride. As for firing me and Jesse, you can't. We've been hired by your parliament to provide security and assistance for the royal wedding and to train the new queen's guard."

Yes, he'd had far too much to drink. He was still sleeping and having the oddest dream.

Weston shook his head. "It's all right there in the paper, if you don't believe me. Now hurry and take that shower. You've got to get home because the formal engagement ceremony is in two days."

Kash opened the paper and stared down at the headline.

Playboy King to Claim His Bride

"I'm not getting married."

Weston stepped up and patted his arm. "You are or you'll give up your throne. I'll explain it all on the plane. The other reason your mother hired me is I have a degree in law. I've read the clause in your constitution that your mother intends to use to force you to marry. I assure you, it will hold up. You can attempt to change the constitution but that requires a two-year review process, another year of public forums, and a vote. You'll be replaced by then. Like I said, I can explain it all on the very long plane trip. Are you all right, Your Majesty? You just went a bit green."

Kash ran for the bathroom.

He'd been right. He shouldn't have bothered to wake up.

Revenge
Lawless, Book 3
By Lexi Blake
Coming June 20, 2017

Passion and danger collide in the latest contemporary romance featuring the Lawless siblings—from New York Times bestselling author Lexi Blake.

When Drew Lawless discovers a fatal flaw in his plan to avenge his parents' deaths, he turns to the one woman he'd promised he wouldn't touch. He offers her a deal, one that will bring her into his investigation, his life, and his bed.

Investigative reporter Shelby Gates never dreamed how twisted the case would become—or how fascinated she would be with Drew. Every day they spend together binds them. And every night brings her closer to realizing he might be the man for her.

As Drew's feelings for Shelby grow, so does the danger. From the streets of Dallas to Austin's high-tech business world, Drew and Shelby play a game begun twenty years before—a game they will win, or die trying.

* * * *

Shelby looked up at him. He'd been silent as she read the contract. Well, the salient parts. She was not to reveal to his family members what she was working on. She was not to reveal to anyone that the relationship with Drew Lawless was a contractual one. She was to keep Drew Lawless informed at all times of her progress on the case and was to allow him to accompany her when at all possible.

In exchange she would receive monetary compensation and a publisher for her book when it was complete.

"Why?" She had a million and one questions, but it was the first one she could think to ask.

"Why you? Or why the girlfriend clause?" he asked, as though they were talking about some academic subject and not a totally fake relationship where they would have fake sex.

"I suppose both." She tried to make herself sound as blasé as he did. Like she received this kind of offer three times a week. No big deal. Just turned down the Google guy last week, buddy.

"You're smart and you're already closer to the truth after a few months' research than I was after years." He leaned back, his eyes steady on her. "And you're good at undercover work."

"Why not hire that security firm to research? From what Carly tells me, they're very good." And the Lawless clan was in tight with McKay-Taggart since Mia was married to one of them.

He nodded. "Yes, and they have years of experience and technical know-how behind them. They're the best in the country and you matched them. You, all by yourself."

She hoped he couldn't see how she flushed. "Sometimes a focused individual can do more than a company. They have to look at big-picture things. I get to think about the small stuff."

"Like what?"

"Like the fact that your father made a dentist appointment the day before he supposedly murdered your mother and killed himself." She had made a study of Benedict Lawless's habits. He'd had an assistant, but tended to make his own appointments when they were personal. The dentist's appointment had been written on his calendar, the bulk of which survived the fire. It had been left in his car and booked into evidence.

"Perhaps he was simply enraged," Lawless offered logically. "He lost control of his temper and impulsively killed her."

It was obvious she was going to have to lay out her case for him. "First, Benedict Lawless had no prior record of domestic abuse. There's typically an escalation that begins with small violence and leads to the final explosion. Do you recall your father ever hitting your mother?"

He took a long breath. "Never. My father was quite gentle, but then we all have our secrets. I was a kid. I saw my parents through the eyes of a worshipful child."

"The evidence can't be denied. There were no reports of violence in your household. So if we establish that your father was neither impulsive nor violent, we have to look at the crime itself. It took planning. The gun had to be purchased. There were no records of Benedict owning a gun until a week before the murder. He purchased that gun for the sole purpose of murdering your mother and taking his own life. So why make a dentist appoint for the week after, and why schedule car maintenance on the Wednesday prior to the killing? Why waste time on a vehicle he wouldn't drive again?"

"Perhaps he intended to set this up as a burglary gone wrong."

Did Drew honestly think she hadn't examined and excluded that scenario? "Then why would he have blocked all the exits and set the house on fire? You want to tell me why you're trying to poke holes in my theories? I thought we were on the same page."

"I'm merely playing devil's advocate." His voice was low, his body relaxing a bit. "And showing you precisely why I wrote that contract. I couldn't have this discussion with a McKay-Taggart employee. I would receive a report and be left out of the intellectual process."

"Somehow I think you could pay them enough to get the working relationship you want."

He chuckled, a deep, sexy sound. "You would be surprised. Thebig guy makes me lo ok like a fluffy kitten. He's also my sister's brother-in-law. If I hire him to continue, he would have to put up a business wall between himself and his brother. Ian Taggart's family is everything to him. I'd rather not put him in a situation where he's forced to choose between his brother and a client. I rather think I would lose, and I don't want my siblings to know I'm continuing the search, for reasons I'll explain to you if you sign the contract."

If he was serious, maybe she should be sure he understood what she would want from him. "Okay, I kind of get that, but there are other investigators out there who wouldn't want to write a story about their findings. You seemed extremely certain you didn't want a reporter investigating. You need to understand, Mr. Lawless, that I will want that story."

"Which is precisely why I'll pay you to write it. And please call me Drew. It's going to be awkward if you continue to call me Mr. Lawless." Because she was supposed to be his girlfriend. "Now for the other why. Why the secondary clause? Why do I need to play out the illusion that I'm your honey?"

He got a wistful smile on his face. "Because it might be fun?"

Going Down Easy
Billionaire Bad Boys Book 1
By Carly Phillips
Now Available

Meet Kaden Barnes. Alpha-licious in the most unexpected ways, Kaden Barnes always gets what he wants.

Enigmatic and exacting, he's unable to keep an assistant for long. Until Lexie Parker arrives. She's no-nonsense, efficient and all business… She's also hot as sin and soon starring in Kaden's dirtiest fantasies.

When their passion for each other reaches a boiling point, Kaden may think he's calling the shots, but for this billionaire bad boy, going down easy has never felt so good.

* * * *

Kaden Barnes walked out of yet another unproductive settlement meeting, his business partners, Derek West and Lucas Monroe, by his side. He exited into an early-morning drizzle. From the wet look of the ground, the skies had opened up while they were indoors, and his foot hit a puddle before he climbed into the waiting Town Car.

Fucking swell. This day was just fantastic already, and it was barely nine a.m. Julian Dane, their former friend, was suing them for a piece of their company and a huge chunk of money. Today's plan had been to set the meeting early, intending to catch him at a weak moment, when he wouldn't be as focused and ready to talk terms. The bastard trying to steal a piece of their empire had a problem with partying and a bigger issue with drugs. As they all knew from experience, mornings were rough on him.

Unfortunately, all the power plays in the world didn't matter. According to their attorney, because Julian had been there during the initial design phase, they'd have to come up with some kind of settlement if they wanted this mess to go away. In Kade's book, any acknowledgment of Julian's supposed hand in the creation of the Blink app was a loss. And Kade didn't like to lose.

He remained silent on the ride downtown to their Soho offices while Derek and Lucas talked about potential offers Julian might accept. Kade was still brewing on that. The man had a cocaine problem. Money would probably be the most welcome solution. Lord knew he hadn't been interested in rehab when offered, and no way in hell would they give him a stake in the company.

"You could have shaved for this meeting," Derek said as they exited the car a little while later.

Lucas slammed the door behind them and laughed. The asshole.

Kade shrugged. "I wore a suit. You can't have everything."

They'd agreed to dress like the adults they were, not the tee-shirt-wearing juveniles they preferred to be, in order to let Julian know he wouldn't be walking all over them. They were taking his lawsuit seriously—because if it dragged out and ended up in court, their company valuation would be impacted. They couldn't afford to let that happen, and Julian knew it. Which meant he had the upper hand.

Still stewing over that fact, Kade followed the others into the elevator. He hit the button for the top floor, heading up to the area above the workspace they shared with employees. The offices were housed in a newly renovated garage.

He strode past the abstract paintings surrounded by steel beams toward his private office and stepped inside. The wall-to-wall windows provided him with a full view of the gloomy rain that matched his mood. All he wanted was to hole up at his desk and work on the funding. No distractions, no bothersome annoyances, no—

"Good morning, Mr. Barnes," a chipper voice said, popping up from beneath his desk.

He blinked in surprise, then narrowed his gaze at the strange woman he'd never seen before. "Who the hell are you, and what are you doing under there?"

"I moved your computer and was plugging it back in," she said, pointing to the far corner of his desk. "You can pull it forward when you need to work. I set the keyboard at a better ergonomic location so it's safer for your back. Not to mention, you'll have easier access to your files when you're sitting at your desk," she explained, clasping her hands in front of her.

His lips firmed, and he was about to rip into her when he realized she looked as if she'd been caught in the morning's downpour. Her brown hair was damp, curling at the ends, and her white shirt had water stains on the front, calling attention to a lace bra and her full breasts. None of which detracted from the beauty beneath the smudged makeup. With big blue eyes and porcelain skin, she was exactly Kade's type.

Not skinny and more than a handful, he thought, his mouth watering at the thought. "And my other question? Who are you?" he asked, his voice harsh in order to cover the sudden rush of desire he didn't need riding him here and now.

"Lexie Parker, your new personal assistant," she said, her voice soft and pleasing, at distinct odds with her bossy personality, if her nerve in rearranging his desk before meeting him was anything to go by. His anxiety and ADHD were off the charts with a mere glance at the new setup, not that he'd admit to such a thing.

When he remained silent, she placed her hand on the stapler—on his now neat desk. Folders sat in precise stacks; his favorite pen was nowhere to be found, probably mixed in with the writing utensils in the holder he never used. His organized disorganization was gone. Not even his meds took the edge off her changes.

"I didn't hire you," he said through gritted teeth.

"I see you two have met," Derek said, joining them in his office and slapping Kade on the back as he drew up beside him. "Think you can hold on to this one?"

Kade unclenched his jaw. "Did I miss the interview?" he asked.

"Lexie is Wade Parker's daughter," Derek said, naming their biggest backer and investor. "She needed a job, and you, my friend, need a personal assistant you can't run off with your not-so-charming personality and demands."

His eyes shot daggers at his partner, who knew full well he liked to choose his own PA, before glancing back at Lexie. She smiled and treated him to a small wave. His dick responded to her smile. The wave irritated the shit out of him.

He turned to face her. "Guess we're stuck with each other."

She smiled, and it brightened her entire face, lighting up incredibly blue eyes. Sky blue, his favorite color. "So what next?" she asked.

"Don't touch my stuff without permission."

She frowned, her eyes narrowing, drawing attention to her dark lashes. "How about you try my changes. If you don't like them, I'll put things back the way I found them." She patted his chair, indicating he should sit.

Well, what do you know? She wasn't intimidated by him.

He met her gaze and grinned, extending his hand. "Just ask before you touch my things next time."

"Yes … sir." They shook hands, and the feel of her soft flesh sent waves of desire rippling along his skin. He jerked his hand back quickly.

Derek chuckled. "I think you two will get along just fine." He leaned in close and whispered in Kade's ear. "And since she's Wade's daughter, you can trust her with your keys. You won't have to pick up your own dry cleaning." Another slap on the back, and he walked out the door.

"Would you like to make a list of what's expected of me?" Lexie asked eagerly.

He groaned. A peppy, sexy personal assistant wasn't what he'd had in mind. Of course, he'd run off the older woman before Lexie (too many personal errands for her taste), the young woman right out of college (she'd come on to him and looked like jailbait, and when he'd not-so-politely turned her down, she'd walked out on the spot), and another PA who hadn't appreciated his request for coffee every morning. She'd said it went against her feminist sensibilities. He'd told her he didn't give a shit and she'd quit.

Lucas claimed Kade had control and trust issues with women and drove them off on purpose. He was right about one thing. Kade didn't trust most females. The first one in his life had abandoned him by choice, and the ones who'd come after had betrayed him. That didn't just jade a man. It embedded an ugly truth deep in his psyche. Women either wanted something or would stab him in the back, one way or another.

His personal assistant, as much as he needed one, had the potential to get too close and intimately involved, at least in his private life. Add in the fact that the woman waiting for his instructions was beautiful, and things were destined to get complicated. But he needed the help, something Derek obviously knew. So Lexie Parker was his, at least for now.

Rescuing Rayne
Delta Force Heroes Book 1
By Susan Stoker
Now Available

As a flight attendant, Rayne Jackson is used to cancelations, but she never dreamed her latest would lead to a whirlwind tour of London with a handsome stranger . . . or a life-altering night in his bed. One evening is all the enigmatic man can give her, and Rayne greedily takes it, despite suspecting it will never be enough.

Heading home after another extreme mission, Keane "Ghost" Bryson hadn't planned to seduce someone during his layover, but Rayne is too sweet to resist. Being a Delta Force member means lying to protect his identity, which is unfortunate, considering Rayne seems made for Ghost, right down to the tattoo on her back. For the first time in his life, regret fills him as he slips away the following morning.

Both are shocked when, months later, they meet again—under the worst possible circumstances. Seems fate has given them a second chance . . . if they can survive the terrorist situation they're in. If Rayne can forgive Ghost his lies. And if Ghost can trust Rayne to be strong enough to endure the secrets and uncertainty that come with loving a Delta Force soldier.

*** Rescuing Rayne is book 1 in the Delta Force Heroes series. Each book is a stand-alone, with no cliffhanger endings.

To sign up for Susan's Newsletter go to: http://bit.ly/SusanStokerNewsletter

* * * *

Chapter 1

Captain Keane "Ghost" Bryson leaned his head back on the seat and closed his eyes, ignoring the rain that was pouring down outside as if someone had turned a faucet on full blast. The gray day seemed determined to wreak havoc on the moods of every man, woman and child inside the crowded airport.

He used to hate flying commercial, but it didn't faze him anymore. As a Delta Force operative, and the team leader, his missions were always top secret and he and his fellow teammates typically flew commercially to get to where a mission would start or to get home.

Ghost had just completed one doozy of a mission and was looking forward to getting home. He shifted in the uncomfortable seat in the waiting area at London's Heathrow Airport. He and his teammates had, as normal, flown out of Turkey into Germany then split up. Fletch and Coach flew to France first and then were headed back to the States. Hollywood and Beatle were going home straight from Germany, Blade was going through Amsterdam, and Truck was taking a detour through Spain.

He could've taken a flight directly to Austin, but the Dallas/Fort Worth flight got in a bit earlier, and had an empty exit-row seat. It was a matter of convenience, but with the rain pouring down in sheets, Ghost thought that maybe he should've taken the later flight after all.

"Is this seat taken?"

Ghost turned toward the low, husky voice that immediately made him think of sex. He'd been aware that she'd been walking toward him, as he was of everyone who moved around him. He was always on alert, ready to take whatever action might be needed. It was engrained in the very marrow of his bones.

A brunette stood next to him. Her hair was pulled back into a bun at the nape of her neck. There were wisps of hair hanging around her face, which had obviously fallen out of their confinement. She was fairly tall, especially in the heels she was wearing. Ghost guessed her to be around five-eight or so. She was pleasantly rounded in all the right places. Her Marilyn Monroe physique was a turn on, as was the bright smile she was aiming his way.

Her accent gave away the fact she was American. She was

wearing a navy blue skirt and shirt, and was pulling a blue suitcase and a small matching bag behind her. Obviously an employee of the airline, a flight attendant, she greeted him warmly.

Ghost shook his head and gestured toward the seat, inviting the woman to sit next to him.

"Thanks."

The woman sat down, opened the small blue bag, and fished out her cell phone. She turned to him and asked, "Going somewhere fun?"

Ghost wasn't sure he really wanted to get into a chat, but he was bored, and he might as well pass the time. He'd never been one to reject an opportunity to talk and flirt with a pretty woman. "Home."

His one-word answer didn't seem to daunt the flight attendant. "Ah, American. Where's home?"

"Texas."

"Really? Me too! How funny that we're going to the same place. Out of all the people I could've sat next to, I picked someone who was going to be on my flight." She laughed. "You are on flight eight twenty-three, right?"

Ghost nodded.

"Cool. But my place in Texas is really more of a place to store my stuff than a home, since I'm usually working. I currently have the European shift. I'm gone more than I'm home."

Ghost smiled inside. The woman was very pretty and her bubbly personality was pleasant. "Yeah, I travel a lot too, so I know what you mean."

She beamed. "Ah, I didn't really peg you as a businessman, but I guess looks can be deceiving, huh?"

"What did you peg me as?"

The woman tilted her head, contemplating his question. Her lips pursed and then she bit her bottom one. Amazingly, Ghost felt himself getting erect.

Jesus, was he that hard up for a woman? He tried to think about when he'd last had the pleasure of a woman's company in his bed, and was amazed to realize he wasn't sure.

"Bounty hunter," she said resolutely.

Torn out of his internal thoughts of when he'd last had sex, Ghost chuckled out loud in surprise at her deduction. "Bounty hunter? Really?"

"Uh-huh."

When she didn't elaborate, Ghost crossed his arms over his chest and smiled at her. "Why?"

"Let's see. Your eyes are constantly scanning the area, even as we talk. You're hyper-aware of everything around you. I bet you knew I was coming toward you before I even got here. You're sitting with your back to a wall, a typically defensible position. You ooze testosterone, you're more muscular than anyone else around here, and you're wearing combat boots."

"And you got bounty hunter out of all of that?"

She smiled at him, leaned back in her seat, and turned toward him. "Yup. Am I right?"

"No."

"So?"

Ghost knew what she wanted, but he was enjoying playing the game. "I'm a businessman."

She looked sideways at him for a beat. "So, you'd tell me but then you'd have to kill me…right?" She grinned, obviously also enjoying their flirting.

"Something like that."

She rolled her eyes. "Okay, spy was my second guess. I'm sticking with one of the two. Bounty hunter or spy. I'm Rayne Jackson, by the way. Spelled with a y and an e. Not like what's currently falling outside." She didn't hold out her hand but looked at him expectantly.

Rayne. Ghost liked that. It was an unusual name for an unusual woman. If she really did think he looked like a bounty hunter, she probably shouldn't have approached him. "Ghost."

"Ghost? Really?" She rolled her eyes again. "Okay then, Ghost.

It's nice to meet you. And I'm amending my guess. I'm definitely going with spy."

"It's good to meet you too," he returned, ignoring her spy comment. It was a bit too close to the truth. "Think we'll get out of here today?"

She smiled at him. "So we're talking about the weather? Okay, I can do that. Are you in a hurry to get home?"

Not knowing why she was asking, but being cautious, Ghost answered, "Not particularly."

"Good, because in my expert opinion, we aren't going anywhere today."

"Hmm. Other than your profession as a flight attendant, what is this expert opinion based on?"

Rayne grinned. "Well, I'm not a meteorologist, but I've been flying through here for quite a while now, and every time it's rained this hard, the flights are either delayed or canceled."

"Shit," Ghost said under his breath. He didn't really need to get home, his team could handle the report back to the lieutenant colonel at the base, but he also didn't need the hassle of spending the night in London either. Damn the others, they were probably well on their way home by now. Stupid English weather.

"Yeah," Rayne commiserated. "Unfortunately, I'm pretty used to it by now."

Just then an announcement came over the loudspeakers in the busy airport.

Flight eight twenty-three to Dallas/Fort Worth is now delayed. Please check the boards for more information.

"Told ya," Rayne said with a smile.

"You really don't care that you could be stuck here?" Ghost asked. "Most women I know get extremely…ruffled…when their plans go awry."

Rayne snorted, and Ghost noted that even the small sound was attractive coming from her.

"No. I don't get…what was your word? Ruffled?" She shook her head. "I certainly didn't picture a man like you using a word like that. Does it usually come up in your super-spy conversations?" Her question was obviously rhetorical, because she continued before he could answer. "No, I don't get ruffled when flights are delayed or canceled. It's all a part of my day. Remember, I'm actually working, not on vacation. In fact, the delays and cancelations give me a chance to get out and see the city where I'm holed up. I've had dinner in the shadow of the Eiffel Tower, taken a gondola ride in Italy, and even smoked a joint in Amsterdam during one layover."

"Hmm, a woman of the world," Ghost joked.

Rayne laughed at him. "Not even close. Don't let my adventures fool you. I'm much happier sitting at home reading a book than going out, but I figure while I'm young enough, and I'm here, I might as well get out and see some of the cities most people only dream about visiting."

"Very mature of you," Ghost said honestly.

"Are you trying to tell me I'm old?" she joked.

"No, ma'am. I know better than to even hint at a woman's age."

"Good. Because at twenty-eight, I'm not old. Not even close."

Jesus, twenty-eight. It seemed so young to his thirty-six, He'd seen a lifetime of things she couldn't even imagine, but his body didn't seem to care. He was attracted to her, there was no denying it. "Twenty-eight…practically a baby."

"Whatever. What are you…thirty-two?"

"Six, but thanks."

"You are not."

"I'm not what?"

"Thirty-six. There's no way."

"So you're saying I'm lying?" Ghost sat up and put one arm on the back of the chair she was sitting in. She was hilarious.

"Not exactly lying, but you might be trying to make me think you're more worldly than you really are."

446

If only she knew how worldly he really was, she'd probably immediately get up and walk away. "I'm thirty-six. Want to see my ID?"

Rayne waved him off, laughing. "No. I'm just teasing you. So...what're you going to do if our flight is canceled?"

Ghost stared at the woman sitting next to him. He made a split-second decision. "Hopefully taking a pretty brunette to dinner and showing her some of the sights of London she might miss if she stayed in her hotel room and read a book."

He watched as Rayne blushed and stared at him for a beat. Then, surprising him, she said, "I'll take you up on checking out your ID now."

"My ID?" The change in subject threw Ghost for a moment.

"Uh-huh. I might go to dinner with you, but I've watched too many episodes on the crime channel. I'll text your name, address, and birthday to my friend back home. Then we can hang out here until we find out if our flight really is canceled. If you continue to be as interesting as you have been the last half an hour and you don't do anything completely creepy or stalkerish, like ask me to take off my panties so you can pocket them, I'd be happy to see the sights of London with you."

Again, Ghost was surprised, but pleasantly. He wasn't sure why, but the thought of Rayne being cautious and safe gave him a weird feeling inside. Knowing she was looking out for herself and trying to be careful was a total turn-on. Surprisingly so. He reached into his back pocket and took out his wallet. He pulled out his Texas driver's license and handed it to her without breaking eye contact. "I have a rule. I don't ask for anyone's panties on a first date."

She smiled, but didn't comment further. Rayne balanced his ID on her knee, took a picture of it with her cell phone, and then typed out a note to her friend on her phone.

Ghost knew the information she was transferring to her friend would never lead back to him. He was using one of his many aliases. Each team member had several they could use to make sure they could travel incognito to and from missions. Ghost felt a pang of regret for lying to Rayne, but he pushed it aside. She was obviously looking for a good time, just as he was.

She looked up at him. "John Benbrook? That's your name?"

"Yeah, what's wrong with it?"

"I don't know." Rayne wrinkled her nose adorably. "It just doesn't seem...like you, I guess."

"Call me Ghost," he demanded. "I don't use John that much anyway." It wasn't a lie.

"Okay...Ghost. Thanks for humoring me with your ID. And I still don't think you look thirty-six."

He smiled at her and put the plastic card back into his wallet. "So...how long have you been a stewardess?"

"Flight attendant."

"What?"

"We're not called stewardesses anymore. We're flight attendants."

Ghost smiled and apologized. "Sorry, my mistake. Flight attendant. How long have you been a flight attendant?"

"Around six years."

"Six years? You started young."

Hearing the question behind his words, Rayne explained, "Yeah, I majored in education in college. I did the whole student-teaching thing, aced the certification tests for the state and the whole nine yards."

"But..."

"But one, I couldn't find a job, at least not in the area I wanted, and two, turns out, I didn't care much for the kids."

Ghost burst out laughing and relaxed farther into his chair. "Seems like that might have been something you figured out before you got your degree."

"Yeah, you'd think, right?" Rayne laughed.

"So you decided to what? See the world?" Ghost asked.

"Sorta. So there I was, with a degree I had no desire to use and no idea what I was going to do with my life. I had a friend whose mother worked for the airlines and I was bitching about finding a job I enjoyed and she suggested the flight-attendant thing." Rayne shrugged. "So yeah, I figured I could see the world while I decided what and where I wanted to work. And here I am, six years later, still seeing the world—or at least the airports of the world—and still trying to decide on what the perfect job is for me."

"It doesn't sound like a bad thing to do for a living," Ghost said.

"It's not. Don't get me wrong. I enjoy what I'm doing, I wouldn't be doing it otherwise, but it's not what I want to do for the rest of my life. I really am a homebody. I might go out and try to see some of the cities that I have layovers in, but it's not much fun to explore by myself and sometimes the cities don't feel that safe."

"If they aren't safe, you shouldn't be wandering around," Ghost told her matter-of-factly.

"I understand that. But some of the places, I know I'll never get the chance to see again."

"That shouldn't matter. You could get killed, or raped, or kidnapped in some of those places…so you might see them, but it's not worth your life or your health."

Rayne nodded in agreement. "You're right. And just in case you're feeling smug that you can order me around, I'd already decided to be a bit more cautious when I'm overseas now that ISIS has gotten completely bat-shit crazy and has no moral compass whatsoever."

Ghost smiled at her cheekiness. "Good. How long before you think—"

His words were interrupted by the automated voice over the intercom.

We regret to inform you that flight eight twenty-three has now been canceled. Please see an airline representative to reschedule your flight. Heathrow Airport apologizes for any inconvenience.

449

Ghost stood up and held his hand out to Rayne. "So, since it's not safe to wander around by yourself…want to explore London with me?"

About Lexi Blake

Lexi Blake lives in North Texas with her husband, three kids, and the laziest rescue dog in the world. She began writing at a young age, concentrating on plays and journalism. It wasn't until she started writing romance that she found success. She likes to find humor in the strangest places. Lexi believes in happy endings no matter how odd the couple, threesome or foursome may seem. She also writes contemporary Western ménage as Sophie Oak.

Connect with Lexi online:

Facebook: https://www.facebook.com/pages/Lexi-Blake
Twitter: https://twitter.com/authorlexiblake
Website: www.LexiBlake.net

Sign up for Lexi's free newsletter at www.LexiBlake.net.

40887116R00269